MURDER
AT THE
LANTERNE
ROUGE

MURDER AT THE LANTERNE ROUGE

cara black

Published by
Soho Press, Inc.
853 Broadway
New York, NY 10003

Library of Congress Cataloging-in-Publication Data

Black, Cara
Murder at the Lanterne Rouge / Cara Black.
p. cm.
HC ISBN 978-1-61695-061-3
PB ISBN 978-1-61695-214-3
eISBN 978-1-61695-062-0
1. Leduc, Aimee (Fictitious character)—Fiction. 2. Women private
investigators—France—Paris—Fiction. 3. Missing persons—Fiction.
I. Title.
PS3552.L297M78 2012
813'.6—dc23
2011037028

Printed in the United States of America

10 9 8 7 6 5 4 3 2 1

In memory of Laura Hruska and the women *Rèsistants* in the Marais—Odette Pilpoul, Raymonde Royal and Paulette Buchmann.

———

For the ghosts

Every bird which flies has the thread of the infinite
in its claw.

— VICTOR HUGO

The Marais

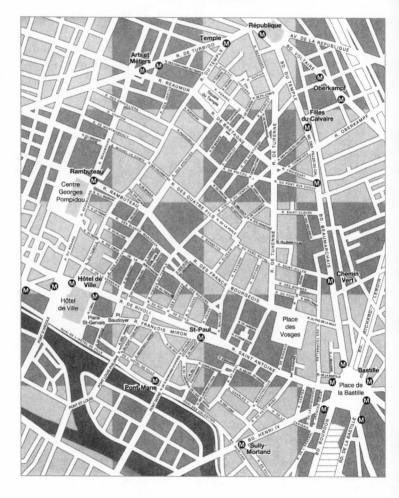

PARIS

JANUARY 1998

Friday Evening

TOO SMALL FOR a bomb, Aimée Leduc thought, nudging with her high-heeled toe at the tiny red box on the cold landing outside Leduc Detective's office. No card. Curious, she picked up the red gift-wrapped box, sniffed. Nothing floral. A secret admirer?

The timed hallway light clicked off, plunging the landing into darkness. She shivered, closed the frosted glass door behind her, and hit the light switch. The chandelier's crystal drops caught the light and reflected in the old patinated mirror over the fireplace.

For once the high-ceilinged nineteenth-century office was warm, too warm. The new boiler had gone into overdrive. Her nose ran at the switch from the chill January evening to a toasty, warm office. She set down her shopping bags—January was the season of *soldes*, the big sales. She'd blown her budget.

Et alors, yogurt and carrots at her desk for the next week.

She slung her coat over the chair and noticed a chip on her *rouge-noir*-lacquered pinkie. *Zut*. She'd have to spring for a manicure.

The office phone trilled, startling her.

"Tell me you found Meizi's birthday present, Aimée," came the breathless voice of René, her business partner at Leduc Detective. "The damned jeweler screwed up the delivery."

"Small red box? You mean it's not for me?" she joked. She shook the box and heard a rattle. Maybe those jade earrings she'd seen him looking at. "You're serious about Meizi? I mean, *that* kind of serious?"

"One day you'll meet your soul mate, too, Aimée."

Soul mate? He'd known Meizi what, two months? But Aimée bit her tongue. So unlike René to rush into something. A surge of protectiveness hit her. She ought to check this girl out, see what she could learn from a quick computer background search. Could be a little ticking bomb, all right.

"Save my life, eh?" René said. "Bring it to the *resto*, Chez Chun."

"But I'm in the middle of a security proposal, René," she answered, hoping he didn't hear the little lie in her voice. She surveyed their bank of computers, which were running security checks, updating client systems she'd programmed before she left. The boring bread and butter of their computer security firm.

"Take a taxi, Aimée," he said, his voice pleading. "Please."

Meizi must have something his previous girlfriends from the dojo didn't. Better to check her out in person. Aimée put the box in one jacket pocket and dug through the other for her cell phone.

"A taxi, with this traffic? Métro's faster, René."

She grabbed her leopard-print coat and locked the office door.

Twenty minutes later she ran up the Métro steps, perspiring and dodging commuters. Frustrated, she found herself at the exit farthest from where she wanted to be, by the Romanesque church that was now the Musée des Arts et Métiers. Harmonic Gregorian chanting wafted in the cold air and drifted into the enveloping night. Petals of snow lodged like nests of white feathers in the bare-branched trees. What a night, the temperature falling, a storm threatening in the clouded sky. The frigid air sliced her lungs, shot up the mini under her coat.

Great. She hadn't thought her wardrobe through, as usual. René had better appreciate this. Listen to sense and slow things down.

She ran across the boulevard into the medieval quartier, still an ungentrified slice of crumbling *hôtel particuliers*, narrow cobbled streets lined by Chinese wholesale luggage and jewelry shops. Red paper lanterns hanging from storefronts shuddered in the wind. From a half-open door she heard the pebble-like shuffling of mah-jongg tiles. This multi-block warren comprised the oldest and smallest of the four Chinatowns in Paris. Few knew it existed.

She reached Chez Chun, the oldest or second-oldest building in Paris, depending on whom you talked to, sagging and timbered beside a darkened hair salon.

Inside Chez Chun a blast of garlic, chilis, and cloying Chinese pop music greeted her. The *resto*, an L-shaped affair, held ten or so filled tables. Roast ducks dangled behind the takeout counter. Not exactly an intimate dining spot.

René cornered her at the door. "Took you long enough, Aimée." René, a dwarf, was always a natty dresser. Tonight he wore a new silk tie and a velvet-collared wool overcoat tailored to his four-foot height.

"Work, René," she said. "I'm still running programs."

He raised his hand. "Routine. We're good till Monday."

She'd never seen him like this. For once work took second place.

"Yet look who came out in the cold," she said, wiping the snow from her collar. "Why so nervous?"

"Her parents."

"Use your famous Friant charm," she said under her breath. She pulled the gift from her coat pocket. "But why rush this, René?"

René reached for the box, a small smile playing on his lips. "Time to listen to my heart, Aimée."

At the table, Meizi, her black ponytail bobbing, smiled at them. A warm smile that reached her eyes. "René said you'd be joining us. We ordered, I hope you don't mind." Petite, not much taller than René, she wore jeans and a green sweater as she stood ladling abalone soup into small bowls. "Love your coat, Aimée. Meet my parents."

"*Bonsoir*," Aimée said politely.

The unsmiling Monsieur and Madame Wu stared at her. "My parents speak Wenzhou dialect," said Meizi with an apologetic shrug. "I'll translate."

Aimée grinned, determined to thaw the atmosphere. Her black-stockinged thigh caught on the plastic-covered seat. Under the disapproving stare of Madame Wu, she remembered René's complaints about how Meizi's parents insisted on chaperoning their dates.

René set the present on the table beside the steaming soup. "Happy birthday, Meizi."

Aimée tried not to cringe. Even if it was only earrings, it was too soon. René was nuts, or crazy in love.

Madame Wu turned and spoke to her husband. Aimée heard her sharp intonation, and could imagine what was being said.

But Meizi's face lit up in happiness as she untied the bow and opened the jewelry box. To Aimée's surprise, it was a ring. A pearl ring, luminous and simple. "How thoughtful, René," Meizi gasped. "I lost my other ring at the dojo."

He winked. "I hope the next one will sparkle more."

Meizi blushed.

Madame Wu pulled the reading glasses down from her short, very black hair—dyed, Aimée could see—and shook her head. Round-faced Monsieur Wu, who was much older, averted his gaze.

Were they criticizing René's gift or objecting to the relationship? Perhaps they didn't want their daughter involved with a dwarf? Despite her own reservations, Aimée felt a pang for René.

"Lovely, *non?*" Aimée said, trying to ease the almost palpable tension.

"Try it on, Meizi," René urged.

Aimée noticed the look René and Meizi shared. Lost in each other. She nudged René. He ignored her.

Madame Wu spoke sharply, and Meizi translated. "My parents say you're too kind, René."

Aimée doubted that. Meizi slipped the ring on her fourth finger. "*Parfait.*" Aimée noticed the bitten nails, the worn calluses on Meizi's fingertips. Meizi set the ring back in the box and passed out the steaming soup bowls. A large serving for René.

Meizi's phone vibrated on the table. She glanced at the number and pushed her chair back. "I'll be right back."

René's hand paused on his soup spoon. "Can't you talk later, Meizi?"

"Won't take a moment," she said. As Meizi went to the door, Aimée noticed her backward glance, her beetled brow, before she stepped outside.

The Wus, not ones for conversation, tucked into the soup. Poor René. Aimée imagined the dinners he'd shared with the humorless Madame and Monsieur Wu. Had she read Meizi, a dutiful daughter, all wrong? A young waitress cleared their bowls, leaving Meizi's, and brought a platter of fragrant roasted duck with shaved scallions. At least five more minutes passed.

"Where's Meizi?" René asked, holding off from serving himself.

"Meizi, *oui*." Madame Wu nodded, her chopsticks working at morsels of duck.

Aimée wished Meizi hadn't left them in this awkward situation. She shot René a look. He flipped his phone open, hit Meizi's number on his speed dial.

A stooped older woman wearing a stained apron entered the *resto*. Madame Wu exchanged an uneasy look with Monsieur Wu as the old woman made her way to their table.

"Who's this, another relative?" Aimée asked.

"The busybody who sells tofu and groceries next to her

uncle's place." René frowned. "Meizi's not answering her phone."

Suddenly, the old woman shouted in Chinese. Madame Wu dropped her glasses on the table.

The old woman continued, bellowing, frantic. Loud murmurs and the clattering of chopsticks filled the *resto*. Surprised, Aimée saw diners throw money on their tables, heard chairs screeching back in haste over the linoleum. As if at some mysterious signal, people reached for their coats and fled in a mass exodus.

Madame and Monsieur Wu stood in unison. Without a word they left the table and were out the door of the *resto* without their coats. Not only rude, but unnerving.

The ring in the red velvet box sat by the teapot, forgotten. Like Meizi's coat on the back of her chair.

"But what's happening?" René said, bewilderment on his face.

Aimée rubbed her sleeve on the fogged-up window to see outside. A red glow reflected in the ice veining the cobble cracks. Firemen, an ambulance, the police?

The young waitress by the door turned down the pop music.

"What's the matter?" Aimée asked her.

"Trouble."

"Trouble as in a robbery?" Jewelry stores abounded in the quartier, which had once been the diamond-cutting district.

"The old lady said murder."

"Murder? But who?"

The waitress shrugged. Her fingers worried a tattered menu. "Behind the luggage shop."

Aimée sat up. "The luggage shop around the corner?"

The waitress nodded.

Meizi's parents' shop. A terrible feeling hit her. Meizi?

René had pulled on his coat and was already halfway to the door. Aimée scooped the jewelry box into her pocket, left a wad of francs on the table, and took off behind him.

• • •

FILLED WITH DREAD, Aimée hurried down the street, following René past the dimly lit Le Tango, a dance club emitting a reverberating drumbeat. No one stood outside. It was too cold for the usual drunken brawls. A horn blared streets away.

A flash of red disappeared around the corner. Madame Wu.

Aimée glimpsed a few Chinese people crowding the short walkway behind the luggage shop. The dark walkway between the buildings was crowded with garbage bins, wood palettes, old cart wheels, the view ending in a dim red lantern shining on back stairs. Not a hundred yards from the *resto*. Her shoulders tightened.

"Meizi lives here above the shop." René panted, his breath frosting in the cold. The windows he pointed to were dark. Where were the Wus?

Aimée fought a rising panic, picking her way through Chinese people of all ages, mumbling and scraping their feet on the ice.

"Has someone been . . . ?" Aimée's question was interrupted by a woman's piercing scream. People jostled her shoulder as they ran away, their footsteps thudding on the snow. Shivering in the cold and full of misgivings, Aimée crossed the now deserted walkway.

Not Meizi, *non* . . . don't let it be Meizi.

A rat, fat and brown, its tail the length of its long, wet, furred body, scurried down the steps over the new-fallen snow. It left a trail of red in its wake.

At the foot of the crumbling stone stairs by Meizi's door, a man's snow-dusted trouser-clad leg sprawled from a wooden palette. She gasped. Bits of gnawed, bloody flesh, orange peels, and black wool threads trailed in the snow. Good God. Her stomach lurched. The rat.

Aimée couldn't peel her horrified gaze from the corpse,

which was half wrapped in clear plastic, the kind used to secure merchandise to palettes. The man's matted red hair, prominent nose, and cheekbones all melded, smooth and tight, under the clear plastic. Her gaze traveled to his wide, terrified eyes, then to his mouth, frozen open in a snowflake-dusted scream.

She stumbled and caught herself on the ice-glazed wall. Who was he? He hadn't been here long, judging by the light coating of snow. Where was Meizi?

"*Mon Dieu*," René said, stepping back. He took a few steps and pounded on Meizi's back door.

No answer.

Aimée gathered up her long leopard-print coat and stepped with care around the dirtied snow, avoiding the overturned garbage bin's contents.

Her insides churned. She shouldn't have looked at the eyes.

A pair of black-framed glasses lay in the snow beside his gnawed calf. Crinkled papers, a half-open wallet. Using a dirty plastic bag to cover her hands, she picked the wallet up. No cash or credit cards. Cleaned out.

"Come on, Aimée," René said. "The *flics* will handle this. We have to find Meizi."

Wedged deep in the wallet's fold she found a creased Conservatoire des Arts et Métiers library card with an address and the name Pascal Samour. The photo showed a younger version of the pale face in plastic before her.

She turned the card over.

"Put that down, Aimée," René said.

Stuck to the other side of the library card by gummy adhesive was a smudged photo of a Chinese girl with a glossy ponytail. Meizi. "But look, René."

He gasped, and his face fell. He stepped back, shaking his head. "I don't understand."

She caught her breath. "He knew Meizi, René. What if she . . ."

"You think she's involved?" he sputtered. "Impossible."

He punched numbers on his cell phone. "She's still not answering. She's in trouble."

At that moment, wide flashlight beams blinded Aimée. She stumbled, dropped the wallet. Static and voices barked from a walkie-talkie: "First responders, truck thirteen. Alert medical backup we're in the walkway."

"Someone reported this incident," the *pompier* medic shouted, his blue anorak crunching with snow. "Was that you?"

Aimée shook her head.

His colleague brushed past her with his resuscitator equipment. He pulled on latex gloves, took out clippers and snipped the plastic away, revealing that the man's wrists were bound behind him. The medic felt the man's carotid artery. A formality. He shook his head.

A shout erupted. A bedraggled figure came down a side staircase shaking his fist. He wore a matted fur coat, a sleep mask on his forehead, and orange slippers. "I'm trying to sleep."

Aimée hadn't noticed the crumbling stairs, the bricked-up windows. Or the *Permis de Demolir* sign on the building. Condemned.

"How many times have we told you to stay in the shelter, Clodo?" said the second medic.

"They took my wine," the homeless man said in a rasping voice.

She wondered why the rats hadn't chewed him, too. "Did you hear anything? Or see this man attacked, Clodo?"

"Every night I hear the angels sing. Then the devils come. Like you." A loud burp.

"*Clochards*." The medic shrugged. "Guess this is one for the *flics*." His partner packed away the resuscitator.

"You're going to leave him like that?" René shivered beside her in the footprinted snow. Aimée scanned the ground, but the wallet with Meizi's picture had disappeared.

"*Alors*, it's not like he's going to spoil in the heat." The words came from an arriving blue-uniformed *flic* with a roll of crime-scene tape. "What's this kid doing here?"

René blinked. His snowflaked eyelashes quivered. He hated being mistaken for a child.

"Need your eyes checked?" Aimée glared at the *flic*.

The *flic* gestured to his partner, who was approaching from the street. Behind him she saw the blue van. The crime-scene unit piled out.

"You two," said the *flic*, "in the van for questioning."

AT THE REAR counter in nearby Café des Arts et Métiers, Aimée squeezed René's arm. On edge, she tapped her stiletto boot heel on the mosaic tile. She wanted to discover where the hell Meizi had disappeared to. And get René home.

Still, if they had to be questioned, the café beat the frigid police van. They'd allowed her to clean up in the café's WC. Two blocks from the scene of the murder, in the warm café by the Métro station, felt like another world.

Several *flics* and plainclothes hunched over espresso at the counter. Their wet coats dripped on the floor. Little pools formed at their feet among scattered sugar wrappers and cigarette butts. Odd, so many *flics* here at this hour.

A clearing throat interrupted her thoughts. "Mademoiselle Leduc, you were saying . . ."

"My partner's in shock." Aimée turned to Prévost, the *chef de groupe* of the Police Judiciaire. Late thirties, stocky and sallow-faced, a permanent downturn to his thin lips. He stood ramrod straight, his close-set eyes not unlike those of the rat that had gnawed the corpse.

"This is a formality, you said," she reminded him. "My partner's got nothing to hide."

Prévost tilted his head and leaned in. She could feel his hot breath on her face. "Do you?"

She slammed her hand on the counter, and Prévost flew back. "Just the run in my stocking," she said.

"Witnesses need to cooperate, Mademoiselle."

Her taxes paid his salary and she didn't care for his attitude. "Witnesses? Talk to whoever called this in. There was a whole crowd in the walkway before we got there."

"Like usual in Chinatown, everyone's disappeared."

Disappeared?

Aimée had an uneasy feeling Prévost had defaulted to them as suspects. Meizi's photo in Samour's wallet didn't make her feel any better. Best to go to the head honcho. "I want to speak with le Proc." She straightened, crossing her arms.

Le Proc, Procureur de la République, the investigating magistrate, attended crime scenes and referred the investigations either to the local Police Judiciaire or Brigade Criminelle, the elite homicide branch. Murder usually went to *la Crim*. But before it got shoved on someone's desk tomorrow, Aimée would prefer to explain her presence at the scene of the crime to *le Proc*.

"We go by chain of command," Prévost said, managing to look bored and tired at the same time.

"I know," she said. "My father was a *flic*. He worked at the *commissariat* at Place Baudoyer."

"*Et voilà*, you know procedure. And I know your relationship with Commissaire Morbier. I wrote it all down," he said with a little yawn, a hooded look behind his eyes. "Le Proc's come and gone."

Great. Time to get René home. Chilled and pale, he slumped on a high stool.

She reached for her bag.

"I'm afraid there's a few more things to clear up." Prévost consulted his notebook. "Convenient, *non*, Monsieur Friant, parking your car near where the body was found? How do you explain that?"

Aimée leaned forward. "*Alors*, ever tried to park here at night?"

"Where's the receipt for your meal at Chez Chun?"

She'd paid cash and run like everyone else. But she felt in her damp coat pocket. The jewelry box.

Prévost's mouth turned down. "You do have a receipt, don't you?"

"*Phfft*. I paid cash."

René averted his eyes.

Prévost balled a sugar wrapper and downed his espresso.

Aimée shoved her empty demitasse across the counter. "Why are you treating us like suspects? Like we told you—"

"Dining with Madame and Monsieur Wu, a nice meal, Monsieur Friant," Prévost interrupted. "Know them well, do you?"

Egging René on, Aimée thought. Pursuing the wrong link, while he should be trying to find the murderer. Typical.

René shook his head.

Prévost jerked his chin toward Aimée. "And you, Mademoiselle?"

"I met them once. Tonight."

"But I'm disappointed." Prévost's brows furrowed. "Weren't you going to tell me about this birthday celebration for Meizi Wu?"

Aimée stiffened. They'd questioned the waitress in the *resto*. How much did Prévost know?

"We'd like to talk with her," Prévost said.

Did he regard Meizi as a suspect? She squeezed René's thigh under the counter. René caught her look.

"So would I," René said, his lips compressed. "*Alors*, during the soup course Meizi took a phone call and left."

"So you know this man, the victim?" Prévost was quick.

René's large green eyes widened. "But I never saw that poor man before."

"Didn't Meizi talk about him? His mistress, lover?"

Aimée's hands trembled. The *flics* had found the wallet and alerted Prévost. Or he was fishing for information.

"What?" René glared. "A man wrapped in plastic doesn't point to an affair of the heart." René's eyes filled with pain, and something else.

"But who's the victim?" Aimée asked. His library card had told her his name and that he'd lived in the quartier. She wanted more from Prévost.

Prévost ignored her question. "Where did the Wus go, Monsieur Friant?"

René shook his head. "Like I told you, I don't know."

"Shouldn't you question the woman from the tofu shop, the people in apartments overlooking the area, the shop owners?" Aimée shook her head. "Someone noticed. Called it in."

A long-suffering look filled Prévost's eyes. "We're talking to all persons of interest."

Wasting time, more like it.

"A man's been murdered," René snapped. "But you're grilling us?"

Outside the clear circle in the steamed-up window, Aimée saw a police truck idling on rue Beaubourg. Moments later it cleared the way for the van from the morgue. A lone passerby watched. A sad end.

"More than one way to peel the onion in Chinatown," Prévost said. "That's what it's about here."

Meaning what, she wondered. "Did you find a weapon?"

"My job's to ask the questions. Not you." Prévost stared at René.

An unmarked van pulled up outside on the street, and three men emerged wearing sweaters, no coats. One yawned, stretched, and climbed back inside.

Her shoulders tightened. Now it fit together. "You're conducting police surveillance in the area, *n'est-ce pas?* The murder's connected?"

"Not for me to say," Prévost said.

His gaze flicked over the men hunched at the counter and

darkened. His thin lips tightened. He glared at her—a warning to shut up? One of the *mecs* at the counter half turned as if he were listening.

Turf issues? she wondered. Bad blood between competing forces? Had they stepped into the middle of a rat's nest?

Aimée noticed René's short legs dangling from the stool, his dripping handmade Lobb shoes. She caught the wince as he shifted. The damp exacerbated his hip dysplasia.

"Different rules apply here," Prévost said. "Gangs, protection. The quartier's infested with gangs and protection rackets. These Chinese glom together like sticky rice."

His thinly veiled racism didn't inspire much confidence. Probably a member of the right-wing France for the French party.

"Quite a generalization, Prévost," she said. He spilled too much for a *flic*. Or he was warning them of the score. Why?

"*Et alors?* I've worked this quartier five years," he said, his tone changing. "My wife's from Shanghai; she says the same thing." He thumbed the pages in his notebook. Wrote something. A professional demeanor now. He slid two business cards over the table.

"What avenues are you looking into?" Aimée asked.

"Too early in the investigation to say." He stood and put his notebook in his coat pocket. "Tomorrow we'll talk at the *commissariat*."

She sensed something else. Something she couldn't put her finger on. What was this surveillance?

The men at the counter smelled of RG, *Renseignements Généraux*, the hydra-headed intelligence branch on Île de la Cité. Not known to cozy up with uniforms at the counter. But if they worked surveillance in Chinatown, had the murder muddied their surveillance? Or was it all connected?

• • •

OUT ON THE dimly lit street, she pondered Prévost's insinuations. Was the murder retribution by a Chinese gang for stepping into the wrong territory? Or for a debt? A woman?

Meizi.

"*Zut*, René, the area reeks of surveillance. We don't know what's going on."

"We're going to find out, Aimée."

"Us?" For once René, Mr. Play-it-safe, wanted to investigate something criminal? Talk about the shoe on the other foot. "You did notice the *mecs* at the counter, René."

"No answer at the dojo," he said. "It's closed."

"You think Meizi would go there?" she asked.

René's green eyes blazed. "Meizi's parents hide in the back of their shop if a customer comes in."

"They don't speak French."

"*Exactement*. Few Chinese here do. Fewer have papers."

René's words were filled with implications she didn't like to think about. "The Wus operate an illegal business?"

René shook his head. "Like we've talked about that during the little time I've had with Meizi and her parents?" He waved his short arm. "This street's full of sweatshops. Hear that?" In the dark street, she heard a low thrum. "Buildings tremble at night, Meizi told me, from machines in basements and attics. Sweatshops full of illegals working in secret. The last thing anyone wants to do is draw attention. Didn't you see how everyone ran away? They're scared."

Or guilty. Aimée's boot heel caught in a drain. She couldn't let it go. "Yet someone tipped off the *flics*," she said. "Ask yourself who, if no one wants to draw attention. The word got out, the old woman gave the warning in the *resto*. If Meizi already knew, or—"

"Somebody wanted the body found, Aimée," René interrupted.

She kicked an iced cobble, regretted it right away. "After she opens your present, serves the soup, Meizi takes a phone call. Disappears."

René ran his fingers through his hair, then knotted his scarf around his neck. "I know she's in trouble."

"An understatement, René. Her . . . friend was murdered behind her family's shop."

"Meizi's my soul mate. She never talked about anyone else," René said. "*Zut*, you met her parents. Strict and traditional. Something's happened, don't you see?"

Why couldn't he get it? "René, the victim carried her photo in his wallet." She wanted to sit him down in the snow, make him understand. "Prévost regards her as a suspect.

He shook his head. Denial. "*Bon*, I don't need your help to find Meizi. Not that you offered, Aimée."

He took off down the iced cobbles, favoring his right leg. He usually tried to hide his slight limp.

Her heart ached. She didn't want René hurt. Her mind raced with scenarios—Meizi, illegal, maybe owing a debt, finding René, a dwarf, thinking him an easy mark. A vulnerable man, due to his stature. What if Meizi had been playing cat and mouse, giving and withholding? Using her parents as a chaperone tactic to ensnare René into marriage for residence papers?

She caught up with him at the corner. Took his arm and stared at him. "I could have told Prévost. I didn't, did I?"

He shrugged her off.

"*Mais*, you're my best friend, René," she said. "I'm in this with you."

Aimée followed his gaze to the Wus' shuttered luggage storefront, the scattered wet plastic bags in the gutter. He flipped open his phone and hit Meizi's number. He shook his head, his brow creased. "Her phone's off."

A light flickered on in a floor window above the shop. Had

the Wus returned? The back walkway was blocked by orange-and-white-striped crime-scene tape labeled *Police Zone Interdite*. But on rue Volta, she saw a side door to the building, grillwork with a lion's face at its center.

Too bad she'd left her lock pick set at the office. She took out her mint dental floss.

"Flossing your teeth?" René quirked an ironic eyebrow at her.

"Stand in front of me."

"Why?"

"Just do it, René."

He stood in the snow caked in the doorway as she knotted the floss and slipped her finger inside the ornate, rusted grill-work. The knot caught on the brass handle, which she knew came standard in these seventeenth-century doors. She tugged, heard a click, and pushed the creaking door open.

"Hurry, René."

AIMÉE HIT THE light switch, illuminating a narrow stair-case winding upward like a corkscrew. The timed light clicked in eerie counterpoint to their footsteps on the cracked, upturned linoleum. Fried garlic and sesame oil odors clung in the shadowy corners.

No answer when René knocked on the shop door.

Aimée studied the ancient gas fixtures poking from the hallway ceiling, the metal spigot dripping into a pail. Just like many an old tenement. She imagined more than a hundred people living in this building, one sink per apartment and a communal WC between the floors.

A hum grew louder as they ascended the stairs, like cicadas in Provence at summer twilight. But in this decrepit hallway, cut by sharp drafts, the hum issued from something else.

"What's the noise?"

"Sewing machines," René said, his voice low.

Sweatshops.

On the first-floor landing, René pointed to an unpainted door. "This one's above the shop."

He knocked. Footsteps sounded behind the door, then muffled Chinese.

"Meizi, it's René."

Aimée's fingers clenched. Now they'd get an explanation, maybe not the one René wanted.

The door opened halfway. A young Chinese man in an undershirt peered from behind. Smells of sleep, of too many bodies and kerosene from a heater wafted out. Behind him she caught a glimpse of a room lined by rough wooden platforms where ten or so men slept. A bared slit of a window, flaking stucco walls. Like a narrow cell. Alarm bells went off in her head.

"I'm looking for the Wus and Meizi," René said.

The young Chinese man shook his head. With an abrupt movement, he waved his hands as if shooing them away. "*Cuò wù!*"

Shaken, René stepped back.

"We mean from the shop downstairs," Aimée said, pointing below. "The Wu family?"

He shook his head again. Fear in his eyes. "Wu, *non*." He shut the door. She heard the bolt slip from inside.

Aimée's stomach sank. She realized this was the only room above the shop. "I don't like this, René."

Heads peered over the banister, figures above them watching.

"*Excusez-moi*," she said, looking up, trying one more time, "we're looking for Monsieur and Madame Wu. Meizi Wu."

Suspicion and fear emanated from the darting shadows; the figures began stepping back and closing doors. She sensed quiet despair in the lives crammed on each floor. Door latches bolted.

An eerie quiet filled the hallway. The Wus didn't live here. She doubted they ever had. "Let's go."

Out in the icy street, René put his gloved hands in his pockets. They walked the block toward René's car. His mouth was tight, holding something back.

"Talk to me, René."

"Those men do the jobs no one else will, work like slaves."

Another side of René, whom she thought she knew so well. The fighter for the underdog. But wasn't he one himself?

He shook his head. "Meizi's in danger."

"What if she's staying with a friend from the dojo?" Aimée said.

René's eyes pooled in anguish. "Already left messages. No one's returned my calls." Suddenly he snorted in disgust. "Look at that!"

His snow-dusted Citroën DS sat wedged, bumper to bumper, between a Renault and a dented blue camionette. A too common occurrence these days, with tight parking in medieval streets.

After a twelve-hour day, all she wanted was to get warm and sleep. "Skin tight," she said. "Start the engine. I'll push."

She put on her leather gloves, hitched up her coat in the cold. René started the engine and hit the windshield wipers, sending sprays of snow. Aimée tried to push the parked camionette so René could pull out.

No luck.

Standing in the street, she guided René centimeter by centimeter as he edged forward, then reversed.

This would take hours. Cold, her legs numb, she spied a jogger coming down the pavement, his breath puffing.

In this weather?

"Monsieur, mind helping a moment?"

Together, they shoved the camionette's bumper back a tad. Then again. Every shove gave a centimeter. Aimée caught her breath, perspiring under her coat. She noticed two figures huddled on the corner. She was about to enlist their aid when she did a double take. She recognized that pink wool cap. *Her* cap. The one René borrowed for Meizi last week.

The darkness shrouded the pair of faces, but she could see the man shove the woman and then shake her. Clinking metal echoed off the stone. He'd thrust a bag into her arms.

Meizi?

Aimée's heart thumped.

Had René noticed?

But now they'd gone. Aimée took off, wishing to God her heeled boots would gain traction on the ice. Snow fell faster now, little flurries whipping off the stone walls. She skidded, threw out her arms to break her fall. A sickening feeling seized her in the long moment before she hit the wall.

Jolted, she took a moment to stand up. At the corner she looked both ways. No one. Had she imagined it? But in the yellow streetlight she made out mashed footprints in the piling snow.

It had all happened so fast, she thought, hurrying back to René's car. Did Meizi have another boyfriend? Or was she in trouble?

"Running off, Aimée? But you need to push again," René said, twisting the wheels. Ice chunks spit and frosted her calves.

Two more shoves of the camionette's bumper and René's Citroën broke free of the logjam.

"*Merci*, monsieur," she called after the jogger, who had already headed off into the shadows.

In the passenger seat, Aimée pushed a wet blonde lock from her mouth and hit the heater. She longed for the leather seats to warm up. "Take a right at the corner."

He paused mid-shift, stepped on the clutch. "Did you see something?"

She hesitated. Should she tell René? Reveal that Meizi had been two-timing him and stringing him along? But she didn't know that. Didn't even know if that was Meizi. Yet.

"My wool hat you lent Meizi—I think I saw a woman wearing it. Up there."

René ground into first and shot down the street.

For forty minutes they cruised the narrow, winding streets, back and forth, up one end of the quartier, down the other. No woman with Aimée's cap, no answer from Meizi's phone.

René pulled up on Quai d'Anjou in front of Aimée's seventeenth-century apartment on Île Saint-Louis.

Before she opened her door, she asked, "Why would she lie to you about where she lives?"

"I know what you're thinking, Aimée," René said, his voice tight. "You're thinking she's involved. But she's not. She's a country girl, innocent. I need to find and protect her."

Not before Aimée found her. She wondered who needed to be protected from whom.

"But we don't know what happened, René."

"Caring for a person means trusting her." René turned on the ignition. "You should try it sometime."

DAWN, LIKE A silver pencil, outlined Aimée's mansard bedroom window frame. Light slanted over Melac's crumpled jeans on the wood floor and glittered off the Manurhin revolver poking from his back pocket.

Aimée felt his warm breath in her ear. His tongue on her neck. His musk scent on her skin.

Delicious. The white feather duvet bunched around her shoulders as she ran her toe along his warm ankle. She grinned to see his eyes were half hooded with sleep.

Trilling came from the phone console on her escritoire. "Room service?" She nibbled his ear. "How thoughtful."

He shook his head and flicked his tongue over her neck. "Remind me to dump that in the river."

The phone clicked and went to the answering machine.

"Aimée?" René's voice, as tense as a taut bowstring. "Meizi's phone's disconnected. I've been out looking for her all night." Pause. "Call me."

The red light blinked on her answering machine. Her throat caught. She imagined René driving in the ice, the cold. Alone. While here she lay, entwined with Melac in her warm bed.

She reached for Melac's cell phone on the Louis Quinze bedstand. Melac's hand shot out to stop her. "Let René handle this. It's our weekend, remember?"

As a Brigade Criminelle inspector in the elite homicide squad, his hours varied according to his cases. He'd come over after his shift the previous night. Tired, she'd hesitated before giving him a brief account over a glass of wine. She figured le Proc would have referred the investigation to the Brigade Criminelle. When she'd asked him why he hadn't been assigned the case, he shook his head. "Work's over, we'll talk later." He'd pulled her sleeve and they'd ended up under the duvet.

"René's upset, I'm calling him," she said, sitting up in bed.

"You agreed with me, remember?" He traced his finger over her lips. "Our first weekend in a month."

"But René's important. And it's still our weekend," she said, rolling over.

Melac messaged her neck. "Leave it, Aimée."

She hesitated, pulled in two directions. But leave René stranded? "He sounds frantic." The cell phone ringing in her hand interrupted her. A number she didn't know. She showed him the screen.

Melac bolted upright and took his phone from her hand.

"*Zut!* Some double standard going on here, Melac?"

"*Oui?*" he said into the phone.

His soon-to-be-ex, Nathalie? She stifled a groan. Or his eleven-year-old daughter, Sandrine? Melac, a devoted part-time father, spent every other weekend in Brittany. This could take forever.

Melac leaned forward, his warm arm slipping away. A chill settled on her skin where it had been. He cleared his throat. "A car in ten minutes?"

Aimée felt a sinking in her stomach. Unfair.

Springing into action, he rose from the bed, grabbed his jeans, and disappeared into her bathroom, all in one motion. She heard running water, his voice on the phone with the taxi company.

Running out. Just like her papa used to do whenever he was called.

He returned a moment later, dressed, looking for his shoes. "Let me guess, you're going to the *boulangerie*." She kept her voice even.

"Sorry." He sat down on the bed, stroked her cheek with his damp, warm hand.

"No croissants?" Her glow gone, she fluffed the feather pillow.

"I'd like to crawl under the duvet and continue where we left off, but I'm reassigned. I meant to tell you." His gray-blue eyes were full of his urgency to leave and worry about other things. Things she didn't know about.

She pulled the sheets around her shoulders. "Don't tell me. A new posting?"

"A promotion, a new six-month assignment," he said. "One I can't talk about."

"Or you'd have to kill me?"

He smiled. "I signed a confidentiality agreement. Took an oath." He stood. "*Désolé*. Don't count on me this weekend."

The call, his sudden departure . . . it all happened too fast. She put on her father's old wool robe, tied the belt. Fear clutched her stomach.

"Were you going to tell me, or just wait until—?"

"Tonight, over dinner and that bottle of Veuve Clicquot in your fridge," he interrupted. "It's a step up for me. Think of the bright side."

Hard to, with an empty weekend ahead.

"Trust me, Aimée."

Trust a *flic*? Never, she wanted to scream. She'd lived this while growing up with her father, the long years he was a policeman, and even after he left the force to be a private investigator—all the nights he never came home, the stakeouts, the toll showing on his face. The terrible not knowing if he'd turn the key in the front door again. Then the bomb explosion in Place Vendôme. His charred body parts . . .

"Trust you?" The words caught in her throat. She'd gone

against her code to never get involved with a *flic*. It never worked out. "Two minutes ago my partner called for help, but that didn't matter. Now your job rang and you're leaving. *Phfft*, like that. At least I know where I stand."

"*Zut!* It's an opportunity I can't pass up, Aimée. Takes care of my alimony. We'll carve out next weekend."

She looked away.

"Didn't we agree," he said, cupping her chin in his hand, "at your suggestion—*non*, at your insistence—that our work took priority? No recriminations if work called. I respect that." His eyes clouded. "Of all people, I thought you understood the demands of my job."

His ex, Nathalie, hadn't.

Part of her wanted to lock the door, barricade him in. Tell him she wouldn't live like this. Break it off. The other part itched to help René.

"Nice to use my own words against me, Melac." She reached for her cell phone.

Melac sat back down on the bed. "I'm not your father." He took her face in his warm hands again. "I always come back. You won't be able to get rid of me."

Melac put on his leather jacket in the hallway. She hesitated. But Melac knew everyone.

"Ever had dealings with Prévost?" she asked. "A *flic* in the *troisième* arrondissement?"

Melac's grip tightened on his scarf, emblazoned with hearts—his daughter Sandrine had knitted it. "Middle-aged, thin lips, married to a Chinese woman?"

She nodded, shivering. She turned the sputtering radiator's knob to high.

"Why?"

"He questioned us last night."

Melac shrugged. "A fixture in that area. Speaks some dialect. A plodder. I worked with him once. There were rumors."

She was instantly alert. "Rumors like what?"

"That he's a frustrated Ming dynasty classical scholar, a disillusioned Orientalist." Melac shrugged. "He liked the horses. And cards."

That gave her food for thought. "Liked? Past tense?"

Melac shrugged again. "Disciplinary action years ago."

"So you're saying he's bent, on the take?"

"I'm saying that's old news. Ancient history."

"Any idea who's assigned to this case at *la Crim?*"

"Not me." He buttoned his leather jacket.

"Smelled like the RG's involved."

"A task force?" He shook his head.

She'd have to ask Morbier, her godfather, a *commissaire.* But he was in Lyon, and hadn't returned her calls.

The taxi's horn sounded from below.

"Go."

He gave her a long, searching kiss. A moment later the hall door slammed shut behind him.

At the window, she watched him leave, but he never looked up. A pang hit her. Like her father. Her mind went back to her last day of *école primaire.* The playground, the swings, landing on concrete. Her skull fracture.

So vivid in her mind, like yesterday.

Her father's worried face drifting in and out. Overhearing the doctor—"The operation's touch and go."

Beside her father at the hospital bed was white-faced Morbier, a man who didn't pray, with a priest. The smell of incense, the cold holy water, administering the last sacrament. The huddling nurse. "The operating room's ready, *mon curé.*"

Then the sun-filled room, her stuffed bear on the pillow, the tubes in her arm.

She remembered her father's smile: "*Ma princesse,* you'll need to quit the acrobatics for a while." The nurse saying, "She needs to take lessons and learn to fall correctly."

Aimée shook her head. She'd made it.

She said a silent prayer Melac would too.

RENÉ'S HORN TOOTED from the quai below her kitchen window. She opened the window to the smell of wet foliage and flashed René five fingers. The sluggish gray-green Seine slapped white crests against the stone banks.

Miles Davis licked the last of the horsemeat from his new Sèvres bowl. In her bedroom Aimée pulled on a cashmere sweater over her black lace top, hitched up her stovepipe, stonewashed suede leggings, and stepped into her friend Martine's high-heeled Prada ankle boots. At the door she grabbed her vintage Chanel jacket. Miles Davis wagged his tail expectantly and sniffed his leash. "*On y va*, furball. Madame Cachou will do the honors."

Miles Davis scampered down the wide marble staircase, his leash trailing on the worn steps grooved in the middle, to the concierge's loge in the courtyard. Madame Cachou's early morning yoga on the *télé* had finished. Perfect timing.

In the loge, Madame Cachou ruffled Miles Davis's ears. "My favorite little man." The concierge, who was in her sixties, perspired in a purple yoga outfit. A matching sweatband encircled her gray hair. "I've lost five kilos, not even a twinge of bursitis." Her eyes narrowed at Aimée's pale face. "You should try it."

That and a lot of things.

Aimée smiled and handed her the leash. "*Merci*, Madame."

Plumes of exhaust came from René's Citroën idling at the curb. Oyster-gray clouds hovered on the horizon. Another frigid day. She stepped over slush in the cobbled gutter, felt the urge for a cigarette, and visualized her concierge's glowing face. She could go without a cigarette. Five more hours and she'd be a month, cigarette-free.

"I forgot Melac had the weekend off," René said, turning

down the radio weather forecast. Another brewing storm. "*Désolé.*"

"Not anymore."

She slammed the door shut. Relationships—she was just no good at them. Never picked the right man. She should know better. And a *flic!*

"The dojo's open for early practice," he said. They counted on finding Meizi's real address in the dojo membership. "Thanks for coming, Aimée." René swung the Citroën into sparse traffic on Pont de la Tournelle.

"You think I'd let you do this alone, partner?" She checked the backseat. "Where's your martial arts bag?"

"Not important. Meizi's in trouble. You were there, you saw—everything was fine until she got that phone call."

Aimée noted the dark hollows under René's eyes. "You look like hell, René."

"Not enough beauty sleep."

She felt for him.

Inside the dojo, the gong signaling a meditation session reverberated. The Thai monk in orange robes raised his folded hands in greeting. The young French nun, her shaved head covered by a wool cap, ran her fingers down the membership ledger. "I don't see Meizi Wu listed."

Odd. "Try W-O-O," Aimée suggested.

René added, "She sometimes goes by Marie."

The nun shook her head.

"But I met Meizi here at practice," René said, exasperation in his voice.

"Check for yourself, René," the nun said, pushing the list over. "But we don't let people drop in on practice; they need to join."

Sandalwood incense wafted from the meditation room.

He pushed the list back to the nun. "But you've seen her. Black ponytail, jeans, petite, a bit taller than me."

"Chinese?"

René nodded.

"But those girls clean the bathrooms."

Startled, René stepped back. "What do you mean?"

"Cash, you know." The nun rubbed her fingers together.

So they paid girls under the table. No tax. No trace.

"But I met her in a martial arts class," he said.

"One of the perks is taking a class for free," said the nun.

A stunned look appeared on René's face, so Aimée broke in. "Don't you have an address? Or a number to reach her at?"

The nun blinked in alarm. "It's not how it looks. We operate on donations, and it helps the girls out. I don't want anyone to get in trouble."

"A bit late for that," Aimée said. "She's disappeared."

René spread his hands, pleading. "We're trying to help her. Please."

The nun looked around the deserted teak-wood foyer. She pulled out a paper from the drawer. "Ching Wao. We call him and he sends girls to work."

"They're illegals?" Aimée asked.

"I don't ask." The nun paused. "But I hope this girl, Meizi, is all right."

RENÉ SPOKE INTO his cell phone outside the dojo as freezing wind off the Seine whipped the quai. He paced back and forth, trying to get reception as the Métro clattered on the overhead tracks from Austerlitz.

Meizi had lied about living above the shop, and about cleaning bathrooms at the dojo. What else was she hiding?

Aimée couldn't bear to see René heartbroken. If she could find Meizi, talk to her, and . . . what? Get her to admit she had another man?

Aimée opened the glove compartment and felt around. Under René's car registration she found his licensed Glock pistol.

With a full clip.

Not only was he a crack shot, René had a black belt in judo. She'd always said he should register his fists as lethal weapons.

René climbed into the car, brushing a soggy brown leaf from the shoulder of his wool overcoat.

"Since when do you carry this loaded?"

"The last time I was shot made me cautious." A grim smile. "You never know what you're up against."

True. Yet it didn't ease her worry that René might go vigilante. She put the Glock on top of his car registration and shut the glove compartment.

"Ching Wao understood when I said Meizi's name." He readjusted the height of his adjustable seat. "The rest was in Chinese. But we'll go to his address on rue de Saintonge."

He gunned the Citroën up the ramp and over Pont d'Austerlitz.

"René, you've known Meizi less than two months."

His jaw set in a hard line. She'd never seen him so upset. "You're thinking she's illegal. I don't care. But I know she's terrified, Aimée. And there's nothing more to say until I get the truth from Ching Wao."

They drove into the honeycomb of narrow streets edging the Marais. Years ago her grandfather had told her the street names reflected the professions of the ancient quartier: rue des Cordelières, road of the rope-makers; rue des Arquebusiers, musket-makers; Passage de l'Horloge à Automates, watchmakers and windup machines. He never tired of reminding her that rue du Pont aux Choux—Bridge of Cabbages—was named after a medieval bridge spanning the open sewers. Or how he'd investigated a case on rue des Vertus—road of the virtuous— where hookers plied their trade.

Traffic crawled, almost at a standstill.

The image of the man's body in the light of the red lantern came back to her. Her stomach clenched. His gnawed flesh, those vacant eyes.

René parked near Cathédrale Saint-Croix des Arméniens, the small Armenian church. No. 21, their destination, sported chipped dark-green doors and a Digicode. Aimée tried to stifle her rising suspicions that Meizi was part of an illegal ring that preyed on Frenchmen. But that was ridiculous; she cleaned toilets.

"Doubt your dental floss will work here, Aimée."

Wrong type of door. Damn, why didn't she carry that casting putty anymore? The universal postman's key, which she still hadn't given back to Morbier, wouldn't work either.

"We'll have to wait until someone comes out," René said.

"I don't like waiting." Aimée took her LeClerc face powder and makeup brush out of her bag and brushed the keypad with powder. She compared the congealed fingerprint oil to locations on the keypad.

René blinked. "Giving the Digicode a makeover?"

"Utility chic, René," she said. "How many combinations can you get out of the numbers 459 and letter A?"

"Two hundred fifty-six," he said, a nanosecond later.

Amazing. She'd need a calculator.

He reached up on his toes peering closer. "Given the alphanumeric proximity and location . . ." His voice trailed off. "Let's try this." He hit four keys.

The small door in the massive one clicked open. "Impressive, René. You got it on the first try."

He stepped over the wooden doorframe and into the damp courtyard of what looked like an old metal foundry. Inside was a glass-roofed atelier, and ironwork everywhere. Beside the dilapidated townhouse on the left stood a Regency-era theater, complete with pillars and arabesque stonework. Amazing what lay behind the walls, she thought.

"Ching Wao? Never knew the name. Never spoke with them," said the white-haired man who met them inside the atelier. "Chinese moved out. Gone." He set down an iron rod, picked up his cup of steaming coffee. Thought for a moment. "Yesterday. Or maybe today."

Aimée scanned the weedy courtyard. "Where's his office?"

"I wouldn't call it an office," he said.

"So what did he do there?"

"Like I know?" he said. "Back on the right by the rear entrance."

A narrow dripping stone-walled passage led to a door labeled Wao SARL Ltd. Through dirt-encrusted windows she saw an empty desk, chairs. She tried the door. Locked. But the window yielded to a push. A few shoves and she'd opened it enough to reach in and grasp the door handle.

"Try his number, René. I wouldn't want to break in while he's on the toilet."

René shook his head. "Number's disconnected."

A grim look settled on his face. "Let me do the honors."

She noticed the bulge in his overcoat pocket. The Glock.

René kicked the door open.

In the high glass-ceilinged room, half-drunk cups of tea sat on the metal desk. Chinese newspapers, a pink plastic hair-band, and a black telephone lay on top. The tea was warm.

"We just missed him," René said.

The only decoration was a world map tacked on the wall. Aimée studied it, and saw circles drawn around cities: Canton, Bangkok, Trieste, Bucharest, Zurich.

Some kind of trade route? Or smuggling stations?

She opened the desk drawers. Nothing.

Aimée didn't know what to think, but it didn't look good.

Back at the car, René shook his head. "There's something wrong."

More than wrong.

"We're going to the luggage shop."

Unease filled her. With René carrying a loaded Glock, things could go very wrong. She thought quickly. "Give me your phone, I'll call the shop and we'll clear this up." She hit the number. She pressed END after ten rings.

"No answer," she said. "*Bien sûr*, the Wus are at the *commissariat* giving a statement." She sighed. "That could take hours."

"So we'll go, find them, and tell Prévost—"

"Forget it," she interrupted. "Right now, they're with interpreters in a back room. Besides, he'll call us in later. Better we hear from them first."

René punched the steering wheel.

"You don't know that, Aimée. I have to talk to Meizi."

She needed to buy herself time, get to Meizi first. "More important, we need to know what this Ching Wao's up to, René," she said. "He rented a space, has a business, employees. Someone has to know about him. There are records. Go look them up."

"That's your game plan?"

"The *flics* and Prévost will keep their mouths shut, but we have a stake in this," she said, wrapping her scarf. "Get on the computer, sniff around. It's the best way to find out."

But René gunned the engine, turned into the narrow street. "I know she's there. They open early for deliveries. Meizi works in back."

Trucks clogged the street. The luggage shop shutters were rolled down.

"I told you, René." She bit her lip. Had the Wus done a runner like Ching Wao? She had to find out.

René peered at the shop front. "*Merde!*"

"I'll sit on this and let you know when she arrives. No reason to wait in the cold street or in the car," she said. "See what you can find out on Ching Wao."

Keep him busy.

"My former hacker student works in records at the *mairie*," he said. She saw the wheels spinning in his mind.

"Brilliant." Impatient, she stared at the traffic on rue de

Bretagne. "I'll get out, grab a coffee and wait. I'll call you the minute they show up."

She jumped out before he could protest. The snow had melted to gray slush on the cobbles, spattering her boots.

Twenty minutes later, after a steaming espresso at a nearby café, she found the luggage shop's shutters open. Men unloaded boxes from palettes in the back of a truck double-parked in front. She shivered, remembering the man's body on the palette last night.

"*Bonjour*," Aimée called out as she entered the luggage shop. But no *bonjour* in response. Were they in the back?

Aimée fought her way down a narrow aisle stacked with roller bags of every size and color. Knockoff faux-leather handbags hung like streamers from the walls above piles of boxes. The smell of incense from a red-lacquered wall shrine competed with the synthetic plastic aromas of the merchandise.

"*Allô?*"

The only answer was the grunting from the martial arts movie playing on the small *télé* behind the counter.

Scraping noises came from an open side door. She peered into the dank hallway running alongside the shop toward the open courtyard. A young woman, wearing a white cap over her black hair, was stacking cartons of sweatshirts against the wall, her back to Aimée.

Meizi.

"Meizi, René's so worried."

A carton toppled.

"*Aiiya!*" The young woman looked up, her cheeks flushed. A round face, uneven teeth, thick black eyebrows. Not Meizi at all.

Aimée hit the light switch, a yellowed enamel knob protruding from the wall. "*Excusez-moi*, where's Meizi?"

Fear filled the young woman's face. She backed away.

Determined, Aimée stepped over the uneven stone pavers. Something crunched under her boots. Spilled pumpkins seeds. "Can we talk a moment?"

"No speak *Français*," the woman called out, and pointed back in the shop.

Aimée had to talk to her somehow. "Let me help you," she said.

She lifted up the carton of sweatshirts. Heavy, like a sack of potatoes. She wondered how a small woman could lift all this. And at the diversity of the enterprise.

"*Non, merci.*" The girl bit her lip.

She wanted Aimée gone. Now.

Rapid-fire Chinese came from the shop. Footsteps. The Wus had returned. Aimée stepped back inside, to more over-powering synthetic smells. Her nose tickled. Two grunting men in parkas carried stacks of cardboard cartons in from the truck parked out front. Order upon order was arriving.

A middle-aged man, the fluorescent light shining on his bald spot, looked up from behind the counter. He switched off the *télé*. "*Oui?*" From his arm hung several fuchsia faux-leather handbags.

"*Bonjour*, would you tell Monsieur Wu I'm here?"

"We only sell wholesale," he said.

Odd. "Is Monsieur Wu in back?"

The man straightened up. "*Oui*, how can I help you?"

But he wasn't Meizi's father, whom she'd eaten dinner with last night. Impatient, she made an effort to keep smiling. "*Non*, I mean the man who owns the shop with his wife," she said. "His daughter Meizi works here."

The man shrugged. "My wife's in China."

Her skin prickled. This didn't make sense. "Wait a minute." She struggled toward the back counter. "You're Meizi's uncle, *non?* I'm looking for her father, the older Monsieur Wu I met last night."

"Last night, we closed six o'clock. See nothing." He smiled. "I tell *flics* this morning, too."

Had she entered some alternate universe?

"What the hell's going on?"

"No problem," he said. "I show you my business license."

"Where's the couple who owns this shop?"

"You see my sales permit, export lading and bills of sale," he said as if she hadn't spoken.

Was he worried about the tax unit, infamous for swoop investigations?

"Monsieur, I asked you a question."

But he turned—not easy in the aisle crowded with stacked and open boxes—and pointed to the framed business license by the cash register. He pushed a worn binder at her and opened it. "All in order." He smiled. "You check. I work here. I Monsieur Wu."

"Then I'm Madame Chirac."

"You look here." He jabbed his ink-stained finger at the sales permit printed with the name Feng Wu.

Why did he pretend not to understand? He played a game and she didn't know the rules.

"I busy. Unpack shipment." His French deteriorated the more he spoke. His face remained a smiling mask. "Wholesale clients only."

She scanned the dates on the license. The sales permit was dated 1995. "Did you work here in 1995?"

He nodded, and glanced at the cell phone vibrating among the papers strewn over the counter. He ran his finger over a payment log.

"I open business in 1995. Work here every day."

A blast of cold air rattled the cardboard. Voices signaled arriving clients.

"The man murdered last night behind the shop knew Meizi Wu. He had her picture."

This Monsieur Wu looked down. "I don't know. I never see him." He folded his hands over his chest. Defensive.

Aimée stared at the business license. The forms in the binder. Everything matched.

But he'd given her an idea. She'd play his game, whatever it was.

"*Mon Dieu*, I can't find anything in here," she said, rummaging in her shoulder bag, pulling out mascara, her checkbook, keys. "Mind holding this just a moment?" She thrust her *rouge-noir* nail polish bottle in his hands. "*Désolée*. Glass, you know, wouldn't want it to break."

The surprised Monsieur Wu held it, his thin black eyebrows raised.

She smiled, gave a little sigh. "*Et voilà*," she said, pulling a card from the collection in her bag. Imprinted with a Ministry logo. Generic. She had one for each ministry.

"You from tax office, no fool me. I cooperate."

She smiled. "Not quite, but that's good you're cooperating, Monsieur." Her smile widened and she plucked the nail polish bottle from his hand, slipping it into a plastic bag in her purse.

"*Merci*." She handed him the card. "We at the office *d'habitation et domicile* take details seriously," she said. "Your residence isn't listed on the permit. That's because you live upstairs, illegally. We checked that room last night and found illegals, sleeping men. Lots of them. We think you're subletting." She shook her head. "Illegal according to the statute AB34, unless your business permit includes a residence permit."

He blinked. For a moment she thought she had him.

"So my team will need to investigate the premises. Write up our report. Say this afternoon?"

She'd stirred the pot. If he'd hurt the Wus, or was in cahoots with them, this would flush them out.

He reached in the drawer and produced a ledger, which he

set on the counter. He opened it and ran his finger down a column. "I live Ivry. Suburb. See rent in this column. My shop pay from my earnings. All here. All correct."

She'd rather see the other set of books she figured he kept. He was prepared. He'd expected a visit.

"*Zut!* You leave me no option. We'll run your fingerprints in our database, and check them against the prints on file for identification." She smiled and held up the plastic bag with the nail polish bottle from her purse. "Glass shows prints so well. Unless you'd like to tell me where you've hidden the Wus?"

He glanced at his cell phone. Then at her. Deciding. "Come back later."

"Why? So you can check with Ching Wao?"

A horn tooted on the street. "Big shipment." And before she could press him, he'd hurried after the delivery man out the door to the waiting truck. But instead of unloading, he jumped in the passenger seat and the truck roared away.

Great. René would have done better getting answers with his Glock. All she'd done was shake the tree, and now the birds had flown.

But frustration wouldn't get her answers. Aimée ducked behind the counter and explored the back of the shop. Boxes, cartons, a cracked, stained porcelain sink. Dark, empty cupboards. Wet mops leaning against the cobwebbed, padlocked back door. No one had used this door in a long time. Barred windows filmed with dirt looked onto the narrow walkway. The place reeked of damp and mildew. No one hid here, or would want to. She followed the cartons into the side hallway. The young woman looked up from the carton she was taping.

"Why are you afraid?" Aimée asked. "Did they tell you to keep quiet?"

The young woman dropped the tape dispenser. Perspiration beaded her lip. "Why you bother me? Why you make problem?"

"Problem? I think you'll have a problem when the *flics* ask to see your ID, your residence permit. Or don't you have one?"

"You no understand." The girl's lip trembled.

"Understand what?" Aimée said. "Look, if Meizi's in trouble, I can help her. So can my partner."

She could tell the girl understood more than she let on. Aimée's scarf fell from her arm. "It's hard feeling alone and afraid. I want to talk with Meizi. Won't you help me, tell me where she's gone? *S'il vous plaît?*"

The girl stepped closer, picked up Aimée's scarf. Met her gaze and pressed the scarf into her hand.

"No good to ask questions. People watch you. Understand?"

AIMÉE PAUSED AT the walkway behind the shop, still blocked off by orange-and-white striped crime-scene tape. She wondered what evidence besides the wallet the crime-scene techs found. Wondered if the evidence had degraded in the melting snow. Or with the rats. Could the *flics* identity Meizi from the picture? It would be almost impossible if Meizi were illegal.

LIKE FINDING A single snowflake in a gray snowpile in the gutter.

Dejected, she walked, glad to get away from the synthetic smells hovering in the street.

Fake. Like everything else here, in this conspiracy of silence.

The feeling she'd been beaten dogged her.

So far she'd learned the Wus didn't live above the shop. Meizi cleaned toilets, Monsieur Wu was a different Monsieur Wu. And things stank.

But she had someone's fingerprints on her *rouge-noir* nail polish bottle. Five minutes later, she'd reached Benoit, a fingerprint analyst in the crime-scene unit on 36 Quai des

Orfèvres. He'd gone to school with her cousin, liked heavy metal. And with the promise of highly coveted concert tickets, agreed to meet her.

With two hours until their rendezvous, she needed to keep busy. Sniff around.

Where rue au Maire elbowed right, she noticed a small hotel, the one-star variety. A *hôtel borné*, her father had called them, a fleabag demi-pension with rooms rented by the hour, typically by working girls, or old men who couldn't afford anything else rented by the month.

The hotel's open door led to a booth, then winding stairs. The smell of turmeric and onion mingled with the sweetish odor of tobacco.

A North African man in a red-and-green striped djellaba smoked a hookah in the cubicle of a reception booth. "We're full, *complet*," he said. "Try later."

Aimée wanted information, not a room. She saw hotel business cards on the chipped counter. Sophisticated for a one-star hotel. "Hôtel Moderne, proprieter Aram," she read. "You're Aram?"

He shook his head.

"Did you know the man who was murdered last night? Or his girlfriend Meizi, from the luggage shop?"

The man shook his head again. Gave a big, gold-toothed smile. "Better you ask Aram. Knows everybody. Here a long time. But he's at *le dentiste*." He pointed to his teeth.

Good chance, then, Aram knew the street talk. Or saw something. At least she figured he didn't buy into the Chinese wall of silence.

"*Mon dentiste. Très bon*," he was saying. "You need *dentiste*?"

"*Non, merci.*"

Did she have something stuck in her teeth? She ran her tongue over her teeth to check. But she'd speak with this Aram, the hotel proprietor, later.

In her heeled boots, she picked her way over the melted slush and puddles, avoiding the cobble cracks. She felt eyes on her back. Visiting the luggage store had set off her sensors. The awareness that she was being watched sent a frisson up her spine.

She noticed the quick looks from shop merchants. Everyone here had something to hide. How would she ever find Meizi when she couldn't even find anyone willing to talk?

The address listed on the dead man's library card was only a block away. She didn't know if he lived alone or had a family, but she'd find out. She'd discover his connection to Meizi.

Diesel fumes lingered like a fog in the narrow canyon of street between the blackened stone facades. Aimée walked along the medieval gutter, a worn groove puddled with melted slush, down a passage to the next street. Here, roll-down aluminum shuttered the shop fronts. The old, faded sign of a printing press appeared above a wall plaque commemorating a member of the French Resistance, Henri Chevessier, shot by the Germans in 1943. A lone pigeon pecked at soggy bread crumbs near a drain. A forgotten islet of quiet.

Rusted metal filagree covered the dusty glass in the water-stained door. Aimée located No. 14 and read the nameplate. Samour/Samoukashian lived on the third floor. A married couple? Dread filled her as she thought of a grieving widow.

She kept her leather gloves on as she climbed the steep, unheated steps. Chipped plaster, scuffed baseboards, and sagging landings in between floors in the old tenement testified to the passing of centuries. Her breath frosted in the air. She needed to swim more laps in the pool and forego macaroons, she realized, breathless.

The third-floor door stood ajar. Alarm bells sounded in her head. She wished she had her Beretta, but it was home in her spoon drawer. Then smells of frying garlic reached her. Her stomach growled.

"*Allô?*"

"*Entrez*," a woman's quavering voice answered. Polished honey-wood floors gleamed under the high, dark-beamed ceiling. Oil portraits and landscapes hung on the whitewashed walls over fragrant pots of paperwhite narcissus. Not what she'd expected. The man had an exquisite apartment. Like a page out of *Elle Déco* in the "Makeover—what you can do to a historic flat" section.

"MADAME, *excusez-moi.*"

"It's Mademoiselle," said the quavering voice. "Come to the kitchen."

Aimée followed the paprika and garlic smells down the hall. Warmth emanated from the toasty floor. She wanted to take off her wet boots and go barefoot.

A tiny, trim woman, with hair as white as the blooming narcissus, chopped carrots and swept perfect orange circles into a bowl. Leeks and greens tumbled from a string shopping bag on the wooden table.

"My knees." The woman looked up. Sharp brown eyes in an unlined face, a small scar running under her chin. She set down the knife and rubbed her hands on an apron with what looked like scientific equations printed on it. "At eighty, I only do the stairs twice a day now—not like before."

Aimée blinked. She felt winded at one go.

"I've told you *flics*, I'm tired of questions," the old woman said. "So if you don't have answers, quit wasting my time."

"I'm sorry, but you don't understand, Mademoiselle Samour . . ."

"It's Mademoiselle Samoukashian, can't you people remember?"

Aimée handed the woman a card. "But I'm not a *flic*. I'm a private detective."

Interest sparked in the woman's brown eyes.

"Then sit down. *Café turc?*"

Turkish coffee? Aimée nodded. "*Merci*. Please accept my condolences."

The woman turned her back on her.

"That doesn't bring my great-nephew back."

Nothing would. At a loss, Aimée hesitated. She needed to plow on and find out what she could.

The little woman slipped the chopped carrots into a long-handled brass pot of boiling water, then adjusted the blue flame. "Drumming up business? But you don't look like an ambulance chaser. Why visit me?"

A sharp-eyed old bird who got to the point, this octogenarian. Aimée draped her leather coat on the thatched cane chair and sat, unbuttoning her vintage checked-wool Chanel jacket, a church bazaar find.

"I'm so sorry for your loss," she offered again, the words sounding trite. She took a breath and continued. "But I presumed Pascal Samour lived here."

"Then you saw my address on Pascal's old student library card, like the *flics* did." She nodded. "*Bon*, I figured you were smarter than you look."

Aimée dropped her bag, but caught it in time before her mascara, encryption manual, and nail polish scattered across the warm floor.

"Pascal lives . . . lived near Square du Temple," said Mademoiselle Samoukashian. "He taught at the Conservatoire National des Arts et Métiers." The engineering school a few blocks away.

"I saw . . . found his body last night."

"But how is it a detective just happens to find his body?"

Aimée couldn't let the old bird intimidate her. She had to find out why Pascal had Meizi's photo in his wallet.

"That's why I'm here, Mademoiselle," she said.

Mademoiselle Samoukashian handed Aimée a Limoges demitasse and saucer. Into it she poured frothing brown liquid, then crowned the coffee with a lip of foam. "Armenian style, with cardamom."

"*Merci.*"

The old woman uncovered a plate of crescent rolls smelling of apricot. "*Dziranamahig.* We're Armenian, Mademoiselle," she said. "My grandparents sought refuge here from the Turkish genocide. And then we were only rounded up again here during the war, that time by French police. Since the last war, I don't trust the *flics*. And I don't trust them now. Neither did Pascal."

The war? "But that was fifty years ago."

"More. I'm hoping you're better at math than that." She shook her head. "Drink. Then I read your grinds. Then we see."

See what, Aimée wondered.

"Please, first hear me out," Aimée said, determined to leave out the horrific details. "Last night, my partner and I were eating dinner nearby in Chinatown when an old woman came into the *resto* shouting about a murder. We followed the crowd behind the luggage shop, and your . . . and we found Pascal. Everyone ran away, but I picked up his wallet to learn his identity. There was nothing in it but his library card."

"That's all you know?" Sadness pooled in Mademoiselle Samoukashian's eyes.

"Meizi Wu's picture was on the back of his card." Aimée took a sip. "Can you tell me about their relationship? Anything you know about Meizi?"

"Ask her."

"Meizi's disappeared."

She nodded, matter of fact. "*Bien sur*, she's illegal, terrified."

Like a steamroller, this little woman. "So you know Meizi?"

"Never heard of her. But that's most everyone in this slice of the quartier. *Alors*, it never changes—immigrants, illegals. Roundups just like in '42."

"Roundups?" Was she really comparing Chinese sweatshop workers today to French Jews deported to extermination camps?

"I know the feeling. Hunted, hiding, moving all the time."
Surprised, Aimée leaned forward. "You do?"

"I was part of the Resistance, you know," the old woman said. "History forgot us: immigrants, political exiles, Communists. A ragtag bunch of Poles, Jews, Hungarians, Italians. Guerilla fighters. Our last names and politics didn't fit in with de Gaulle's myth of *la grande Résistance Française*. My cousin Manouchian, the Armenian poet, led thirty successful attacks against occupying Germans. But do schoolchildren learn this?" She shook her head. "His group was betrayed, branded as criminals by the Vichy collaborators—you've heard of the infamous Affiche Rouge poster? Those were the Communist Resistants. And they were all executed. No one talks about it."

So the old woman related to Chinese illegals. Did she know Meizi? Was she trying to protect her, hide information?

"Meizi must feel so alone. Lost."

"But there are always places to hide, to meld into the woodwork, like we did." Mademoiselle Samoukashian shrugged, her eyes far away. "Pascal was a funny boy. Sweet but odd."

From the sound of it, the woman would tell the story in her own way. Aimée needed to be patient. She took a sip of coffee, a thick mixture like silt with a cardamom aftertaste.

"His parents had him late in life," Mademoiselle said, glancing back at the pot before continuing. "My nephew, his father, was held in a Siberian POW camp until the sixties. Never was the same, but don't get me started. Pascal's mother died from TB in a sanatorium." She shrugged. "He came to live with me until he passed the exams for Ecole Nationale Supérieure d'Arts et Métiers."

The prestigious *grande école* of technical engineering. "Quite an accomplishment," Aimée said, wondering how this fit in.

"But Pascal still lives . . . lived nearby. Always fixed this, took care of that." Mademoiselle waved her hand around.

Aimée took in the recessed halogen lighting, felt the

warmth from the floor, surveyed the high-tech console of buttons labeled Heat 1, Hall, Boiler.

"Pascal did all this. You've noticed, eh?"

And lusted for a renovation like this for her own seventeenth-century flat. Right now Aimée would settle for consistent heat in their office.

"Beautiful and innovative," Aimée said, noticing the high-tech chrome laptop, a model that their part-time hacker Saj kept mentioning. The woman was more tech-savvy than most people half her age. "I imagine, a small repayment for devoting yourself to his upbringing."

She snorted. "Not so much. No one called me the nurturing type, but I provided. I managed stage sets at Théâtre de la Gaité Lyrique, the wardrobe. Pascal used to play back stage sometimes, but he grew up across the square in the Musée des Arts et Métiers. After school I'd find him there. The machines, gadgets stimulated his mind. Too much."

Aimée turned this over. "By that you mean . . . ?"

"He loved making 'inventions.' Obsessed." The old woman rolled her eyes affectionately. "Following the beat of a different drummer, as they say. Never played in the park with the other boys. He told me, when he was still a boy, that one day he'd work at the Musée. Because the Musée still kept alive the spirit of science, art, and invention of the medieval guilds that built the cathedrals. Can you imagine a teenage boy saying that?"

Mademoiselle Samoukashian gave a little shrug, sipped her Turkish coffee.

"Yet as a youngster he wore the dunce hat in the corner of the classroom, a *tête de Turc*."

Aimée nodded. "Me, too, for daydreaming." She took another sip. But she wondered at the point of this fable. What agenda lay behind this, other than reminiscing about her murdered great-nephew? Maybe this woman just needed to vent.

"But what an accomplishment, that Pascal entered a *grande école*," she said.

"*Mais oui*, but only after two years of competitive prep to pass the *mathématique supérieur*," Mademoiselle Samoukashian said, a hint of pride in her voice. "Another exam with a technology component for Arts et Métiers. Of the two thousand who pass the test, they accept six hundred."

"Sounds grueling." She was painting a picture of Pascal, Aimée realized.

"It was only the beginning!" she scoffed. "Then, a *grande école*. Before his first year, their assignments included figuring out how to write verses of Gothic script on matchsticks with a Rotring pen nib. He needed a magnifying glass to even see what he was writing, never mind figure out how to write it." She shook her head. "The *bizutage*, the ritual hazing, got worse in his first year. A strange group, if you ask me. Medieval."

Aimée needed to steer this back to Meizi. "Mademoiselle, the investigating *flics* suspect Chinese in your nephew's murder."

"You're the detective," she said without skipping a beat. "You found his body. What do you think?"

Aimée had thought a lot of things, all related to Meizi. Hoped to God she wasn't involved in his murder. Thoughts, like air, came cheap. "That's not my job. I'm looking for Meizi."

"Pascal never drank, hated gambling. He was so shy and awkward around women," said Mademoiselle Samoukashian. "No Chinese would kill him. No one here, young or old, trusts the *flics*. *Alors*, he spent all his free time volunteering at the Musée."

Whatever his involvement with Meizi, he had kept it from his great-aunt. Aimée had a thought. "Mademoiselle, with Pascal's *grande école* credentials, I wouldn't have thought he'd teach at an engineering trade school. Couldn't he have had any job he wanted?"

Mademoiselle Samoukashian bristled, her eyes sparkling

with anger. "Aimed higher, you mean. Command a top salary. Serve and sup with the elite."

Aimée wanted to kick herself. Tactless again. "*Desolée*, I didn't mean that the way it sounded."

"Of course you did." She shrugged. "You're not the first. Blame my Bolshie upbringing, but Pascal did me proud. He wanted everyone to benefit, not just a sliver of the top crust."

Mademoiselle Samoukashian took Aimée's demitasse, studied the dregs coating the sides. Nodded.

"I see a road. A long road. A wall, rounded like a tower. You are going to see a person. A place."

Foreseeing such a vague future in coffee grinds, Aimée thought, was less than helpful.

"Weren't you the one in the paper?" Mademoiselle Samou-kashian said suddenly. "A kidnapping, murder case before Christmas?"

Aimée cringed at the memory—her godfather, Morbier, had been a suspect in his girlfriend's murder; then there were the high-profile repercussions of recovering a Spanish princess who had been kidnapped by Basque terrorists. Aimée had hated the reporters besieging the office, the new flood of calls for help from distraught families of murder victims. She had promised herself all that was over. She'd never do criminal work again. And she'd kept that promise for all of a month.

"My firm does computer security," she said.

"But you're also a licensed private detective," Mademoiselle said, looking at Aimée's card. "According to this."

Aimée could learn nothing else here. She stood, slid her arms in her coat sleeves, and took a step toward the old woman. "Wonderful café, Mademoiselle."

"But this woman, this Meizi, you said there's a connection to Pascal?"

Aimée nodded, hoping this had jogged her memory. "Maybe you remember something Pascal said?"

Mademoiselle Samoukashian clamped Aimée's hand in an iron grip. "But you're looking for her. You think she saw who murdered my Pascal."

"I don't know," Aimée said.

"God shouldn't let a child die before his parents," Mademoiselle Samoukashian said, her voice small. "But I don't qualify; I just raised him."

Aimée leaned down and hugged her where she sat in her thatched chair, felt the thin shoulders, the heaving chest of this tough little old woman. Like her own grandfather, who'd stepped in to help raise her when her mother left. He'd pitched in when Aimée's father was on a stakeout, taken her to piano lessons, the auction gallery, supervised her homework.

When Aimée looked up, she saw tears pooled in those dark brown eyes. A look of despair.

"I don't trust the *flics*," Mademoiselle Samoukashian said. "Won't you help me?"

"I'd like to, but . . ."

"How much?" She reached under the piled napkins, pulled out a rubber-banded wad of francs. "Never mind, take it," she said, and thrust it into Aimée's hand.

"Mademoiselle, I can't take your money."

"My rainy-day money? What good's it to me now? You're already on the case." She squeezed Aimée's hand. "Find who murdered him."

Aimée looked away, torn. How could she investigate the murder for this old woman when her best friend's girlfriend might be the culprit? A bad feeling seeped in her bones. She was fraught with worry that she'd find Meizi involved.

"I can't guarantee you satisfaction. Or that we'll find his murderer. These cases . . . you don't want to know."

"Pascal was murdered behind a building, and I don't want to know?" The old woman leaned toward her, her eyes sharp. "I want justice."

"I'm truly sorry, but . . ." She paused. Pascal could have had a double life. Better to save his great-aunt from knowing. "Unless there's something pointing to—"

"But he was afraid."

Aimée blinked. "Afraid? You must tell the *flics*."

"You think I didn't? Did they want to listen to an old woman, clouded by grief, ranting about his project?"

"What project?"

"I don't know, but he kept a safety deposit box. In the Crédit Mutuel on rue Réaumur."

"I don't understand."

"A month ago, he told me if anything happened to him— his words—to open the safety deposit box." Mademoiselle Samoukashian rose. "Of course, this Meizi's hiding and scared. You find her, discover what she knows. I've got an appointment with the bank manager to open the safety deposit box today. Then I'll show you."

Aimée's heart tugged. She felt for this old woman.

"Don't do this for me, please. Do it for my Pascal."

Aimée's mind went back to the plastic-wrapped body dotted with snowflakes. That mouth opened in a silent scream. Those eyes frozen in terror.

She nodded. "No promises, Mademoiselle, but . . ." She hesitated. "Call me and we'll meet."

In the hallway, Aimée paused, loath to leave this grieving woman, her warm and inviting apartment.

Mademoiselle Samoukashian took her black purse from the coat rack by the door. She opened her wallet, a Fendi knockoff, and rifled through photos. "Here's Pascal in the school play. Oh, here's a science project based on a Knights Templar gadget. This one was taken at graduation."

Saddened, Aimée glanced at the thumbed and faded schoolboy photos, the progression as Pascal grew up.

"The Arts et Métiers campus at Cluny," Mademoiselle

Samoukashian said, flashing a photo of a group of young men on the ramparts of a castle. "Horrible place, in a medieval abbey. He hated it there," she said. "Let me give you one. So much better to remember him by than . . ." Her voice trailed off and she handed Aimée a photo of Pascal, wearing glasses, standing in what appeared to be his office. The Pascal Aimée preferred to visualize: big eyes, wild red hair, smiling.

"*Oui, merci.*"

A green carry-all bag hung under a jacket from the coat rack. Faux reptile, just like one she'd seen in the luggage shop. Her heart skipped. Here was a connection to Meizi.

"Pascal's bag?" Aimée asked.

Mademoiselle Samoukashian gave a tired shake of her head. "Force of habit." Her gaze looked faraway.

What did that mean? But if this belonged to Pascal, she wanted to examine it.

"May I look?" she said, not waiting for a reply.

Aimée's hand came back with a *carnet* of Métro tickets, a Eurostar ticket to London, a wad of francs. This put a new spin on Pascal's murder, only she didn't know how.

"Pascal planned a trip?" Maybe escape with Meizi?

Mademoiselle Samoukashian shrugged. "That's my middle-of-the-night bag," she said. "Pascal bought it for me. The ticket's got my name on it, if you notice. Also shoes, a change of clothes. We always kept a bag ready. You never knew when they would come. If we'd be warned in time."

Aimée stared at this little woman. "You prepared for roundups? But the Occupation's over, Mademoiselle."

"Not for some of us."

Aimée's heart churned. And it made sense.

Aimée kissed the woman's paper-thin cheeks, a smell of Papier d'Arménie clinging to her. "No wonder Pascal loved you so much."

"YOU'RE POPULAR, CLODO," said the volunteer at the Salvation Army shelter desk. "A *flic* left you a message. Someone else, too."

Clodo stiffened. Already? January bit with cold teeth if the *flics* wanted to talk to him. He needed to get the hell out of here.

Clodo waved his blistered hand. "I'll let my agent handle them." His lungs burned, his eyes teared. He needed something warmer to wear.

He rooted in the clothes donations pile, grabbing a scarf. Pink and thick cashmere. He wrapped it around his neck.

"Hot enough water in the showers today, Clodo?"

Always a new volunteer. Kids who knew nothing about the streets. Or life.

"Not bad," said Clodo.

Time to move. Once a week he came to this shelter in the east exit of the closed old Métro station. A shower, a meal, clothes, a warm place. But he hated the questions, the checking up. A few years ago, the city let the homeless sleep in alcoves on the platforms when the thermometer hit four degrees centigrade. Not anymore.

The volunteer refused to be put off. "The *flic* said it's important, Clodo."

As if he wanted to talk to a *flic*, after last night.

The *salauds* kicked him out from his spot on the stairs, which had been covered and dry. They'd questioned him about the *mec* the rats feasted on. Clodo, he minded his own business. Had to survive, didn't he? He learned that in the war.

A racking cough overtook him. Damn lungs.

The kid pointed to the nursing station. "Get your cough checked out, Clodo."

Like hell he would. He needed a drink. "Lend me some *fric*, eh. My cough syrup's ready at the pharmacy."

"You know we can't do that." The kid looked away. "But I can check on beds tonight in the Bastille shelter."

Damn do-gooder. He needed a drink. He snorted and mounted the stairs to Boulevard Saint-Martin.

Later he'd sleep in the old ghost station. He knew the subterranean web of tunnels like the holes in his shoes. Had slept there during the air raids in the war, while the British bombed the train supply depots. People forgot that. They forgot how once neighbors, shopkeepers, postmen, and bourgeois families all huddled together in the deep stations—République, Temple, Arts et Métiers, and Saint-Martin, the ghost station. They forgot how the aerial bombing reverberations rained powder over their faces. The terror.

But he didn't forget. He didn't forget his parents, either. Communists, rounded up the day his Aunt Marguerite took him to the doctor for his seven-year-old checkup. They'll come back, she'd said. But they didn't. She worked nights playing the accordion and singing at the dance hall on the Grands Boulevards. He'd go to the shelter with Madame Tulette, the concierge.

"Watch where you're walking, old man." In the sea of passersby, a man in a suit jostled Clodo into a half-frozen puddle. The pavement rumbled and warm gusts shot up through the grill from the Métro running below. He leaned against the kiosk to catch his breath. Horns blared.

He remembered his aunt coming home at dawn with a tired smile and a package of butter, bread, a tied length of *saucisson*. The contents varied. Sometimes he'd meet a soldier in the bathroom on the landing. Green-gray uniforms with lightning bolts; then, after *la Libération*, the uniforms were blue with stars.

One day he'd found an envelope with money from his aunt on the kitchen table. "Getting married in Canada. Will write from Quebec." But she didn't. After *la Libération* he found his parents' names on a deportation list of Jewish Communists.

Seized by another fit of coughing, he grabbed at the magazine rack. The kiosk vendor raised his fist. "Buy a paper or move on."

"Who reads that shit anymore, eh?" he snarled back, pulling his frayed fur coat tighter and shuffling away.

He anticipated snow. The chill air sliced his lungs as he breathed. Just as it had that other January—under another cloud-frosted sky—when he'd quit school.

Old Madame Tulette's son ran the silversmith's courtyard atelier and gave him odd jobs. He worked when he wanted. The years went by; *les Chinois* moved in and took over the building. The pain went to his legs, the women he slept with didn't invite him home as often, and he ended up on the streets. Not that he minded a bottle of wine under a roof of stars in the summer, or the shelters in winter, like during the war. But nowadays his joints ached. His perfect spot on the alley steps—layered with cardboard, newspapers, and blankets—was ruined.

"Clodo? Got wax in your ears? Can't you hear me, Clodo?"

The blue-uniformed *flic* shook his shoulder. "Why don't you tell me what you saw last night."

"You kicked me out, remember?"

"We took you to a warm shelter. Let's talk at the café. Try to remember, eh? You must have heard something, seen a Chinese girl. Help me, won't you?"

Help him, and get wrapped in plastic?

Like the other one?

Clodo lifted his bag and joined the *flic* at the zinc counter. "Order me a *café crème*. I need the WC."

And by the WC, he slipped out the back exit.

DOWN IN THE passage, Aimée fought the urge to light a cigarette. The pack of crumpled Gauloises lay, like a talisman, in the bottom of her bag. Just knowing its proximity reassured her, gave her the power to choose to smoke or not. She inhaled the crisp, cold air and exhaled, her breath like smoke.

She hit René's number on her cell phone. "The bags aren't the only faux things in the shop, René," Aimée said, unfurling her scarf. "The Wus aren't the Wus."

René cleared his throat. "Try making sense, Aimée."

"Visualize the new Monsieur Wu I met: middle-aged, shorter, speaks good French, with an attitude."

"New?"

She recounted what happened in the luggage shop. "Smelled bad, René. He'd prepared."

"And you bought it?"

She rooted for her gloves. "Hard to dispute after he showed me his business license, permit and ledger showing he's owned the shop since 1995."

"But he could have hidden the real Wus. Maybe he waited until after you left. Hurt them."

"I checked everywhere," she said. "There was nothing in back, just storage. So I took his fingerprints. My contact in the crime-scene unit will run the prints to find out his real identity."

Silence.

"*Alors*, what if he's the real deal?" she said. "For argument's sake, René, suppose the Wus we met are as faux as my leopard coat?"

Pause.

"I'll get back to you when I find something on Ching Wao." He hung up.

A taxi idled on rue Beaubourg and she hailed it.

"FNAC at Bastille," she said to the driver.

He hit the meter. "Shopping in those crowds?"

"Just the ticket window, five minutes. Then 36 Quai des Orfèvres."

Aimée hated waiting in the dark bowels of the prefecture by the crime-scene unit. Its bunker-like underground atmosphere was reinforced by narrow corridors, dim lighting, and serious uniformed law enforcement rushing in and out, carrying on hushed conversations under oppressively low ceilings.

Beside her, a glass case displayed the history of French criminology techniques. Notably those of Alphonse Bertillon, a police officer and biometrics researcher who—according to the placard in the case—created anthropometry, the identification system using photos and physical measurements to identify criminals. He was the first person in the world to use fingerprints to solve a crime—right here, in 1902, in the small, glassed laboratory, so the sign boasted. She'd researched Bertillon in a premed course and realized today they'd call him a racial profiler.

"Aimée, I'm fitting you in." Benoit, sporting Levi's under his lab coat, gestured her down the hall. A lank lock of brown hair fell across his forehead and pockmarked cheeks. "I was just about to lift prints off a batch of counterfeit francs."

"Can you do that?"

"Call me an optimist."

"Then call this slicing butter, Benoit."

He opened the lab door. Glanced around. Then motioned her inside. "Remind me why I'm helping you. Again."

"Can you spell M-O-T-L-E-Y C-R-U-E?"

His eyes popped. "You got the tickets?"

Scalper prices for a sold-out show at the new Stade de France next month had emptied her worn Vuitton wallet. And then some.

"For you, Benoit, the best. Front stage section in arena seating."

"We'll rock the place."

"Better you than me." Not her type of music.

The green-walled laboratory, small by some standards, housed up-to-date forensic fingerprint wonder machines, many of them British.

"Tell me you got a good set of latents."

She held out her *rouge-noir* nail polish bottle. "At least he held the whole thing in his hand."

"Position it for me the way your perp did."

She donned a set of blue plastic surgical gloves from the box on the counter. Careful not to smudge the bottle, she showed him, shaping her hand around the baggie.

He got to work dusting the glass surface with powder.

Nothing. Her heart dropped.

"Patience." Benoit redusted from another pot, then flipped on a blue light. "For you, Aimée, the works. Any idea what he'd been touching before?"

She thought back. "Plastic bags and synthetic materials."

"Meaning?"

"Those faux designer bags. Fuchsia, if that helps. The shop counter, a ledger written with a ballpoint pen."

He pulled a swing-arm magnifier over the bag, studied it. "*Voilà*. Micro traces of blue ink, I'd say, in the index fingerprint ridges. A little smudged on the thumb whorl."

"You'll run them now?" she said. "I need the works, Benoit."

He shrugged. "I'll need some help."

"That's on you." She held up the tickets. "But this guaran-tees you a hot date." Now she knew what it looked like when fingerprint techs salivated. "By the works, *bien sûr* you'll include the police database registry listing all *cartes de séjour* and pending applications, business permits and licenses."

Government bureaucrats loved paper. Logged applications, maintained files, registries and databanks. Any official request or form left a paper trail. Even the *objets trouvés*, or lost-and-found, had ledgers corresponding with police reports dating back over a hundred years. And that was just in the on-site storeroom.

"So how soon . . . ?"

"You're in luck." He snorted. "Demontellan's playing the piano now."

Playing the piano, the old term used for checking finger-print files.

"He's the best," Benoit said. "Knows the cards by heart."

Her heart fell. "Don't tell me you still match prints manually?"

"We use three match systems in total. More than the cow-boys, the Brits, or Interpol."

Thorough. No doubt he could do more. It never hurt to ask.

"Impressive." She wrote down Meizi's name in the spilled, white fingerprint powder. "Run this name while you're at it, eh?"

Benoit pushed his hair behind his ears. Winced.

She waved the tickets, still in the FNAC ticket envelope, until he nodded.

"This way."

"WE GOT A HIT. Now I call this synchronicity," said Demontellan. "My wife bought her bag in one of those places. A faux Fendi, whatever that means." Reddish-pink keloid scars ribbed what had once been Demontellan's ear and trailed down his neck into his shirt collar. A victim of the bombing, a few years earlier, in the Saint-Michel RER station, he'd been luckier than the others on the train. Demontellan wore thick-lensed, seventies-style glasses. His magnified eyes reminded her of an unblinking mackerel. His index finger stabbed a file labeled *Wu, Feng, age 29*.

He opened it to the record within. *Domiciled Ivry, owner of Lucky Luggage, rue au Maire.*

"But he's not twenty-nine years old," Aimée said loudly to Demontellan's ruined ear.

"Don't shout," he said. "My hearing's superb."

"*Desolée,*" she said, abashed, averting her gaze from the painful-looking scar tissue.

"Everyone does that at first," he grinned. "Bet my hearing's better than yours. I'm bionic. Cochlear implants."

Not knowing whether to laugh or applaud, she shrugged. "We're all special, Demontellan. Any photo of him?"

"For that let's take a little stroll." He led her to a bank of metal file cabinets, chose the W section, and pulled open a drawer at shoulder height. Oatmeal-colored fingerprint cards, filed by surname, stretched before her, some with worn, dog-eared edges, others crisp.

"My father used these," she said, amazed.

"For cross verification purposes, and individuals not entered into the main system, it does the job. *Zut*, I can match a card's prints faster than anyone can boot up, log in, enter the system, and search a database."

She nodded.

"That's if we had a current computer database," he grinned. "*Alors*, the Brigade Criminelle still types reports on Remingtons."

Archaic, like everything else at 36 Quai des Orfèvres.

"Plus I know the smell. I sniff better with these."

For any good *flic*, it came down to the nose. One's sense of smell developed over years, illustrating Oscar Wilde's aphorism, "Nothing worth knowing can be taught." A good *flic* could pull out a detail cataloged in the recesses of his mind. A name or an address cross-referenced to a memory, a whisper in a bar from an informer. The methodical, painstaking accumulation of details— piecing them together, building evidence, a case.

Computers didn't do that.

"W. Woo. Wu." Pause. "Here we go." Demontellan pulled out three cards. "Wu, Meizi, age 36; Wu, Feng, age 29; and Wu, Jui, age 30."

Aimée stared at the cards. None of the photos matched Meizi or her parents. What in hell was going on here?

"Demontellan, I suggest you route these to Prévost at the *commissariat* in the third."

"Think I do magic, too?"

She grinned. "You could head the report, 'Question of identity regarding witnesses and suspect in the homicide case reported last night." And conclude that the identity is inconsistent with fingerprints on file."

"Did Prévost request this?"

"He should have," she said. "But I'm sure you'll craft it so he thinks one of his men did. Cite a paperwork request lost in the shuffle. I'm sure you know how to word it."

Demontellan took off his glasses and wiped them with a handkerchief. "You must hold something over that boy."

"And he must hold something bigger over you," she said.

Demontellan gave a knowing smile. "It's evened out." He paused. "That help you?"

"The more I dig, the deeper the hole." Her finger traced the stiff edge of the Meizi Wu card. "Proving no one is who they say. But this gets me no closer to finding Meizi Wu."

He jerked his thumb toward his desk. "Benoit left you a file. On the house, he said."

She thumbed through photocopied business licenses, *carte de séjour* applications, work permits. All faux Wus. Ching Wao probably drove a Mercedes with the proceeds.

Disappointed, she picked up her bag from Demontellan's desk, and saw that a paper had slipped out.

A national museum employment application for a maintenance position at the Musée des Arts et Métiers. The application was for a Wu, Meizi, dated two weeks earlier, and listing as a reference Pascal Samour, faculty department head at CNAM.

Her heart raced. Pascal Samour had given Meizi a recommendation. While Demontellan was photocopying the application and fingerprint cards, Aimée checked the in-box on his desk.

Two current reports from Prévost's division. Taking advantage of Demontellan's turned back, she scanned the contents. And almost whistled.

"*Merci*, Demontellan," she said. "Get creative with Prévost. He needs the mental stimulation."

"NEW SPARK PLUGS, oil change. Your scooter will run like a dream, Aimée," said Zaco, wiping his greasy hands on his overalls at her local garage on the Île Saint-Louis.

Zaco told her the same thing last month. Her secondhand pink Vespa, Italian and temperamental, broke down with annoying regularity.

"*Merci*, Zaco." She knotted the cashmere scarf around her neck, donned her leather gloves, hit the kick-starter, and headed over Pont de Sully. She wove her scooter through the narrow backstreets to her office. The wrought-iron balconies cast long shadows in the gray winter light. She longed for the sun, even a glimmer.

Scenarios played in her mind. Was this a simple case of Meizi cheating on René? Maybe complications arose, as they usually did. Wrong place, wrong time? Say Meizi used the Wus, whoever they were, for a front. But why? To wangle René into marrying her? To use him for citizenship?

Or could Meizi's boyfriend, or the man who mistreated her, have threatened to hurt René?

Layered over that was the RG surveillance of the quartier. Did Samour's murder connect? Why had Samour recommended Meizi for a job?

All Aimée had were questions.

• • •

AT LEDUC DETECTIVE, warm air and a floral fragrance greeted her. At least the office heat worked. Unlike last winter. She hung up her damp coat, put her scooter keys in her bag.

"About time," René said, looking up from one of the three terminal screens on his desk. Beside him, Saj, their permanent part-time hacker and analyst, sat on a tatami mat with his laptop—his preferred mode of working. Despite the season, Saj was barefoot.

Aimée bit her lip, adrift on a sea of conflicting emotions. She was not eager to voice more suspicions of Meizi, fracture her crumbling image, or hurt René. Every part of her wanted to protect him.

"Those came for you," Saj said, unfolding from his lotus position and gesturing to her desk, where a bouquet of lush rose-blushed hibiscus sat. Who in the world sent hothouse hibiscus in January? She opened the card, which came from the florist on rue du Louvre.

> *I'll make up for this weekend in Martinique. Clear your calendar mid-February.*
>
> —Melac

Her heart jumped. Melac, Martinique, and sun. All in one? Guilt worked wonders. The card fell from her hand.

Saj caught it. Grinned. Flashed the card for René to see.

"Road trip, Aimée?" René asked, his eyes narrowing.

Could she afford to take time off?

"We've got two projects for the end of the month," René said, his voice strained, "and a possible third if we land the Sofitel security contract."

Routine computer security surveillance. Nothing he and Saj couldn't handle for a week. Had Meizi's disappearance, compounded by his hip pain, made him irritable? Or did she detect a note of jealousy? For a moment guilt invaded her.

She couldn't worry about that.

"Time to deal with that later, René," she said, slipping the card in her bag. "We've got more pressing things to discuss. Let me get you two up to speed. First, the Wus are not who we thought they were."

René's face reddened. "Lies." He slammed his fist on the desk. "You can't prove that."

She pulled out the copies of the fingerprint cards from her bag, spread them on René's desk. "Matter of fact, I can."

René leafed through the cards. Shook his head. "Who the hell are these people?"

"Illegal émigrés, I don't know," Aimée said. "Meizi could be part of something larger."

A hurt look wrinkled René's brow.

"Think back to the map in Ching Wao's office, the circles around cities," she said.

"Maybe they're part of a smuggling ring," Saj said, lifting up a newspaper. "The front page today in *Le Monde* has an article on rhinoceros horn pirated from China. It's prized for increasing virility."

Saj and his daydreams. "Meizi cleaned toilets, for God's sake," Aimée said. "Who knows what else. Didn't you notice her calloused hands, her bitten nails?"

A ping came from Saj's computer.

"Got a hit." Saj pointed to his terminal. "This Ching Wao seems to be a man of many talents."

Maybe many faces. She brightened. From the keystroke recovery program he ran, she could see the telltale sniffing in the network. "Sniffing keystrokes, Saj? Nice high?"

Saj gave a sideways grin, pushed his dirty-blond dreadlocks behind his ears. "Network eavesdropping's a nicer term, Aimée.

Here's Ching Wao's wholesale prêt-à-porter business on rue de Saintonge."

Interested, Aimée leaned over Saj's laptop. She remembered the frightened girl stacking cartons of hoodies. A connection?

"That's all?"

"The beginning, Aimée."

"Pascal Samour bought his great-aunt the exact green bag they carried at the luggage shop," she said. "That's the second connection between Meizi and the murder." She set down the recommendation letter. "Now the third: Pascal Samour recommended her for a job at the museum where he volunteered."

René snapped, "You're implying Meizi was his girlfriend, that she led me on, two-timed me, *non?*"

Aimée averted her gaze. "*Non,* you've said it René."

"How could Meizi, not much taller than me, murder a man? Or wrap him to a heavy wood palette with industrial plastic?" René's voice trembled in anger. "*Et puis,* make it to the *resto* in time to order and be ready to serve us soup when we arrived without breaking a sweat?"

"I'm saying we find her, René," Aimée said, keeping her voice even. "Find out why she ran away after receiving that phone call. But don't you wonder why no one is who they say they are, why people's identities change like cards?"

"You're neglecting the dead man's phone, assuming he carried one." Saj pulled his dreadlocks back and tied them with a bandanna. "What if he called her for help? It's close, you said. So she gets there and he's being attacked."

"We're spinning theories until the autopsy reveals the cause and time of his death." Aimée set her bag down on her desk and scrolled through her cell phone contacts for Serge, her pathologist friend at the morgue. But his voice mail answered. "Taking a personal day. If you need immediate consultation, contact admin affairs at 01 55 34 78 29."

Great. Up the river without a paddle, until she got a hold of him. Unless . . .

Thoughts spun in her mind.

Saj reached for a steaming cup of green tea."But what if the killer picked up the victim's phone and called the last number he'd dialed—Meizi's?"

"That's assuming he had a phone, Saj," René said, shaking his head.

"Say that call alerted her," Aimée said, sitting down to think. Saj was just supposing, but his ideas weren't completely wild. "Before she left the *resto*, Meizi looked back, worried. I don't know how to explain it." Aimée shrugged. "Say she ran by, saw or heard the murderer, then called it in?"

"But Meizi trusts me." The hurt in René's tone stung her. "She knows I'd do anything for her. Why wouldn't she tell me?"

Trusted him to a point.

Maybe the man Aimée had seen on the corner was her pimp. But she kept that to herself. René's Glock bulged in his jacket pocket. He was ready to blast his competition.

Meizi lied about where she lived, what she did. Aimée had no doubt she'd strung him along. And her unsmiling parents?

René shook his head, adamant. "The *flics* found her photo, they suspect her. Of course she's hiding."

"But like you said, wouldn't she call you for help? Try to explain?"

"There's only one reason why she hasn't called—she can't."

No work would get done until they found Meizi. Part of Aimée dreaded knowing; the other wanted to resolve this for René. Stand by him when it hit the fan.

The opening strains of something by Mozart trilled from René's pocket. Hope filled his face as he clicked open his cell phone.

"*Oui?*" He turned away. "Now?" He edged off his orthopedic

chair. Flipped his phone closed. "Prévost wants me to sign my statement."

Aimée stood up and reached for her coat. "Let me drive."

"No need." René gave a grim smile. "New developments," he said.

"You think he'd share them after he treated us like suspects?" Aimée asked. How many times had she heard the same tired technique? "It's a ploy."

"He needs to know about the Wus."

"Taken care of, René," she said. She explained what she'd gleaned from the hurried look at Prévost's reports in Demontellan's in-box; Prévost, as *chef de groupe*, had convinced le Proc that his investigative unit of the Police Judiciaire knew the quartier, had language skills and informers for a more efficient investigation than *la Crim*. "In other words, Prévost talked his way into control of the investigation."

"So?" René bristled.

"Even the tofu seller lied to Prévost, from the report I saw." Aimée shook her head. "Doesn't bode well. By now, after years in the quartier, he should have established rapport—run small investigations, know the prostitutes, the gamblers, the bartenders. If any were arrested, he'd have made deals with the prosecutor and turned them into informants."

"But Meizi's in danger." René buttoned his Burberry overcoat. "This is his job."

His job to protect a suspect who fled?

"Don't count on it, René."

But a cold blast of air came from the hallway as René slammed the door behind him.

"One must have a clear mind to discover the true path," Saj said, a dreamy look appearing in his eyes. Not this again. "Disturbed auras cloud this room. Divisive forces," he said. "We'll channel clarity, meditate on the white light." Saj unrolled his meditation mat.

"Like I've got time for that now?"

"René's pulled by forces of samsara." Saj nodded to himself. "You need it, Aimée."

It couldn't hurt. Right now she'd try anything. She pulled off her boots and sat down cross-legged. "The abridged version, Saj." More her style to discover facts, links, and let them percolate.

"Lift your diaphragm," Saj said. "Take a deep, cleansing asana breath."

She took a breath. Another. Centered on the air filling her lungs.

"Focus on your pulse, the in and out, the area above your middle chakra."

She closed her eyes. Saj's exhortations on breathing, along with the whine of a siren outside on the street, faded.

Another breath. A humming resounded in the recesses of her mind, growing louder, pervasive. Sewing machines. The terrified girl folding hoodies. Mademoiselle Samoukashian's words came to her: *but there are always places to hide, to meld into the woodwork* . . . Now it was the Chinese—blending in, working, hiding in plain sight. Just part of the daily bustle of the quartier.

By the time Saj sounded his gong, her mind had cleared. And she had a plan.

"*BONJOUR.*" AIMÉE SMILED at the stocky man puffing on a hookah in the reception cubicle in the hotel around the corner from the luggage store. "You're Aram?"

He nodded and inhaled, the water bubbling. He exhaled a long plume of smoke, scrutinizing her with his close-set brown eyes through the haze. Fruit notes laced the thick tobacco aroma. Not unpleasant, but it would cling to her skin, her clothes.

Aram smiled back, his teeth gleaming. "May I help you, Mademoiselle?" About five-foot-eight. Brown, wavy hair; a sparse beard and thick jowls. Familiar, but from where?

"He's expensive, your *dentiste?*"

"Not when his cousin eats my couscous every night on his security guard break."

Her ears perked up. Nice gig. "And that's where?"

Aram scratched his beard. "*Vous êtes du type curieux, non?* Lots of your kind sniffing around here."

She threw up her hands. "Can't hide anything from you, Aram." She pushed her *détective privé* card across the gouged counter. "Like it says, I work privately."

Aimée had a business to run, and a missing Chinese woman to find before her partner went off the deep end. Worse, she was now caught up in helping the little old woman, Pascal's great-aunt, to find justice. Those eyes. She shouldn't have looked at his eyes.

"I shouldn't say this, client privilege, et cetera," she said, "but I think you've noticed him, Monsieur Friant. He favors velvet-collared Burberry overcoats. About this tall." She raised her arm to her waist.

"A lot of people walk by here," he said, pushing the hookah to the back of the office. "And if I have?"

"Confidential, of course, but a matter of the heart." She gave a little sigh. "His girlfriend worked in the nearby luggage shop. She's disappeared."

He'd understand that.

"But that didn't come from me," she said. "*Alors*, I'm knocking on doors here. No one talks to me. Word is you're connected. I'm prepared to pay."

Aram grinned a white smile. He'd taken the bait. She reached for her wallet.

"This? You think I believe your little card? Cheap trick."

Her hand froze in her bag.

"See, I have nice cards, too, like three-star hotels. *Un mec* prints them for me around the corner." He fluttered his ringed hand, a dismissive wave. "Good luck knocking on doors, Mademoiselle."

But she remembered now where she'd seen him before—the stark hospital emergency room, her cousin Sebastien's faint pulse when he almost OD'd, the small-time dealers who informed for immunity. Aram. Only his teeth hadn't been so white then.

"Now I wouldn't like to crimp your drug trade," she said, pulling out her wallet, "by ruining your evening delivery schedule and alerting the *flics*. Or tell my RG contact how you finance your cheap couscous." She stared hard into his face. "But I could."

He returned her stare, his dark eyes never leaving hers. The wall clock above the counter ticked. The sizzle of something frying came from the back window, which overlooked a shoebox courtyard and kitchen.

"Big talk, Mademoiselle. You've got nothing."

"Want to chance it?" She leaned forward.

"I run a hotel," he said.

"Once a dealer, always a dealer. But I should thank you," she said. "No hard feelings. Best thing that could have happened to my cousin Sebastien, your old client. You ended him up in rehab. Six years now and he's straight, runs his own business. He's getting married, too." She shrugged. "*Zut*, Aram, your sideline doesn't interest me. It's better we help each other."

"Go bother someone else, Mademoiselle."

"My client doesn't trust the *flics*," she said. "I don't blame him. But the *flics* won't leave Chinatown alone after last night's murder." She watched his eyelids flicker. "You know how set in their ways they get. One-track focus. Don't you want them out of your soup?"

"So you think I know who killed him?"

"Do you?"

He shook his head. "Might have, as I told the *flics*, if I'd been working that day. Instead I had front-row seats." He pointed to the Palais des Sports boxing match poster on the wall: The Mad Moroccan vs. Steel Punk. "Bought my tickets six months ago."

"And who won?" She would check.

"The Mad Moroccan delivered."

"I need to find Meizi Wu," Aimée said. "I think she knows what happened."

"Who?" His gaze strayed to her wallet.

Don't play with me, she wanted to say. She hoped she'd hooked him and just needed to reel him in.

"As I said, from the luggage store." She paused. "She may use another name."

"No one is who they say they are, Mademoiselle."

She nodded. "True. About five feet tall, black ponytail."

"Generic. Look on the street. Describes a good quarter of them."

She pulled her wallet back. "I've got more details. First I need to know if you're interested."

He met her gaze. "Five hundred francs interested."

Expensive.

"Two fifty up front," she said, "the rest when I find her."

"I can't guarantee . . ."

Aimée slid the francs over the counter. "She speaks good French."

"Narrows it," he said, pocketing the francs.

"She's part of Ching Wao's cleaning operation in the thirteenth arrondissement," she said.

"Ching Wao's gone. *Phfft*." He opened his palm.

"Tell me something I don't know, Aram. When I got there, his tea was still warm."

A gleam of admiration flashed in Aram's eyes. "*Bon*, he pulled girls from several sweatshops. Mixed and matched. For another hundred, there's a list for you."

"And a way in?"

"That's extra."

Saturday, Noon

ANXIOUS, RENÉ LOCKED the door of his Citroën on a side street near Leduc Detective. Prévost had been called out. René had given his statement to a sergeant who'd turned a deaf ear to his questions. So far no one from the dojo had heard from Meizi. After obtaining the address of the property management agency that had rented the space to Ching Wao, he found the office closed for the weekend.

Meizi didn't answer her phone.

He stepped over an icy puddle in the cobbled street. And slipped. He grabbed the wall, a sharp pain shooting up to his thigh. René hated days like this, the permeating dampness. He longed for his hot water bottle and an Epsom-salt bath, the only relief. He glanced down narrow, congested rue Vauvilliers, thinking of the long three blocks to reach Leduc Detective.

His mind went back to the e-mail his friend Marcel had sent him last night from Silicon Valley.

You'd love it here, René. Three new start-ups approached me today. Cutting edge, opportunities mushrooming, venture capitalists and tall, blonde Californiennes, the beach forty minutes away . . . There's these two mecs from Stanford, crazy with search engine concepts, smart . . . calling this little idea Google.

Not for the first time, René wondered why he slogged through damp, cold Paris when he could be enjoying the beach and sun, the chance to bite into a new field as it developed. Join the ground floor of these start-ups. Mountain View . . . where the hell was that, and how far from the beach?

But he knew the answer.

He trudged ahead, concentrating on avoiding the ice, the slush, the slick pavers. He turned the corner and found his way blocked by a delivery van. The chill blast of wind cut René's cheeks and sent shooting cold up his legs. Why hadn't he taken a taxi?

Then he realized he'd circled back the way he'd just come from in this warren of streets. Right back to his parked car. *Merde!* He shooed away a fat pigeon in his path. At his height, his gaze barely reaching over the parked car hoods, everything loomed gigantic. He never let on to Aimée how often he got lost on foot.

Or his feelings for her, which simmered just under the surface—until he met Meizi. Meizi gave him happiness he'd never known before. Or would give him, at least, over time, once her parents warmed to him. But she'd forgotten his ring on the table.

Had she dumped him, just like that? A horn blared, interrupting his thoughts. His phone trilled in his pocket.

Meizi. Excited, he hit answer.

"Are you all right?" he gasped.

"As soon as you give me a clue concerning the spyware tracking popping up on your desktop, René," said Saj.

Disappointed, he stood on the damp pavement in the slush and biting cold.

"Network it to your terminal, Saj," he said. "Have you dug up anything on Ching Wao's business license?"

"A common name, it turns out."

"So let's narrow them down."

Time to get to work.

Saturday, Noon

HALF AN HOUR later, after a plate of spiced lamb couscous, Aimée sat at a Formica table in a back nook adjoining the hotel's kitchen.

"There are only three addresses on the list," Aimée told Aram over her tiny glass of sweet mint tea.

"Be happy you've got that," he said.

"Pretty expensive, Aram."

"So's the payoff I make to stay open. Factor that in."

"Protection money?" Aimée pulled out her tube of Chanel Red, swiped her lips.

"At first I refused, but fires in my kitchen changed my mind."

"You're not saying the *flics*—?"

"Chinese mafia," Aram interrupted, lowering his voice. "I pay, like everyone on the street. They extort, kidnap shop owners' kids if they don't pay. Demand the gold bars under the bed and a cut in the business." He sipped his tea. "The quartier's wrapped up tight, all 'in-house.'"

No wonder the *flics* got nowhere.

"And the girls?"

"I don't know, don't ask."

"For the meal, Aram." She slid ten francs over the table.

But he shoved the money back. "I invited you."

Service compris? She liked that, but wrote it off to ingrained Arab hospitality. "*Merci.* What's the word on the street about last night?"

He smiled. Again that white smile. "No one sees. No one hears anything. The usual."

"Let me understand this. You're saying if someone did witness the murder, they—"

"Shut their mouths." He sliced his index finger across his neck. "*Compris?*"

She suppressed a shudder, picked up her bag and pushed back her chair from the table. Paused at the distant look in Aram's close-set eyes.

"That incident with your cousin, not my doing," he said. "Just so you know. The hard stuff, not my thing."

She believed him. "But I'm proud of Sebastien. He heeded the wake-up call."

"Not many do." And from the downcast look, she realized Aram knew of what he spoke.

AIMÉE HEADED HER scooter up rue des Vertus, past the Tai Chi practitioners in the Square du Temple, where denuded trees shivered in the wind. Across from Eglise Sainte Elisabeth, she turned right at la poste, whose grilled doors were open to a line of seniors snaking out to the street. Lining up for their monthly pension checks. Even in this weather!

A few brave brasserie patrons sat outside on rattan chairs under flapping awnings. Here the one-way streets were double-parked, and Aimée narrowly missed a woman pushing a stroller. She had to hop off her scooter and thread it through cité Dupetit-Thouars by foot. Narrow lanes of shuttered shop fronts sported peeling posters and flaking stucco, just as in black-and-white Brassai photos of prewar Paris. A *luthier*, a stringed-instrument maker, still operated behind dark windows. Otherwise, the old shops looked deserted, awaiting the gentrification heralded by the bright, white facade of a trendy kitchenware shop.

She parked her scooter on the slush-covered cobbles at the

curb. Down another open passage lined by two-story buildings, she found 55. Children's voices came from an interior
courtyard.

She pressed the button and the dark-green door clicked.
Pushing it open, she found another arched door, its sign
engraved in gold letters: Lestimet, Custom Racing Cars.

Posh and exclusive. Not her destination.

"Lost, Mademoiselle?" A Frexpresse deliveryman appeared
at the door.

"My friend's meeting me."

She gestured to a smaller door, unpolished and water-
stained. "Maybe I'm wrong," she said, making this up as she
went along, "but I thought she said it was for rent."

He nodded. "It's been vacant on and off for years. Bad leaks.
Not on my pickup route anymore."

Talkative, this man. Didn't he have deliveries to make?

"Really?" She kept her eye on the door, hoping someone
would come out so she could sneak in.

"You're better off somewhere else. A real headache, I've
heard." He leaned forward as if in confidence. "You know, it
was a nightclub during the war. They kept it secret from the
Boches. Supposedly Maurice Chevalier liked the girls there.
Then squatters for years."

Perfect venue for an illegal sweatshop.

She waited until he'd waved good-bye and buzzed himself
out, then put her ear to the door. Ticking noises, the smell of
leather.

The door opened and she caught herself before she fell inside.

"*Pardonnez-moi,*" she said to the surprised middle-aged Chinese woman hurrying out. When she didn't stop, Aimée
walked inside.

In the weak light falling from the glass-roofed atelier, thirty
or so Chinese women of various ages worked at industrial
sewing machines. She scanned the downturned faces. No one

looked up, all intent on feeding thin pigskin leather under the punching needles. Mattresses were stacked against one water-stained wall.

Mon Dieu, they slept here. They must work in shifts.

In a corner, a group hand-stitched delicate leather straps onto handbags they took from an overflowing bin. These handbags, Aimée realized, sold for thousands of francs in Place Vendôme. It sickened her, almost as much as the pervasive leather odor.

But no Meizi. *Merde*.

A woman in the corner watched Aimée, saying something under her breath to the woman beside her.

Aimée scanned the walls for a schedule, anything listing workers. Perhaps her timing was off, and Meizi worked the night shift? She saw only a calendar, still turned to December, with a picture of a faded Christmas tree. She peered around stacks of cardboard boxes labeled: Fontain, *luxe à la mode fabriqué en France*.

Over the punching machines she heard someone approaching. Best defense was a good offense, her father always said.

She pulled out her phone. Hit mute. "The orders?" She spoke into her silent phone. "But I'm here!" She whipped around to face a short Chinese man in red-framed glasses, with spiked, blond-tipped hair.

"*Attends*," she said as he opened his mouth. She rolled her eyes and raised her hand. "Of course I'll ask him," she said into the phone, nodded as if listening intently, then clicked off.

"Monsieur, I'm Melanie, Fontain's new distributor," she said breathlessly and shook his hand. "I won't take your time except to check if the order's ready."

He blinked.

"Don't tell me it's not ready?" she said in feigned dismay. "Tonight's order?"

"But it's supposed to be packed, ready for shipment."

"Shipment?"

Wrong. She had to salvage this, keep him off-kilter.

"New policy," she said, thinking fast. "We're treating these leather bags as if they could be shipped overseas. Like the Italian brands. Impresses the retailers."

Nonplussed, he shrugged. "Not my end."

"So you're telling me what, it's not ready?"

"Ten P.M. tonight," he said. "Like usual. What's going on?"

"That's what I'd like to know."

"Let me call the office, check on this."

She could only keep this up so long before she blew it. "The schedule's fixed?" She looked around. "So you've got another shift in tonight to guarantee the order's ready?"

"But who's your contact, anyway?" His eyes narrowed behind his glasses. "Why don't you know how we process standing orders?"

She'd ruffled his feathers. Stupid.

She stepped forward, waved her finger close to his red glasses. He didn't like that, she could tell. "Off point, Monsieur." She raised her voice: "I'm asking how you'll fill the order with only this crew. You have more people coming in, yes or no?"

He stepped back. Nervous now. Reached for his phone.

She punched numbers on her cell phone. "*Bon*, we're canceling the order."

A long moment passed. Several heads looked up, then back down at their machines.

"*Mais Mademoiselle, pas de problème*," he said, clicking off his phone and now fawning. "Six of our finishers arrive in an hour to add the final touches, do quality control."

He didn't want to lose the order he thought she had power over. He smiled. Small teeth.

Scared. Good.

"Not those young ones who clean toilets for Ching Wao! We expect experienced hands."

He blinked again. "I don't know what you mean." But he did. "They've all worked with me before . . ."

"How long?"

"On this fine detail? The lining, the seams? Three, four years. We only use the older women."

And then it hit her. All the women were wearing cotton gloves. "Do those gloves protect their hands?"

"But Mademoiselle, cotton lisle absorbs moisture and oils from the skin to prevent stains and protect the leather. Our workers do precise work, keep their hands supple."

He approached a woman at the nearest machine. Motioned for her to stop and take off her gloves. "See?"

Disgusted, she looked at the smooth, pale hands. Not work-worn like Meizi's. But she'd found out what she came for.

"*Bon*, I'll keep this between you and me," she said, then turned on her heel and hurried out before he could stop her.

She ran through the next coved door, down the narrow passage and to her scooter, not pausing to catch her breath. All that to find Meizi didn't work here.

She battled a mounting feeling that going around intimidating sweatshop managers would get her nowhere. She hated snooping, invading the lives of women forced to work in underground sweatshops. A wild-goose chase? Smarter to cut her losses and think of another way. But which way?

She pulled her scooter off the kickstand, turned the ignition, and squeezed the clutch into first gear.

One address down. Two more to go.

AIMÉE STRODE INTO the cobbled Passage du Pont-aux-Biches, which led up to a steep stretch of staircase and rue Meslay, a cache of designer wholesale shoe stores. Her friend

Martine labeled it "the stairway to heaven." But Aimée didn't have time for shoes now.

Two men in overalls hauled an antique harp through the doorway of No. 32. She followed the grunting men and paused in the courtyard. Pots of geraniums lined the damp butterscotch stone walls. Upscale and bourgeois. Not what she figured for a sweatshop.

"Up here, Messieurs, top floor." A gray-haired woman smiled and beckoned from an upstairs window.

"Up yours, Madame," muttered one of the men under his breath. Had Aram steered her wrong?

Aimée closed her eyes and listened, distinguishing the sounds of the movers mounting the creaking staircase, the rush of water in courtyard pipes. And then she heard it. A faint, continuous clicking.

The clicking grew louder as she followed them to the back of the courtyard. Behind it a coved walkway nestled into the remnants of an old wall. The clicking drifted up from a grilled vent set in cracked stone. She lowered her head to duck into the dark stairway, treading over the uneven dirt to find herself in a humid warren of caverns. Vaulted stone arches supported the low ceilings. It was positively dungeon-like. She remembered a school field trip to an old château where, during the Terror, revolutionaries chained aristocrats to metal rings on the walls. Not too different, she thought.

Bare white bulbs dangled from the ceiling, illuminating squatting young Chinese women surrounded by red silk flowers—hundreds of them, exploding with color in the dank cavern. She scrutinized the young women's faces as their fingers worked nonstop, twisting bright red flowers onto green wire stems. By an arch she saw a ponytail bent down over a pile of flowers.

"Meizi?"

A few women looked up with questioning eyes.

"Lunchtime?" an older woman said. She made a gesture of eating, and several others laughed.

Aimée stepped around the flowers and bent down. "Meizi, are you okay?"

The young woman looked up. Glasses, brown birthmark on her cheek. "Boss eat lunch. Back soon."

Shaken, Aimée sat back on her haunches like everyone else. The women watched her with curiosity, not fear.

"Beautiful flowers," Aimée said. "Do any of you know Meizi Wu?" She pointed to the woman's ponytail. "Hair like hers?"

A few smiles. The women kept twisting the stems.

Didn't they understand? Did they think she was crazy? Or both?

But she had an idea.

She rooted in her bag. Found the red velvet jewelry box she'd forgotten to give back to René. Held it up.

"Meizi forgot her birthday present." She cleared her throat and sang, "Happy birthday to you, happy birthday to you, happy birthday dear Meizi . . ."

More smiles. One woman nudged the pixie-haired woman next to her, who smiled.

"Meizi Wu," she said, pointing to herself.

A joke? But no one laughed.

"I mean Meizi Wu, who worked for Ching Wao."

She nodded. "Me."

Another idea flat on the dirt. Aimée shook her head. "*Desolée*, but . . ."

"You look." In her silk-stained hand, the woman held a *carte de séjour*. It showed her photo with the name Meizi Wu, and the same address on rue au Maire. The luggage store.

Startled, Aimée leaned forward. As Aram had said, no one was who they said they were. Yet she could work this for information.

Aimée took out the luminous pearl ring. "*Belle*, eh? It's for the other Meizi. Give me Ching Wao's number, okay? I want to tell him."

She shrugged. "I don't know."

"Don't know, or don't want to tell me?"

"Boss call him." Her face was blank now, no longer smiling.

But she had to get information. Something. "Where do you sleep?"

She pointed to the address.

"No, you don't. Tell me the truth." Aimée set the ring back in the box.

"You say you give me." Her eyes teared, and Aimée's heart clenched.

"We live at Chinese evangelical church," said the woman next to her in accented but proficient French.

"Who are you?"

"Nina's my French name," she said. "We're Christian. We study and pray with a pastor, who gives us a dormitory. No one works for Ching Wao, if they can avoid it."

"But these flowers—"

"Bad times now," Nina interrupted. "We do piecework. Have to." She paused. "Ching Wao's contact gave her this card yesterday. Our families pay lots of money in China for this. We don't ask questions. You'll give her the ring?"

"Cash is more useful." Aimée pressed a hundred francs into the girl's hands. "But she got a raw deal with that card. The *flics* suspect Meizi Wu in last night's murder on rue au Maire. Or didn't Ching Wao tell you?"

Nina spoke rapidly in Chinese to the increasingly frightened-looking girls.

"Something bad might have happened to the other Meizi," Aimée said. "I need to find Ching Wao."

"No one knows where he goes."

Great.

"Can't you think back, remember something, anything? What if she's hurt, or being held prisoner?"

Nina shook her head. "Bad people. Better stay away. You're a French woman. You don't know."

Like that made a difference to Meizi? Aimée wanted to shake this woman.

"But Ching Wao pays all of you centimes while he makes thousands of francs," she said, her voice rising. "A man extorts money from this girl's family for the *carte de séjour* of a murder suspect? But you think I don't know, or can't understand, or not want to help?"

Her speech was met by silence, broken only by the clicking of wire and shushing noises of silk. A chill went up her spine. She turned around.

A Chinese woman stood with Styrofoam containers of takeout food, glaring at her.

"Private business," she said. "You better leave. We have a permit to work here."

Aimée doubted that. But she was tired of seeing fake papers and arguing with people who would disappear.

She left another hundred francs by the girl's leg, then stood and made her way out.

In the dank passageway, she felt a tug on her coat sleeve.

Nina pulled her close. "Ching Wao gets girls from Tso, a snakehead. Bad teeth. Everyone knows him on rue au Maire."

And then she'd gone.

"TOUGH GOING, RENÉ. The two sweatshops I checked out were dead ends," she said into her phone. She pulled her collar up against the damp chill. "But I discovered Meizi's *carte de séjour* has gone to another Meizi."

"Sweatshops?" René said. "Start at the beginning, Aimée."

She gave him a brief account, told him about Aram and Tso, the snakehead.

"Breaking bread with a dealer who sold drugs to your cousin?"

"He's a source, René." One of the reasons she hated criminal investigation. Yet, down and dirty resulted in leads and information, her father always told her. You just take a long, hot shower later. "Not that I'd do it again, though he does serve a mean couscous."

"You believe this Aram?"

"I believe he dislikes paying Chinese protection money," she said. "Let's call it a mutual non-admiration society."

"So he'd know this Tso," he said. "We have to prove my Meizi's innocent."

Silver rivulets of rain snaked down the apartment windows overlooking Passage du Pont-aux-Biches. Aimée's shoulders slumped. Why couldn't René get it?

"But Chinatown's a closed world," she said, frustrated. "I'm getting nowhere."

"Has that ever stopped you before, Aimée?"

Saturday, Noon

CLODO BURPED. HE was safe from the *flic*, celebrating down in the Métro on the bench of the line 9 platform at République station. He steadied his shaking hand around the bottle of red, trying to rid his mind of what happened last night, the *mec*'s cry for help.

Unsuccessful, he watched the surge of passengers. That poor *mec* didn't deserve suffocating like that. Who did?

The burnt-rubber smell from the train brakes lingered in the fetid air. The *parfum* of his childhood, of the underground. A warning buzzer sounded and the doors shuddered closed. Then the train rumbled off, gathering speed.

Clodo swigged from his bottle on the deserted platform, watching the train's red lights disappear in the dark tunnel. In the distance he heard the grating of a shutter being rolled down, closing off this section.

Now he could get some sleep.

Snatches of conversation heralded the crew who maintained the subterranean world—three hundred stations, more than two hundred kilometers of routes unseen by *flics*. The Métro workers were simple to avoid if one knew the station maintenance closure schedule via the homeless grapevine. And Clodo did, courtesy of a fellow clochard. On the weekends, no line work, apart from stock and service repair runs, would run on this route, which branched toward Strasbourg Saint-Denis.

Ever since the war, he'd dreamed of working in the Métro. It was a second home to him, in a way, after the nights taking shelter in the station. Always good with his hands, he'd applied at the Vincennes train repair center, but without a school certificate he had no chance.

He downed the dregs from his bottle, tossed it in the bin. Time for his stash in the Métro tunnel.

And to barter the cell phone he'd found on the steps near the body. Wouldn't do the *mec* any good now. But Clodo would raise a bottle to his memory.

At the mouth of the tunnel, he ignored the yellow sign saying *Passage Interdit au Public—Danger* and the blinking signal-switch panel. He followed the narrow walkway hugging the curved wall of the Métro tunnel. The service walkway supported a small, green, illuminated track that stretched ahead in the darkness. Clodo inched his cold fingers along the grimy wall for several yards until his thumb caught on the flaking mortar. He wedged out the loose brick and reached into the niche for the bag.

His stash.

As he replaced it with the *mec*'s cell phone, the tunnel filled with blaring white light and a terrifying whoosh as a repair train thundered through like a luminous snake. He saw the momentary silhouette of a figure before the bright light passed. He closed his eyes, grabbed the wall. Wind blew grit in his nose and ears. The walkway vibrated beneath his feet.

Merde. He moved faster. The walkway led down three steps to the rails. Candles flickered ahead on the ghost station platform, silhouetting blanketed mounds. The enclave of the homeless. Not far.

With the forecasted drop in temperature today and the shelters full, it was too much trouble for the Métro *flics* to rouse the drunken and unwashed. Clodo clutched his stash inside his fur coat, knotted his pink scarf, and steadied himself, careful to avoid the live third rail. 750 volts of electricity. He'd seen a man fried last year. Lying on the rail, his hair standing up like a porcupine's.

Raised drunken voices and red wine smells told him he'd arrived. Graffitied posters and water-stained advertisements from the forties still clung to the walls. Forgotten relics, like those who clustered here for warmth, but intimately familiar to Clodo. He remembered his mother swearing by Persil soap, like the old pockmarked green bottle half visible on the tattered poster. It was one of the few things he remembered her saying.

He gathered crumpled newspapers and torn cardboard, nodded to Fichu, who huddled in several khaki sleeping bags.

"Want to rent me a bag, Fichu?"

"If the price feels right," Fichu mumbled. "What you got, Clodo?"

Clodo sat down. A wave of dizziness, then a fit of coughing overtook him. Damn lungs burned.

He fumbled in his coat, keeping the bag from Fichu's view. Pulled it out.

"What the . . . ?"

In his hand was a sealed Plasticine bag of white powder.

"I don't do sugar, Clodo."

"Some bastard took my bottle," Clodo said. "My wine's gone."

"Left you with something you don't want to keep." Fichu shook his head. Bleary-eyed, he rubbed his nose. "Dope dealers here these days. Strangers."

Clodo struggled to his feet. "We'll see about that. He owes me, the *salaud*," he said. Then he remembered. "Interested in a cell phone, Fichu? It's fresh."

"Like I'd get reception down here?"

Clodo shuffled to the end of the platform. Another fit of coughing overtook him. The tunnel reverberated with the roar of an approaching train.

"Looking for this?" a voice said behind him.

Before Clodo could turn, he felt a hand on his back. Then a push. Felt himself flying in front of the blinding light.

"BUT I TELL *flic* this morning," said Madame Liu, "I no see *le petit*, or you. I go to funeral service last night."

Aimée stared at Madame Liu, the manager of Chez Chun, a tiny woman with an upswept hairdo of lacquered curls. Her hair didn't move when she shook her head, but her jade bracelet jingled as she speared a receipt on a nail.

"Can I speak to the waitress who worked last night?"

"She live far away, work Monday."

Convenient.

"But *flics* tell her my food make *le petit* sick. True?"

No one forgot René. Aimée shook her head. Looked outside on the narrow, slush-filled street.

Aimée pointed to the shuttered luggage store. "But you must know the Wus and Meizi. Any idea where I can find them?"

"Quartier change. New shops. People come and go."

"What about this man with bad teeth. Tso?"

Madame Liu averted her eyes. "I semiretired."

Aimée wouldn't know it from the way Madame Liu whipped around cleaning tables. She noticed the woman's knuckles had whitened around the dishtowel she clutched. Was she hiding something?

But it made her think. This narrow street was the shortest route from the Conservatoire to Pascal's great-aunt's.

"Have you ever seen this man?" She showed Madame Liu Pascal's photo.

Madame Liu lifted her reading glasses from the chain around her neck. Stared. "Him? No eat."

As she suspected, Madame knew him. A local in the quartier. Aimée suppressed her excitement. "Last night? What time?"

"Not eat here." Madame Liu took her reading glasses off. "Busy, now prepare for dinner."

"Where did you last see him, Madame Liu?"

"Not sure."

"Here in the quartier? On the street?"

"Dead man, right?"

Aimée nodded.

Madame Liu grabbed a dry dish towel. "Come back later."

Aimée had to get some kind of information from her. "But the *flics* suspect a Chinese gang killed him."

"*Flics* don't speak good Wenzhou dialect."

"They're lazy, too," Aimée said. "But that's between you and me."

Madame Liu leaned forward. "*Flics* like my noodle soup. Like no pay."

She imagined Prévost enjoying a free lunch. *Flics* took it as their due, and her godfather Morbier was no exception. That grated on her.

"Me, I pay for information. I keep it quiet, too."

Aimée pulled fifty francs from her wallet. Set it on the table. This search was getting expensive, and her bank balance was getting low, but she pushed that out of her head. "Do you know anything about his family?"

"Family? He have very old auntie?"

Aimée nodded again. Not only was Madame Liu a good observer, but she knew who lived in this village-like warren of medieval streets.

"He teach class and eat here Fridays. Order #32 shrimp wonton soup."

"So last night . . ."

"Every Friday, but not last night."

And he was murdered around the corner.

"But did you see him yesterday? Going in the luggage shop to see Meizi, to buy a bag for his auntie?"

"Sad for auntie. Nice lady." Madame Liu rubbed the towel over the cracked tiled counter.

"His auntie knows no Chinese would hurt him," Aimée said. Time to stretch the truth. "But I need Meizi's help to prove that to the *flics*."

Madame Liu nodded to a young man arriving in the back door.

"He walk by maybe seven o'clock," Madame Liu said. "No stop like usual. I go funeral service. That's all."

At seven in the evening it would have been dark, the shops closed.

"Was he with Meizi? Black ponytail, sweet face, jeans and green sweater?"

Madame Liu shrugged. "He wave. Alone. That's all."

On the way to meet his killer.

Aimée looked out the window again. Saw how close the luggage shop was. Her mind went back to last night, this table: Meizi ladling the soup, her face lighting up upon seeing René, how her smile reached her eyes. Not the face of a woman who'd killed a man and wrapped him in plastic before dinner. When Meizi excused herself to take a call, Aimée couldn't help believing, she intended to return to her birthday meal, her present, and René.

"My restaurant full soon, dishwasher sick. I'm busy."

In a swift movement Madame Liu joined the young man at the counter, turning her back on Aimée.

RENÉ WATCHED THE Chinese man standing in the shadows. The red-orange glow from a cigarette bobbed as he spoke into a phone. His Mercedes jeep idled at the corner. René wanted to get close enough to see the man's teeth.

A moment later the man flicked the cigarette in the gutter, buttoned his sleek leather jacket, and headed for his jeep, and René finally caught a glimpse of his face. Black hair, fashionable stubble shading his face. Yellow, crooked teeth.

Tso. The snakehead. The man who Aimée had discovered sold Meizi's papers.

René turned the key in his Citroën's ignition. He followed slowly, keeping a car between them. The jeep paused off rue Beaubourg, and two men leapt out of the back to unload boxes. A delivery. Then another, until an hour had passed. Never once had Tso gotten out. Antsy, René wished he'd hurry up and get to his destination. Then René would show him what bad teeth really were.

After the next delivery, the men disappeared and the jeep took off. René followed, staying two cars behind this time. The jeep turned into the narrow one-way rue de Montmorency and maneuvered into a parking spot.

René pulled into a red zone.

By the time Tso locked the jeep, René stood poised in a doorway, ready. But Tso crossed to the other side of the street. René looked both ways, keeping to the ancient buildings.

Tso turned at the corner, stepped into a *café tabac*. René considered his options. Grab him when he came out or follow him. More chance of finding Meizi if he did the latter.

"*Pardonnez-moi*, have a light, Monsieur?" asked someone behind René. Before he could turn, a blow hit his sternum, knocking the air out of him. Slicing pain doubled him over. His arms were grabbed behind him.

He heard laughter, "*le petit*," something in Chinese.

With every bit of strength he could muster, he kicked out, connecting with a leg. Hearing a cry, he kicked again and again, until his arms were released. Remembering his judo, he jabbed a crosscut in his assailant's ribs. Aching pain shot through his hip as he twisted away on the wet pavement. Tso and another man loomed over him.

René pulled the Glock from his pocket. Aimed up at Tso's face. Those bad teeth. "Tell me where Meizi is, or—"

Tso ducked, tossed his cigarette, and both men took off running. Clutching his chest, René got to his feet, took a step, and folded against the wall. By the time he managed to straighten up and reach the corner, they'd gone.

But René heard the unmistakable sound of a door shutting. Mid-block, if he calculated correctly. Not much good to anyone right now, he limped into the *café tabac*.

"A brandy, *s'il vous plaît*," he said, punching Aimée's number on his phone. "Make it a double."

"BUT ACCORDING TO Aram, the sweatshop entrance is on rue du Bourg-l'Abbé, René." Worried, Aimée surveyed René as they sat in the small *café tabac*. "On the next block."

"So Tso took a shortcut." Perspiration beaded René's forehead and his breath came in short gasps. "But it was him, bad teeth and all."

Aimée's glass of fizzing Badoit water glistened under the café counter light. "You don't look too good, René."

"I'll feel better if you try the front entrance," he said. "Call me and I'll come."

She doubted he could walk without pain right now. She shook her head. "Stay on this stool, *compris?* Watch from this window until one of them leaves and call me."

She eyed the café's rear galley kitchen, where a sagging apron, a pair of overalls, and a white butcher-shop coat hung from the coatrack. "You work in a charcuterie, Monsieur?" she asked the man behind the counter.

"Not me. Next door." He flicked a thread of blond tobacco from his rolled cigarette. "After a *pichet de rosé* the butcher always forgets it."

"*Bon*, let me borrow it."

"Eh? It's not mine."

She slapped twenty francs on the counter. "Then I'll rent it."

Drumbeats thrummed from Les Bains, the club in the old

bathhouse on rue du Bourg-l'Abbé. The building entrance on the right was boarded up. No luck there. The one on the left, shrouded in scaffolding, was also boarded up. The only way to the sweatshop in the rear courtyard was through the club.

"No date?" asked the mascaraed transvestite at the door. His Sisters of Perpetual Indulgence name tag read Lola.

"Not yet, Lola," Aimée smiled.

"We'd love to let you in, but the benefit is reservation only. Sold out." Lola gestured with an orange-lacquered nail, which matched his eye shadow, to the poster announcing "Afternoon Tea Dance! HIV caregivers support benefit competition."

Where were her sequins when she needed them? But Michou, René's transvestite neighbor, entered these contests all the time.

Aimée opened her coat, revealing the white butcher's smock. "I'm a health inspector."

"*Mon Dieu*, but we're up to code!"

"I know you passed inspection, Lola." Aimée gave a little sigh. "But I'm inspecting the toilets in the rear courtyard. Some complaints, you know."

A couple, tottering on high heels and wrapped together in a feather boa, passed her.

"We don't want any trouble," Lola said.

"Of course you don't, that's why you'll let me do my job," she said, slipping a fifty-franc note in the donation box.

"We're all about cooperating." Lola swept his arm at the ushers. "Let this girl in. She's in a hurry."

Out on the dance floor, couples gyrated under a flashing disco ball to "I Will Survive" as a large-shouldered blond, in a skintight red velour jumpsuit with the highest heeled boots Aimée had ever seen, lip-synched along.

She felt a tap on her shoulder. "Don't tell me your dance card's filled."

She turned to face a person wearing a white Courrèges tunic with the signature geometric design. Vintage and delicious. But those cheekbones looked familiar.

"Where's René?" He pecked her on both cheeks. "Careful, I just powdered."

Viard. The police crime lab head on rue de Dantzig. And Michou's partner. "It's complicated, Viard. Where did you get that Courrèges?"

"If you're a good girl, I'll let you borrow it," he said, his hips swaying to the music. He gestured to the lip-syncher. "Michou's on next."

"Right now I need to get to the back."

"She's not that bad. She's a professional, you know."

She and René had seen Michou's show in Les Halles many times. "I know, stunning. But there's a clandestine sweatshop only accessible—"

Viard put his arm up, pearl bracelet sliding. "Like we can help those poor people?"

"But I can. So you've seen them, Viard?"

A moue of distaste showed on his crimson mouth. "How can you miss those grinding machines?" Viard said. "It's in the courtyard behind the men's. As sisters under the skin, we let them use them, you know. There's Michou!" And he danced off.

She found the door marked Exit near the men's, pushed it open to a damp alley narrowing between the buildings. Cracked concrete and crumbling stone walls led to a thin courtyard surrounded by bricked-up windows, already dark in the fading afternoon light. Behind her sounded the distant strains of "I Will Survive"; before her the *chomp*, *chomp* of machines. She felt the vibration in the soles of her boots.

She entered the door at her left. Inside, Chinese men in sweat-stained T-shirts fed plastic sheets into twenty or so cutting machines. She recognized the plastic, which matched the luggage she'd seen. The hot oil and synthetic odors choked her. Good God, how could the factory owner let human beings work in this air? In this noise?

An older woman peered down at her from a stairway. Coiffed black hair, jade bracelets on both wrists, red silk scarf trailing from her neck, and thin painted eyebrows. Aimée sucked in a breath as Madame Wu pointed a bamboo back scratcher at her like a weapon.

"You lost? Bathroom that way."

"We meet again, Madame Wu. Seems there's quite an extended Wu clan in the quartier."

Aimée recognized the girl behind her—it was the girl who had been packing hoodies at the luggage shop, who'd warned Aimée off. The girl's eyes widened in fear, then flicked upward. She caught Aimée's eye and shook her head.

"How many Madame Wus are there?" The humming of sewing machines spilled down the rotted hallway.

"This building's private property. *Privé.*"

"You're the owner then, Madame?"

The small eyes narrowed. "Manager. You go now."

"But we're old friends," Aimée said. "Call this a health inspection. Lots of complaints. Just think of the unsafe working conditions for your employees."

"I call *sécurité*." The woman hurried down the steps in small, brocaded house slippers. "Private property, not for public."

"But this isn't up to code, Madame." Aimée pointed to the fuse box with rusted wires trailing from it. Telltale signs of illegally tapping into the electricity source. "Dangerous." She wagged her finger. "Where's Meizi?"

The woman whipped out her cell phone, hit a number on her speed dial.

"Not cooperating, Madame?" Aimée reached for the fuse box switch. "Then I'll need to shut you down."

The woman jabbed the bamboo back scratcher at Aimée,

just missing her eye. Aimée pulled the bamboo from her hand, knocked the cell phone to the floor, and grabbed the woman's wrists.

"Get Meizi," she said to the girl. The girl backed up, frightened.

"Now."

"Tso!" the woman shouted, struggling. Tough and wiry, like an old hen.

Aimée twisted the woman's arms behind her and, in a flash of inspiration, stuck the bamboo between her jade bracelets, which trapped her like handcuffs. She looked around, but the girl had disappeared. With a deft movement she twisted the bamboo between banister posts and stuffed the woman's red silk scarf in her mouth. That should keep Madame Wu quiet for a while.

Footsteps pounded on the stairs. Aimée looked up to see a man, hooded eyes, a cigarette between his crooked teeth.

"If you're security, then I'm the electrician," she said.

"*Gweilo*." And then she saw the raised knife in his hand.

She yanked the fuse box handle. A sputtering fizz, ear-splitting grinding sounds. The light from the bare bulb flickered before the building plunged into darkness, machines grumbling to a painful halt. In the sudden quiet, Aimée could catch the soft conversations of workers, the drumming of Madame Wu's feet. And that persistent humming, which came from somewhere above.

She had the advantage now; the man would have to come down the steps. She pulled out her penlight, set it on the last step, flicked it on, and stepped away.

Cold air gusted past her face. In the dim light she made out the flash of his knife. She gave a quick kick upward, contacting what she hoped were his ribs. A crunch, and a yelp of pain.

She didn't have much time. Who knew how many of his cohorts waited upstairs? Her fingers found the penlight on the dusty floor, then his knife. She shone the beam in his eyes, put the knife tip to his throat, and stuck her hand in his back pocket. Thick wads of hundred-franc bills, a cell phone.

"Bonus time for your employees," she whispered in his ear. "Number five on the list of secrets of successful bosses."

He yelled.

She silenced him with another kick, this time to the temple, and his eyes rolled up in his head. Out for the count, but for how long? She had to hurry. She ran up the stairs, shining her penlight over each rotted step. The humming grew louder, and she followed it up to the third floor. She needed to find Meizi. And a way out. She hoped to God the frightened girl hadn't sounded the alarm. She hit 1-6 on the man's cell phone.

"Police," the voice answered. "*Je vous écoute.*"

"Rue du Bourg L'Abbé," Aimée said, "in the courtyard behind Les Bains, there's a man with a knife attacking—"

"I'll transfer you."

"Listen, he destroyed the fuse box," Aimée interrupted. "It's dark, we can't . . . he's coming . . ."

She clicked off, hopeful for a quick response time, since the *commissariat* was located around the block. She didn't know what she'd face inside. And she couldn't wait.

A line of light shone from under a door. She tried the handle. It didn't move.

She closed her eyes, tried to center herself. Focus.

Then she kicked the door in.

CLODO BLINKED AT the bright white light. He was cold all over. Even the blood coursing in his veins felt cold.

"He's responding," a voice said, and the white light receded. "Two more milligrams of morphine."

"Can you feel this, Clodo?"

He floated on a river, strains of an accordion drifting in the air. Sun speckles shivered on the water's surface.

"Feel what?" Clodo asked.

"Good." The voice moved away. "Rest for a while."

His aunt—he was dancing with his Aunt Marguerite, a long, thick braid down her back, and it was 1942. His parents watched them, laughing and drinking wine. It didn't matter that he'd never danced with Marguerite before. Or that his parents were already gone in 1942. Light glimmered on their wineglasses; his mother crinkled her nose like she always did.

"Try not to move, Clodo."

"But why not?" he said. Joy filled him. They were there all together at the river. "I'm at the *bal musette*."

Footsteps. "Never seen one survive." A muffled conversation. "He thinks he's dancing, doctor."

"His dancing days are over," a man was saying. "If you think he's up to it, I need to question him."

"We're monitoring his morphine drip," another voice said. "Give him some time. The first few hours post-surgery are critical. No drug stills the phantom leg pains after amputation."

What were they going on about? Now he was dancing with his mother, her flower-print sundress twirling as they spun to the music, her head thrown back, happy and laughing. But her face changed. Now it was the man, and he was yelling. Yelling until the plastic silenced his screams.

RENÉ PUSHED BACK the brandy snifter on the zinc counter, his gaze raking the street, the doorways.

"Call me Bruno," said the man rinsing tall beer glasses behind the counter. He was in his fifties, with the red, veined nose of a drinker. "Likes to dress up, your friend."

"At every opportunity," René said, declining another brandy.

"She a secret agent?" Bruno winked knowingly. Too many Bond movies, René thought.

"A force of nature," René said, "but why don't you tell me about the one with bad teeth who bought cigarettes."

"He do that to you?" Bruno shook his head. "Seen him a few times. That's all. No shame, these people, attacking your kind."

His kind? All his life René had struggled against ignorant perceptions, to prove his stature made no difference. He'd studied martial arts at the dojo, achieved a black belt to prevent trouble. If only the cold hadn't affected his hip this way.

"Implying that I can't take care of myself?" René said.

"I call it unfair the way these *Chinois* take advantage," said Bruno, on the defensive, "that's all."

"So he's done this before?"

"They're taking over the quartier, buying up the shops," Bruno said. "Me, I'm the only family business left, apart from Chartier, the butcher."

Seeing he had a captive audience, Bruno warmed up. René

listened with half an ear to his litany against immigrants, until Bruno's words caught his attention.

"Colonized the quartier, the *Chinois* have." Bruno tipped back his *bière*. "*Prête-nom*, rent a name, *compris?*"

René thought he knew what Bruno meant, but shook his head.

"They use a legal name to run a business. Not the real proprietor. Some big entrepreneur in China, more like it."

Had Meizi's luggage shop done this? René wondered.

"Yet no one does anything." Bruno sighed. "Only one thing riles a phlegmatic Parisian to action."

Not selfish with his opinions, this Bruno, René thought. "So you mean transport strikes? Or the cost of Gauloises going up?" René rubbed his hip.

"I mean officials getting a free apartment." Bruno shoved the morning edition of *Libération* across the counter. "Huge flat, complete with balcony terrace, private garden," Bruno said, "while it's us taxpayers footing the bill."

Nothing rubbed a Parisian raw more than a plutocrat with a *maison secondaire* in the country who enjoyed a government-paid apartment in Paris.

"Part of the perks, *non?*" René's eye scrolled the article.

"There's perks. Then there's excess and being found out, like this ministry official Roubel, with his pied-à-terre on the Seine."

Why the hell hadn't Aimée called?

AIMÉE SCANNED THE attic room, the mattresses on the floor lumpy with sleeping figures. She registered the sharp drafts of air from holes in the roof, the peeling wallpaper, the pot bubbling on the stove and emitting chili paste odors. The humming of sewing machines in the adjoining room.

She wove among the mattresses, checking the faces. No Meizi. *Merde!*

Any moment Tso could show up, summon reinforcements.

At the sewing machines fifteen or so women treadled the old-fashioned foot pedal sewing machines and stitched zippers. Hoodie sweatshirts were piled beside them on the floor.

"Meizi?"

No one looked up.

If Meizi wasn't here, she'd made a huge mistake. She pushed down panic.

"Police!" she shouted, flashing her PI license. "Show me your identification."

Treadles ceased as the sewing machines stopped. She heard rustling from the mattresses. A cry.

"Ask our boss, Tso," said a young woman in a blue hoodie, her hair in a ponytail not unlike Meizi's. "He have our papers."

"Not Meizi Wu's papers. Where is she?" Aimée said, making this up as she went along.

"Don't know."

"I don't like your lies," she said, then sniffed. "Or the soup."

She pounded her fist on the stove. "Tell me or I'll take you all to the station right now!"

Terror showed on the women's faces.

"A girl in back," said the one in the hoodie. "Don't know name."

"That's better." Aimée stepped back and opened the door. Looked down the hallway. "Now get out."

The young woman moved closer, and her stale breath hit Aimée in the face. She stared at the white butcher's coat. "You not police!"

The blue hoodie wanted to argue with her?

"Undercover *narcotique*." She thrust several hundred francs in her hand. "Talk to Nina at the Chinese church. She'll help you."

The young woman stood dumbfounded. Loud voices came from below.

"Or you want to get arrested in a drug bust?"

Without another word, the women rushed by her, stampeding down the hall.

Tso and Ching Wao made a staggering sum, she realized, considering all the women here and in the sweatshops. Aimée picked her way through the piled hoodies to a pantry. Under a skylight was a sink filled with hundreds of zippers. Beside it, Meizi, her ankle chained to the pipe on the floor. Like a dog.

Horrified, Aimée knelt down. "Meizi, are you all right?"

Meizi nodded, her eyes wide. "Something's happened to René?"

Had she tried to protect him and failed? Aimée's earlier suspicions evaporated.

"He's a black belt, remember?" She smiled reassuringly.

Noises came from the attic. They didn't have much time. Aimée pushed the door shut and kicked at the pipe under the sink. "We'll talk later. First we need to get out of here."

"But I can't leave."

After all this, Aimée had no intention of losing her. "*Au contraire*." She kicked the pipe until it shuddered apart and lifted off the chain. For good measure, she took the broken segment of rusted pipe. If only she'd kept Tso's knife.

"Tso's coming back," Meizi's voice trembled. The chain was still hooked around her ankle.

"I took care of him, for now," Aimée said, "but it's the *flics* you need to worry about." She glanced around. "Any screwdriver here?"

Meizi's shoulders heaved. "They want to deport me?"

"Worse, Meizi," she said. "You're a suspect in Pascal Samour's murder."

"Who?"

"Don't play with me," Aimée said, some of her distrust returning. "The body in the walkway behind your luggage shop."

Meizi shuddered.

Aimée tried the adjoining door.

"*Non*, Aimée. We'll go out the skylight!" Meizi looped the greasy chain and tucked it in her pocket. "We sneak out that way all the time. That's why he chained me."

Aimée climbed on the sink rim, praying it would hold her, unlatched the skylight and propped it open with the pipe.

The slanted blue-gray slate roof overlooked the courtyard, which was filled with the *flics*. To her left were more skylights. Afraid of heights and up on a rooftop. Again.

Meizi grabbed a hoodie from the pile, and a Tati shopping bag with her things. "There's a way over the gutter. Come on, Aimée."

She could do this. Had to. Frigid air gusted over the rooftops. The cold slate froze her knees. Aimée kept her eye on Meizi's back and the stovepipe chimneys ahead.

And then Meizi disappeared. Like smoke.

Aimée found herself poised over a hole in the tiled roof.

"Down here, Aimée!" Meizi shouted.

Aimée gripped the edge of a roof tile, breathing in rank odors of mildew, and dropped down, catching herself before she fell on a picture frame. She landed in a dim attic next to a half-sheeted piano.

She hit René's number. No reception. They'd have to risk going to the café.

"Let's go."

But Meizi blocked the door of the small attic. "You can't tell René."

She wondered at Meizi's stubbornness. If they didn't get out of here . . . but she decided to play along.

"Do you want your parents caught in a raid?" she said. "Held at Vincennes detention center, checked for valid identity papers, their shop records audited?"

Meizi's face blanched.

"They do have papers? And you?" She knew the answer, but had to get Meizi out of here. "Or are you illegal?"

The truth shone in Meizi's eyes. Illegal. About to bolt. Aimée grabbed her shoulder. "I don't care. But I can help you."

"Help me? But you'll tell René."

He knew most of it already.

"*Non*, you will. Then I'll introduce you to a lawyer specializing in asylum requests."

Tears pooled in Meizi's eyes. "No good. It doesn't matter about me. Tso's cousin threatened my parents, my family in China. One message and they're—"

"So your parents aren't here," Aimée interrupted.

Meizi's hand went to her mouth. Shook her head. "You don't know the way snakeheads operate." Sobs racked her shoulders.

Aimée's mind went back to Madame Wu's unsmiling face, René's disappointment at the long hours Meizi worked. How the "parents" chaperoned her everywhere.

"They're not your parents," Aimée said. "You work for them, and this Tso controls you."

"Tso controls everyone here, the ateliers in our building, the whole street." Meizi took Aimée's arm. "They keep me in the shop, speaking French, making a good face for the customers, the *flics*."

Sirens whined outside. A questioning look appeared in Meizi's large eyes. "What's happening? Is this a raid?"

Smart. She was putting this together.

"I guess you want to find out the hard way," Aimée said. "Or do you want my help?"

Meizi hesitated, then tucked the chain, which had fallen out of her pocket, into her jeans' waistband and opened the door.

"This way," Meizi said.

They ran down the corridor, descended three flights of the twisting staircase to the street door. "Out here."

Aimée sucked in her breath. Cold, crisp air hit her lungs. Late afternoon light glinted off the damp cobbles. She could see the café. Perfect. They'd reach René . . .

A siren whined. Flashing red lights appeared from a police car. They had to get out of here. Now.

She grabbed Meizi's hand, pulled her into the crooked passage. They ran past a woman shaking a tablecloth from her window and emerged on the next street. Panting, Aimée stopped and caught her breath.

Passersby in dark overcoats leaned into the wind, which rippled the red awnings of the belle epoque hotel across the street. She clutched Meizi's arm and tried René again as they started into the lanes of traffic. She ran with her cell phone to her ear, just avoiding the Number 38 bus.

Faded gold letters on the facade advertised Hôtel Bellevue et du Chariot d'Or. In the marble foyer, festooned with turn-of-the-century colored glass, she set her bag on the reception desk. "A double room, *s'il vous plaît*."

"No luggage?" The concierge, a middle-aged brunette with Slavic cheekbones, crunched her consonants.

"Does it look like it, Madame?" she said. "We missed our train." Aimée glanced at the room tariffs posted on the wall. Old-world, all right; the kind of hotel that a few generations ago lodged patrons for the myriad theaters on the Grands Boulevards.

She set down the slimmer wad of Tso's francs and showed her ID with its less-than-flattering photo and filled in the form. "We're hungry. Room service available?"

The woman sniffed. "*Bien sûr*, if you like *omelettes à l'estragon*."

They took the groaning cage of an elevator to the second floor and navigated a maze of hallways to a bare-bones room facing rue de Turbigo. If René would answer his phone, she wouldn't have to go back out in the cold. She ransacked her mind for the name of the *café tabac*; finally, it came to her—Café Saint-Martin, the name of the street it was on.

Aimée dialed the black melamine rotary relic room phone, but only got Reception. "Mademmoiselle, could you look up a listing for me?"

The receptionist sighed. "That's five francs extra."

"Connect me," Aimée said, then added, "*s'il vous plaît*."

A man's voice answered. "*Qui?*"

"Monsieur Friant, *s'il vous plaît*. He drank a brandy at your counter not twenty minutes—"

"Ah, *le petit!*" he boomed. "Why didn't you say so? And you're the secret agent. The butcher needs that coat back."

"And if I talk to Monsieur Friant, he'll get it."

"*Attends.*" Banging as he dropped the phone. Crunching in her ears.

"What have you done, Aimée? The place is crawling with *flics*."

"Try to answer your phone sometime, René. Damn irritating."

Pause. "I'll reinsert my SIM card. The phone fell during my . . . altercation."

"Tso's taken care of, for now." She looked at Meizi, who sat in the room's only chair, fingers tensed on the armrests. "Someone wants to talk with you."

"Meizi . . . you found Meizi?"

"Room 22, second floor, Hôtel Bellevue et du Chariot d'Or. Around the corner, on rue de Turbigo. You can't miss it."

Aimée checked her face in the mirror over the lavabo, her raccoon eyes. A mascara mess. She splashed water on her face, rubbed off the smudges, lined her eyes with kohl, and applied lipstick. Then poured Meizi a glass of water and took out her lock-picking kit.

She knelt down, examined the lock chained around Meizi's ankle, and chose a double-edged snake rake from her kit. With a swift jiggle the lock opened. Meizi rubbed her ankle.

"Now you're going to tell me about your boyfriend, Meizi."

"But René's my boyfriend." Meizi's eyes batted in fear.

"I think you have things to tell me about last night," she said, smoothing the duvet. "Why you disappeared from the restaurant. Why I saw you wearing my hat on a street corner. Why that man pushed you."

Meizi's lip quivered. She eyed the door. "I don't want to talk about it."

"But you will, and before René arrives in five minutes." Aimée pointed to her Tintin watch. She handed her the water glass. "I won't let René get hurt, Meizi. You're going to tell me what's going on."

"You don't understand."

"Then take a drink and explain it to me."

Meizi's hands shook. "It's my family. *Non*, I have to go."

"Go where?"

Meizi squirmed, terrified and shaking. How could she make Meizi open up?

"There's a surveillance operation in the quartier. Plain-clothes in cafés," Aimée said. "In parked vans, wiretapping the shops, the ateliers."

She knew the first part was true. Had seen more vans this morning. Figured the second part was close.

"But if I don't work off the debt, my family's dead," Meizi said. "If I don't cooperate, they send me to Marseille."

"Marseille?"

"That means, you know . . ." Meizi's voice lowered. "To be a . . . prostitute. Truckers at the highway rest stops, massage parlors in Aubervilliers." She shook her head. "I hear stories. Girls don't come back."

No brothels anymore. Everything was mobile; girls switched and moved at a cell phone call's notice. An ongoing headache for vice, according to Melac.

An idea formed in Aimée's mind. She took Meizi's hand, squeezed it. "I'll help you," she said. "After you tell me about Pascal Samour's murder."

Meizi blinked, thought. Took a sip of water. "The funny Frenchman with red hair?"

"You knew him, *non?*"

"He eats . . . ate at Chez Chun all the time. That's all."

Frustrated, Aimée leaned forward. The bedsprings creaked. "Quit lying. Samour recommended you for a job at the Musée."

"*Vraiment?*" Meizi brightened. "He offered, but I never thought he meant it."

"And that photo he carried of you?"

"Photo?" Meizi's brows knit.

"The photo of you in the shop."

She nodded. "That's right. I remember his friend had a new camera, he played around, took some shots."

His friend? "Do you remember this friend's name, what he looked like?"

"But that was two weeks ago, maybe. Lots of people come in the shop. I don't remember."

Aimée stored that for later. Now she needed to take advantage of the few minutes before René arrived.

"Think back to last night, it's important," she said. "Tell me what happened. The phone call."

Aimée saw a blossom of blood appear on Meizi's bitten lip. How she glanced away.

"I don't want René hurt either, Aimée."

"*Alors*, tell me the truth. The dead man's great-aunt deserves to know, don't you understand?"

"The *flics* make controls," she said, "stop people in the Métro, on the street. Check for identification, the *carte de séjour*."

"So the call was to warn you?"

Meizi nodded. "I had no ID. Nothing."

"Why not?"

"Someone borrowed my card. We share. So I ran."

"But behind the shop you saw the killer."

"Killer? I ran away from the *flics*," she said. "Tried to reach *les tampus*, the girls in Belleville who've paid off Tso and work legally. But their room's empty. Gone. I had nowhere to go."

"Maybe you saw and didn't know it," Aimée said. "Think back, Meizi. The street, it's dark, cold, snowing." She did her best to lead her. "You'd left your coat in the *resto*, but the caller tells you to run, you're afraid, you turn the corner, and then . . ."

"Noises like ripping plastic," Meizi said.

The killer would have worked fast to subdue Pascal and then wrap his head in plastic. Aimée couldn't stop herself from picturing those eyes.

"What else, Meizi?"

She hesitated. "A homeless man sleeps behind the shop on the back steps. He sings, that's all."

Aimée remembered the man, too. How the first-responder medics called him Clodo.

"I think you're smart, Meizi," Aimée said. "So smart you want me to think Clodo's involved. But I doubt it."

Meizi fingered the duvet.

"Tso's men murdered Samour, *non?*" Aimée said. "Under Ching Wao's orders. You witnessed them and they threatened you."

"The snakehead's cousin?" Meizi's mouth opened in surprise. "But Tso's afraid of the tax men. So's Ching Wao, with all his Mercedes. The unreported earnings from their protection rackets. It's about money."

Money. Like always.

"No one dies in Chinatown," Meizi said.

"What do you mean?"

Meizi took a long gulp of water. "A valid *carte de séjour* is valuable. They sell them."

"He's sold yours already, you know that? You're not 'sharing' anymore."

Thin vanilla light pooled on the wood floor. The radiator grumbled. Meizi pursed her lips. "You won't tell René?"

"Tell René you've got another man?"

Meizi shook her head.

"He knows you're not who you say you are."

"I can't let René know."

"That Pascal got you a job?"

"*Non,* that I lied about my parents. He'll never believe anything I say. Please, just until I figure this out."

Aimée nodded. "And in return?"

"Listen, one section of the Chinese cemetery at Ivry is full of unmarked graves," Meizi said. "Potter's field, that's what you say?"

Paupers, no family. Aimée shuddered. Did Tso threaten Meizi and these women with an unmarked grave? "So you're saying . . . ?"

"When someone old dies or commits suicide, papers get passed on."

For a culture that reveres its ancestors, this seemed a sacrilege, and a high price for living in France. But a leverage point she could use with Prévost.

"Tell me more about their protection racket."

"The luggage store is a front," Meizi said reluctantly.

"In what way?"

"Like half the shops. A way to launder money from Wenzhou. Tso makes them pay 'insurance.'"

"But what did Samour have to do with it?"

Baffled, Meizi shook her head. "Nothing. He's . . . he was some kind of scientific engineer, *non?*"

"What aren't you telling me, Meizi?"

"I don't know what you want to hear, but . . ." Her throat caught. "Tso's suspicious. He thinks I'll run away. Had that man follow me. That's why I wore your hat." Meizi's lip trembled. "René's the only person I know here, the only one who cares. I'm short, too." A smile flitted across her face, then it was gone. "He has a good heart."

Meizi gulped the water, determined to go on.

"René struggles to overcome things," she said, her voice dropping. "He thinks he hides it, but I see his lonely side. I feel lonely too. Lying to him makes me sick inside. Now he won't trust me."

Touched, Aimée nodded. "René calls you his soul mate, Meizi. Just talk to him."

Her phone beeped. A message. She'd forgotten she'd muted her phone. She heard Mademoiselle Samoukashian's voice: "Meet me at the *mairie,* upstairs, Salle Odette Pipoul. I need to see you. Now."

Had Mademoiselle Samoukashian discovered something?

A knock sounded on the door. Aimée put two hundred francs and her card in Meizi's hand. An idea had formed. "Call Tso. Tell him you're afraid, hiding. But promise to tip him off before the big raid happens. Convince him, Meizi. Say you don't know the details yet but you'll warn him," she said. "He'll call his dogs off. He'll need you."

"He will?"

"Trust me. Buy a pay-as-you-go cell phone. Call me. I have a plan."

She checked the peephole, then tossed her lipstick tube to Meizi. "A little color does wonders, Meizi. Keep it."

She opened the door and smiled at René.

"*Merci*, Aimée." His brow was beaded with perspiration. He held a bouquet of blue forget-me-nots.

Aimée leaned, kissed René on both cheeks.

"Expect room service in a few minutes." She winked. "And a few hours alone."

A man in a windbreaker huddled with the receptionist at the lobby desk. His stance, the way he nodded, pricked up Aimée's antennae. A moment later he sat behind a wilting palm and pulled out a newspaper.

This didn't feel right. Listen to your gut, Morbier always said. Instead of crossing the lobby, she kept to the wall by the manager's office and slipped into the door marked *Service*.

She hurried down a corridor full of room-service trays to another flight of stairs. As with most hotels, the back environs never matched the exterior. Cracked concrete partially covered the faded whitewashed brick walls leading to a turn-of-the-century laundry, complete with airing cupboards and ancient ironing boards.

She followed a faded red-and-yellow line to the next level. Evidence of an exit or an old bomb shelter, she figured. Matching painted arrows led down the stairs to a subterranean series of brick rooms. Bed frames, chairs, racks with dust-furred wine bottles. Hotel storage.

Notausgang—emergency exit, from the little German she remembered—was painted above an alcove. She waded through plastic bags and old pipes to find a padlocked slatted-wood gate.

Cold gusts of mildewed air came through it. At least it was a way out. With a padlock shim from her lock-picking kit, it took less than a minute to gain entrance to a dark, wet cavern. Her penlight revealed browned notices in German script with SS lightning bolts. And a partially bricked-up staircase.

A prickle ran up her spine. No time to linger among Nazi ghosts. The bricks yielded after several kicks. Up the staircase, to another gate that jiggled open. She found herself in a smoke-filled room. Poker players sat around a table under a low-hanging green light. She nodded to the surprised men and kept going.

FIFTEEN MINUTES LATER she entered the courtyard of the neo-Renaissance *mairie*, the town hall laid out like an H in the florid style favored in the nineteenth century. She mounted the marble staircase of honor, passing the acting sentinels: two buxom female bronzes. Over-the-top, as most of these architectural homages were. Promoting a feeling of grandeur where citizens of the quartier attended to mundane affairs: school registration, housing, senior services, marriage and death certificates.

In the Salle Odette Pilpoul, Mademoiselle Samoukashian sat on a gilt-backed chair that was all but swallowed up in the grandeur of the room: maroon velvet floor-length curtains, stained-glass windows, a massive fireplace at one end, a stage at the other. Why meet here? Aimée wondered.

"I did my homework." Mademoiselle Samoukashian gestured to a pile of newspapers. "They archive them downstairs."

Copies of *Libération*, headlined "Kidnapped Spanish Princess Found" and "Basque Terrorists Linked to ETA Discovered by Leduc Detective."

"I knew I remembered you from the papers," the old woman said.

Outed, Aimée shrugged, then pulled up a little gilt chair. "It was personal, Mademoiselle." A little over a month ago she'd almost lost Morbier, her godfather. She'd protected him and saved his career by a hair's breath. Too close. "My godfather—"

"*Bien sur*, family, I understand," she said. "I accessed Pascal's safe deposit box."

"*Vraiment?* Aren't the banks closed on the weekend?"

"Not if you know the manager," said Mademoiselle Samoukashian. "He's Armenian." She waved her age-spotted hand. "Not only did I change his diapers, I hid his father during the war. With Odette Pilpoul."

Aimée was impressed, and wondered what memories this musty *salle* brought back to her. "Mademoiselle, it sounds like you're connected to the quartier's history."

A small sigh. "Not that I care to remember those days." She shook her head. "All the hotels requisitioned for the Wehrmacht's telegraphists, their drivers, the Luftwaffe pilots, bordellos for the soldiers. Even took over the Conservatoire." A shrug. "Odette and I printed false identification papers in the printing press below my family's apartment. We targeted disruptions at the Centre Téléphonique et Télégraphique, their communications headquarters on rue des Archives. A 'nest of saboteurs' was what the Gestapo called the quartier." Her eyes were far away. "We rendezvoused at the pharmacy on Boulevard de Sébastopol, next to the German recruiters. Who'd know it now?"

Mademoiselle Samoukashian shrugged. "But some of us paid."

Was another old war story coming? Aimée crossed her legs on the small, creaking chair.

"My cousin Manouchian, a poet. And the man I loved, a Jew. Others. But I missed the bus and was too late to warn them," she said, her voice trailing off. "*Alors*, all that's left now is the plaque on the building, a mass grave."

An almost palpable sadness radiated from this little woman.

She pointed to a sealed manila envelope on the table with the words: "to be opened in case of my death only by one whom my great-aunt trusts." "I'm late again," she said. "But please read what's inside, Mademoiselle. I haven't opened it."

Aimée's brow lifted. She was intrigued. "Why?"

"Pascal made me promise," she said. "If you don't help me, no one will. His project will be ruined."

Aimée stiffened. "A project? You think it connects to his murder?"

"I want you to find out."

Pause.

"The museum fascinated him," the old woman said. "I told you. He'd volunteered the past two years, cataloging their holdings during their renovation. He was so excited last week about some discovery there. *Alors*, won't you respect his wishes?"

Aimée stalled, uneasy. "First tell me why he gave Meizi a recommendation for a job there."

"This Chinese girl?" Madame Samoukashian shrugged. "*Bien sûr*, the Chinese are immigrants like us. I raised Pascal to think of others, not just himself. But look what it got him."

What did that mean? "I don't understand, Mademoiselle."

"*Non*, I shouldn't say that. Who knows? Find this girl and ask her."

"I did."

"And?" Mademoiselle Samoukashian leaned forward, expectant.

"She heard noises and ran away. At least, that's what I've learned so far." And she believed Meizi.

"Of course, she had no papers," Mademoiselle Samoukashian said. "I told you. Who'd stick around?"

Aimée took the manila envelope off the table. "Shouldn't you give this to the *flics*?"

"Like I trust them?" A bitter laugh. "Now it's the Chinese. Before it was the Jews, Eastern Europeans, and us Armenians.

But it hasn't changed. They don't like people to know they held deportees here, downstairs at the old *commissariat*. My father and mother were in a cell until they had enough to fill a train for Drancy. Next stop the ovens." The anguish hardened in Mademoiselle Samoukashian's brown eyes. "But we're not here to talk about that."

Aimée slit the sealed flap open. Inside she found a note, dated two weeks earlier:

> *Whatever you do, smile at my great-aunt, tell her I meant to fix the loose tiles in the kitchen. At my Conservatoire office ask Coulade for the green dossier. You'll find keys for my flat under the geranium pot on the 3rd floor of 19 rue Béranger. Give Becquerel the 14th-century diagram you find. He'll tell you what to do next. Say nothing to my great-aunt, for her safety. No matter how she grills you. Now hug her for me. Pascal.*

Aimée's hand shook. Under the envelope lay a check for five thousand francs made out to Leduc Detective.

"You know what to do?" Mademoiselle Samoukashian's voice quavered. "But you can't tell me, *n'est-ce pas?*"

Aimée nodded. "For your safety, Mademoiselle." She averted her eyes. "Who's Becquerel?"

Mademoiselle Samoukashian shook her head. "Professor Becquerel? But he passed away last week. He was ninety. Pascal's last professor."

Too late. Aimée felt a cold pit in her stomach. Becquerel led nowhere.

She leaned down to hug the old woman, again felt her thin shoulders. "Pascal said he meant to fix the loose tiles in the kitchen," she said, trying to smile. "May I take you home?"

Mademoiselle Samoukashian shook her head. And when she spoke, Aimée heard the grit in her voice. "You've got more important things to do, Mademoiselle."

THE FIRST FORTY-EIGHT hours of an investigation were crucial. After that the trail iced up, the odds lowered for tracking down a witness, a name, an accurate memory. As time passed, leads dropped to zero. Almost twenty-four hours had passed since Pascal's murder.

Aimée pulled out her cell phone and made two calls. Both went to voice mail. Frustrated, she left messages as she skirted past the old covered market, the Carreau du Temple.

A homeless man—or SDF, *sans domicile fixe*, the politically correct term—camped on a ventilation grate. Most people still referred to the homeless as *clochards*. This man held a cracked transistor radio to his ear. The radio weather report cackled in the afternoon air.

"Clear afternoon skies, crisp, and ten degrees warmer tomorrow, *ma chère*." He winked at Aimée. "Plan ahead."

She was trying to. "I'll get out my beach umbrella," she said, reaching in her pocket and handing him change.

"Me too. *Merci, ma chère*." He grinned, a weathered look on a youngish face. Fallen on rough times, as so many had these days.

And then she got an idea.

"Haven't I seen you over there?" Aimée asked, gesturing back across the park of Square du Temple.

"Dry and warmer here," he said.

"And no problems, eh, like last night? The murder."

He shrugged. Turned the radio volume down. After all, she'd paid—the unspoken rule—and it was time to deliver. "I heard about it."

She crouched down, careful to keep her stilettos out of the grate holes. "What did you hear?"

"The regulars scattered. Won't go back."

"Like Clodo?"

"Clodo? We're all Clodo to the *flics*." His mouth turned down in a frown. "Tell me you're not a *flic, ma chère*."

"*Moi?* You're joking." She took more change from her pocket. "I mean the *mec* sleeping on the steps behind the building near rue au Maire. Fur coat, pink scarf."

"The crazy one?"

Weren't half the ragged men on the street crazy? Shuffling and mumbling to themselves? But then sometimes she did too.

"Angels worried about devils?"

"*C'est lui*," she said. "I'd like to talk to him."

"Usually goes underground at the Fantôme. Most do."

Some code? "Where's that?"

"Métro at Saint-Martin."

She thought. "But there's no station there."

"Closed in 1939. A shelter in the war. Abandoned now, but they know ways in." He shook his head. "Not your type of place, *ma chère*."

She grinned. "But I'm a Parisian rat."

He shrugged. "Up to you."

"So how can I talk to Clodo?"

"The Métro opens at five thirty A.M."

"But why don't you go to the Fantôme?"

The crow's feet in his weather-beaten face deepened. He pointed to a window of the third-floor apartment building across from the Carreau, rose-colored curtains. "My daughter lives there. I don't like to be far away."

"Could this help?" Aimée said, laying fifty francs on his sleeping bag. He gestured with a grimy hand for her to come closer. Welcome heat from the grill vent toasted her face.

"I heard Clodo's in a bad way," he said. "In the hospital."

Startled, she leaned closer, trying not to breathe in his unwashed smell. "After last night?"

"Clodo sidelines in cell phones. Where he gets them . . ." A shrug.

So that was where Samour's cell phone went.

"Word says a dealer confused Clodo's stash niche for his powder, *ma chère*," he said. "A misunderstanding."

News via the homeless grapevine traveled fast. "That put him in the hospital?"

"Got him pushed on the Métro tracks today."

"A bit harsh for a misunderstanding," she said, interested. "Sounds like retribution."

"That's life on the street."

"More like under." She didn't buy it. "Sounds to me like someone wanted to silence him after he witnessed the murder."

"Tell me, *ma chère*, would you believe Clodo, who talks to angels and devils?"

More than she'd believe the *flics*.

The man peered around her shoulder, his attention on the window. His face crinkled in a smile. For a moment he looked almost lordly, as if surveying his territory from his rumpled sleeping bag. "Light's on. My daughter's doing her homework, nice and early. Good, she looked tired today."

His voice was like that of any father. And it saddened her. But she sensed he knew more. "Could we trade a new radio for that phone Clodo found?"

He shrugged. "Not my thing, but I'll check into it. No promises."

"But I'll depend on you for the weather forecast so I know what to wear." She winked. Slipped him her card. "Why don't you use that and let me know."

He winked back.

This smelled like it went somewhere.

AIMÉE PICKED OUT Coulade, surrounded by students, in the office at the Conservatoire National des Arts et Métiers, adult division. The narrow two-person office he'd shared with Pascal—she recognized it from the photo. She sat down to wait in the anteroom, a high-ceilinged affair painted a faded institution green. A welcome warmth radiated from the chipped heater. She took off her coat and rolled up her sweater sleeves. A few minutes later, the students left, papers in hand.

"*Oui*, Mademoiselle?" Standing at the office door, Coulade gave a quick glance at the card she handed him. He was in his late twenties, black hair sprouting from a widow's peak, stocky of frame under a dark sweater and tweed jacket. A typical academic. He looked rattled. "I'm sorry, nothing to do with me."

"But I think it does," she said.

Coulade took in her stovepipe suede leggings, his gaze resting a moment on the low V-neck of her black cashmere sweater.

"Since Pascal Samour's murder—"

He stiffened and put his finger over his mouth. "Inside."

Mock drama, a chance to grope her? She didn't like him already. But she stepped inside the office. She needed answers and access to Pascal's work computer.

Coulade's face blanched in the hanging fluorescent office light. "We kept this terrible news from the students. I took over his symposium today. There are thirty-five students finishing their exams. And my notes . . ." He scrambled around amongst the papers on his desk. ". . . somewhere . . ."

Overwhelmed, she saw that. Nervous? Or guilty?

"This won't take long," she said, scanning the two cluttered desks. "Where's the green dossier?"

"Eh?" His eyes gravitated again toward her neckline.

Her dislike for Coulade grew by the minute. "Pascal said you had the green dossier."

"He told you that?"

Why couldn't Coulade answer a question?

Coulade grabbed a pile of notebooks. Checked his watch. "Listen, I'm late. There are waiting students."

"But Samour—"

"*Zut!* We share this office, but I'm only here part-time. My day job's teaching at the lycée. I don't know of any green dossier."

"Two weeks ago there was one," she said.

He expelled air from his mouth. "*Et voilà.*" He gestured to the files. All blue. "I've got no clue what Samour meant."

Her stomach turned. "You really don't know?"

"No idea," Coulade said. "He was an absentminded type. Half the time, his head spun with ideas and he'd forget to write anything down. A dreamer."

But it still didn't explain Samour's letter. "When did you last see Pascal Samour?"

Coulade hurried to the door and beckoned her to follow. "Last week, *non*, Monday. We were supposed to meet here yesterday, but . . ." His face fell. "I couldn't."

Coulade had to know more. Even if he didn't realize it. She wouldn't give up. "Meet regarding what, Coulade?"

"He didn't tell me." Coulade shrugged, eyed the door.

"Think back to the green folder."

"Green folder?" Coulade shook his head, his face blank.

"Color-blind, Pascal. All our folders are blue." He waved toward the file cabinets. "But these folders, all they have are student grades. No way you're allowed to look at them. *Compris?*"

Another bump in the road. A road going nowhere. She wanted to get Coulade's eyes off her chest and nail his feet to the floor.

"*Alors*, Coulade, last night my partner and I discovered Samour's body chewed by rats in the snow." She stepped closer and pointed out the thick bubbled-glass window. "*Juste à côté*, not far from here. I think you know more than you're letting on."

"Eh?" Coulade ran his hand nervously over his neck.

"He told me to talk to you."

Coulade reached for the door handle. "But I don't—"

"*Bon*," she said. "I'll let the *flics* know you've got something to tell them. Let you sweat it out at the *commissariat*."

Coulade stiffened. "Nothing to do with me, I tell you."

"Too bad. I'm surprised they haven't questioned you." She shrugged. "I play fair, but they don't."

Coulade blinked, hesitating. "Half the time I didn't know whether to take him seriously or not. He'd found this document misfiled in the Musée's holdings. Or so he said. Ranted about how he'd found a link. But he needed more."

She suppressed a shiver. "A link to what?"

Coulade shrugged. "Some design he worked on. But it never made sense."

"I need something more specific."

"He hadn't put the pieces together. Or so he said." Coulade shrugged again. "Yesterday he left me five messages here at the office. I'd turned off my cell phone."

"Messages saying what?"

"To meet him here. He sounded excited. Paranoid, if you must know. Couldn't leave specifics on the message, he said.

Mentioned a fourteenth-century document. That's all. But I'd taken my students on an all-day field trip to the Meudon Observatoire." Coulade looked shaken.

"What time did he leave the last message?"

Coulade checked the pile of pink message slips on his desk. "Looks like five P.M."

"Did he mention Becquerel?"

Coulade shook his head.

There was a knock on the office door.

"If you'll excuse me," he said.

Aimée looked around the office. Sparse. Only one computer, on Coulade's desk. Her heart sank.

"Didn't Pascal work on a computer?"

"His laptop," Coulade said. "Refused to use these antiquated ones the department furnishes. But he kept his at home, I think."

He ushered her out and locked the door behind them. His footsteps beat a quick tattoo down the drafty hall toward a crowd of waiting students.

What wasn't he telling her, she wondered. She waited until he turned the corner, reached in her bag and took out her lock-picking kit. Into the old-fashioned door lock, she inserted the snake rake, then the W pick, and jiggered the mechanism. She heard the tumbler turn.

"Mademoiselle?" a voice called from the hall.

She whipped around, keeping her back to the door and her hand on the lock picks.

An older woman, her hair in a bun held in place with a pencil, waved at her. "Professor Coulade's received an urgent message."

Aimée smiled. "If you hurry you'll catch him. Left at the end of the hall."

The woman clucked like a hen. "If it's not one thing, it's the other. We're swamped. I don't suppose you could bring him the message?"

"*Desolée*, Madame, I'm en route to the archives," she said.

The woman's ample bosom heaved, perspiration beaded her brow. She shrugged, then hurried past Aimée.

After the woman's footsteps faded, Aimée turned the knob, removed the wires, and entered the office. That done, she reinserted the wires and locked the office from inside.

She needed to hunt for this green dossier.

But Coulade's computer screen blipped. A swirling desktop image of a trebuchet, the medieval slingshot-like weapon used to hurl boulders at fortified battlements, floated across it. In his hurry Coulade hadn't logged out. She hit the cursor. Apparently he didn't have time to organize his files. There was data info all over the screen. A bonanza.

The key turned in the lock. *Merde!* Coulade had come back.

She depressed the key combination to store his log-in, then dove under Pascal's metal-frame desk at the end of the narrow office.

Not a moment too soon.

"Everything's handled," Coulade was saying. "We'll shift assignments, I found a substitute—"

A woman's voice broke in. "Professor Coulade, the last exam's begun. The departmental guidelines outline specific procedures."

Aimée pulled at her sweater, which was bunching up her back in the cramped space. Her hands were coated in dust. At least the desk panel hid her from view. She wished she could hear their conversation better.

"But my mother-in-law suffered a heart attack." Coulade opened his desk drawers.

"What can you do for her at the hospital?" The woman's tone indicated his duty was here to the students.

Aimée agreed. She'd never understood the clannishness of French families. Perhaps because she'd only known it from the outside.

"If the department questions or invalidates the exam proce-dures, the students will have to postpone until a retake next semester," the woman pleaded. "We can reschedule the eve-ning symposium session, but—"

"If none of this had happened . . ." Coulade's words trailed away.

As if he blamed his murdered colleague for the inconvenience.

"Jean-Luc's substituting, thank God," he said. "He's more qualified than I am. A *grande école* graduate and friend of Samour. No problem. I confirmed with the registrar."

"But Professor Coulade—"

"Madame Izzy, for the tenth time, I'm part-time, not a pro-fessor, and all of this takes too much time from my family. My wife's distraught."

Or did Coulade want to distance himself from the murder, the complications?

Aimée heard the trilling of a cell phone.

"*Oui?*" Coulade's voice rose. "But you don't mean . . . I'll try."

Then the shuffling of feet as they left the office. The light switch flicked off and the office plunged in darkness, and the lock clicked. She didn't have much time to trawl Coulade's desktop for a misnamed file. She hoped, since Samour sus-pected danger, he'd have sent this file to an unsuspecting Coulade. Made a backup.

Coulade's password prompt yielded to her keystrokes, and seconds later his swirling screen saver appeared: *Engineering Tech. Slide Rule. Calculation Theorems.*

In the heated office, which now felt stifling, she rolled up her sweater sleeves higher and pulled out discs from her bag. The heat made her sleepy. She needed an espresso, but there was no machine in the sparse office. Trying to stay alert, she inserted a disc and let the machine go to work copying the data. Later, Saj could weed through the program for a link to Pascal.

Now to Samour's metal desk, which was cluttered with administrative memos, requisition lab slip receipts, and student papers. She picked his locked desk drawers to find more of the same. No laptop. Nothing to do with the museum holdings.

Frustrated, she searched his bookcases, documents, the blue files. Engineering manuals, phone books. Nothing interesting, until she found a frayed leather volume, nineteenth-century by the look of it, entitled *Guilds in the 14th Century*.

Had Samour meant this, she wondered, leafing through the gilt-edged, tissue-thin pages. A bookmark inside bore the logo of the occult bookstore on rue aux Ours.

She stuffed it in her bag, glancing at the time.

There was a click and whir as the copied disc ejected. She slipped in the second disc, which installed a spyware tracking bug. Hoped to God it worked as fast as René promised it could.

Her cell phone rang in her pocket. Quickly she hit mute. She debated not answering it, but Prévost's number showed.

"Mademoiselle Leduc. You left me a message?"

"*Oui.*" She stepped to the back of the office, lowered her voice. She needed an excuse to discover more about his investigation. "I've remembered something."

"*Un moment,*" Prévost said. She heard rustling, what sounded like his hand over the receiver.

In the meantime, she checked Coulade's computer. A long moment until INSTALLATION COMPLETE popped on the screen. She hit eject. Another whir as the second disc popped. She scooped them both in her bag.

"Mademoiselle?" Prévost was back on the line.

"Doesn't procedure dictate the Brigade Criminelle handle Samour's murder?" she asked. From the crime report on Demontellan's desk at the prefecture, she knew Prévost had inserted himself in the investigation. But why? She wanted to know more.

"Who says they're not, Mademoiselle Leduc? For now you

deal with me as *chef de groupe* of Police Judiciaire. Things have come up," he said, suddenly hurried. "I don't have time. Come at seven to the *commissariat*."

She checked her Tintin watch. More than an hour. Almost enough time, if she left now, to check out Samour's apartment and visit the museum.

The line buzzed. He'd hung up. Great.

Minutes later she strode down the overheated hallway. Students blocked the corridor, grumbling over the late-afternoon symposium postponement. Near the open door of the back exit, several students wearing parkas stood around smoking, instead of venturing into the chill, moss-carpeted courtyard outside.

And the feeling of being watched hit her. She shuddered. But among all these milling students? Had she grown paranoid?

She passed a classroom and peered in the open door. Heads bent down over wooden desks built in the last century. She remembered those small desks. Murder on her long legs.

"Time's up," said a clear male voice. "You've earned a five-minute break."

She peered inside at Coulade's replacement. A tall, blond man gathered papers from the podium. If she hurried she'd manage a few words with him.

Shoulders jostled her. By the time she'd negotiated the stampede of outgoing students, she no longer saw him.

"Mademoiselle, you dropped this."

The man held up Samour's book.

Azure-blue eyes, a grin. Muscular shoulders under his denim jacket. Good-looking in a Nordic way, and an engineering genius to boot, she figured.

"*Merci*. I heard from Coulade you took over the seminar." She thought fast. "You're Pascal Samour's colleague?"

"Pascal's my old Gadz'Arts classmate." His eyes flickered in pain. "Such a tragedy. I still can't understand it."

"Gadz'Arts?"

"Silly term." He shook his head. "It's from *gars des arts*, guys from the arts. Just what we call ourselves. But we graduates remain close. Our training and traditions bind us like family." He shrugged. "That's why I wanted to help out."

"So this adult school and your *grande école* are connected?"

"Confusing, I know," he said with a small smile. "This school was originally charged with collecting inventions and gradually became an educational institution, a *grand établisse-ment*, a loose affiliation to us at Ecole Nationale Supérieure d'Arts et Métiers. Liken this to an adult trade school granting doctoral degrees."

She wondered at an engineer from an elite school teaching in an adult trade school. Service to the community?

But he knew Samour. This man was no doubt a source of information. And he had a test to give.

She smiled. "Do you have time for an aperitif later?"

If he was surprised, he didn't show it. He handed her his card, a slow smile spreading over his face. Jean-Luc Narzac, Communications Division, Frelnex.

The telecom giant.

"Not that I'd turn down an *apéro* with a woman like you, but why?"

"It's regarding your classmate, Samour."

"You work in the Conservatoire, Mademoiselle?"

Not yet. But it gave her an idea. "A consultant. I'll explain. Tonight?"

The hall buzzer sounded. Students tramped and engulfed them. He checked his watch.

"Let's say nine P.M."

In the ten minutes it took to reach Pascal Samour's street, Aimée came up with a plan and made three phone calls, one of them to the Musée des Arts et Métiers. She scanned Pascal's building on rue Béranger. The dark-blue doors hung open, revealing a long, cobbled courtyard. The concierge was making a half-hearted attempt to sweep the slush to the gutter. The scraping noise grated in Aimée's ears.

A typical late Saturday afternoon on rue Béranger, the inroads of *les bobos*, the *bourgeois-bohèmes*. Families braved the crisp cold to guide toddlers on tricycles; middle-aged women in long down coats with shopping carts returned from the market. Newspaper delivery trucks double-parked mid-block outside *Libération*'s headquarters, near an indie art gallery. A leashed dog sniffed a lamppost, and a mufflered child laughed and ran ahead of his parents. Another world from Chinatown only a few blocks away.

Inside the cavern-like portal, she glanced at the mailboxes, high-security tungsten with each resident's name in neat, black capital letters. SAMOUR, PASCAL, she noted. *Escalier C, 3ème étage.*

The concierge, trim for his fifties, set the shovel against the mailboxes with a thump. He squinted curiously.

"Looking for someone, Mademoiselle?"

In all the wrong places, she almost said.

No reason to share her goal of a murdered resident's apartment. Sooner or later, she hoped much later, the *flics* would affix the notice with telltale red wax signifying a deceased resident and seal the apartment.

"Why, I just found my friend's apartment . . . Escalier C." She flashed a bright smile. "*Bonne soirée, Monsieur.*"

She stepped past him into the courtyard. Escalier C, the last on the left, was a circular, tower-like outcrop with a dizzying climb of seven stories. The polished brown stairs, sagging from wear in the middle, wound upward like a snail shell. This rear area around the courtyard had to be seventeeth-century if not older, she thought. And not remodeled since then.

On the third floor she caught her breath, found the long-handled key under the flowerpot. Anxious, she let herself in. In contrast to his great-aunt's flat, Pascal's was a cold room with a high-timbered ceiling.

Ransacked too.

She gasped. An IKEA bookcase overturned, a drawing table upside down, an armoire open, shirts and jackets littering the floor.

She reached for her keys, bunching them between her fingers, and scanned for an intruder. But the door had been locked, she remembered.

In the galley kitchen, emptied spice bottles and spilled pasta were strewn over the counter. Iron sconces on the stone walls held broken candles. Behind a battered bamboo screen she found an overturned iron bed frame, sprinkled goose feathers from a ripped duvet, a slashed mattress with ticking bulging out.

Living in a tower didn't appear comfortable. Even the destroyed furniture gave off an unlived-in feel.

For twenty minutes she searched every nook and cranny in the single, cold room. No laptop. No green dossier.

She needed to put the little she knew together. Yet what good would that do, if the killer had the laptop or whatever Pascal wanted her to find? *Non*, she needed to think as Pascal would. Or at least try to.

A geek with searing intelligence, a highly trained technical engineer from a *grande école*, a loner. A man who taught at an adult trade school when his fellow graduates took jobs in high positions at companies like Frelnex.

Pascal, afraid for his life, had left a message two weeks ago instructing its recipient to find a green file, come to his apartment, and talk to Becquerel. But Becquerel had died. Hence, she figured, his repeated messages to Coulade yesterday.

And no green file. Or fourteenth-century document.

But why make it all so mysterious? Why not give concrete details? Unless . . .

Something happened yesterday. Unable to update Coulade, he'd seeded info in several locations. Pieces of a damned puzzle.

Yet, to find what?

A project his great-aunt had mentioned—concerning a museum file he'd told Coulade he'd discovered.

Frustrated, Aimée righted a chair by the window and noticed blue dust on her fingers. She smelled it. Chalk dust.

She paused at the lead-framed window and, with her gloved hands, opened it and pushed the shutters back. The view gave way to scattered low buildings, the crescent edge of a courtyard, a glass-roofed atelier below. The approaching dusk darkened exposed patches of earth. Unusual to find open space in a dense quartier like this, where every meter was utilized.

But more unusual were the diagrams in blue chalk on the curved stone wall below. Blue chalk lines intersected and arced in what reminded her of a star chart. An amateur astronomer, a stargazer? But she saw no telescope, no binoculars.

A configuration. But of what she had no clue.

Pascal would be a puzzle lover, she figured. A dreamer, Coulade had said.

But driven and edgy in his work? If this was a guide, a map, she wondered again why he'd made it so difficult. Especially since he'd suspected the danger.

Too clever for his own good? Or afraid of discovery and running out of time?

She breathed in the cold air. Her mind cleared. The diagram was so familiar. But from where?

She pulled out her palm-sized digital camera, René's latest must-carry gadget, shot photos of the wall diagrams, a few of the room layout, the view from the window. If she hadn't found answers here, she'd picked up a sense of how to look for them.

She locked the apartment door behind her and descended to the ground level.

Her breath caught.

Prévost, a blue-uniformed *flic*, and a *mec* she recognized from Brigade Criminelle strode across the courtyard.

She ducked into a cove containing garbage bins, crouched on the damp flagged floor behind a broken chair. Odors of last night's fish clung in the corners.

Prévost huddled in conversation with the plainclothes, who wore a bomber jacket just like Melac's—a definite undercover trademark. After a long moment, the *mec* handed Prévost an envelope and jerked his thumb upward. Prévost turned on his heel and the man headed toward the tower entrance. And toward her.

Pascal had left her the key, and his great-aunt had hired her to investigate. By all rights they'd given her access to the apartment. But try explaining that to *la Crim* or a *flic*. One she didn't trust.

They could accuse her of violating procedure, regulations, the order of the law, or of ransacking a victim's apartment. With no time or desire to engage in semantics, she kept her head down, hoping her knees didn't give out.

Five minutes later, after the last footsteps sounded on the staircase above, she crossed the courtyard. She checked for Prévost or police presence on rue Béranger. None.

Turning left, she headed toward her parked scooter and called René. René was better at puzzles, loved a challenge. His phone rang and rang. Too late, she remembered the hotel . . .

"Can't you give us some time, Aimée?" René answered, irritated.

"*Desolée*, but it's important," she said, checking her Tintin watch. "You're going to get a call."

"From who?"

"I'm volunteering and you're going to give me a stellar reference, René."

"Gone crazy, have you?" A sigh. "Consider our accounts, our security projects out for bid. Accounts who'll pay real money."

"The volunteer coordinator from the Musée des Arts et Métiers will call, can you remember that? I'm volunteering to assist in digitizing the museum holdings during their renovation," she said. "Pro bono, of course, a service to the community. Tell her how Leduc Detective welcomes opportunities to preserve history and culture for the next generations—"

His line ticked.

"Right on time." She prayed this worked out. "A glowing recommendation, René."

She heard the click of heels behind her. A woman walked into an art gallery. "Call me back. I'm en route there now."

She shouldered her bag, double-looped her scarf, and turned the key in her scooter's ignition.

"Seems they're desperate since the last volunteer left. You got the job," René said, ten minutes later. "Digitizing the catalog collection, sorting through centuries."

She figured as much.

"She wants to meet you. I said you've made time in your busy day, et cetera." Pause. "This involves Pascal Samour, n'est-ce pas?"

"Bien sûr. It's the only way to find out."

"Find out who murdered him by volunteering at the museum?"

"Long story, René." The image of Pascal Samour's corpse flashed in her mind. "I took the job. Five thousand francs retainer." Not to mention Tso's cash "retainer," but she kept that to herself. "You in, René?"

"The old lady reminds you of your grandfather, n'est-ce pas?"

Maybe she did.

"And Meizi's still a suspect," Aimée said.

Pause. "I'm in. See you at the office in a few hours."

"OUR MUSEUM DEPARTMENT appreciates your donation of time and expertise," said Madame Chomette, the curator, a tall, slender woman with white hair pulled back in a sleek ponytail. She was dressed head-to-toe in black, which highlighted the silver teardrop pendant hanging from her neck. "I think that's all, Mademoiselle Leduc. It's been a long day."

All? Aimée stared at three centuries of the Musée des Arts et Métiers' cataloged holdings to digitize.

"We hope you don't mind the accommodation, as we can't transport the documents. Legal issues."

Madame Chomette gestured to the alcove office carved out behind a Gothic strut pillar. Worn Latin was just visible in the floor paver. The extensive renovation of the museum revealed that the walls stripped down to eleventh-century stone. Thoroughly medieval, apart from the power strips and space heater.

"Tomorrow we'll have a desktop operational for you and functioning within the museum network."

Aimée wouldn't hold her breath. After one look at the antiquated system, she'd decided to bring a laptop or three for backup.

Now to the meat, and finding Samour's project. "To prevent duplicating Monsieur Samour's efforts, perhaps you could tell me where he left off?"

She wondered if Madame Chomette was in on this, or a friend of Samour's. Or both.

"So sad. Such a loss." The conservator paused. "But I'm new, on loan from the archives to finish things up by the reopening deadline." She gave a small shrug. "I met Samour last week for five minutes. But each person who worked on this logged the details."

"Who did he work with?"

Another shrug. Madame Chomette glanced at her watch. "He was a wonderful help, that's the memo I got. I'm late for a meeting. *Desolée*."

Did this woman really not know? Aimée tried again. "I'm looking for a fourteenth century document."

"The museum building was a church until the sixteenth century, so our holdings don't go back that far," Madame Chomette said. "We concentrate on inventions and machines from the eighteenth century on."

"Could there have been another collection? A mistake? Or might it have been misfiled?"

Madame Chomette shook her head. "Not to my knowledge."

Was Aimée some pawn in an elaborate setup? She wondered at how eagerly they'd accepted her services. Or was this more paranoia?

"But open one of our storage cellars and you'd be amazed at what's in there," Madame Chomette said, perhaps noting the dismay on Aimée's face. "Believe it or not, the Archives Nationales kept things here during the Occupation. It wouldn't surprise me if some were left. In most cases no one's looked at these things in a hundred years. We're overwhelmed and so grateful for your generous offer. It's a true gift, this expertise you'll furnish."

Aimée believed the woman. Felt a brush of guilt for her ulterior motive, but groaned inside. It sounded like an exercise in futility. Still, she had to begin somewhere.

"I'll program a laptop and start tomorrow."

"*Merci.*" Looking again at her watch, Madame Chomette motioned her out. "Vardet, the security guard, will furnish your badge and outline security protocol."

COMMISSAIRE MORBIER NODDED to the driver of the unmarked police car. "Relay to dispatch that I'm detained. Breaking revelations in the investigation, the usual."

He'd miss another *commissariat* meeting he couldn't afford to miss. Like every other hurry-up-and-wait bigwig caucus he'd missed in the throes of this damned investigation.

"*Compris*, Sergeant?"

Trained to cover Morbier's ass, the driver nodded. Morbier glanced at his cell phone. Two calls from Aimée. Nothing he wanted to deal with now.

He powered off his phone and slammed the car door. Set his shoulders for this grief-therapy session that Honfleur, the police psychologist, mandated. Otherwise he'd face a week at the stress unit "intensive" outside Paris. The last thing he wanted.

His breath steamed in the cold, twilit air. He walked back a half block to the Sainte Elisabeth church in case the driver kept him in his rearview mirror. Morbier gripped the stair railing, taking each ice-slicked step one at a time. I'm just another old man, he thought, frustrated, terrified to break a hip. All of a sudden the thick, carved wooden doors slapped open. Two laughing boys ran out like rifle shots, just missing his leg.

Had he ever been that young, or moved so fast? He straightened up in the cold church vestibule. Melted candle wax and frankincense, smells so familiar, rooted in some saint's day, he forgot which. The traditions of his childhood.

Deep notes sounded from the organ above. A refrain played again and again. Saturday evening organ practice, Morbier thought. "The Lord washes away our sins," a staccato voice joined in.

No bets on that from his corner.

On the community notices tacked near the side chapel, under the flyer for Narcotiques Anonymes, he found "Grief Group Meeting, Room 2, Rear Stairs."

Merde. More stairs.

The room held twelve or so men and women, gathered around the pastries and coffee on a refectory table. A wall poster invited parishioners to bring guitars to Sunday sing-along Mass. Surprised, he noticed people of all ages.

"The pastries come from the *pâtisserie* on rue du Temple," he overheard a young woman saying, "off Place de la République. Wonderful *pain au chocolat* . . ."

She looked up. Clear, steady gaze. Warm smile. "We take turns providing refreshments," she said, not showing surprise that an extra-old codger had just appeared. Morbier hadn't signed up. Almost backed out at the last minute. "Welcome, I'm Jeanne. The coffee's not bad. I made it myself."

After a round of introductions—first names and how long they'd attended the grief group—Jeanne stood and smiled. "We'd like to welcome the newcomers to share if they wish. Speaking and getting support is what we're all about here."

Not that he had any intention of "sharing" with strangers. A typical bunch of whining types with time for a pity party. He noticed a patch of mildew on the wall below a simple wooden cross.

"For a year I couldn't face this hole in my life," Jeanne was saying, "always being reminded by the little things."

Alors, just what he'd expected.

"I was so ashamed when I burst into tears at everyday, mundane things," Jeanne said. "His tie I found behind the armoire, the one I'd forgotten to dry-clean. His crumpled Post-it about my library fine, which I found in the bottom of my bag. How I still listen to his voice on our answering machine."

"Me, too." Several heads nodded.

"My life's like treading underwater and not breaking the surface," a voice added.

"They dismissed my brother's death as an industrial accident," said another. "The elevator controls failed . . . nothing even left to bury."

Morbier lapsed into his own thoughts, an opaque, dismal netherworld. The ache that hadn't gone away since Xavierre's murder. His survival was work. Good thing they'd kept him on the internal corruption investigation.

That or he would have shot himself.

And left a mess for Aimée to face. Coward that he was, he still hadn't told her. About the past.

But if he did, she'd never speak to him again. Never forgive him.

"You said something, Monsieur?"

Had he? He felt the others turning toward him. He'd forgotten where he was.

"Please, continue." Jeanne smiled. "This is a safe place."

Feeling like a fool, he took a breath. Steeled himself and looked up. He saw sad faces, beaten expressions, a quiet desperation mingled with kindness. Better say something.

He cleared his throat. "I can't talk about losing my . . . . It's been over a month."

"Grief holds no time line," Jeanne said.

The middle-aged woman next to him reached out and squeezed his hand. "I couldn't talk about losing my husband or hear his name for six months. Bottling up my grief made me ill. But I'm making up for things now. Learning. I won't let my feelings go unsaid."

Morbier chewed his lip. He felt a wetness on his cheeks.

Tears dampening his wool scarf. And pain flooded him. "I'm afraid if I die I still won't have said what I need to." Then he couldn't stop talking. The floodgates opened. "Xavierre, the woman I . . . I loved, was buried in Bayonne. With work . . . I can't even visit her grave."

And somehow, later, he found himself wiping his face with a borrowed handkerchief, drinking coffee, and agreeing to bring pastries the following week. Also arranging to meet Jeanne, who lived in his quartier, to talk over a glass of wine. Something to look forward to, instead of another long evening alone.

Emerging into the darkness, he descended the ice-slicked stairs feeling lighter. Knowing he could cope, at least for tonight. For the first time in a month, he took a deep breath and didn't feel the slicing pain of regret.

A woman stood in his way by the church railing. She tossed a newspaper in the trash bin. Her figure, the posture, that slant of the head . . . familiar. Where did he know her from?

"Attending church now, Morbier? I thought you were an atheist."

He hadn't heard that voice in years. That American accent. His mouth parted in an O of amazement.

Different hairstyle, clothes. Cheekbones more prominent. A face-lift, he figured. Unrecognizable except for her voice. And the carmine-red lips.

"And I thought you were dead," he said.

And buried.

"Rumors of my death have been greatly exaggerated." A tight smile. A lost look flitted across her eyes, and then it was gone. "For now."

She scanned the lit street. Then turned and in a deft movement slipped something in his overcoat pocket.

"Follow the instructions."

"That ended years ago, Sydney." He shook his head.

"I can't shield my daughter now. Or protect her. Not anymore."

"Protect her?" He snorted. "You abandoned Aimée."

The wind sliced his face.

"You're the last person . . . the only one I can turn to now, Morbier."

His skin prickled.

"Aimée's in danger."

Then it all came back to him. He was stung to the bone. "You think I'll fall for that again?"

She stepped back in the shadows.

"Then her blood's on your hands."

OUT IN THE street, Aimée stamped the ice from her boots. She turned the key and pulled her scooter off the kickstand. Trying to avoid the slush, she zigzagged in the worn grooves of melting ice. A sputter, choking, and her scooter died. Out of gas.

Great. She flipped on the reserve tank, prayed she had a quarter of a liter and some fumes. She sloshed the scooter back and forth to get the juices flowing.

Again she sensed someone watching her. The shadow of a figure appeared on the pavement. An uneasiness dogged her.

Had Prévost followed her?

She whipped around. An old man, his collar pulled up against the cold, clutching a Darty bag, a Miele vacuum attachment poking from the top.

Get a grip. She needed to calm down, reason things out. Get back to Leduc Detective and show René the blue chalk diagrams.

Another scooter's roar filled her ears. "Need help?" asked the helmeted figure, pulling over.

"*Non, merci.*"

But the rider pulled the helmet off. A fortyish woman, who shook her blonde curls and smiled. Kissed Aimée on both cheeks.

Did she know this woman?

"We're going to Café Rouge. Behind you. We're old friends."

"*Quoi?* Who are you?"

A little laugh. "But a wonderful new hair color. Chic, I like it."

She hadn't been to the *coiffeuse* in six weeks. And then she felt her wrist seized in an iron grip.

Aimée struggled to shake the woman loose.

"What the hell . . . let go!" Panicked, Aimée looked around. No one on the street now.

"Stay calm. Cooperate." Laughing now, the woman swiped the curls from her face with the other hand. "My instructions say we'll sit at the café's back table. They're watching, so smile."

This smelled bad. Security forces bad.

"And if I don't?"

"A broken wrist. Unpleasantness." She winked. "We wouldn't want that."

Not smart to struggle if they'd gone to these lengths.

"But my scooter—"

"Will be taken care of," the woman finished.

The woman propelled her arm in arm, as if they were old friends, into the café. Grinning, a whispered aside. "Smile."

Aimée sat down on the banquette under a beveled mirror. Before she knew it, the woman had disappeared and a man sat down next to her. She recognized Sacault, a member of the DST, Direction de la Surveillance du Territoire, the national security branch under the Ministry of the Interior. He wore a brown suit. Brown-eyed, hair to match. Anonymous. He'd pass for an accountant. Muscular, mid-thirties, not an ounce of fat on him.

Sacault snapped his fingers at the man behind the counter. "*Deux cafés, s'il vous plaît.*" He turned back to her.

"Am I going to like the coffee here, Sacault?" she asked.

"Please listen. Ask questions after. *D'accord?*"

She suppressed a shudder. "Now I know I won't like it." She gestured to the man behind the counter. "Make mine a Badoit, *s'il vous plaît.*" She glared at Sacault. "Whatever's going on, you know that I only talk with Bordereau." Her lap-swim partner, the only one she trusted in the DST. She'd helped Bordereau before. And he'd returned the favor.

"Bordereau's busy," he said. "I'm the one you talk to now. We employ watchers, handlers . . ."

"And tough blondes."

He continued. "Consultants on all levels. This morning, we had a cast of consultants for four hours until you showed up. Imagine what that costs?"

The DST could afford it, and more. A drop in the ministry bucket to them.

"Like that's my problem?"

"You didn't know?" Sacault cut in. "Sad news. Pascal Samour, your friend, died serving his country."

She gasped. Pascal worked for the DST. Her heart thumped. "My friend?"

"Went to his flat, didn't you?"

Now she understood why they strong-armed her. But how much did they know about her connection, his great-aunt? She shook her head, determined to keep her cards close to her chest. "*Alors*, I'm sorry about Samour, but there's a mistake."

"Samour worked on something important for the security of our country."

She clenched her knuckles under the table. The project. "What's that got to do with me?"

"We've got more resources than you, but we need the pieces you can offer in the investigation to find Pascal's murderer."

Since when did the DST concern itself with a homicide? Already she didn't trust Sacault. But had Pascal worked for them? It boiled down to Samour's project. Or Sacault was lying. Or both.

"I don't understand."

He paused. "I think you do."

She didn't want to understand. She scanned the café. Empty. A chill ran up her arm. It made some kind of sense.

"Pascal died for his country," he said. "I'm to remind you that your father worked for the forces in a similar consultant capacity."

"So the DGSE claimed. I don't believe it." She'd refused a work "offer" from Direction Générale de la Sécurité Extérieure military intelligence last month. Then, as now, she had no intention of taking them up on anything. "So you're implying you at DST get in bed with the other big boys at DGSE when it suits you?"

He averted his eyes. Had she touched a nerve? A bitter rivalry existed between the DST and the DGSE, their military counterpart at the Ministry of Defense. Hatred described it better.

"For all intents and purposes, I liaise with the DGSE," Sacault said.

It cost him to say it, she could tell. Napoleon's design to pit various forces against each other worked to this day. Like so much of the little dictator's centralization in France. "Too bad," she said. "Not a partnership I'd relish."

"*Alors*, you're in place," Sacault said, his mouth tight. "Don't ask me why. We want you to continue."

How much did he know? She held her question until the waiter uncapped the moisture-beaded bottle of Badoit, poured her a glass, and retired.

"In place? I don't understand, Sacault."

"Your connection to the Musée des Arts et Métiers."

"Connection?" She sat back, felt a gnawing at her stomach.

"We know it's not your thing," His lips pursed. "Not something you want to do. But we need your help to bring Pascal's killer to justice."

"You're right, Sacault." She hit her fist on the table. "It's not the way I work. No contract with the DST. Not my style."

She pushed her chair back and stood up.

"But if you cooperate, this will open channels," he said, plopping a white sugar cube in his espresso and stirring with the little spoon. His tone was everyday conversational. "High-level security dossiers with intel might be interesting to you."

She froze. He swam in the big league, like his predecessor, Bordereau. Was he implying what she thought he was?

"Concerning my . . . my family?"

A brief nod. He glanced at his vibrating phone on the table.

She remembered the ten-year-old letters from her supposed brother, the postmarked American stamps, the faded, childish scrawl.

"But the handwriting expert said there's no proof I have a brother," she said. She swallowed. "Do you know something more?"

"I know nothing about a brother," he said, giving her a quizzical look. "But I could open other doors."

He glanced at his still-vibrating phone on the table. "*Un moment*, I need to take this call."

He stood and disappeared into the back.

She sat back down. Her mind traveled back a few weeks, before Christmas, to the crowded café with fogged-up windows. Paul Bert, the handwriting expert, hunched across from her with an open file on the marble-top table.

She'd leaned forward, wanting him to be wrong. "Didn't laser techniques identify the paper's age, the ink, the handwriting?" She paused her hand on the wineglass.

"*Eh voilà*, inconclusive results, Mademoiselle." Bert exhibited all the charm of the wooden chair he sat on. And the warmth.

Empty-hearted, she'd stared at her untouched glass of Bordeaux, the café light fracturing on the rim.

These faded ten-year-old letters had led nowhere. A dead end to a supposed brother. No trail to her American mother, a seventies radical, still a fugitive on the World Security watch list.

She shook aside the memories, her brief hope gone.

"Do we have a deal?" Sacault sat down across from her.

Jolted back to the present, she noticed how he slid his phone in the pocket of his suit jacket.

"Information concerning your family in return for cooperation."

Her mind spun with temptation. And simmering anger. For years she'd gotten nowhere. Time to test him. "A bit unusual coming to me now after all these years. Why?"

"Right place, right time."

Intrigued now, she smiled.

"I want access to Interpol, MI6. CIA," she said. "Show me proof. Or nothing."

He met her gaze. Inclined his head with a slight nod.

Too easy. She should have asked for more.

"So you can reopen my mother's files, grant me access?"

"On Sydney Leduc?" he said. "I said open channels, establish communication. But no guarantees."

"Meaning?"

"I'm a fixer," Sacault said. "I can make things happen. Or not. That's the limit of my capability."

Her pulse thudded. "That's too vague," she said. "Give me specifics."

He sipped his espresso. "For example, access to a buried surveillance report, a sighting, a tracking log. Those types of things."

Was her mother alive?

In his echelon, the shadow world, business was conducted behind closed doors, favors granted and repaid, a nod here, a career step up or down, the give and take of information. Priceless. Unavailable to outsiders like her.

"*Compris?*" he said. "You accept or not?"

She'd be a fool not to grab this shot, never get one like it again. But everything cost something, one way or another. To pay the devil? What the hell was she supposed to do? Foreboding hit her deep in her bones.

"Tell me what Pascal Samour worked on," she said.

"I'm a fixer," Sacault said again. "Furnished with limited intel. All I know is that Samour worked on a project vital to the country and he died for it." His voice was businesslike. "Now, I received the call to assemble an operation. Recruit operatives, consultants, work the setup, get them in place. According to my instructions, you're already in place at the museum. We agree, and I set up meets."

"That's it?"

"Routine." He downed his espresso.

"Give me proof."

"Your handler will contact you. With proof."

He stood. The café had begun to fill up.

"One more thing," he said. "You'll have no cell phone contact on this. Remember in here." He pointed to his head. She felt something slide into her hand. A matchbox with a red rooster on the cover. "Follow your instructions. Then destroy it."

He'd counted on her cooperation. How transparent could she be? Ruffled, she wanted to slap it on the table.

But he'd gone.

She sipped the fizzy Badoit as everything whirled in her mind: Pascal murdered a few blocks away, his great-aunt, a fourteenth-century document, Pascal's job recommendation for Meizi, Prévost's role in the investigation, the strange chalk diagrams on Pascal's walls.

Pascal Samour spawned more secrets in death than in life.

Events had ratcheted up another level. If Pascal worked on a project for the DST, that explained why they'd surveilled and recruited her.

They were after what he'd hidden.

She shuddered, fingering the matchbox in her palm. Hesitated. Most access to intelligence dossiers came after the deaths of those involved. Even then, it could still be decades, given sensitive security issues.

Her hands trembled. Could she face the truth? Did she really want to know? Deep down the little girl in her longed for her mother to walk around the corner. The hope never died. She'd never move on.

She slid open the cardboard matchbox. A slip of cigarette paper with writing on it.

Café des Puys 10 p.m.

Nothing else. Disappointment filled her.

Out on the slick, wet pavement, she found her scooter parked and locked by a bare-branched plane tree. She glanced at the fuel meter. Full.

She quivered inside. Any of these passersby—the woman pushing a stroller, the middle-aged couple with a Westie on a leash—could be surveilling her. Any or all of them.

If she didn't push those thoughts down and jump back on the train, she'd get nowhere fast.

The method of Pascal's murder troubled her. The way he'd been wrapped in plastic, his hands bound behind him on the palette. The murderer had been sending a message, but what, and to whom?

The charcoal clouds trembled and the sky opened. Frustrated, she pushed her scooter under a glass marquee and watched the rain. After a call to the *commissariat* for the case number, she rang the Institut Médico-Légal's number and hit the laboratory extension. Two rings. A clearing of a throat, water running in the background. "*Oui?*"

"Serge, *s'il vous plaît.*"

"Try Monday."

"Maybe you can help me," she said.

"We're short-staffed."

She needed answers. And now.

She clicked her phone. "That's my other line. Look, this won't take long. It's concerning the autopsy results for a male, late twenties." She paused, rustled her checkbook near the receiver. "A Pascal Samour."

"Who's this?"

Rain splashed on her boots. "I'm Prévost's admin assistant, from the *commissariat* in the third," she said. "He didn't tell you?"

"Tell me what?"

"I'll check the paperwork, but it's somewhere in the request," she said. "The priority request for Samour's autopsy results this morning."

"Like I've had time to write the report?" he said. "I'm subbing for the interim assistant."

At least he'd performed the autopsy. As interim staff, he wouldn't know all the procedures. Or she hoped he wouldn't.

"*Mais alors*, you should have said so." She gave a short laugh, looked at the report number she'd written on her palm. "It's case number 6A87. Just shoot the prelim over. Serge does it all the time."

Pause.

"Prelim without pathology?" he said. "No analysis of nail scrapings, stomach contents? That's all I've got."

"That will do for now." She let out a sigh. "Or read the results and I'll type in the prelim. Add the path later."

"Call back. Give me ten minutes," he said.

And search for the nonexistent request?

She recognized the low thumping of hydraulic-pump pressure hoses washing down the autopsy tables, the dissecting tools, the tiled floor. Once, during her brief year in premed, her class spent a morning at the morgue. That's when she'd met Serge.

"Prévost's on my back screaming priority," she said. "I'd like to mention how helpful you're being. What's your name?"

"Carton, but . . ." Pause. "*Un moment*."

She prayed he'd find it. And before Prévost got wind of this. She shivered in her wet boots under the glass awning.

Carton cleared his throat. "Considering the snow, the temperature, the conditions, we put time of death at one to two hours before discovery."

So he put time of death between seven and eight P.M.

"Does that take into account the plastic wrapping? Wouldn't that keep in the body temperature?"

"Plastic?" Carton said. "I'm working from a cadaver, you understand. And given that this death occurred outside in the snow, the body would cool faster than the usual degree and a half, two degrees per hour. Let's see, it says leg flesh was gnawed. There's a note that says 'rat meat.'"

She cringed.

"Cause of death asphyxiation," he continued. "Apart from the ligature marks on his wrists, no abrasions or contusions were present."

Unease flickered through her. She hadn't seen the ligature marks. All she remembered were the eyes. "So you're saying . . . ?"

"I'm saying nothing," Carton said. "The burns take longer."

She grabbed her scooter's handlebars. "Burns?"

"Traces on his right index and middle finger. Not fresh, hard to tell," he said. "The tissue after microscopic examination will indicate the age of the injuries, the healing time. We never commit until the pathology report. Even then this looks cut-and-dry."

Cut-and-dry? Samour was wrapped in plastic.

"Take it up with Serge. You got the prelim results. What you wanted, *non?*"

Not what she wanted at all.

RENÉ SMOOTHED MEIZI'S black hair on the pillow. Her soft breaths of sleep ruffled the duvet. He could watch her for hours.

She shivered in her sleep, a cry catching in her throat. A bad dream? He stroked her flushed cheek until her shoulders relaxed and she turned over.

At peace.

He straightened the duvet, tucked it under her chin. To keep her warm. Safe.

He wrote her a note. *Call me at the office when you wake up. Stay here and order anything you want. Bises, René*

René dressed and checked the window. The usual early-evening hum—buses, pedestrians, the lingerie shops open late. He surveyed the street, for a watcher at the corner, for Tso or one of his men.

Only shoppers, *resto*-goers catching the bus or hurrying to the Métro. A waiter wearing a long white apron stood on the pavement under an awning smoking a cigarette.

Satisfied Meizi was safe, he leaned down, inhaled her warm, sleepy scent. Kissed her. She stirred slightly, a smile on her face.

René hung a Do Not Disturb sign from the hotel room door handle, put ten francs on the room service tray with their dirty dishes, and padded down the hall.

SOMETHING NIGGLED AT Aimée. She still hadn't pinned it down by the time she turned her key in Leduc Detective's door. Her stomach growled. The couscous felt like a long time ago.

René sat sipping an espresso at his desk, his expression distant. Saj shot her a knowing look. Winked.

"Let's cut to the chase," René said. "I want to get back to Meizi."

"So you two talked . . . ?" She let her words trail off.

A little smile appeared on his face. "You could say that."

She pulled out the book she'd taken from Samour's office and thumbed to the chapter he'd bookmarked. Medieval glass-making guilds. She set it down and lifted a fresh demitasse of espresso from their machine.

"Meizi's safe for now." René's brow furrowed. "But we're not immigration. Aimée, unless you know a higher-up and can pull strings, I don't know how to protect her."

The only string she could pull was Morbier's. The wrong one. And he didn't answer the phone.

With Meizi safe in the hotel, she had some time to figure out what to do. Fleshing out the plan to keep Tso at bay would have to wait. Right now she needed to concentrate on Samour.

"There are complications, René." She plopped a sugar cube in her cup, stirred, and took a sip. "Samour worked for the DST, died a patriot."

"So now he's a patriot?" René sputtered, spilling espresso on his tie.

"So they say." She sat on the edge of her desk and outlined what she knew: Mademoiselle Samoukashian's discovery of Pascal's safety deposit box, his letter, his repeated messages to Coulade, something about a 14th-century file, Pascal's ransacked apartment, her arrangement of digitizing holdings at the Conservatoire's *musée*, Sacault's recruiting her. She left out thinking about her mother.

"Both Samour's great-aunt and the DST are clients now?" René said.

She handed him Mademoiselle Samoukashian's check. "The DST's concerned with Samour's project, whatever it was. His great-aunt wants his murderer brought to justice." Aimée paused in thought. "And the murderer wanted to silence Samour."

"Didn't the DST tell you what he worked on?" René asked. "Give you a lead?"

"Typical need-to-know basis," she said. "Sacault, the fixer, played it safe."

"How would you have known what to look for, if we didn't have what Samour's great-aunt showed you?"

Aimée shook her head. "Welcome to the gray world. You learn as you go and the rules change all the time. For once, we're ahead of the DST, unless they know all this already. But I doubt it." She pulled out her camera. "Check out the diagrams on Pascal's courtyard walls. Anything strike you?"

"Context is everything," René said, flicking through the digital photos.

"Ideas on how to decipher this?"

"A few." He inserted a cable from his computer to the camera. "I'll scan the photos. Enhance them." He rubbed his hands together, almost in glee. "Only requires me to write a program to customize my search." He savored a challenge.

She handed Saj the disc she'd copied from Coulade's computer. "Pascal might have sent Coulade information, hidden in another file on Coulade's desktop. See what you can find."

Saj nodded.

"I installed René's spyware on his computer, too," she said. "Should be up and running."

Saj inserted Coulade's disc into his laptop. "Nice bugging job, Aimée."

She tamped down her impatience. "We need to link the laptop I bring to the Conservatoire back here," she said, downing her espresso.

"Done." René pointed to the laptop on her desk.

Thank God René seemed back in form.

"Aimée, shouldn't we ask Saj if he's willing to get involved?"

Saj's hacking skills had proved so valuable that the ministries he'd hacked had recruited instead of prosecuted him. And kept him on a leash.

"*Bien sûr.*" She hoped the irritation didn't show in her voice. "Up to you, Saj."

"In for a centime, in a for a kilo," Saj said, "as my *grand-mère* would say."

"Franc," said René.

"*Quoi*, René?"

"In for a centime, in for a franc," said René, lips pursed.

Saj stretched his arms over his head. "I'm implicated already since, at René's insistence, I'm a salaried part-timer. Signed paperwork."

René shook his head. "How else could I pay you?"

"*Bon*, no one here's broken the law," Aimée said, and took another sip. "Yet."

Saj was clicking keys, scanning his computer screen, now a forest of Coulade's icons.

"Not only do we keep tabs on the *professeur*, we can browse his domination fantasies and collection of erotica, circa 1930," Saj said, with a tone of distaste. "Do I have to weed through everything?"

"We need to find out," she said. "So *oui*, get weeding."

A quick knock. Leduc Detective's door opened to a gust of chill air from the hall. Martine Sitbon, Aimée's best friend since the lycée, strode inside, dressed in black denim from the pointed toes of her high heels to her oversize newsboy cap.

"*Mais alors*, not ready, Aimée?" She leaned and kissed René on both cheeks. Winked at Saj. "We're late. Hurry or nothing will be left on the rack."

Now she remembered. The last day of January *soldes*.

René's mouth turned down. "With all this work?"

"It's once a year, René," Martine said.

"Twice." Saj grinned.

"July doesn't count. That's *vacances*." Martine turned to Aimée, her red mouth set in a pout. "But this sale's invitation only. Don't you still need a dress for Sebastien's wedding?"

Merde!

"With that bulging armoire full of clothes?" René said.

"That's my work wardrobe, René!" Aimée shot him a look. "I'm the maid of honor." She rooted under her desk for her vintage ostrich-skin Vuitton travel bag, a ten-franc bargain from the octogenarian in her building who'd nearly thrown it in the trash.

Saj nodded. "Fully loaded, I'd imagine? That bag's lethal and guaranteed to clear crowded aisles."

"Silk lingerie sales get ugly. You have no idea, Saj." Martine tugged Aimée's arm. "The line's all the way around Les X."

Les X lay underground in an old wine cavern, a mix of vintage, retro, and last season's gently worn couture jumbled with Tati polyester and Monoprix seconds. A Left Bank fashionista secret.

"We're pros," Martine said. "With synchronization, it won't take long."

Aimée grabbed her coat. "Keep working. After I meet Pascal's Gadz'Arts classmate, I'll know more."

The image of Jean-Luc floated in her mind. His warm smile, self-assurance—the antithesis of his geeky classmate, Samour. An unlikely friendship forged by class ties? Soon, she'd meet him for a drink and find out.

René frowned. "Check in before."

Her cousin Sebastien had asked René to escort her to the wedding. She paused at the door.

"René, have you gotten your tuxedo alterations?"

René's hand went to his mouth.

"YELLOW LIGHT, MARTINE," Aimée said, knuckles clenched on the Mini Cooper's lime-green dashboard. Martine had only passed her driving test last week. Aimée wished they'd taken the Métro.

She glanced at the time. Fifteen minutes to her aperitif with Jean-Luc. In the blurring fog, the streetlights gave off a tobacco-yellow haze.

"An off-the-shoulder seventies Dior organza . . . and in winter blue, *parfait!*" Martine was saying. She downshifted, the orange tip of her cigarette long with ash. Aimée regretted forgetting her nicotine patch.

"You didn't do badly yourself, Martine," she said, gesturing to the car's backseat overloaded with shopping bags.

Martine rolled down the window, threw her cigarette out into dank mist. She shivered as she rolled it back up. "Shouldn't Melac escort you to Sebastien's wedding instead of René?"

She shook her head. Wary. Martine's longtime mission, to find Aimée a man, was now focused on Melac and his ex-wife.

"I didn't ask him."

"Why not?"

"My father almost missed my baptism. You can't count on *flics* to attend weddings, or funerals either. Not to mention Melac's just been promoted. All hush-hush," Aimée said. "Now he can't tell me what he does, or . . ."

"He'd have to shoot you?" Martine grinned. "Not that you want to know."

Aimée pushed aside her worry about Melac. Time to compartmentalize. Concentrate on what she'd ask Jean-Luc. Then check in with René to see if Saj had connected the dots, what the diagram signified. How this tied into the DST recruiting her. So much to think about.

But for the moment she tried to ignore Martine's pack of Murattis near the gearshift.

"There's another angle behind the DST, Martine. I feel it."

Earlier, while trying on outfits in the dressing room, she'd filled Martine in on Pascal Samour's murder, Meizi, and the DST.

Martine hit the horn at the bus cutting in front of her. "Better idea, give me access to Meizi," Martine said. "Perfect for an exposé on sweatshops. I'll write a series on working conditions, the luxury items made in China and finished here, the snakeheads. No names, of course."

She'd whetted Martine's appetite. Her plan. "Need to stretch your journalistic chops?"

"Call me tired of seven-minute fluff pieces on Radio France."

Aimée grinned. "Deal."

Martine shrugged and hit the horn again. "Watch your back with the DST. You need connections in high places. De rigueur, but have you seen any real proof on your mother?"

An investigative journalist, Martine broadcast on Radio France and nourished her network of connections.

"What if it's all lies, Aimée?"

Aimée's hand trembled.

At the red light, Martine forgot the clutch and stalled the car. "I don't want you disappointed again. Or hurt. Desolée if this sounds brutal, but what's the point if your mother's dead? A five-year-old surveillance report doesn't bring her back."

The wisp of hope reopened the wound in her heart. The wound that never went away. She wondered if she could face that.

"Don't you see, they want to use you?"

Her shoulders stiffened. "Tell me something new, Martine."

"And you'll beat them at their own game, Aimée?" Martine let out the clutch, ground into first. "All those psychological profilers sitting on Aeron chairs in think tanks outside Versailles, funded by you and me. Dissecting your personality, your vulnerability."

Common intelligence practice, Aimée knew.

"They could rehash old intel, smother it with béarnaise sauce, and serve it fresh. Reel you in. Over and over."

"Nothing's free." Aimée pulled down the visor, flicked on the light, and checked for lipstick on her teeth. "Plan two steps ahead, Papa always said."

A scooter cut in front of them and Martine braked just in time. "*Idiote!*"

"*Bien sûr!* That's it." Of course. The DST had attached a GPS to her scooter. Stupid. Why hadn't she figured that out before?

"Your plan?"

Aimée shut the visor. Hesitated. Sacault's matchbox message had contained a time and location. Nothing else.

"The DST's got me under surveillance. My scooter, my office . . ." She looked at Martine meaningfully.

Martine blinked. "Stay at my place, of course."

"Martine, the first place a profiler would look is at my best friend's."

"So what will you do?"

"Do you still have your learner's driving permit?"

Martine nodded. "Check my wallet."

Aimée rifled through Martine's Hermès. "May I take a press ID, an old one?"

"Will I regret this, Aimée?"

"Just insurance."

Aimée put both Martine's old *Libération* press ID and the permit in her bag. "I need to play the game by my rules. Not the other way around."

All of a sudden a figure darted into the narrow street.

"What the hell?" Martine yelled.

Illuminated in Martine's headlights was a man, on the cobbles directly in front. Aimée's stomach jumped to her mouth. She knew they were going to kill him.

"Don't hit him! Martine!" Aimée shouted. Each detail imprinted in her mind, as if in slow motion. The man's camel-hair coat and dark leather buttons came closer. And closer. Martine punched the Mini Cooper's brakes, skidding on the slick cobbles. With a squeal they veered toward a lamppost. Whipped forward, Aimée threw up her arms and hit the windshield. Pain crunched her wrist. The lime-green Mini Cooper scraped the lamppost, then shuddered to a halt. And stalled.

"He ran out of nowhere," Martine gasped, her knuckles white on the steering wheel. "Into the street, just like that!"

Shaken, Aimée rubbed her wrist.

"*Mon Dieu*, are you all right?"

"Just a bruise, Martine." Aimée unsnapped the seat belt. It could have been worse. The camel-hair coat under the wheels, and herself through the windshield.

"He just jumped out," Martine said again, gesturing to the man, his light-brown coat now bobbing through the crowd.

In a hurry, that one, Aimée thought.

Martine set the gear in neutral. Turned the ignition. The engine responded.

Had he been following them? But she couldn't think about that now.

"And I'm late. I'll walk," she said, trying to ignore the pain. "It's a few streets away."

Aimée reached for her Vuitton carryall.

Martine lit a cigarette, her hands trembling, and shook her head. "At least you bought the winter blue for Sebastien's wedding."

And the little black Agnès b. dress, the vintage YSL beaded turquoise bikini Martine insisted was necessary for the Martinique beach in February, plus strappy heeled sandals for next to nothing. With the huge markdowns, she couldn't resist. She hated to think of her bank account.

"Let me drop you at Arts et Métiers."

All Aimée wanted to do was get out of this tiny car and put ice on her wrist before it swelled like a balloon. "Faster to walk from here, Martine."

Horns beeped behind them. Aimée pulled herself out, straightened up.

"You sure you're all right, Aimée?"

Her boot caught in the gutter and she cursed her three-inch high heels. "Fine, Martine."

With a wave Martine ground into first gear and took off.

A siren whined. Aimée buttoned up her long leather coat against the permeating damp. Why had she worn a black lace top and skimpy cashmere sweater with the temperature dropping and zero visibility?

She hurried in the shadows past buckling seventeenth-century buildings and grimy, dark alleys. Turning the corner in the fog, she found her way blocked by several men. They wore thin jackets and were stamping their feet on the cracked pavers, their breath like steam in the dim streetlight. Their angry-sounding rapid-fire Chinese dialect echoed off the high stone walls.

"*Excusez-moi*," she said. Tso's men? Unease filled her as she edged by them. Suspicion, or something else she couldn't name, painted their faces. A second later the men backed off and melted into the doorways, their words evaporating with their breath.

Another world, she thought. These few blocks were a slice

of an old Chinatown—where Wenzhou immigrants settled after the First World War to work in the factories. A little-known enclave tucked near the Arts et Métiers, and not the most welcoming.

The street twisted and into view came a small Chinese store with red banners proclaiming the Year of the Tiger in gold letters. Beyond that was an old diamond merchant, now a wine bar. Her destination.

JEAN-LUC TRACED THE wineglass rim with his finger. His brow creased. "I didn't understand Pascal. Never could. Now it's too late."

Aimée wished the stiff, tooled leather of her chair didn't scrape the back of her knees. That the glass of wine didn't cost what she'd paid for the marked-down beaded YSL bikini. That the ice pack on her wrist would stop the swelling.

And that she'd reapplied her mascara.

Easy on the eyes, this Jean-Luc, still wearing his jeans jacket. In the light of the sputtering votive candle, she saw his blue gaze go to his cell phone on the table. "Sorry, but I'm expecting a call. A work crisis." He gave an apologetic shrug.

She'd need to hurry this up. A copy of *Charlie Hebdo*, the controversial satirical cartoon weekly, lay on a low table. Out of place, she thought. "How close were you to Pascal?"

"Us Gadz'Arts, *alors*, we're a *fraternité*." Jean-Luc combed his damp blond hair back with his fingers. "I know we appear odd to outsiders. Rituals form our traditions."

Medieval. Tight-knit and insular for today's world.

"I feel responsible," Jean-Luc said. "Like in some way I let him down. Gadz'Arts weld together into a family . . . yes, we call it that. It's our life."

Important to him, she could tell. "For the rest of our lives we help each other, network, line up jobs, act as godfathers to each others' children. That's what hurts."

She nodded. Remembered Madame Samoukashian's words about the initiation rituals. "Pascal didn't seem the group type. What do you mean by welding?"

He shrugged again. "Everyone goes through *bizutage*, initiation, it's a rite of passage, a bonding ritual."

"Hazing? That's bullying."

"Not at all, there's a definite distinction," he said. "But none of this is new. For hundreds of years, all Grandes Ecoles have conducted tests of courage."

True. She remembered her first year of premed, the escalating insults and humiliation. But that hadn't been what made her decide to leave premed. It was the cadaver dissection.

"Our rituals follow the spirit of our school."

"In what way?" She needed to draw him out. Took a sip of the smooth, clear pinot gris. "Like secret handshakes, that kind of thing?"

He gave a small smile. "No comment. It's based on discipline. But if you understand our history, the purpose . . ." He sounded almost religious.

"Which is?"

"The Duc de la Rochefoucauld founded our school in the eighteenth century, initially as a military academy. We evolved into the *Ecole Nationale Supérieure d'Arts et Metiers* after Napoleon visited and decided France must cultivate industry and engineering methods, as well. Soon they were developing the machines that launched the Industrial Revolution."

Skip the propaganda, she wanted to say.

"Even now a Gadz'Arts comes out able to design, fabricate, and operate complex machines and systems," he said. "Who else does that today? We're not only mechanical engineers but high-level technicians."

Rigid and prescribed. Entering young and impressionable, graduating out the back door in a cookie mold. Not how she'd describe Pascal, from what she had seen of his life.

"Hands-on training, you mean?"

"From mathematical concept to execution. And some go on to hands-on jobs. Not that most of us need to. We teach . . ."

"Or run engineering departments, like you," she said. "Sounds more managerial to me. Why didn't Pascal go that route?"

"Did he care about money?" He shook his head, answering his own question.

She leaned forward. "What did Pascal care about?" This oddball genius.

Pause. Jean-Luc averted his eyes, sat without speaking.

"Besides machines and inventions, I mean," she prodded.

Jean-Luc was withholding something. "I don't know. As I said, I failed him. But if he'd just talked to me . . . He wanted to tell me about a project, I think. But I'm not sure. He only left a message."

Aimée contained her excitement. "What happened?"

"Just a message. Something to do with the museum. Coulade mentioned he got a message, too." Jean-Luc checked his cell phone. "But you work at the Conservatoire. No one seemed to know you."

Of course he'd check. "That's due to my firm's pro bono work," she explained. "We're digitizing the Musée's catalogs, a few tie-ins with the Conservatoire."

"*Encore*, Monsieur, Mademoiselle?" The white-aproned waiter hovered with the bottle of pinot gris. Aimée kept her breath even. His cell phone vibrated.

"*Desolé*, I've got a meeting," he said.

"*Non merci*," she said. "The bill, *s'il vous plaît*." She leaned across the low table. "Did Pascal's message deal with his research, Jean-Luc?"

Had Pascal reached out when Coulade didn't return his calls?

Jean-Luc sat back. "You're concerned. But why?"

The tinkle of a piano, the low chords of a bass, and the shushing of a snare drum floated from a side alcove. Jazz. Soon the place would fill up.

She debated revealing her investigation. Pondered how to word it. "We're searching for a file lost in the digitization process. I'm puzzled about what a fourteenth-century document signified to a modern-day engineer. Why Samour thought it important."

"Lost? You think Pascal stole it."

Interesting reaction. She needed to allay his suspicion and get information. And come up with a quick lie.

"Samour requisitioned this file as department head. Seemed anxious. We're trying to furnish it." Now she'd enlist his sympathy. Try to. And lie more. "Our firm's hoping to get the museum's website contract," Aimée said, thinking quickly. "This means a lot to us. I wondered if you could help?"

"But as I told you . . ."

"I appreciate your time, forgive my persistence," she broke in with a smile, "but if you can shed any light on what he might have meant . . . his contact with your former professor, Becquerel?"

Jean-Luc shook his head.

Becquerel seemed a dead end in more ways than one.

"You cared for Pascal, I see. Took over his class today," she said. "It would be a way to help his project. See it through as he would have wanted for the Conservatoire. For the *musée* that was so important to him."

She saw Jean-Luc weigh the option. Had she laid it on too thick? Or played enough to his Gadz'Arts traditions?

"He left a message on my machine at home last night," he said finally. "I recognized his number, but heading my new division at work leaves little time for anything else. My cat doesn't know me anymore."

"That might have been Samour's last call," she said. "Don't you remember what he said?"

A sadness crossed Jean-Luc's face.

"He garbled his words. Sounded excited. But he wanted to meet. I remember, *oui*, at his work studio."

"You mean at his apartment on rue Béranger?"

Jean-Luc shook his head. "He had an atelier, I don't know where."

An atelier?

"Something about a document. Encrypted, maybe? But I'd have to listen again," he said. "Do you think he meant this one you're looking for?"

Careful to keep her excitement in check, she nodded. "Could you listen again and let me know?"

A little smile. He touched her hand. Warm. Smooth for an engineer. She saw a cut on his wrist near his cuff link. "Cutting and pasting blueprints," he said, noticing her gaze. "Blame my training."

Didn't he have minions for that?

"And you?" He gestured to the ice pack melting on her wrist.

"Close encounter with a windshield, due to my friend's new driving skills." But her mind went back to the man darting in the street. Had he been following her?

"Now you've got me thinking," Jean-Luc said. "I want to help. Tomorrow I'm in an all-day symposium. Let's meet after. Dinner?"

She'd hoped sooner. But she'd learned that a desperate Pascal had reached out to Jean-Luc about an encrypted document. And that he had an atelier. The key was to find it.

Saturday, *10:15* P.M

AIMÉE CHECKED HER Tintin watch. The DST contact
was late. She stood at the counter in Café des Puys on rue
Beaubourg. The café was near rue Saint-Martin, the old
Roman road, and had been a café in some form for several
centuries, owned by successive waves of immigrants: Auverg-
nats, Chinese, and now Serbs, as evidenced by the Serbian
national soccer pennants plastering the wall.

Before she could order, the waiter slid an espresso over the
counter. "Compliments of the house."

Her nerves jangled. "*Merci.*"

She undid the sugar wrappers and plopped two cubes in her
cup. Stirred. She scanned the café as she waited for the
espresso to cool. An old woman with a poodle on a leash, two
men in security uniforms, and a young couple holding hands,
eyes only for each other. Who was her contact?

She laid odds on the young couple.

She noticed the square of chocolate on her saucer and
smiled at the waiter. He nodded. She opened the packet and
saw a slip of paper insid.

Go to Théâtre Dejazet, Place de la République

Great. More cold and damp. She downed her espresso and
pulled her long, black leather coat tighter. Left a five-franc tip.

Several blocks away, theatergoers spilled over the series of
steps leading to Boulevard du Temple, once referred to as

Boulevard du Crime. Not that long ago, either. Now few under forty attended the theater. She stood shivering, wishing this were over, that she could go home.

Fog shrouded Place de la République and muted the noise of night buses.

"Intermission and right on time," said a familiar voice. The same blonde woman, smiling. Clad in a blue cocktail dress and matching shawl, she walked down the steps and opened her evening bag. "I'm dying for a smoke."

"We meet again," Aimée said, gritting her teeth.

"Like one? Or still not smoking?"

"I like to live dangerously," Aimée said, accepting a filtered Gauloises. And a light. She felt a jolt to her lungs. The rush of nicotine.

"Keep the pack."

"Don't you have something for me?"

Aimée felt a matchbox in her hand. She slid the box open. Stared at the writing on a cigarette paper. "A website?"

"The proof's there. And don't forget to smile."

Smile? "You bugged my scooter. Don't even think of following me."

But the blonde woman had mingled with theatergoers who were descending the steps, pulling out lighters and sucking smoke. A moment later she'd disappeared into the crowd.

Furious, Aimée ground out the cigarette with a high heel, put the matchbox in her pocket, and headed past the theater toward her cousin Sebastien's atelier. She wished she'd kept the ice on her wrist longer.

At least she could get warm and use his computer.

But Sebastien's framing atelier was dark. She hit his number on her cell phone. His phone rang and rang. No answer. Not even voice mail.

She paced the cobbles by Sebastien's and noticed the

stained glass atelier next door. Thinking about the chapter in Samour's book gave her an idea. She'd talk to the stained-glass artist tomorrow. What else could she do?

Still no word from Prévost. She needed to protect Meizi, make good on her promise to Mademoiselle Samoukashian, and ensure Prévost's cooperation in the Chinatown surveillance raid. She headed down the dark street toward the bus stop a few blocks over and hit Prévost's number.

"*Commissariat, bonsoir.*"

"Officer Prévost, *s'il vous plaît.*"

"At a meeting," said a young voice. A yawn. "Leave your number and he'll get the message."

"Too late. His informer's in trouble," she said. "Patch me through to him."

"Who's this?"

"Big trouble, *compris?*"

Pause.

"Now!"

She heard a click. Buzz.

Prévost answered on the first ring. "*Oui?*"

Finally.

In the background she heard what sounded like the click of chips, the slap of cards. Gambling. Hadn't that gotten him into trouble before? But she could use that.

"Who's this?"

"It's Aimée Leduc," she said. "We need to talk."

"About your statement?" She heard surprise in his voice.

"I mean the surveillance mounted in—"

"What's that got to do with you? Keep your nose out of this."

"But you wouldn't want another mark on your record, would you?"

"What?" Voices rose in the background. Chinese voices. A chair scraped over the floor.

"Gambling again?" she said.

"What the hell . . . listen, we'll talk tomorrow." Quiet now. He'd left the table.

"So you'll shine me on again?" she said. "I can lead you to the snakehead who controls boutiques, sweatshops in a three-block radius. Big promotion for you, Prévost. And I wouldn't need to mention your love of cards."

Pause. "You're guessing."

"You want more?"

The street was quiet. Too quiet. She kept her voice low, hurried around the corner. Another deserted street lit by misted globes. Footsteps sounded behind her.

The hair rose on the back of her neck.

She sped up. Three more winding blocks to the bus that would drop her close to Île Saint-Louis.

"More like a source, Mademoiselle Leduc. Hard evidence."

"How about nameless bodies lying in the paupers section at the Ivry cemetery," she said. "Front page to the right investigative reporter. Especially since the funeral parlor's right under your nose in the quartier. Or maybe they finance your chips."

She heard a car door slam, footsteps behind her again.

She made her feet go faster, one eye out for ice while she scanned the darkened windows and the parked cars for movement. Whoever they were, they were good.

"What do you want?"

Right now, dry shoes and a warm fire. And quick. But she saw no taxi in sight.

"A woman protected," she said. "The date of the raid."

"We'll talk. But not now."

Pause. Voices.

"Getting the snakehead and his boss, that's gold, Prévost."

More voices. She had to convince him. Give him something to get information. She took a stab in the dark. "There's a witness to Samour's murder. Haven't you questioned him?"

"Who?"

"Clodo, the homeless man in the stairs."

Pause. "Not anymore."

Footsteps sounded close behind her. She didn't like this. Without turning around she walked faster. Her gut told her to get the hell to the Métro.

"He's in custody? Then he's told you—"

"Pushed on the Métro tracks. At Hôtel-Dieu."

"But have you questioned him?"

"Clodo's not in any condition to tell anyone anything soon. If ever."

Her blood ran cold. "The murderer tried to kill his witness, Prévost."

"More like he fell on the rails drunk or during a fight. A coincidence."

"No coincidence, Prévost," she said.

"What judge would listen to him? I need proof."

Proof? Prévost might need evidence to make a case. She didn't.

Hampered by regulations, paperwork, the endless questioning and rehashing of witness statements—vital time lost. No wonder, despite the cloud of suspicion trailing him, her father was glad to leave the force.

"You want evidence? How about the cell phone Clodo took from the murder site?"

Pause. "Cell phone?"

She hoped the homeless weatherman would come through.

"Help me and I'll help you," she said. "Look, Prévost, you need my information to look good with the RG, don't you?"

He cleared his throat. "More like I owed your father. I'll call you tomorrow."

Owed Papa? "What do you mean?"

But he'd hung up.

Taken up with Prévost's call, she'd forgotten the footsteps behind her. Stupid not to pay attention. To have her arm weighted down with the heavy Vuitton.

Up ahead, light spilled out of massive portals into the street. Chamber music drifted from a courtyard. A man in a tuxedo escorted a laughing woman, a fox-fur wrap draped over her shoulders, to an approaching taxi. Not far now.

And then she was grabbed from behind. Pulled into a walkway between the buildings. Shoved face-first against the pitted wall. Her gasping scream broken by the force of a body pinning her to the dripping stone. Someone had followed her to finish the job, just as they'd finished Samour. One of the huddled knot of Chinese men she'd run into earlier?

Terror filled her. Broken glass crackled underfoot and a rat scurried away by the garbage bin. Hands clasped her wrists in an iron grip. Big hands. A man's hands. Her bruised wrist flashed with pain as her arms were bound together with tape.

Then her head was pulled back. Smooth sheet plastic was wrapped over her mouth, her eyes, her face. Pulled tight, smothering her. She couldn't scream, couldn't breathe. Frantic, she elbowed back with all her might. Again, into his chest as hard as she could, struggling to suck air. Nothing but her tongue on plastic. Panicked, she bit down hard. Only felt smooth plastic.

She kicked back with her heeled boot. Tightness in her chest, her lungs. Voices, laughter, and she didn't feel the man anymore. Footsteps . . . fading away. Groggy, she sank down on jagged glass. Her mind fogged.

She pressed her face on the glass shards, rubbing against a jagged tip, frantic to poke a hole and get air. She felt the sharp point near her nostril. Rubbed harder, the glass cutting her face. A trickle of air. She fought to breathe, her mind slipping away.

MORBIER WIPED THE perspiration from his forehead with a handkerchief in his chief's overheated office in the *commissariat*. His back hurt, and the small chair groaned under his weight. After too much wine, he had to force himself to concentrate. To push Aimée to the back of the line.

Morbier shifted his legs, wishing the meeting had ended thirty minutes ago. Irritation shone in Loisel's small, ferret-like eyes. The mole on his left cheek reminded Morbier of a chocolate smudge. For the umpteenth time, he battled the urge to use his handkerchief and wipe the man's cheek.

"So how do I substantiate allegations of police corruption, Commissaire?" Loisel asked. "Anything old-fashioned, like attending meetings with documentation? Or evidence? Remember those?"

Morbier had obtained illegal phone taps, and telephoto surveillance of the suspect's contacts. Incriminating, but nothing Loisel could use. Still, it was leverage for Morbier.

"My neck's on the block and I don't like it," Loisel said. "You've had free reign until now, but the stratosphere's changed."

His predecessor, Langouile, tasked Morbier with investigating rife police department corruption. It touched the top toes, demanding tact. Morbier met resistance and evasion, hit each bend on thin ice. And with nothing he could use legally.

"What about your *indicateur?*" Loisel asked, tenting his fingers.

Morbier's top informer had been found in the Seine, in the salvage net at Evry. A good man. On the force for ten years and with access to high-level reports. But Morbier had arrived too late. It sickened him. The man left a wife and two young children.

"They got to him before I did."

"So you have nothing besides a dead *indicateur?*" Loisel's tone was cold.

"Don't forget I spent time downstairs in Le Dépôt. A little hard to work when I was a suspect in jail." Due to circumstantial evidence, there had been accusations that he'd murdered the woman he loved. All engineered at the hands of the top brass he wanted to topple. But he had no concrete proof of that either.

"This would go quicker and without the mess," Morbier said, shooting Loisel a look, "if you ordered a legal wiretap."

"I didn't hear that, Morbier. *Alors*, deal with your personal issues, satisfy the police psychologist's mandate, then give me concrete evidence for a court of law."

Telling him to deal with his issues? That his informer had died for nothing?

Anger rippled inside his chest. That man had dedicated his life to the law, but had it protected him? No, only the big men at the top. Like always.

But Morbier wouldn't let this go. He had to pierce this cloud of grief, stop drinking every night, move on. His job depended on it. And so did Aimée's life.

"Give me two men I can trust, Loisel."

"I need results, Commissaire. Or this investigation shuts down due to lack of evidence."

Repeating himself, too. Covering his ass. Sweat popped on Morbier's brow.

Loisel sighed. Sniffed. "Drinking, too. Your memory holding up these days?"

Morbier bunched his fist to knock the smug look off Loisel's face until he noticed Loisel writing on a scrap of paper. Loisel shoved it across his magistrate's teak-wood desk.

One name.

Loisel tore it up. A sweep of his ferret-like eyes to the tall window and a quick flick of his pointed finger told Morbier the office was bugged. Ears listened from the *centre d'écoute* under Napoleon's tomb at Les Invalides.

Merde.

"A full report with developments and proof," Loisel said, "by this time tomorrow night or your investigation goes away."

Morbier nodded, trying to get a read on Loisel. But he'd already picked up the phone and gave a dismissive wave.

The name that Loisel had written down had shocked him. But if this man cooperated . . . No time to delay.

On his way down the worn stairs, Morbier tried Aimée's number. No answer. Typical.

Saturday Evening

AIMÉE RUBBED HER face against the glass, gnawing to make the tiny slit in the plastic bigger, sucking for air. Air, she needed more air. With her throat dry and her wrists bound, she sawed harder against a sharp sliver of glass, like a knife to her nose. More and more, until the plastic tore open from her nose to her mouth. Gasping for air, she lay facedown in the walkway. Fetid air reeking of garbage, but never so sweet. Her chest heaved. Twisting around, she leaned against the stone wall in the frigid cold. Three minutes later, she had sawed her wrists free and pulled the torn plastic from her face.

Sticky with her own blood, she crawled over the uneven cobbles. Somehow her Vuitton was still there. Her suede leggings were shredded, her coat stained with dirt. She struggled to pull herself up and staggered to the street, looking for help. But the loitering taxi's door slammed and it pulled away, tires hissing on the wet cobbles.

Merde! All those generous tips. Where was her late-night taxi karma?

At least the taxi had scared him away. A minute later and she would've been a goner. But she had to get out of here.

Two long blocks away on rue de Turenne, there was still no taxi in sight. She heard the low whoosh of brakes, water splashing from a puddle at the bus stop. But the lighted Number 96 bus took off. She waved and made herself run after it, pounded on the door. By a miracle the driver stopped.

"I shouldn't do this," said the young bus driver, taking a look at her and shaking his head. "Either you've escaped from an eighties punk party, or you're making a getaway."

"The latter, *merci*," she gasped, holding her sleeve to her bloody nose, and fed her ticket in the machine.

At a window seat, her shoulders heaving, she scanned the street. No one. Her hands trembled as she fingered the camel-colored thread caught in her fingernail. The thread from the attacker's coat. The man who ran in front of Martine's car.

In her apartment, after a hot, steaming bath, she applied arnica to her wrists and antibiotic cream on the cuts on her face. Prayed she had enough concealer to cover them tomorrow. Then she huddled under the silk duvet, the raw pain dulled with Doliprane.

For a moment it had seemed so close. Pascal's obsession with a fourteenth-century document. The connection right before her eyes. But that and a ticket got her a bus ride.

The killer had attacked her. That meant she was getting close. Too close for comfort.

Let it simmer, her father always said. Then, step by step, fit the pieces together. But at least she'd found a piece of Pascal's puzzle.

Tomorrow she'd scout out Becquerel's connection, find something.

She felt the empty space beside her, the depression in the mattress where Melac's leg should have been twined with hers. His scent remained on the sheets, on the towels in her bathroom. His half-squeezed toothpaste tube of Fluocaril lay by the sink.

Miles Davis's wet nose nuzzled her ear. His tail flicked the duvet until he settled in the crook of her arm by the laptop. She had her man, four legs and all.

Did the DST really have info about her mother? She booted

up her laptop and hesitated, her fingers hovering over the keys. She chewed her lip. Only one way to find out.

She typed in the website address from the matchbox. A page popped up on the screen: a typewritten copy of an MI6 surveillance report dated five years before. The heading: *Sydney/Sidonie Leduc aka Lampa. Subject sighting location—Merjoides Hotel, Istanbul, lobby. Meeting with known arms dealers ___ ___.* The names had been blacked out. No photos. Duration of incident: seven minutes. A seven-minute sighting in a hotel lobby.

A five-year-old report and it told her . . . what? Maybe there was nothing else to tell. The DST set up a website, as Martine had said, and fed old reports to hook her.

The sharp pang of longing hit her. If her mother had been alive five years ago, why hadn't she ever contacted her?

Just once.

AIMÉE INHALED THE algae-scented wind, watching wavelets crest on the Seine below. The oyster sky mirrored the gray-tiled rooftops overlooking the quai. No snow, the ice had melted, as the homeless man had forecast. Perfect for a wool coat, scarf, boots and a *chocolat chaud.*

Miles Davis's leash tugged her toward the damp stone steps leading down from Quai d'Anjou. He did his business under the bare-branched lime tree. Like every morning.

Her phone rang.

"Got dinner plans, Leduc?" her godfather Morbier asked.

A bolt of surprise shot through her. But she had a rendez-vous with Jean-Luc. Vital for information on Pascal.

"Matter of fact, I do."

"Another bad boy, Leduc?" He coughed. "Given up on Melac? Non, I don't want to know. Lunch tomorrow, *d'accord?*"

"Anything to do with why you haven't returned my calls, Morbier?"

She debated telling him about the attack last night. But that necessitated telling him about Pascal's murder, the DST, her mother.

His voice interrupted her thoughts.

"See you at 1 P.M., Chez Louis."

A three-star Michelin *resto?* "It's not my birthday."

Pause. He cleared his throat again. "It's been a while, we should talk."

Talk? Morbier, the original clammed mouth? This sounded serious. Or was that a trace of guilt she sensed? She could use that to her advantage.

"But you can bring me a present. The Hôtel-Dieu report on Clodo, a homeless *mec*, thrown on the Métro line last night." God willing he'd made it through the night. "Can you arrange for me to visit him tomorrow, Morbier?"

"What's this Clodo got to do with anything?" Pause. "You're not inviting him to lunch?"

"Not in his condition." Let him wonder.

"No promises, Leduc." He clicked off.

As always, he kept her wondering. He'd engineer repayment. Nothing came free from Morbier.

She stared at the torpid gray currents. Morbier was the last link to her parents. Her only family now, besides her cousin Sebastien and René. Morbier had been her father's first partner. The only one left who'd known her American mother. Not that he'd talk about her. He'd avoided Aimée's questions for years.

She was bending down to scoop Miles Davis's morning contribution into a plastic Printemps bag when her eye caught on the trash bin. Another matchbox was visible under the metal lip. Apprehension rippled through her shoulders.

They watched her, knew her schedule, her movements. If they were so good, why hadn't they prevented her attack last night? She bit her lip. Before she defeated them at their own plan, she needed to discover it.

She dropped the plastic Printemps bag in the bin at the same time as she slid the matchbox in her pocket. *Comme d'habitude*, she left Miles Davis with Madame Cachou, her concierge, and followed her morning routine. Hitching up her leather skirt and black lace tights, she climbed on her Vespa and scootered across arched Pont Marie, the wind hitting her cheekbones. By the time she parked her now debugged scooter on rue Bailleul, she had a plan. Instead of turning to Leduc Detective's door, she stopped at the red-awninged corner café.

"*Un double*, Aimée?" Zazie, the owner's redheaded daughter, asked.

"Make it *un double chocolat chaud*." Aimée's smile turned serious. "You're not at school, Zazie?"

"It's Sunday, Aimée." Zazie made a face as she knocked out the coffee grinds with a loud thump. "We let Papa sleep in. Not everyone works all the time like you do."

Everyone else had a life.

"I'm in the lycée now," Zazie said, "or did you forget that too?"

And grew up. It felt like yesterday that Zazie had to stand on a stool to serve from behind the counter.

"Of course not." How could she have missed Zazie's touch of mascara and blush, and her red hair now tamed with clips?

"Nice blusher," Zazie said. "New tone?"

Aimée nodded. At least her makeup covered the cuts.

At the counter stood several suits and an older couple arguing over last night's game show, *Questions pour un Champion*. Two men in windbreakers entered, accompanied by a rush of cold air. They took a table by the window overlooking rue du Louvre, read the menu with studied preoccupation. Too obvious on an early Sunday morning. Even on a bad day her surveillance skills were better than theirs. What did this cost the government?

"*Merci*, Zazie." She sipped her *chocolat chaud* and left ten francs on the counter. "Your mother working the accounts this morning?"

Zazie nodded. "*Bien sûr*."

"I'll just stop by, eh?"

Zazie set the dishtowel down on her school *cahier* and winked. "This way."

Aimée followed her through the narrow passageway by crates of Orangina. She nodded to Virginie, who was sitting in the cluttered office with Zazie's toddler sister on her lap, and headed to the back service door.

"Plan B, *n'est-ce pas*, Aimée?"

"Good memory, Zazie. A detective always needs a Plan B."

And plans X, Y, and Z.

"Those two men who just came in are following you?" Zazie said.

Sharp, too. "Let's hope it's only two." Aimée pulled out her LeClerc compact, touched up her lips with Chanel Red. "When you take their order, count to ten and keep them busy. Eyes away from the window, okay?"

Zazie nodded, serious. "This goes on my recommendation, *non*? I'm ready to go undercover, pass messages anytime."

Aimée blinked.

"For my internship in your office next summer."

Didn't she want to be a dancer? Or was that yesterday?

"PROFESSOR BECQUEREL?"

The pale-faced twenty-something shook his head. He ground his cigarette under his heel in the Ecole Nationale Supérieure d'Arts et Métiers laboratory courtyard and stuck the butt in the pocket of his smudged, gray lab coat. "He died in the nursing home. No family. Sad, they said."

Aimée hoped she hadn't made a trip to the *grande école* in the 13th arrondissement for nothing. And so early on a Sunday morning.

"Didn't he maintain an office?"

"Here we're all third-year Gadz'Arts," he said. "There's no space for old, retired professors, even legends."

"Whom could I speak with who knew him?"

"Only the laboratory's open today. Just students." The young man shrugged. "The school held a memorial for him a few days ago."

That gave her an idea. "Where do they keep the remembrance book?"

"*Quoi?*"

She noticed the ink stains on his lapel pocket. A slide rule sticking out of his pants. A textbook geek.

"People who attended the memorial would sign a remembrance book, *non?*"

He shrugged. "Check with the office." His wristwatch beeped. "*Excusez-moi.*"

But the offices were closed. Five minutes of directions from the concierge and a long corridor later, she found her goal. A high-ceilinged foyer led to a musty nineteenth-century salon dominated by the bronze statue of Duc de La Rochefoucauld-Liancourt, who founded the school before the Revolution. Later, at Napoleon's request, he focused on a trained military-style corps of engineers. Or so the inscription read.

The busts, portraits, and names on the wall spoke of the expertise of the celebrated Gadz'Arts. And the power and prestige. She stood back to note the graduates, from the designer of First World War fighter planes to the engineers of the Suez Canal, and get a sense of Samour's connections.

Another wall listed more recent graduates. On supervisory boards, heading engineering firms, or captains of industry with firms like Renault. Impressive and all over the map.

Below she found a photo of a hollow-cheeked, bespectacled man with the handwritten Gothic script: *Alphonse Becquerel, a pioneer who knew no boundaries in the field of optics and technology.*

She opened the slim leather remembrance volume sitting on the podium. Inside were pasted articles from Becquerel's long engineering and teaching career. Memorials from past students listed by graduating year—all in the stilted Gothic black-ink script. A curious familial feel to the notes, but hadn't Jean-Luc called it a fraternity, a family?

Yet not Pascal's name. Odd not to attend the memorial of a man he revered and trusted. She filed that away for later.

Determined to come away with something besides the sneeze building in her nose from the dust, she stuck the remembrance volume in her bag. In the first office she found, she smiled at the cleaning woman. "I'm in a hurry for the professor. Any copier available on this floor?"

The cleaner, a smiling middle-aged woman wearing a head scarf, gestured across the hall. Twenty francs poorer, Aimée left the remembrance memorial and walked out of the Conservatoire with the copied contents in her bag.

The cold gray outside made her think of the approaching gray monochrome of February. A month of beating rain and the highest rate of suicides. Around the corner she passed *Le Monde diplomatique*, the leftist *intello* monthly lodged in an old dairy. A remnant of the village the quartier was until the seventies demolition and tower blocks.

But the zinc counter at the café hadn't changed in years. The milk steamer whooshed, the steam radiator hissed. She hung her coat up on the rack.

"*Un express, s'il vous plaît.*"

The girl with thick black eyeliner behind the counter put down her *Marie Claire* magazine and nodded.

From the side alcove the news blared on the *télé*—World Cup fever for the national team, Les Bleus, overtaking the ongoing five-month-old Princess Di investigation. Then, a brief bulletin concerning the street closures that would clog northeast Paris on Monday, and the hospital workers protest in the morning. What else was new?

No mention of the Pascal Samour homicide.

Aimée studied the remembrance book pages and picked out the name of the one graduate in Pascal's year. Tristan de Voule of Solas Energie. More approachable, she figured, than the older directors of megaconglomerates. She'd start with him.

The girl served Aimée's espresso and went back to reading *Marie Claire*.

After some dialing, she found no Tristan de Voule listed, but directory assistance connected her to Solas Energie.

Then a twenty-four, seven answering service. After being routed through two receptionists, she reached his administrative assistant.

"Monsieur de Voule's in the field," said the assistant. "His schedule is booked all week."

Great. A busy engineer or head honcho working on the weekend. She thought fast.

"A pity. I'm calling on behalf of the tribute we're setting up in Professor Becquerel's name. He attended the memorial and expressed interest in contributing."

"I'll relay the message, Mademoiselle."

"Of course, but he told me how he looked up to the professor." She scrambled for something more convincing. "Wanted to do a more personal tribute. But I've misplaced his cell phone number."

Pause.

"Last Wednesday at the memorial here at the Conservatoire," Aimée continued. "You know how close the Gadz'Arts grow to their mentors."

"I'm not allowed to give out his number. Company policy."

No doubt the admin fielded calls for donations all the time.

"I understand." She had to persist. "But you could take mine. It's close to his heart, he told me. 06 38 35 15 78. Before tonight, if possible."

A little sigh. "*Bon.* I'll pass on your number, Mademoiselle."

She stirred her espresso and read. Alphonse Becquerel, a descendent of Henri, the physicist who shared the Nobel Prize with Marie and Pierre Curie. Devoted himself to light and optics, mostly in corporate research labs connected with technology. A pioneer in communications systems.

She got little from this bare-bones description. More emphasis seemed placed on his leadership of student organizations. In his later years he'd taught one high-level class on theories in relative connectivity.

Whatever that meant, she thought. But René would know.

She hit René's number on her speed dial. Only voice mail. Why didn't he answer?

She glanced at her Tintin watch. If she hurried she'd make her meeting with Prévost. Her cell phone trilled.

"René, where are you?"

Pause. Grinding metal sounded in the background.

"*Excusez-moi*, but I thought . . . I'm calling concerning Professor Becquerel?" said a deep voice. "A mistake . . ."

Stupid. She hadn't thought he'd return her call so soon, if at all. Instead of preparing a story to elicit info about Pascal, she'd flubbed it. She'd have to salvage this.

"*Pas du tout*, Monsieur de Voule," she said. "Forgive me for not checking my caller ID."

"I'm not sure I remember you at the Memorial. Did we meet?" he said. Polite, cautious, and smart.

No way around this but to plunge right in. And stretch the truth.

"I worked with Pascal Samour volunteering at the museum." A little lie.

Scraping noises. A long pause.

"I don't understand, Mademoiselle."

"Matter of fact, I still do. But his murder—"

"Murder?" She heard shock in his tone.

"You didn't know? But as Gadz'Arts, his classmate, I thought . . ."

A sigh. "It's complicated. Pascal's not on the Gadz'Arts list. No wonder he didn't attend the memorial. But why call me?"

"Now I don't understand," she said. "A list?"

A snort. "I'm a *crapaud*, a toad. Not that I bought into the traditions, just enough to get by. Pascal never did. So he's unofficial. An HU."

"Which means?"

Pause.

"The Mentus, upperclassmen, enlisted cadres to prove themselves. If you resisted, you'd be labeled 'outside the factory,' *hors usinage*, HU, like Pascal. Me, I did the minimum, a *crapaud*, so I made the list."

"Pascal's not part of the family, then?" She sipped her espresso, trying to understand.

"That's one way to put it," he said. "This lore goes so far back." He gave a little sigh. "Ritualistic traditions passed on in a mysterious booklet with arcane symbols, mystical directions. We were pressured to wake up before dawn, wear long robes, learn chants." His tone was embarrassed. Almost apologetic. "Exerting constant pressure on us until our class coalesced into a unit, a cohesive mold."

Not a system Pascal seemed to have fit into. "Sounds like the military," she said.

"Cadres were coached to do the dirty work. 'Killers.'"

Her breath caught. "Killers?"

The girl behind the counter peered up from her *Marie Claire*. Aimée turned away.

"I mean, it was perfect preparation for the cutthroat corporate world. Daring each other to man up, take risks," he said. "Prove they're worthy, part of the group. This notion of group loyalty and camaraderie through shared suffering. Ridiculous when you think about it."

Pause. The clanking and shouting of men came from the background.

"I'm sorry about Pascal," de Voule said. "He looked up to Becquerel. A mentor, even to HU."

"Outcasts like Pascal?"

"Look, I'm at a work site with heavy machinery lined up."

"Pascal confided his project to Becquerel," she said quickly. "But I think it links to the contract we're working on for his department. Can you think how Becquerel would have been involved?"

"Beats me, Mademoiselle," de Voule said. "The professor looked toward the future. He was a visionary. Foresaw computing systems, communication networks, fiber optics years ago."

She grabbed her brown lip liner and wrote "communications networks, fiber optics" on a serviette.

"One more thing. His friend Jean-Luc Narzac, a fellow classmate, you know him, of course?"

Pause.

"Narzac? Haven't seen him in several years." De Voule's tone had changed. "The team's waiting for me, Mademoiselle."

He'd shut down.

"May I just ask what you do, what your company does?"

"Solar energy." Pause. "I tried to recruit Samour, a brilliant research analyst and engineer. But he never cared for an office, four walls."

"He liked them rounded, Monsieur," she said. "He lived in a tower, did you know that?"

"I'm sorry." Another pause. "But I can see him living in a tower, now that you say that. A visionary much in the mold of Becquerel. Both seeing the roots of tomorrow in the science of the past. I can picture him living in a fourteenth-century tower."

Now she was alert. "Fourteenth century?"

"Samour was obsessed with the fourteenth century," de Voule said. "It was his passion, studying arts and sciences from that period. According to him, no one's ever invented anything new since then. Was going to set out and prove it, or so he said when I offered him a job. It's my company, I told him, you could make your own hours. But he followed his own path."

"His great-aunt said the same thing," Aimée said. "Becquerel knew what he was working on, but with his death . . ." She paused. "Did Pascal have enemies?"

Her phone clicked. Another call. She ignored it.

"Look, it's terrible. But I don't know. Sorry if I'm not helpful." She sensed there was more he wanted to say.

"*Au contraire*, you've told me a lot. If there's anything else that comes up for you, you've got my contact number."

She slapped five francs on the counter and listened to the message. Mademoiselle Samoukashian, and she sounded afraid.

AT THE APARTMENT door, Mademoiselle Samoukashian took one look at Aimée's raised Swiss Army knife and stepped back. "Overreacting, Mademoielle?"

"You sounded worried, you stressed urgency," Aimée said. "Has something happened?"

"In the kitchen," she said, "but put that away first."

Aimée slipped the knife in her purse. A high, warbled bleeping, like birdsong, came from the high-end laptop.

An e-mail received.

Mademoiselle Samoukashian blinked and sat down. "That's from Pascal." She pointed to the screen. "His e-mail signal. I've gotten two of them today."

"You're sure?" Aimée asked, startled.

She nodded.

Pascal kept busy for a man on the slab at the morgue. A coldness spread in her stomach. "And you didn't open them?"

"I wanted to show you."

Seating herself on the stool, Aimée stared at the address: Pascal@wanadoo.fr.

There was an attachment. A virus, a sick joke? Or had someone hacked his account already? She'd view the message before deleting it.

If something has happened to me, give this to Becquerel. He can lead you in the right direction.

But Becquerel was dead.

"I just asked one of Pascal's Gadz'Arts classmates about Becquerel."

"And?"

"Nothing." Aimée pulled out her cell phone. "I'll need to confer with my partner."

Mademoiselle Samoukashian nodded, her gaze glued to the screen.

René answered on the first ring.

"Any idea how Pascal could e-mail his great-aunt with an attachment a moment ago?"

Pause. "He had a dead man switch on his computer account," René said. "Common practice for nerds to store secrets in encrypted files. Each time you log in, it resets the clock. But if you don't log in within a certain period of time, it sends an e-mail. Then deletes files, if he programmed it that way. No telling how long ago he set this up."

"So he could have programmed this a week ago, two weeks ago?"

She heard the clicking of keys in the background

"Shoot it to me right now with the attachment. Hurry."

She typed in René's address. Hit FORWARD and said a little prayer. "Done."

René sucked in his breath. "Let me find a program to figure this out."

"How long, René?"

"An hour, a day. Call you back." He clicked off.

Aimée looked up. "I have to go."

"You'll find who murdered Pascal?" The old woman's voice quavered.

Determined now, she nodded. "Count on it, Mademoiselle Samoukashian."

RENÉ RUBBED HIS shoulders. Two hours of endless configurations spent over Samour's decrypted attachment and he still couldn't get a grip on it.

At least he'd left Meizi safe at the hotel.

And his hip ache had subsided to a dull throb once he'd borrowed the portable heater from Luigi's travel agency down the hall.

Aimée's mahogany desk was piled with samples of their new security prospectus. Hadn't she promised to come in? And why hadn't she updated him on the museum?

Saj sat monitoring the spyware installed on Coulade's computer.

"Any activity?"

Saj shook his head. "Not so far. I'm also trawling Coulade's desktop files. Nothing interesting pops out."

"What do you make of this, Saj?"

Saj's sandalwood prayer-bead bracelet clacked as he peered over René's laptop. "Hmmm . . . I'm hungry."

"That's all you can say, Saj?"

"A recipe." Saj handed him a battered takeout menu. "Which reminds me, feel like ordering in?" Saj stretched his tanned arms high over his six-foot frame, cracked his neck. His billowing white muslin Indian shirt blocked René's view. How could he wear almost nothing in January?

René stared at his screen, at the reams of code from Samour's attachment. A cipher.

"Say that again."

"We had sushi yesterday," Saj said. "What about the new South Indian vegan?"

"No, I mean recipe."

"See those interesting code breaks?" Saj pointed to the flat lines of script.

His curiosity piqued, René highlighted a section of the attachment that he'd already pored over several times. "You mean this?"

"Think of it in 3-D. Add dimension."

René slotted in a disc. Hit the icon to open the program. "Like this?"

A raised bed of points and concave lines appeared.

Saj shook his head. "Try a line separation."

Excited, René scrolled down and hit another key.

The script aligned to borders and line breaks.

"Reminds me of my grandmother's recipe book," Saj said, pulling up a chair. "Those configuration symbols start each line."

Symbols. "Meaning what?"

"I'd say they represent numbers, quantity, or measurements, René. Symbols grouped in those kinds of configurations often indicate Roman numerals." Saj nodded, pulling a scarf around his shoulders. "Or medieval drams and weights, I'd guess here."

"Say fourteenth century?"

"Why not?"

René grabbed the takeout menu. "Order anything you want, Saj. We've got a long day ahead of us."

"Officer Prévost, *s'il vous plaît*," Aimée said to the blue-uniformed *flic* on duty. The *commissariat* on rue Louis Blanc had been designed by Gustave Eiffel, and its corners needed dusting.

"Mademoiselle Leduc?" said the fresh-faced recruit who'd missed a spot shaving his chin. He opened a file and slid a typed *procès-verbal* form across the high counter. "Routine, please sign and date your statement, *s'il vous plaît*."

"But we had an appointment," she said. She'd counted on worming the surveillance info out of Prévost. He'd promised her.

"You're late. He left for a meeting."

Merde!

Aimée scanned the typed up statement, noting the case number and file with a pen on her palm. Reading her statement, her mind went back to the snow dusting the plastic on Pascal's unseeing eyes, the chunks of his flesh gnawed by rats. Her attack last night.

"Prévost?" an officer was saying on the phone from the other end of the reception counter. Her ears perked up. "He's on call today. Out to early lunch."

Meeting, my foot, she thought. He'd avoided her.

She scribbled her name. Pushed the statement back to the officer. Smiled.

"I'm starving." She rubbed her stomach. "Know a good place around here?"

The *flic* paused in thought. A challenge for him, she could tell, a new graduate from the police academy who'd been transferred to Paris and no doubt ate in the police canteen in the basement.

He shrugged.

"But *flics* know the best places to eat," she said, pushing it.

"Some of the older ones talk about a cassoulet place on Quai de Valmy. But I don't know."

She winked. "*Merci.*"

Several blocks down rue Louis Blanc she saw the red awning of a bistro, Chez Pépé, cuisine de Bourgogne. Definitely a place for cassoulet. She hoped to God that Prévost ate here. Not a moment later she recognized his sparse hair, that raincoat ducking out the door. She revved into second gear and, her luck still holding, found a narrow space to wedge her scooter into, next to the zebra crosswalk.

To find Prévost *and* a parking place—the gods were smiling on her. She set her helmet in the carrier, edged sideways between the cars to the sidewalk, and stepped into melted slush up to her ankle. Another pair of boots, vintage Fendis, ruined.

Prévost stood in Chez Pépé's doorway, speaking on his cell phone and gesturing with his free hand. Before she reached him, he clicked his phone shut and went back inside.

A moment later Prévost shot out the doorway again, keys in hand. He unlocked the door of an unmarked Peugeot, started the engine.

The gods had stopped smiling.

She ran back to her scooter, wedged it out, and prayed Prévost hadn't made the traffic light. She gunned the scooter down the quai until she saw the Peugeot ahead. A bus cut in front of her. By the time she reached the next intersection, the Peugeot had pulled ahead. She punched the handlebars in frustration. As the light turned green, she popped into first gear and caught up with Prévost.

The threatening clouds chose this moment to open up. Rain pelted the canal's surface. Blinking rain away, she followed Prévost for fifteen wet minutes until he parked on narrow rue du Pont au Choux.

Next to the maroon storefront of Tartaix Métaux Outillage, the commercial metal shop, Prévost pushed open a wormholed faded-green door. She parked her scooter on the pavement, propped it up on the kickstand. Rain dripped from her shoulders. She shivered and ran across the street.

But the door shut behind him. Did he live here?

Instead of waiting in the deserted street for Prévost to emerge, she entered Tartaix Métaux's glass-paned doors. The shop's interior appeared unchanged from how she remembered it from childhood visits with her grandfather: the floor-to-ceiling drawers, long wooden counters reminding her of a bistro, a sales wicket resembling the old Métro ticket booths piled with catalogs.

"We're closed, Mademoiselle."

She noted the blue-coated assistants stocking items from stepladders. "But I didn't see a sign, Monsieur."

"We're doing inventory," said a man, wiping his hands on a rag. "Come back tomorrow."

A side door opened, bringing with it a wet rush of air. Prévost stood under the dripping eaves, huddled with an Asian man.

Her grandfather had known the owner; they'd been old drinking buddies. She could use that.

"Does Monsieur Colles still work in the back?" She flashed a smile and her card.

"Some problem, Mademoiselle?" The stooped, graying man eyed her.

"Not at all, Monsieur," she said, peering over the workman's shoulder. From Prévost's gestures, rigid body stance, and raised voice, she figured they were arguing. The Asian man stepped back, shaking his head. He wore a rain-spattered blue workcoat, and round, silver-framed glasses that gave him an academic air.

A brief glimpse before the courtyard door slammed shut.

"Routine, Monsieur," Aimée said, emitting a bored sigh. "An insurance scam hit several firms on the street. My firm's making inquiries."

He nodded. "Second door to the left."

She stepped to the rear amid rows of aluminum tubing, copper wire, and chrome and bronze strips on shelves reaching to the slanted glass ceiling. The reek of soldering metal and the whining grate of an electric saw assaulted her senses. Familiar, so familiar. She thought of her grandfather's watchmaker friend, who would come to scour these shelves for bronze.

Inside the open office door she saw a thirtyish man, shiny bald head, black turtleneck, and readers perched on his nose. He looked like a film director. She remembered the massive walnut desk he stood at.

"But I'm looking for Monsieur Colles?"

He gave her the once-over. "My father." Glanced at her card. "Leduc Detective. But I knew old Leduc . . ."

"My grandfather. I'm Aimée Leduc." She smiled. "Forgive me, I came here on false pretenses."

"Followed in his footsteps, eh?" He grinned. "Sit down."

"*Non, merci.*" She pointed out the window to the courtyard. "That man the *flic's* talking to, he's your employee?"

Colles Junior's eyebrows shot up in his forehead.

"Cho? Three years now." His eyes narrowed in suspicion. "What's this about?"

"He's not in trouble. Please understand. But I'd like to talk with him."

"Why?"

She looked around the office. Little had changed. "My client doesn't trust the *flics*. In this case, I don't trust the one who's talking to your employee."

He sat down in the heavy wooden chair. "Big eyes. Yes, I remember you visiting with old Leduc and the watchmaker from rue Chapon. My father, like Riboux the watchmaker, is long gone."

She nodded. "My grandfather, too." It took her back to her childhood, visiting here one afternoon during a sudden hailstorm in May. "Aimée, we call it *les saints de glace* if it hails in May," her grandfather had said. "That means the farmers harvest crops later."

Colles sat down, indicated she do the same.

"But you've followed in your family's footsteps, too," she said, hoping to warm him up. Enlist his aid.

"At the end of the nineteenth century, seven hundred and fifty thousand artisans and craftsmen lived and worked in Paris," he said. "Many lived in ateliers, like my great-grandfather did upstairs. Raised families. Now it's diminished to ninety thousand, and fewer each year." He shrugged. "But my father loved his friends and a good excuse to open one of his bottles of Montrachet."

The soft wooden floor creaked under her feet as she remembered. She noticed the bronze coils and intricate inner springs of the blond-wood clock that Riboux had touched with his work-worn hands. "But I can still see the watchmaker repairing this." She gestured to the tall seventeenth-century longcase clock. "I sat crosslegged on this floor, fascinated, just watching him with his old repair diagrams."

Diagrams.

Samour's chalk diagrams jumped out at her. She caught herself, looked out the window. Prévost was nowhere in sight. "Look, forgive me for barging in and being abrupt about this, but what do you know about Cho?"

"Determined, too. Like your old grandfather." Colles Junior leaned back in the chair. "Cho was a metallurgist back in China. Highly educated. A shame we can only offer him technical work beneath his skills. He's legal. I sponsored him."

She paused. "Then why . . . ?"

Colles Junior snorted. "He hawked faux designer bags on the quai. Had a brush with the law. How he got here from China, I don't know. He was living with ten in a room, they took turns sleeping."

She nodded. No doubt Cho owed the snakeheads. And Prévost used Cho's brush with the law to turn him into his *indicateur*. An informer.

That's how it worked.

Now she knew she needed to speak with him, to get on the playing field with Prévost. Find out his investigative path in Samour's murder.

"You owe me nothing, but seeing as we have a past," she said, and grinned, trying on the charm, "would you mind asking Cho into the office so I could talk to him without others around?"

"Why don't we have a drink first?"

Aimée groaned inside. Not too hard on the eyes, but not her bad-boy type. And she needed to find out Cho's connection.

She edged closer to the desk. "*Desolée*, but I'm investigating my client's murder. If Cho knows anything, it's imperative we talk. And that he trust me." She glanced at her watch. "I'm already late for the autopsy." A little lie she figured didn't matter. She counted on that to put him off for now.

And it did. He'd averted his eyes. "But how can you think Cho knows anything about that?"

She shrugged. "The *flics* do." At least she hoped Prévost did.

She noticed the wedding ring on his finger before he covered his hand. But he caught her look, and she saw a slump of defeat in his shoulders.

"*Alors*, just five minutes," she said. "Please."

He buzzed the intercom.

"Ask Monsieur Cho to step into my office."

Not a moment later, Cho walked inside smiling. She noticed

scarred flesh on his wrist that his work coat didn't cover. "Monsieur Colles, we're still working on the custom order . . ."

Colles Junior rose and waved his hand. "*Pas de problème.* Talk to the mademoiselle here."

Cho's eyes widened.

Colles stopped at the door. "Not my business, you understand. But her family knew mine, and, well . . . I took the liberty of saying you'd cooperate." At a loss for more to say, he left and closed the door.

Aimée smiled. "Nothing you say will leave this room, Monsieur Cho."

Cho stared at her. Light glinted off his silver-rimmed glasses.

"Monsieur Cho, I'm a private detective investigating the murder of Pascal Samour. On rue au Maire on Friday night, I think you've heard."

Cho stood as still as a cat watching a mouse. As silent, too. Well, she could play along.

"It's not my business if you're Prévost's informer in Chinatown," she said, taking a hunch.

"Why should I talk to you?" he said.

"Didn't your patron, your sponsor, request you to assist me? I'm not with the *flics.* But I can give you more reasons." She returned his stare. "I want to find who murdered Samour. I don't think he gambled, or was jealous over a woman, but no one will talk to me." She shrugged. "Prévost holds something over your head, *non?*"

"You're threatening me?" Cho said at last.

"Not me. Prévost's pointing the finger to Chinatown. Even if you help him, there's no guarantee against immigration crackdowns." She let that sink in. "Or raids in the quartier."

"I'm legal," Cho said.

"But what about the others? The ones who helped you when you hawked bags on the quai, the ones who fed you?"

Cho blinked. He averted his eyes. Then came to a decision.

"You think I have a choice?" Cho's low voice was laced with inflections, a singsong French. "Here, like in China, even when you play the game, tiptoe in the political minefields, they hold something over you and pull you in every time."

Recruiting him as an informer, Cho meant. She edged around the desk. Lines creased the bridge of his nose, radiated from the corners of his eyes. Older than she had first thought. Tired.

"I'm sorry, Monsieur Cho."

"My laboratory, our chemistry department at the university in Wenzhou . . ." He shrugged. "The deals I made to keep operating our laboratory sickened me."

"So what have you heard?" she asked.

Cho stared at her. "We never bring attention to Chinatown. Too dangerous. If French people kill French people, it's not our business."

"Why do you say that?"

He shook his head. "No one is who they seem."

"I know about the false identities, the unmarked graves at Ivry, the shops fronting money-laundering operations, the protection racket." She tapped her heel. "I need more, Monsieur Cho."

"Look deeper," he said.

She didn't have the time for a philosophical exploration. "Deeper?"

Cho backed up toward the door. "My room's on rue des Vertus. If a Chinese murdered this man, I would have heard, as I told Prévost. I need to get back to work."

She believed him. "What's behind the surveillance?"

"The sting operation?" he said. "The usual roundup of little fish. Why do you care? Your neck's not on the line."

Cho needed convincing.

"Call this a love bite, do you?" She pulled her scarf down, showed him her bruises. "Whoever murdered Samour thinks otherwise. I was attacked last night. And Meizi, who worked in the luggage store, is in danger."

"Don't tell me you want to warn her?"

"Protect her if I can. But I need your help."

Cho hesitated. "The owners of the handbag, luggage, and costume jewelry shops hide their profits." His voice lowered. "Never pay into the fisc for illegal workers. You're right, most of it's a front for laundering money from China."

Meizi had told her the same thing.

"But what about Tso, the snakehead? Ching Wao?"

"Both would provide a goldmine of back taxes and penalties," Cho said. "If the tax men find proof, they'll freeze their network's bank accounts. That's all I know."

And then he'd gone out the door.

She caught up with him in the wet, footprinted hallway. Slid her card with a hundred-franc note in his hand. "I'd appreciate a call if you hear anything."

He shook her hand off, a flash of pride in his eyes. "I cooperated for Monsieur Colles."

Again, she'd put her foot in it. Offended him. "*Desolée*, Monsieur Cho, I meant no disrespect." Why had the few interviewing skills she had deserted her?

"Now if you'll excuse me," he said, taking out a notepad with measurements from his jacket pocket.

One last effort. She pulled out the photo scan of the chalk diagrams. "Can you tell me anything about this?"

"This? A diagram."

"Recognize anything?" Aimée asked.

He pulled off his glasses and peered closer. Shrugged.

"What about this?" She pulled out one of René's photo scans of the chalk diagrams.

He pointed his smudged forefinger to the border. "Formulas."

"These?" She stared closer at what could be elongated symbols. Why did they seem so familiar? "The ones that look like old French?"

"Partially, and engineer shorthand." Cho gave a little smile. The first time he'd thawed. "Electrical engineering's not my field." Interested now, he studied the diagram. "But we metallurgists sometimes worked with similar equations."

"So what can you tell me?"

"It's hard to say." He shook his head.

Take a guess, she wanted to yell. Instead, she managed a smile. "But with what you know, your expertise . . ."

"Clearly these symbols represent an alloy. But this . . . maybe glass?"

She stared at the diagram, wishing she could see what he saw.

"If I enlarge these, could you tell me more?"

"The diagram looks like a map. But this? Your best bet, Mademoiselle?" Cho put his glasses back on. "Find an electrical engineer."

Aimée double-knotted the cashmere scarf around her sore neck, donned her leather gloves, and wove her scooter through traffic on chilly Boulevard de Sébastopol. Thoughts of sunny Martinique and Melac spun in her mind.

Her cell phone rang. With one hand she answered it.

"Saj cracked the encryption, Aimée," René said.

Finally.

"See you in five minutes." She clicked off and veered around a bus and gunned her scooter.

Aromas of cilantro and curry drifted from the Indian takeout cartons on René's desk. Saj stepped on a Louis XV chair, spread a damask tablecloth over the gilt-framed mirror hanging above the fireplace. He then angled his laptop on Aimée's desk. "I cracked a portion. A part's missing. I figure if he'd encrypted this a week, two weeks ago—"

"Then found the other part yesterday," she interrupted,

taking off her leather gloves, "it wouldn't be in there. I'll get going on that at the museum."

"What's wrong with your wrists?" René asked, looking at her bruises.

It all came back to her—the panic, struggling to breathe, her bound hands, biting at the plastic, rubbing her face against the sharp glass shards, crawling in the wet walkway. She knew if the couple hailing the taxi hadn't frightened the killer off she wouldn't be here now. She stilled her shaking hands and told him.

"Samour's murderer attacked you?" René's eyes widened.

The memory of the thread from his coat stuck in her fingernail came back to her. "I'm close, René."

"Too close," he said. "Have you told Prévost?"

"Not yet," she rubbed her wrist, "but I will, and I'll discover when the raid's planned." She had to move on. "But how's Meizi?"

A little smile painted René's face. "Safe." Then it disappeared. "For now, Aimée."

Right now Saj's discovery of Pascal's encryption was more important.

"Ready, Saj?" she asked.

He hit a key on his laptop, projecting an image of a bordered manuscript. Her mouth dropped open. Tight lines of black-ink script, ancient-looking and illegible to her, marched across the page, reminding her of the tiny, sharp curls of a monk's illuminated manuscript. Accompanying the script was a drawing that looked like a primitive blueprint, for what she didn't know.

"But that looks like Latin." Not her strong point.

Saj bit into a potato pakora. "Latin's the standard, the lingua franca. Samour encrypted a recipe."

"Like a medieval Paul Bocuse?" René stared at Pascal's encrypted attachment under the chandelier, enlarged on the damask tablecloth. "Cookbooks in the fourteenth century? That looks like an oven."

Aimée peered closer. "But what is it?"

"I'd say an alchemical formula," Saj said.

"Alchemy?" Aimée sat up. "You mean wizards, Merlin, eye of newt and mad monks?"

"Why not?" Saj's eyes gleamed.

René frowned. "It could as easily be a poison. Or a machine."

"Saj, let's forget the woo-woo." Aimée pulled Samour's book on medieval guilds from her bag and opened to the chapter he had marked. Glassmaking—a coincidence? "To me it's more concrete." Her gaze caught on a subchapter heading. "Listen."

She read out loud, "'Glassmaking guilds guarded secret alchemical formulas and techniques used in the prized leaded-glass-paned windows of cathedrals.'"

René's eyes widened. "He lived in a tower, didn't he?" René lifted up the diagrams he'd scanned from her digital camera. "Drew these. We just don't know the connection."

Aimée grabbed a pakora. "And we need to connect the dots." Cho's words came back to her: alloy, glass, formulas. "Look at the elongated swirls, René. They're symbols, part of an equation or formula. For an alloy, or glass . . ."

"A machine or a concept," René interrupted, his voice rising. "Lost in the past, misfiled in the archives. Why didn't we see it before?"

She nodded. Saj clicked the brown beads around his wrist. A sign his chakras were aligned, or were out of alignment, she could never remember. "But the formula's incomplete," Saj said, moving the cursor down. The page ended in what was obviously the middle of the text. "I found corresponding alchemical symbols and phrases," Saj said, "in Nicolas de Locques's *Les rudimens de la philosophie naturelle*." He patted a thick leather-bound volume under the curry takeout container. "Published in 1655."

"That tail of newt, eye of toad nonsense again?"

Saj expelled air. "This explanation of the symbols cut my work in half, let me tell you. Samour used de Locques's book as a guide. The same Latin words appear here in Samour's incomplete segment."

Her excitement mounted. "Pascal searched for the missing part of the formula. He knew there was more, and where better to find it than in the museum's archives."

"Formula to what? Alchemical stained glass?"

"Why not? This connects somehow," she said. "I'll comb the museum holdings, Saj. I'll find it."

"*Et alors*, so we know everything Pascal knew?"

She paused in thought. "But not the formula's significance," she said. "Something so important that Pascal was murdered for it."

This added up. But how?

"A nerd who grew up in the museum's shadows," Saj said, "an engineer who's obsessed about a lost alchemical formula?" He shook his head. "It doesn't add up."

"As René pointed out, he lived in a tower," Aimée said. "His former classmate spoke of his obsession with the fourteenth century." At her desk, she downloaded Saj's enhanced encryption, then powered off her laptop. But Saj's words raised more questions.

"Picture Samour, tech-savvy, skilled at encrypting, spending time and energy on a lost formula." She shook her head. "What would it get him, Saj?"

Saj stretched. "*Bon*, in academia he'd publish a paper, write a treatise. Or a book," he said. "What about Becquerel?"

His last professor. "Dead in a nursing home at ninety last week."

"So another blind alley," Saj said, looking at the remembrance pages Aimée had copied.

"Or the usual academic battle," René said. "Say Pascal tried to garner department funding after discovering a lost medieval stained-glass formula."

People killed for less. But that held less water than their poorly functioning radiator.

"It's more than just that if the DST wants me to monitor Samour's activity at the museum."

Saj whistled. "So any ideas?"

"Besides checking my horoscope?" She rubbed her bandaged wrist. "Keep monitoring Coulade's computer."

So far all that they'd discovered put her back in the dark.

"The conservator mentioned that the Archives Nationales used the museum's storage during the war," she said, racking her brain. "They don't know half of what's in it, either."

"Pascal programmed a dead man's switch to e-mail this encryption," Saj said. "He insisted Becquerel be contacted. Becquerel's role was pivotal to Pascal, yet . . ."

"Well, everyone talks about Becquerel's innovation." René pointed to the copies from the remembrance book. "'A pioneer who knew no boundaries in the field of optics and technology.'" He looked up. "Thinking what I'm thinking?"

Aimée nodded. "Fiber optics?"

"It's an avenue to explore," he said.

Saj grabbed his laptop. "Let me see what I find."

BEFORE GOING TO the museum, Aimée hoped to find answers in the stained-glass atelier in her cousin Sebastien's damp courtyard. Disappointed, she stared into the darkened windows. Knocked. No answer, nor at Sebastien's atelier either.

Great.

She pulled her coat tighter and in the *porte cochère* scanned the mailboxes. Listed under Atelier J, Stained Glass was an alternate delivery address at a Galerie Juno on rue des Archives. A place to start.

Three blocks away she found Galerie Juno, with a sign in the door that said Open by Appointment Only.

Merde. Before she met Prévost she needed answers. And a game plan.

She punched in Galerie Juno's number on her cell phone, and heard a recording of Vivaldi's *Four Seasons* and a voice saying, "Leave a message, *s'il vous plaît.*"

"Bonjour, I'm interested in the stained-glass artist who has an atelier on rue de Saintonge," she said, hoping that the gallery would answer. That she wasn't speaking to the wind. "I'm at your gallery and want to make an appointment."

The message clicked off. Full.

Lace curtains moved in the window next door.

Smiling, she put her face to the window.

The lace curtains parted to reveal a young woman with blue braids wound shell-like above her ears, and matching lipstick. A punkette wearing a dirndl, no less.

The window frame cracked open. "Juno's working in back." She jerked her thumb. The window slammed shut, and there was the sound of a lock tumbling.

Aimée pushed open the door, stepped over the frame into a courtyard lined with potted plants. Miniature bonsai trees in animal shapes—a rabbit, a bird. Whimsical.

Keeping her heeled boots out of the cracks between the worn pavers, she reached the atelier in the rear. On the wall were framed certificates from the Artisan Glassmaker Association, a notice of completed apprenticeship to a master glassmaker. Both with the names Juno Braud.

She'd come to the right man.

Hot molten-metal smells filled the atelier. Bundled lead rods stood upright like a forest against the glass walls. A man in overalls worked copper foil along the edges of a piece of blue glass using a soldering iron.

"Monsieur Juno?"

A wayward brown hair hung over a work mask that covered half his face. He looked young. "*Attends,*" came the muffled reply.

He set the soldering iron down on a brick, switched off the generator box. "*Oui?*" He'd pulled his mask off. A slash for a mouth, a cleft palate. Sad, it could have easily been treated by surgery in childhood.

"Sorry to bother you," she said, focusing on his eyes. "My cousin Sebastien's in the atelier next to yours."

He tapped his thick fingers. "So?"

Impatient. She'd make this quick. "He suggested you could help me. Those for sale?" She gestured to a shelf of shimmering indigo-blue glass boxes.

"Rejects."

"But they're beautiful."

"Imperfections, the glass bubbled . . ." He paused, a nervous swipe of his hand over his mouth. "But that's not why you're bothering me."

She gave what she hoped he took for an enthralled gaze. "I need your expertise for five minutes. And I'll buy those." She pulled out the copy she'd made of the Latin alchemical formula. The black-and-white encrypted copy. "Could you tell me about this, besides the fact that it's incomplete?"

"Where did you get this?"

She could go two ways here: offer some version of the truth, or coax him and see how far she got.

"Does it matter?" she leaned forward. "Is it valuable?"

"Would you ask me if it weren't?" He stared at it. "It's medieval symbols, an archaic formula, I'd have to guess."

"Meaning it's a formula for a stained-glass window in a cathedral?"

"Did I say that?" For a moment she thought she'd lost him.

But he sat down on a battered stool, ran his fingers over the paper. Nodded. "The Revolution disbanded guilds in 1791. The guild emblem's unique."

"Meaning?"

"This guild, deTheodric, was one of the oldest, going back to the thirteenth, fourteenth century. They were known for working with the Templars. Not much survives of their work now, though," he said sadly.

What did the Templars have to do with anything, she wondered. But Samour lived in what had been the Knights' old enclave.

"But why the Templars?"

"Stained glass was for cathedrals and monasteries." He ran his fingers over a warm metal frame. "Apart from the aristocracy, tell me who else financed cathedral building? Promoted and used the artisans, the trades and the guilds?"

She figured it was a rhetorical question.

"The Templars ran it all. That's until the Pope outlawed the Templars and took over their coffers." He paused. "Like I said, little's left of deTheodric's work. They went the way of the Templars in 1311. Disbanded or executed, some accounts say."

But a connection had to exist. "It's your métier, what do you think?"

"There were stories," he said, his words slow. A shrug. "But all glass artisans hear them."

"Like what?"

He let out a puff of air. "Well, all trades and guilds were regulated at the time. Statutes and regulations in force until the Revolution. The powerful guilds paid the most tax and kept their craft secrets. Think of the windows at Chartres, no one's replicated their technique." He shook his head in rueful respect. "Or Abbé Suger, who developed that resonant blue 'sapphire glass' used at Saint-Denis."

"But wouldn't the techniques be passed down by word of mouth?"

"Or they died with the alchemists," he said. "Like so many things, secrets lost, shrouded in time. Who knows?"

Something tugged in her mind.

"Art can happen by mistake," he continued, a distant look in his eye." In the thirteenth century, for example, a monk dropped his silver button into the glass and created indigo for the first time. We only found this out two hundred years ago. This discovery gave us a chance to make the indigo the hue guilds used before the Revolution in 1791."

She heard other things in his voice now. A quiet excitement, almost awe. Any self-consciousness about his cleft palate had disappeared.

"For me it's expression, glass gives form to beauty," he said. "A painting with light. Not like the one-dimensional painting, where light shines on it. With glass, the light shines through."

A purist, she thought, immersed in his trade.

He gestured to the diagram and its rows of Latin. "Of course, as journeymen we visited this guild's masterpiece, a church window, the only one left of their work."

Her pulse raced. "But you said this guild collapsed with the Templars."

"Rumors handed down through time hint at conspiracies, plots . . ."

She straightened up. "Secret lost formulas?"

"So you think you've got one here, eh?"

"You tell me."

He grinned. "But even so, it's incomplete. Worthless."

She pulled several hundred-franc bills from her wallet. "Say the other part of the formula were discovered. How valuable would it be?"

"More than a historical treasure." His eyes gleamed. "Think of modern stained-glass windows made from an original ancient formula. The enhancement of cathedral restoration techniques."

Ancient techniques for new windows in old cathedrals—interesting—but not sexy enough. Or worth murder. There was more, she knew it in her bones.

"Hasn't anyone analyzed the components of this guild's masterpiece?"

"A hundred feet up in the nave? Any exploration would damage the glass. It's protected under historic preservation."

Her mind went back to the Templars, the end of the guild. An angle to explain the questions swirling in her mind. "What if this powerful guild owed the Templars for some reason? The Templars demanded their secret formulas as payment. After their downfall the formula was lost and with it the guild's influence?"

"Everything's possible."

"This window's far away?" She imagined a long trip to Chartres or to a countryside cathedral hours away.

"You call Saint Nicholas des Champs far?"

Six blocks away and across from the Musée des Arts et Métiers. A block from where Pascal spent his youth.

"*Mais non*, it's on my way to work."

WITH THE WRAPPED indigo boxes in her bag, a perfect wedding present for Sebastien, she caught a taxi.

Her cell phone rang in her pocket. René's number showed on her caller ID.

"Has Saj found Pascal's file on Coulade's computer, René?"

He sighed. "Not yet."

Too bad. Impatient, she rolled and unrolled the encrypted page in her hands.

"Meizi keeps asking when you'll help her," he said, worry in his voice.

"As soon as I reach Prévost and find out the timing of the police raid. Tell Meizi to trust me, René."

"You're popular," he said, sounding anxious now.

Her throat constricted. The men she'd lost in Zazie's café?

"Two men?"

"I got rid of them."

But for how long?

"Hold on, there's another call," René said.

She checked from the taxi window. If they were following her by car, they were stuck in traffic. But it bothered her.

"Pull over, Monsieur," she told the driver.

"*Ici?*"

She paid, took her bag, and slammed the taxi door. Horns blared.

"Where are you, Aimée?" René asked.

"A block from the museum."

She was around the corner from the church. But she didn't have time.

"Right now you need to go to church," she lowered her voice into her cell phone. Huddled in a doorway from the wind.

"Church?"

"Saint Nicholas des Champs. In the ninth chapel transept you'll see a star-shaped stained-glass window," she said. "Crafted by the same guild in Pascal's encryption."

"But what does that mean?"

"The glass guild disbanded with the Templars, but the formula connects somehow. The star, remember, in the formula?" She heard the rapid keystrokes over the line. It sounded like René was running searches. She tried to put this together. "If Pascal discovered properties in this alchemical recipe that could be used in something significant now . . ."

"Like you said, that would explain the DST's interest."

"Let me know as soon as you find it, René."

She knew it existed. She was certain.

Pause. "Zazie called from the café," René said. "Told me to tell you two men are sitting watching our door."

Damned irritating. Aimée sucked in her breath. She needed a cigarette.

"You know what to do, René," she said. "Go out the back."

Sunday, Noon

RENÉ LOOKED BOTH ways before stepping into rue Bail-leul. The thwack and scrape of the street sweeper's green plastic-pronged broom provided counterpoint to the shouts of the man unloading crates of wine from a truck into the café's rear.

All clear. At least his hip was cooperating today. He needed sun, heat, and the last installment for his Citroën. What he had was the DST on Aimée's tail, the uneasy feeling Meizi was keeping things from him, and a crazy errand in a church.

He shut the Citroën's door, keyed the ignition, and blasted the heater. His leather-upholstered seats heated up within a minute. One out of three wasn't bad. He shifted into first and turned right into rue de l'Arbre-Sec.

"STAND HERE, MONSIEUR." The young, black-frocked priest gestured René toward Chapelle Saint-Sauveur, the ninth of the twenty-seven side chapels. "Few visit our petit jewel. Or ask about it." The priest, who had sideburns, let out an appreciative sigh. "Beautiful, *non?*"

From his vantage point, all René could see was a dance of silver-white light shivering on the worn stone-slab floor.

"Look higher in the apse, Monsieur, past the left chancel columns."

Not for the first time, René cursed his short legs. He leaned back, staring upward at the vaulted Gothic arcs of stone. He saw only soaring light framed and half blocked by the damned columns.

Rows of votive candles flickered in this cold south-wall chapel. The musky drafts of incense, fading floral scents from sprays of drooping winter lilies—all smells he remembered from childhood. And his mother's whispered novenas in the chapel of the count's château, where she prayed his legs would grow.

René gestured to the prayer kneeler. "Do you mind if I try a better look, *Monsieur le curé?*"

"*Pas du tout, Monsieur.* Please call me Père André, we're modern these days."

René untied the laces of his handmade Lobb shoes. Using the prayer kneeler's straw seat for a step, he climbed onto the ledge of the recessed niche below a statue of Mary. He balanced on the ledge below her blue robe and craned his neck.

He saw a cluster of grisaille glass panels. But crowning it was a blossom-like luminescence of white emanating from a star shape high in the church nave. An intense shimmering.

"All of God's children should gaze on this," said the priest. "The unwavering radiance speaks of strength. It lifts the soul."

René wondered why this small, glittering star shone unlike the other panels.

The priest crossed himself and waved at a few teenagers near the baptismal font. One held a guitar. "Time for our folk music practice," he said. "We strive to involve our young community. We sing and celebrate the early Sunday Mass. You should come."

Priests never changed. Always recruiting a new flock.

"Do you know the window's history, Père André?" Saying that felt foreign to him.

"I'm new to the parish. We've run out of guides." He paused. "Ask Evangeline."

The priest gestured toward a room labeled Saint Nicolas des Champs Altar Society and joined his teenagers.

Evangeline, a lace mantilla over her gray pageboy coif, wore a chic purple wool suit. René found her reaching on tiptoes into the altar linen cabinet. Only a head taller than René, she was short-statured like others of the generation that grew up during the war. She gave him a lopsided smile. "I'd ask for your help, *mais alors*, you'd have the same problem."

René pulled a wooden chair to the cabinet, undid his laces again, and climbed on the chair. "*Pas de problème.*" She handed him the ironed altar linens. One by one he organized them in the old bleach-scented cabinet. "I'll have to ask for something in return, you know," he said, wishing the room had heat.

"Name your price," Evangeline said.

"Know the history of the star in the stained-glass window?"

Evangeline handed René another stack of linen. "Early fourteenth century. An anomaly, considering the surrounding sixteenth-century chapel. The records from that time . . . *phfft*, gone." She shrugged. "We know the church's foundations date from the eleventh century, then a hodgepodge of Romanesque, Gothic, Renaissance, and the bell tower later. Why?"

"I'm researching fourteenth-century glassmaking guilds." That much was true. "That star window is so different from everything around it. . . ."

"Striking, that sparkle. So different, like you say. Not like any other glass I've seen. Yet you're asking the wrong person. Who would know now?"

"Have you heard any legends or stories about this window?"

She paused in thought. "Funny, someone else asked me that."

Had Pascal been searching for the window's secret? René turned and looked down at her. "Reddish hair, glasses?"

"Your associate?"

Saddened, René gave a brief nod. "But what did you tell him?"

"The same as you." Her expression became bashful. "It's nothing, but after vespers at night, when I change the altar linens, well . . ."

"Go on, Evangeline," he said.

"The light streaming from the star," she said. "It's almost as if the star grabs the streetlight from outside. Somehow transfuses, brightens, or magnifies it, sending a sheer white light beam. That's not explaining it well. But there's a radiance, a clearness. Power." She gave another lopsided smile. "Silly, eh?"

René stepped down from the chair. Sat and tied his shoes, his mind working. "I think I know what you mean. *Merci*."

THE WORDS PLAYED in René's mind: grabs, transfuses, magnifies. Power. Pascal had found part of the formula for this special glass hidden in the museum's archives and . . . what? Tried to replicate it? And couldn't?

The question rearing up in his mind was why a fourteenth-century document had been hidden in a museum devoted to the pre- and post-industrial revolution. Pascal must have stumbled across the stained-glass window formula either miscataloged or hidden centuries ago in the Archives Nationales, stored during the war. And as Aimée had intimated, found its relevance today.

René gunned down rue Saint-Martin heading toward the Archives Nationales. The archives held a place to work in peace and find answers.

Sunday, Noon

AIMÉE PARKED HER scooter at the museum's entrance. Her mind spun. They still hadn't found Pascal's laptop or figured out what the diagram meant, or heard what Clodo had witnessed. Let alone identified the murderer.

But the DST was on her tail. She'd promised Meizi protection before she could guarantee it. She hadn't discovered the time of the raid or any other information Meizi could feed Tso. She shuddered. If Meizi got caught, René would never forgive her.

She left another message for Prévost. Why had she ignored his comment that he owed her father and not questioned him? Chinatown had never been her father's beat.

Yet she'd set wheels in motion—herself connecting with Jean-Luc, Saj working on the encryption, René at church. But the DST expected information and she needed to give them something.

AIMÉE WORKED OFF two laptops in the vaulted Gothic nave, wishing the faded tapestries didn't smell their age. She'd spent hours alone in the dark alcove transferring the Musée des Arts et Métiers' archaic database to the new digital operating system. On the other laptop, she ran a concurrent search for a fourteenth-century document. Fruitlessly.

She backed up a 1695 water pump invention to the digital archive. Hit SAVE. Done.

She pulled her silk scarf tighter against the chill and sighed. Only three more centuries to go. Her boots rested on a smooth paver engraved with Latin, a remnant of the original tenth-century abbey. Norman columns blended into the Gothic priory, evidence of the Parisian habit of building on centuries of history. She was surrounded by history.

And by ghosts.

The creakings and shiftings in the building unnerved her. What sounded like whispers came from the adjoining chapel. The wind? She stifled her unease and focused on her screen. But after several hours, her stiff neck decided for her that the rest would have to wait. Time to go.

Her cell phone vibrated in her pocket.

"Still working, Aimée?" asked René.

"Just backed up the seventeenth century," she said.

"Any luck finding Pascal's file?"

"Not yet, *desolée*," she said. "Nor the log he supposedly signed in on. Odd. Hope you had better luck with the stained-glass window."

"I spent the afternoon at the Archives," he said, excitement in his voice. "Get this, Aimée. Pascal's diagram is a map."

"A map?" Why had Pascal made this so difficult?

Gargoyle-like stone carvings stared down at her, their disembodied faces like masks in the stonework. She rubbed the goosebumps on her arms.

"Long story," he said. "The map leads through the medieval sewers."

"They didn't have sewers then, René."

"*Zut*, I know. Now it's the sewer, going right to rue Charlot, rue Meslay, and along rue Béranger, where he lived."

"No sewers for me."

Or army of rodents wintering underground. She'd faced enough of those already.

"There's more," René said. "There is one remaining Templar tower Napolean forgot to destroy. The church's stained-glass window lies in a direct line from the south end of its old wall.

The wind rattled the scaffolding bars lining the nave. Her mind went back to her conversation with Jean-Luc at the piano bar: Samour's message to Jean-Luc mentioning an atelier. Another piece fitting in Samour's damned puzzle.

"Of course, that's it," she said. "His work studio, René. Where is it?"

"73 rue Charlot. Bring his keys."

He clicked off before she could ask him if he'd reached Meizi.

All of a sudden there was a high-pitched whine from a distant fuse box. Then the building plunged into darkness. A power outage.

She froze, rigid with fear. She was wrapped in darkness, alone, just as she'd been last night. She recalled the sensation of those huge hands around her neck, the plastic bag over her face, straining to breathe. Had he come back to finish the job? Move, she had to move. Quickly she closed the programs on her laptop, not wanting to linger under the groaning scaffolding lacing the nave. It seemed as if it could topple any minute in this blackness.

Or did she imagine it?

She shuddered. The only light came from the stained-glass window in the chapel. Beautiful and unnerving.

"Monsieur Vardet?" she called out to the security guard. Her voice echoed in the nave. She didn't like this.

The soft flutter of snow settled like a sigh on the protective plastic sheeting, and again she saw Pascal's eyes under the snow-dusted plastic. "*Sécurité?*" Where was Vardet?

"*Par ici*, Mademoiselle, no cause for alarm," Vardet's reassuring voice answered. "You'll need to exit through the refectory. Let me show you out."

Thank God.

TEN MINUTES LATER, Aimée stood in the *porte cochère* of 73 rue Charlot under a clicking timed light. The snow lay upon upturned cobblestones like confectioner's sugar in the deep courtyard.

"This leads to the tower in the remaining bit of Templar wall, Aimée." René pointed to the mildewed wooden door. "Try Samour's keys."

She felt in her bag for the keys she'd taken from under the geraniums, inserted the largest, old-fashioned one, like the key her grandmother used to the cellar on her farm. She heard a tumble as the well-oiled lock turned.

Winding stone steps, deep and narrow. No handrails but uneven walls to feel their way upward. Like entering the Dark Ages.

On the first landing stood a hinged wooden door with a

beaten metal clasp. Original, no doubt. She inserted the key again, turned it, and pushed the door open to a mustiness laced with chocolate.

René hit a wall light switch, flooding the circular tower room with light. Aimée saw a blackboard covered with formulas in blue chalk, and an open laptop with a blinking green light on a long trestle table. Next to it, a distilling apparatus. Test tubes, glass flacons, and copper wires. An alchemist's lab down to the medieval walls. Then she saw what looked like a small, industrial, high-temperature stainless-steel oven.

She gasped.

"That's it, René." She ran forward, excited. "The drawing in the encryption."

She sniffed the contents of the cellophane bag by the laptop. Chocolate. Popped one in her mouth. "Dark-chocolate espresso beans. Pascal had good taste."

"Thinking what I'm thinking, Aimée?" René asked.

"That Samour distilled his own absinthe? Not quite."

But René had opened up the screen on Samour's laptop.

"Look, it's the same alchemical formula Saj deciphered. Why did he hide this, yet . . ."

"More than why, René, *from whom*," she said. "Trawl around and see if you find more."

She stared at the formulas in intricate blue chalk. Meaningless to her. A funnel of white sand, technical magazines, a fiber optics newsletter on an Aeron chair. An incongruous collection until de Voule's words came back to her.

"He told his classmate no one has invented anything new since the fourteenth century. What if he tried to prove that here?"

René rolled his eyes. "By making stained glass in an ancient alembic? Melting the contents in that machine?"

She remembered the preliminary autopsy report. "He had burn marks on his hands," she said. "It could have come from this heater. The guilds worked with little more than sand, potash, and fire."

René put his camera in her hands. "Check out the real masterpiece, from the church. The camera captures little of the star's clarity. But you get the idea."

The stained-glass window images conveyed bright, streaming light. "Such radiance. Amazing."

Perplexed, she picked up the magazines. "It's all here, but we don't understand."

"Think where we are." René's finger traced the diagram. "Inside the fortified walls of an old Templar enclosure."

"*Et alors*, I took that history class, too, René." She ran her fingers over the smooth glass alembic. "But it proves what?"

"We're in the last remaining Knights Templar tower." René grinned. "It's part of the prison where Marie Antoinette and her children were kept."

"Not all that Holy Grail business."

René snorted. "Think of the Templars as investors in startups," he said. "They had more money than kings, or the Pope."

"So you took Medieval Studies 101 at the Sorbonne?"

"Fundamentals of Economics, second semester." René went on, "So the Templars were venture capitalists, this tower was their Silicon Valley. Instead of developing microprocessors, the Templars built cathedrals, castles, a whole series of industries. They employed the guilds for research and development in architecture, weapons, communication."

Pascal would have appreciated René's enthusiasm for his project. René got to work on the laptop. Pulled his goatee. "No wonder there's been no more activity, his laptop's frozen."

"Try mine. See if you can unfreeze and network."

René stood engrossed at the trestle table, comparing Aimée's backed-up work from the Musée. She checked the magazines, the newsletter. Nothing jumped out at her. She tried to make sense of this, put things together.

Finally, René broke the silence. "Samour's search prints show all over the Musée files you digitized today, Aimée."

So Samour had been looking. "That's what I'll tell the DST."

"Make sure that's all you tell them. We found this tower on our own." René plugged a cable from Aimée's laptop to Samour's. Hit several keys. "I'm rebooting his laptop and will network it to ours." He tugged his goatee again. "Why didn't Mademoiselle Samoukashian tell you about this tower?"

"Pascal protected her," she said. "Considering his diagrams and secrecy, it's like he wanted to discover something here."

"Or prove it before he showed anyone," René said.

She picked up the newsletter, thumbed through it until an article caught her attention. "Aren't fiber optics made of glass?"

René looked up, nodding. His eyes met hers and widened.

She lifted a slim, colorless strand, little thicker than a hair, from the drawer. "Like this?"

René blinked. "Fiber optics is a hot market in telecommunications these days," he said. "Bundle that up with more strands and it will carry up to ten million messages, using light pulses." He shot her a look. "Not chump change either."

"*Bon*, I'll ask my dinner date about it," she said, applying Chanel Red to her lips. "He runs one of those things."

"The same *mec* from last night?"

Odd, she could have sworn René sounded . . . *non*, not jealous, he had Meizi. But concerned.

"How's Meizi?"

His brow creased. "I'm worried. She's at the hotel, but doesn't answer the phone."

Aimée buttoned her coat. "You're staying until I come back?"

"Until I find something," René said, a grim set to his mouth. "I'll have Saj bring what he finds over and we'll work on this together."

A quiver ran down her spine. "Whoever murdered Samour didn't find this place, René. The murderer is still looking."

"Then make sure you're not followed, Aimée." René pulled out the diagram. "According to this, if you go left in the courtyard there's an exit to rue de Picardie."

Her heeled boots clicked down the tower's steep, damp staircase. And then she missed a step, lost her balance. She caught a rusted ring in the wall and held on for dear life. No broken bones, no fall, but a scuffed leather heel and a pang in her sore wrist. Damn medieval towers.

Her phone beeped. One new message. Prévost.

"Give me Clodo's phone and I'll tell you when the raid's scheduled."

Nothing else.

She hit callback. Tried to leave a message, but his voice mail was full.

She had to find Clodo's phone.

"WHAT'S THE WEATHER report tonight, Monsieur?" She smiled at the homeless man on the grate at Carreau du Temple.

"Radio's broken, *ma chère*."

"This should help," she said, laying twenty francs on his sleeping bag. "How's your daughter?"

"Doing her homework." His face lit up.

"Don't you have something for me?"

He handed her the prepaid phone card she'd given him. "*Desolé*, I couldn't find a phone cabin. Everyone has mobiles."

Disappointed, she wanted to kick the grate. She needed a bartering tool for Prévost. A way to protect Meizi.

"But you're interested in this, *non?*" A cell phone. "I can't vouch it's the one Clodo took, but rumor goes it is."

"Brilliant." She slipped him a hundred francs. "Don't forget I count on your weather predictions for my wardrobe."

Now she had something to bargain with Prévost. Finally, the trail smelled like it went somewhere.

But she was late. At the small square, she spied a taxi, ran to catch it and jumped in, and overtipped the driver for the short six-block ride.

But the maître d' at the bistro shook his head. "*Desolé*, the monsieur changed your dinner reservations to seven thirty. An urgent meeting. He apologizes."

More than an hour away. Why hadn't Jean-Luc called her? Then she remembered she hadn't given him her number. Stupid.

But she had his. She got only his voice mail, left a message to call her.

"Why don't you wait at the bar? I'm sorry, Mademoiselle, blame it on the symposium. The attendees booked the whole bistro."

She glanced around. Suits in earnest conversations, consulting handheld calendars under the dark oak beams. Great. "Any idea where the symposium's held?"

He shrugged.

So now she'd have to wait in the crowded bistro where she couldn't hear herself think, or roam the dark, wet street?

She didn't think so. She wedged a place at the bar by an engineering type, a young man with thick-framed glasses, an ill-fitting suit, and licorice-black hair.

"My friend Jean-Luc's late to meet me from the symposium." She smiled.

"Which symposium?" he asked, his eyes catching on her cleavage. The pianist in the corner struck up "L'Heure Bleue," the Françoise Hardy version.

"You know . . . he's with Bouygues . . . I forgot . . ."

"Do you mean fiber optics in today's world? Or fiber optics infrastructure in the Third World?"

Fiber optics. "I'm not sure."

"No matter, they're both held at the old cloister, on rue des Archives. Cloître des Billettes."

Close by.

He smiled, revealing a set of braces that caught the light. He looked twelve. "Like a drink?"

"Next time."

She'd crash the symposium and find Jean-Luc. Too bad she didn't have her business suit.

Three blocks away, she only had to wait a few minutes before a group of men exited the arched doors of the cloister. She slipped inside. Quiet reigned, broken only by the drip of melting snow on worn pavers. She passed under the fifteenth-century vaulted arcade surrounding the small courtyard.

She half expected robed religious figures treading in prayer. But at the far end, a door opened to a crack of light and voices. A place to start, she thought. Inside, she found a cavernous chapel with men huddled by pillars, signs posting seminars in various rooms, and a label reading Wine Reception on the sacristy door. But the sacristy was empty. Jean-Luc could be in a meeting anywhere here, or somewhere else entirely.

But she could learn about fiber optics. She consulted a symposium schedule in the main chapel and headed to the first room on the right. The meeting had broken up. A few people lingered by a grouping of red velvet gilt-backed chairs, thick binders under their arms. Above them on the sandblasted stone wall, a canvas banner read: Information Highways—Fiber Optics in the 21st Century. René would eat this up. And ask for another helping.

A man in a suit was speaking. "As outlined in our presentation, clients should connect with solar companies like ours via infrastructures with up-to-date fiber optics . . ."

Weren't solar and fiber optics two different things? Her eyes began to glaze until she saw his name tag: *Rimmel, Solas Energie.* De Voule, the Gadz'Arts she spoken with on the phone, headed the company.

"*Excusez-moi*, Monsieur." She smiled, stepping into the group. "That's like connecting apples and oranges, *non?*"

He took in her leather pants, faux fur coat. "If you interns bothered to attend our presentation, the correlation would be obvious." A sneer appeared on his long, pale face.

Intern? Thank God the concealer had masked the shadows under her eyes. She'd buy it by the kilo.

"Who do you work with, Mademoiselle?"

She thought quickly. "Jean-Luc at Bouygues," she said. "Have you seen him?"

"The symposium's finished for today," he said dismissively.

His condescending air rankled, yet who better to ask about fiber optics than one in the business? "I'm assembling a marketing proposal for a fiber-optics campaign, Monsieur. I'd like to get a handle on it. Maybe you could elaborate?"

His sneer relaxed. He seemed the type who enjoyed imparting his expertise.

"Third World countries, without existing infrastructure, can put fiber optics in place immediately without expensive adaptations to outdated and often malfunctioning systems," he said, flicking lint off his tweed jacket.

Patronizing, too.

"The goal would be to provide renewable energy coordinating with a basic delivery infrastructure," he said. "The horse with the buggy."

A young engineer type nodded. "Brilliant. Basket the services."

"And corner the million-franc market," said an older professor type next to her. "However, given the unstable politics and the issues you outlined, cost-wise that makes coordination inefficient."

"At present, but . . ."

Her eye wandered to a tall man who'd entered the room and gestured to Rimmel. She could only make out part of his name tag, but he was from Solas Energie. He appeared to be in a hurry. She followed him outside to the drafty corridor.

"Monsieur?"

He turned. Tall, wide-shouldered, late twenties with a shock of reddish-brown hair parted to the side. And she deciphered his name tag illuminated in the light.

"So we meet, Monsieur de Voule," she said, handing him her card. "I'm Aimée Leduc. We spoke on the phone concerning Pascal Samour."

His forehead crunched in thought as he read her card. "A detective? But you said you worked at the Conservatoire . . ."

"True on both accounts, Monsieur." Behind him on poster board was the list of symposium meetings. "Your firm stands to make millions in Third World countries. . . ."

He blinked. Swapped his briefcase from one hand to the other, glanced at his watch.

"So do many others," he said. "Everyone here, in point of fact."

"But you specialize in solar energy," she said. "What do fiber optics have to do with you?"

"For example, Mademoiselle, installing a solar-energy harvester in the middle of the Sahara or Gobi Desert sounds obvious. Free sunlight, immense profits. Yet an isolated energy source does little in the grand scheme, makes no sense if you can't connect with a delivery system down the road. My firm found out the hard way." He gave a little shrug. "We're trying to convince telecommunications to band this together or it's not worth the investment development."

"Meaning?"

"Unless dramatic developments in fiber optics make it economically feasible for China or African countries to build and maintain telecommunication systems, it's a moot point. No one likes to hear that here."

Money. Did it all come down to money?

She tried a hunch. "So how was your classmate Samour connected to fiber optics?"

"I'm confused. Weren't you concerned with a fourteenth-century document? Some pie-in-the-sky dream of Pascal's?"

He'd avoided her question.

"He was murdered, Monsieur de Voule. I'm looking at all angles."

"You're implying what?"

"I found pieces, but not how they fit into the puzzle," she said. "Weren't you just away on a work site?"

He nodded. "Going back tomorrow. But I need to meet with staff at this event. And if you'll excuse me . . ."

She couldn't let him leave like that. "Hear me out for one minute, please."

"You're trying to tie in Pascal's murder somehow, aren't you?" De Voule said, his tone exasperated.

"If Samour discovered an economically feasible fiber optic and manufactured it cheaply, who'd want it?"

"Apart from corrupt governments, the military, and politicians who pocket UN subsidies for grain and health services?"

Hmm, not so much money there after all, she thought. "So you think his murder's personal?"

"I don't know."

"He confided in Becquerel," she said. "But with his death, that leads nowhere."

He looked stricken. "That led you to me." A small sigh. Rimmel's tapping foot echoed in the corridor, and de Voule looked up. "*Desolé*, Pascal and I were close in school, but it's been several years. I've got an appointment."

"His great-aunt said that Becquerel mentored him."

De Voule paused. "Petite Madame Samoukashian?"

"She hired me. You know her?"

"Best soup in the world." Memories flooded his eyes. "They

presented her with the *Légion d'honneur* for her work in the Resistance, you know. But she refused it."

"She was a *résistante?*" Aimée knew but wanted to draw him out.

"A hero," he said. "She ran a clandestine safehouse network in the Arts et Métiers."

Aimée thought back to her feisty nut-brown eyes, the determination in her thin shoulders.

De Voule shrugged. "But she said she wouldn't accept until the government acknowledged the role her cousin Manouchian, the Armenian poet in the Affiche Rouge, played during the Occupation. And until they reburied the group with honors, since the Germans executed them and dumped them in a mass grave."

Surprised, Aimée took de Voule's sleeve. "Pascal meant everything to her. She believes his murder is due to a project he was working on. We found material relating to fiber optics. Can't you think back? Anything would help."

He shrugged.

"Your classmate Jean-Luc thinks otherwise."

He shook his head. "Jean-Luc and Pascal didn't get along. Well, except when Pascal could help Jean-Luc."

Before she could press him, Rimmel took his arm and they left. She pondered his last comment. Spite? But he seemed honest and revered Pascal's aunt.

The rooms in the cloister had emptied. Feeling chilled, she wanted to warm up and go over Pascal's laptop with René. She paused to pull her coat around her, then tried Jean-Luc's number.

A phone trilled somewhere. The ring tone, a techno beat, escalated, echoing in the vaulted stone corridor. Pleasantly surprised, she followed it to the sacristy.

"*Desolé*, Aimée, I'm late," Jean-Luc said. "Where are you?"

"Right here." She smiled, waved to him and headed to the sacristy bar. "I could use a drink right now instead of dinner."

"I apologize." She noticed his flushed cheeks, the rapid rising of his chest under his suit jacket. "But how did you find me?" His eyebrows rose on his forehead.

"No apology necessary," she said, uncorking a dense red Burgundy and pouring two glasses. She glanced at the label. Not cheap. "We couldn't talk at a crowded bistro, anyway. They suggested I'd find you here."

She handed him a glass, determined to relax him. Probe for information and check it against de Voule's words. She clinked his glass. "Salut." She let him take a sip. Then another. "Symposium overload or work issues?"

"Department miscommunication," he said, a tired edge to his voice. "Nothing I can't handle. But I'm still new at this."

"You're not trying to avoid me?" She gave a little laugh. "Look, I wouldn't want you to feel I'm hounding you. You're so busy . . ."

"Not at all." A crease worried Jean-Luc's brow. "Now that I've listened to Pascal's message, it's adding up. But not in a good way."

Alert, she poured more Burgundy in his glass.

"I feel terrible," he said.

Aimée tried to look understanding. "Something bothered you in Pascal's message, didn't it?"

"That's just it, it's my fault. He needed my help."

"Needed your help?"

De Voule said it had been the other way around. Which one told the truth? Which should she believe?

Jean-Luc sipped. Pushed his blond hair back. "A month, *non*, six weeks ago, they promoted me to division head. A new division concerned with logistics. In telecommunications that translates to nuts and bolts, infrastructure, systems placement . . ." He took a breath. "I'm boring you, *desolé*. Here I am still talking work after the all-day symposium."

"A fiber-optics division, that's what you're getting to, *non*?" Aimée took a linen napkin and set the bottle on it.

Jean-Luc blinked. "How did you know?"

She pointed to the fiber-optics symposium banner.

"*Alors*, I'll cut to the chase," he said. "Added responsibility, and one I qualified for, but of course I'm learning as I go. My team's brilliant."

"Composed of fellow Gadz'Arts?"

He gave a brief nod. "That's where Pascal came in," Jean-Luc said. "He visited me at my office several weeks ago. Turns out he worked on a fiber-optic formula and wanted my advice."

The connection. Aimée willed her fingers to remain steady on her glass.

"Anything specific you can tell me?"

Jean-Luc shook his head. "Pascal caught me between meetings. A five-minute conversation." He shrugged. "To play fair, I couldn't reveal the company's plans. I can't say I understood all the projects we'd undertaken. That's why I attend these symposiums, to get up to speed."

"That's it?" Aimée felt hope slipping away.

"Three days ago, he begged me to meet at his office," Jean-Luc said. "But I'd just gotten back from our new lab in Strasbourg. Then Friday night he left the message, excited, saying he'd found something, a fourteenth-century technique that could be the missing fiber-optic link. He needed to show me, show me before . . ." His lip trembled.

"Please go on, if you can," she said, hating to push him. "Before what?"

He nodded. "He said, 'before they find out what I've done,' almost as if he'd stolen something."

"You're sure?" Yet according to the DST, Pascal worked for the security of the country.

"But I don't know who or what." He squeezed her hand, then let go. Large, tapered fingers, worn fingernails. Even as department head he'd said he still did the dirty work. "Then this afternoon." He downed his wine, his brow furrowing. "I couldn't find reports in my briefcase for today's presentation. Gone. My secretary checked, but I hadn't left them at the office."

He shot her a troubled look.

"Vital reports?" Aimée asked.

"Topics relating to our presentation," Jean-Luc continued. "We're on the cusp of discoveries in fiber optics. But of course, no detailed specifics. We're sharing the current trends with the participants." His phone vibrated. He glanced and ignored it. "It's like a knife in my heart. I can't believe Pascal would have taken the reports from my office. I don't want to believe it. But if I'd met him Friday, defused the situation, convinced him to own up or . . ." Pause. "But I'm projecting."

Had Pascal stolen reports? She needed to think about this new spin.

"I'm still not understanding how this links," she said. "Was he obsessed with the project?"

"A geek, you mean?" Jean-Luc's tone changed, verging on sarcastic.

Realizing she'd struck a sore point, she shrugged. "I'm quoting your fellow Gadz'Arts, de Voule."

"We're all geeks, some of us more obviously than others," he said. "Fascinated by engineering and the arcane." He shook his head, almost apologetic now. "No one wanted to date *mecs* like us in engineering school."

So he spoke from experience? Had he in his youth resembled Pascal: glasses, wild hair, a distracted and bookish look? If so, he'd changed. Pascal hadn't.

"*Vraiment?* You?" She'd ease a smile onto his face. Get him to talk. Reveal more about Pascal. Learn what she didn't know, why he suggested Pascal stole. "More like a catch, I'd say."

He grinned. "And you?"

"Me?" He turned the tables in a neat switch.

"So you're taken, Aimée?"

By a man married to a job he couldn't talk about? Who might never have a weekend free but asked her to go with him to Martinique?

"Relationships? I don't get them." She shrugged.

"But I can tell," he said. "*Alors*, give me credit for trying."

He hadn't tried very hard. And his being department head of a conglomerate, not bad boy enough for her.

"Weren't de Voule and Pascal outsiders?" Aimée asked, persisting. "De Voule said you and Pascal butted heads. That you used him. How do you explain that?"

"*Crapaud!* You believe de Voule? Consider the source." Jean-Luc downed his wine. "*Alors*, de Voule inherited his father's company. Lucky for him. A mediocre engineer, a passable technician who paid lip service to our traditions to bolster his credentials. His firm's in financial trouble. Their ministry project defunded. Yet he thinks himself too good for a Gadz'Arts, can you imagine?"

"Yet Pascal didn't buy into any of it, did he?"

"We knew where we stood with him."

She poured more wine. The bottle was almost empty. "Did you use Pascal?"

"*Moi?* The other way around. I felt sorry for Pascal. These flashes of brilliance he had, with no discipline to follow through. His scattershot approach. We were so different from each other, but I understood him. His obsessive tendencies from a solitary childhood. Like my own. Now I hate to think he repaid me by . . ."

"Stealing reports? Is that what you're implying?"

"I hope to God not." He glanced again at his cell phone, worried. For a moment vulnerable. "Another work crisis."

Overwhelmed by responsibility. She could relate to that.

"Forgive me, but I need to go over tomorrow's project." He gathered his overcoat from the rack. A camel-hair coat. It was one of several similar coats on the rack, but her stomach went cold. And she remembered the man darting in front of the car. The thread in her fingernail after the attack. "That's your coat?" Had it been him? Her throat caught.

He snorted in disgust. "Can you believe that?" He pointed to a grease stain. "A brand new coat—I only just bought it this afternoon. Dirty. Teaches me not to shop the sales again."

"Today?" A tingle in her ankles rose up her legs.

"Before my seminar. A new coat, to make a good impression. And look." He shrugged for a moment like a little boy.

Relief flooded her. It couldn't have been him.

"Look, if my reports surface in Samour's files, will you tell me? Keep it between us? No need to implicate Pascal now."

Not to mention keeping his company ignorant of this. But she understood.

Jean-Luc kissed her on both cheeks. Lingering kisses, and then he'd gone. She wanted him to be wrong about Pascal. Very wrong.

AIMÉE STOOD AT Café des Puys, running her chipped *rouge-noir* pinkie over the zinc counter. What she wouldn't give for that cigarette in her bag.

One drag. That's all.

Anxiety settled over her mind as she wondered about the DST's agenda, their claim to Pascal, de Voule's firm's financial trouble, Jean-Luc's intimation that Pascal stole his fiber-optics report. They each had different reasons for lying. Who to believe?

Just as she was about to reach for the pack the blonde had given her, the waiter slid an espresso in front of her. So instead, she took sugar cubes from the bowl. No chocolate on the demi-tasse saucer this time. No instructions either.

"Monsieur, *un chocolat?*"

"All out," he said, without looking up.

Alors, she'd appeared as instructed. Done her part. Foolish to think the DST could lead to her mother. Secret meetings, games, all smoke and mirrors. She'd promised Mademoiselle Samoukashian she'd find Pascal's murderer. But she still hadn't connected the pieces, or found out who murdered him. Or why.

Tired, she downed the espresso, slapped five francs on the counter. The next time the DST made contact, she'd tell them where to go. About to leave, she glanced up. In the café mirror her gaze caught that of the man sitting in the back.

Sacault. Same brown suit. A matching brown wool muffler.

Color coordinated as usual. She sat down across from him. "Glad you're here. Makes it easy to say adieu."

"Don't you have news for me?"

She set down the tiny GPS tracker she'd found under her scooter's headlamp. "Your surveillance techniques don't impress or protect me. Nor do your old recycled surveillance reports," she said. "After meeting the blonde last night, I was attacked. Consider me done."

Sacault slid a gift-wrapped box with a blue bow across the marble-topped table. "Open it."

Presents, a three-star *resto* tomorrow . . . bizarre goings-on. "But it's not my birthday."

"Pretend."

"You're good at that." She stared at him. "Like that supposed five-year-old surveillance report on my mother. Posted on a website that disappeared before I could track it. Or how you altered the date." She shook her head, shoved the gift back at him. "Quit gaming me."

"You'll like this. Guaranteed."

Reluctant yet intrigued, she untied the bow, tore the paper, opened the small box. A small mirrored ball with pink strands shooting out of it. Sacault reached and hit a button. The strands lit up, glowing dark pink at the tips.

"A Barbie gift. How thoughtful."

"Give me the customary thank-you *bises*."

Surprised, she felt Sacault's cheek near hers. She pecked both of his cheeks. "Look familiar?" he whispered. "Samour worked on micro fiber optics. Much smaller than these."

Similar to the one she'd found in his atelier tower. "So?"

"Take out the card in the box and smile."

She opened the card. A postcard-sized black-and-white photo of a woman, slightly out of focus, her arms folded, standing on Pont Neuf. Aimée's hand quivered.

"Approximate date on that's within the last six months."

He shrugged. "From a freelancer. No time-date on his camera. We assume it's your mother."

Her heart thudded. "But you've no proof. A freelancer?"

"Surveillance paparazzi who sell to the highest bidder," Sacault said. "They photograph known hot spots, people of interest, the works. I found this in a file last night. We sift for anything useful. Make a purchase. He's in prison now."

Sacault didn't often say so many sentences together. She believed him.

She swallowed hard, her gaze unable to leave the photo. The woman leaning on the Pont Marie, across from her apartment on Île Saint-Louis. Did it explain that sense she felt in the street, coming out of a shop, or running to the bus—that feeling of being watched? But it didn't explain why her mother hadn't come forward, made contact. If this was her.

"That's it?"

"The most current. Make of it what you will. We'd be interested in talking with her, if she ever contacts you."

Startled, she sat back. "So you can put her in prison?"

"To keep her from prison. She's more valuable outside. Trust me." He tapped his spoon on the demitasse. "Now what did you find about Samour?"

Trust him? She trusted him as far as she could spit. No reason for him to know they'd discovered a strand of fiber optics in Samour's tower atelier.

Yet.

Clodo's phone burned a hole in her bag—her trump card with Prévost. She wanted to copy the numbers and listen to it.

But she had to give Sacault something to keep him off her tail.

"I've digitized a century of holdings at the Musée. Documents, machines," she said. "Two more centuries to go. So far, Samour's Internet fingerprints are all over what I've cataloged and probably what I haven't. He was searching." She flicked the pink fiber-optic strands of her gift. "For something to do with this?"

Sacault said nothing.

"Didn't you just say he worked on fiber optics? I don't get it."

"It's not for you to get."

"First you hint this relates to fiber optics, now you back-pedal. Wouldn't it make more sense to clue me in on what I'm looking for?"

"So you found his laptop?"

"Did I say that?"

"How can you verify his 'fingerprints'?"

She thought quickly. "I traced it back to his office computer account at the Conservatoire. Spill, Sacault, make my hunting effective."

"Ministry sources are interested in a developing fiber-optic project Samour worked on. It's gone. With him."

She sat up. Had Samour stolen Jean-Luc's info at Bouygues to further his project? "Isn't that in private firm domain? Or do you all cozy up together?"

"Something like that," Sacault said. "All you need to remember is he worked for us. Died doing duty for his country."

"But how . . ."

Sacault stood. "See you here tomorrow night. Bring something concrete."

AIMÉE HUDDLED BY the medieval well in the old wall under the *café tabac* awning. Her knees trembled.

If her mother was alive . . .

Her cell phone trilled. Jolted out of her reverie, she recognized René's number.

"Aimée, Meizi called," he said, worried. "She's frightened. You promised to help her."

Damn Prévost. He hadn't called, hadn't alerted her to the raid. It could be going down tonight.

She had to find him. "Order her room service at the hotel," she said. "Keep her occupied."

"She's threatening to meet with Tso."

Meet him? "But she can't, René. Not in person. She's to call him, once I've found out the time of the raid. Tell her everything will work if she stays patient."

She scanned the street. Stepped into a puddle in the gutter. Cursed and hailed a taxi.

"No need to swear, Aimée," René said.

"Any joy from the laptop?" she said, opening the taxi door. "And any way you could tell if this formula's stolen?"

"Stolen? Anyone's guess. But I'd say Pascal fabricated a tool that conducts light like the ancient guild's window."

And he hung up.

Now it was all making sense.

"The *commissariat* at Château-Landon, *s'il vous plaît*," she told the taxi driver.

She hit Prévost's number again.

"I'm en route to your office, Prévost."

Blaring horns sounded in the background. "Count that a wasted trip."

"Where are you?"

More blaring horns. "*Libération*. On the rooftop. But give me ten minutes, I'm in a meeting . . ."

She clicked off.

"Change of plans, Monsieur," she said, touching the taxi driver's shoulder. "*Libération* on rue Béranger. Fast as you can."

He nodded, shifted into fourth gear. "Once a good newspaper, when it was Sartre and the sixty-eighters. But now . . ." A shrug. "Too conservative for me."

She let his patter drift over her, not paying attention.

"You're a reporter, eh?" They passed Samour's building. "Working on a story?" he asked as he pulled up.

"You could say that," she said, reaching in her worn Vuitton wallet for a tip.

"Tell the story of the little guy, the ordinary *mec*," he said. "You know, that's what your paper was all about. Back when writing meant something."

He declined the tip. "Buy yourself a coffee, write something meaningful. Change things for people who need it, eh?"

"I'll do my best." She squeezed his shoulder, thought of Martine's idea for an exposé on Chinatown sweatshops. "It won't be for lack of trying, Monsieur. *Merci*."

Libération took up eight floors of a former parking garage. She showed Martine's old press pass and the guard waved her on.

Instead of waiting for the elevator, she spiraled up the ramp, passing offices, photo archives, various news desks. She was dizzy by the time she reached the top. A few scattered reporters worked at computers. "I'm looking for Officer Prévost."

"The *flic*?" a head popped up from a terminal. "He's enjoying our view. Best in Paris."

She had to hurry. At the nearest empty news desk, she took a memo pad, dusted off the cigarette ash from it, scrolled Clodo's cell phone and copied the numbers. Two messages on it, the voices fuzzy, indistinct. *Merde!* She rifled through the desk drawers for a tape recorder. Martine always carried one, didn't every reporter? No luck. Just a phone console with an answering machine. But that could work.

She punched in the console number from her cell, waited until it went to the answering machine, hit the cell phone's message replay and held it close to the console to record the messages. Murky, but René's software could isolate the voice from the noises, from the whining siren in the background.

She scanned the news desks. Then bent down, popped the tiny cassette out, and put it in her pocket.

She wended her way among partitions reeking of day-old coffee to a wall of glass sliding doors. She slid one open and stepped out on the rooftop terrace. Paris spread out below her as far as she could see, glittering pricks of light floating in the cotton-like mist. The wind knocked her off her feet.

She grabbed the railing. Held on and righted herself.

"What's so important? What are you doing here?" Prévost ground out his cigarette with his heel. His muffler whipped his face.

"You didn't know my father in the force," she said. "He was before your time. Liar, you didn't owe him."

The words came out before she could stop them. Before she could ask why he'd avoided her.

"So you came to accuse me?" He shook his head. "That's what this is about? But true, *oui*, your father was before my time. He left the force disgraced."

"Cleared years later, Prévost, due to me," she said, the wind catching her words. "No thanks to the department."

"I would have left in disgrace, too," he said, "without a way to support my family. But I didn't have a father with a detective agency to slide into."

She held up her hand. "So you're vindictive against my father?" Her jaw trembled. "My dead father? And for some strange reason—"

"He helped me," Prévost interrupted. "We never met. Never even talked. But your father consented, years after his discharge, to return and verify to Internal Affairs that I wrote a report routed to his department. Crucial to his investigation." Prévost shrugged. "He could have refused. But as one officer to another he did a hard thing. He did the right thing."

Aimée's jaw dropped.

"I kept my job thanks to him. You probably don't understand," Prévost said. "Or want to understand. I detailed men to watch you. For your safety."

Her shoulders stiffened. She doubted that. Where were they when Samour's killer stretched plastic over her head?

"Too convoluted for me," she said. "I don't understand."

"The DST's tailing you," he said. "But I couldn't be seen to be involved with you."

Tell me what I don't know, she almost said.

"I don't know what in hell's going on, but for your father's sake I've tried to keep minders on you. To give the DST notice that other eyes watched. To keep their toes clean."

That's what all this was about, why she felt watched all the time—the DST and the *flics*? Yet she'd still been attacked.

"Wait a minute. If the RG's involved, it's a pretty crowded field . . ."

"Let me finish. The RG set up the Chinatown surveillance six weeks ago. Six weeks of their ass in my face. Then the DST horn in."

"Like your turf war's my business, Prévost?"

Prévost's coat whipped in the wind. He grabbed at his wool hat. "Look, I quit the cards, what you heard was a sting," he said. "But your father would never let me repay him. Just passed on the word that he had to do the right thing. So I wanted to do the right thing, to help you."

Prévost's jaw shook. It meant a lot for him to say it.

"But the DST want me to lead them to Samour's murderer," she said. "It's what Samour worked on, don't you see?"

But this triggered a new thought. She shut her mouth. What if it flipped the other way around, in a ploy to lead them to her mother?

"Samour was a adult trade school teacher, for God's sake." Prévost shook his head. He was shaking. He'd felt an obligation, tried to help her. Even if he'd barked up the wrong tree.

"If it means so much, you knowing my father was a good man," she said, "pay it back by protecting Meizi Wu. Can you do that for me?"

"A person of interest? She's a homicide suspect."

"More like a witness who ran away scared," Aimée said. "You think she could shrink-wrap a man taller than herself?"

Prévost shrugged. "The investigation's widened. I can't talk about that. But no guarantee I'll find her before the raid at nine P.M."

Less than two hours. Right now she didn't know how else to make good her promise to Meizi and protect her family in China.

"Play it so the snakehead Tso and Ching Wao hear Meizi's in custody. On the deportation list back to China. You give me your word?"

"Then consider your father repaid."

"Deal." She smiled. "I promised you Clodo's cell phone in return, didn't I? Rumor goes he picked this up near Samour's body. That's why he was pushed in front of the Métro."

She put the phone into a surprised Prévost's gloved hand.

Prévost's hat flew off in the wind. Like a fluttering black crow dancing over the slanted rooftops. They both watched it until it disappeared.

"Clodo didn't make it."

Sad. "That's why you need this to find the killer, Prévost. This should help."

"So you just happened to tap into the homeless network?"

"*Mais non*, I just asked my weatherman for help."

WITH THE RAID less than two hours away, and no answer on René's phone or word from Meizi, she turned the corner heading to Pascal's atelier. At least she'd get Saj started on isolating sounds in the microcassette recording. One step closer to finding the killer.

Her phone vibrated in her pocket. She looked at the incoming number. Unknown.

Her hope rose. If this was Meizi on the pay-as-you-go phone, she could give her the specifics about the raid, what disinformation to feed Tso. Assure her that her friends and family were safe.

"Meizi?" she said.

A man's throat cleared. "You gave me your card."

She recognized Cho from the metal store. "Monsieur Cho?"

"I think the symbols in the diagram . . ." He paused, choosing his words.

"*Oui*, go on."

"I think they represent a fiber-optic cable, one like I read about."

"And you're telling me now?"

"No repeaters, which would give it very high bandwidth. Triple what's in use right now."

What did that mean? "So you're saying what?"

"A pipe dream so far, but single fiber-optic cables like these could stretch the length of the Atlantic without a relay system."

"That's a good thing?"

"Revolutionary." Another pause. "The girl showed it to me."

"A girl?" She stepped back and bumped into the dripping wall. "Wait a minute, you mean the diagram I showed you . . ."

"Not that. Another one. The girl didn't know what to do with it. She was afraid."

"What does she look like, Monsieur Cho?"

"She found this by accident in the sweatshirts she sewed. The dead man put them in her pile." He went on to describe Meizi. "She didn't realize until the other night."

"And you didn't tell me?" There was silence on the other end. "Where's the diagram, Monsieur Cho?"

"I don't know."

"Who else knows?"

"No one." Pause. "I'm telling you because Monsieur Colles helped me. And I think you're the only one who can protect her."

"Why?"

"Tso's men are on the streets looking for her."

IN THE TOWER, she handed Saj the microcassette. "Can you clean this up and try isolating a voice from the background sounds?" Tired, her shoulders heavy, she stood in Pascal's tower atelier. "It's a garbled recording from either Samour's or the killer's phone. We need to hear it."

"René's grabbing a scanner at the office," Saj said, sitting up and punching his cell phone. "I'll tell him to pick up a sound-tracking program."

While he did that, she scanned the laptop screens. "But that was on Coulade's screen saver." She cleared the papers and diagrams aside on the trestle table.

"Samour used the trebuchet picture for his screen saver," Saj said. "Hiding his message under multiple layers of encryption. See how the computer assigns every pixel three numeric values? They correspond to the amount of red, green, or blue in the color the pixel displays. By changing those values by a shade, Pascal hid the ones and zeroes of computerese in the picture's pixel numbers, but without altering the picture's appearance."

Hiding it in plain sight.

"It's steganography, embedding messages within images. The point of encryption is to hide the content of the message. Using his great-aunt's password, I found the key to unlock the encryption program. *Alors*, it's a bit more complicated than that and took me a while, but . . ." Saj pointed at the screen. "The Latin's quite simple."

"The ingredients, you mean?"

He nodded. "Sulphur, lead, sand, and it goes on."

Her eyes locked on the emblem above the formula: letters intertwined in a symbol. Her mind raced. She'd seen that before.

"Hold on." She pulled out Pascal's book. Found what she was looking for. "*Et voilà*, that's the glassmakers' guild emblem. So this is proof he'd found part of the lost formula and come up with . . ."

"This portion." Saj clicked the screen to reveal a modern diagram. "According to my postmodernist programmer, that's part of a fiber-optic formula. One of incredible strength and clarity. So strong that information could go hundreds of thousands of kilometers without repeaters, like relay stations, in one piece."

That echoed what Cho said.

"Worth millions," Saj went on. "The military, governments, private sector, everyone wants this. Didn't he contract with the DST?"

She still had doubts. "Could he have stolen a trade secret, incorporated and refined it?"

"Intellectual property from the guild expired a few centuries ago," he said. "But trade secrets? I don't know."

So close. They were so close, except for this missing piece.

She hit René's number. "How soon will you get here, René?"

"Just left Meizi. I'm grabbing a scanner and sound program from the office," he said.

"Tso's men are looking for her."

Pause. "Didn't you take care of him?"

"Thought I did. The snake wiggled out." Aimée paused. "Meizi told you about the diagram she found, *non*?"

"What?"

A sinking feeling hit her.

"Samour put a diagram in her pile of sweatshirts."

"How do you know that?"

"Cho the metallurgist."

"Who?"

Worried, she pulled on her coat, headed to the door. Meizi had kept the information back from her and René. She grabbed her bag. "Prévost's informer. But she didn't say anything?"

Green light from the laptop screen smudged the tower's walls.

"You're implying Meizi thinks it's valuable, that she'd use it as a bargaining chip with Tso?" René said, his voice rising. "But you're wrong, she trusts us to help her."

Then why hadn't she called? Right now a terrified Meizi wouldn't know the deal Aimée had made with Prévost. She might give Tso any information to protect her family. Get caught in the raid. . . . Aimée hoped it wasn't too late. She had to convince her, get the diagram.

"Let me know the minute you isolate the voices, okay?"

She slammed the tower door.

AIMÉE IGNORED THE hotel elevator and took the stairs two at a time. She knocked on Meizi's door. No answer.

"Meizi, it's Aimée."

A maid pushed a cleaning cart down the hallway.

"Forgot my key," she smiled. "Mind letting me into my room?"

"Who says you're a guest here?" The maid's eyes narrowed in suspicion. "People pick up their keys at reception."

After a tip, Aimée figured. Aimée gestured to the room list hanging from the cart.

"See room number 32, Sitbon," she said, flashing Martine's press card. "My friend's asleep. Do me a favor and open the room."

The maid shrugged. With a ten-franc tip, she unlocked the door.

The duvet was ruffled and soap stained the mirror over the lavabo. Meizi had forgotten a red sock.

What did she expect? Tso's men were after Meizi. She had to find her before they did. Before the raid. If only Meizi had confided in her or René. Trusted them and just stayed here safe.

She rooted in her bag for Tso's cell phone. Scrolled down the list of numbers he'd called. She'd work from that. First she needed a Chinese speaker.

But Monsieur Cho didn't answer his phone. Panicked, she ran out of the hotel room and down the stairs, narrowly missing an elderly couple in the hallway.

• • •

"*S'IL VOUS PLAÎT, Madame*," Aimée asked the same Slavic-cheekboned receptionist.

The receptionist stood with her back turned at the whirring fax machine. Aimée scanned the lobby for watchers. It was deserted.

"Madame?" Was the woman ignoring her on purpose?

"Your friend's gone out," she said.

"How long ago?"

"Said to tell you she's getting a cell phone."

And walking into danger. But not if Aimée could stop it. She stepped out the front door, and at a glance took in parked cars and pedestrians but no vans. As she passed the Métro at Arts et Métiers she noticed a parked van on the boulevard. Wires and antennae. A surveillance van. Minutes later she reached Chez Chun's fogged-up windows, caught her breath and entered.

"Madame Liu, *s'il vous plaît*." A waitress slicing smoked duck behind the takeout counter jerked her thumb toward the back.

Madame Liu, who was stirring a pot of congee, looked up. Her black curls didn't move. She frowned. "I get health-code violation if customer here."

"Please, I need to talk with you, Madame."

Steam rose and pots clattered.

"Busy now. My cook sick."

Aimée glanced around. The small kitchen was a hive of activity—workers at the range, washing dishes, waitresses grabbing plates.

"How will you keep your *resto* open without these people?"

Alarm crossed the little woman's eyes. "You try to shut me down?"

"I want to help so you won't be shut down." Aimée took Madame Liu's wiry arm and led her past sacks of rice to the rear door. A damp alley. Her mind went back to last night, the plastic, fighting to breathe. She shook it aside.

"*Alors*, Madame, we'll help each other."

"I answer your questions before."

"Within an hour the police will raid the quartier," Aimée said. "Spreading the net to catch big fish like Tso, but your little fish will be caught too. Unless you help me."

Madame Liu's eyes narrowed. "Not my business."

"The staff's your business," Aimée said. "If you don't believe it, see for yourself. Go near République, out on rue Beaubourg. Check out all the parked surveillance vans."

Madame Liu's fingers grabbed the dishtowel in her hands. Weighing her options, Aimée figured.

"Or do you like paying protection money to buy Ching Wao's Mercedes?" Aimée tapped her heel on the damp cobbles.

A shout came from the kitchen. Madame Liu's brows knitted in alarm.

"*Mais alors*, Madame, there's not much time."

Madame checked her watch. A long moment passed before she nodded. "What you want?"

Aimée explained what she wanted her to do. Asked Madame to repeat it. Satisfied, she handed Tso's phone to Madame.

Madame Liu glanced at her watch again. Nodded and hit the first contact number. She spoke the brief message in Wenzhou dialect. Then the same message again for the next three numbers.

"Remember what I said," Aimée said. "Close in ten minutes. Only inform people you trust."

Madame Liu nodded.

"You catch killer for great-auntie?"

"Not yet." Aimée pulled out the phone's memory chip, ground it on the cobble under her heel. Pulled her own out and left a message for Prévost.

Aimée turned to head down the alley.

"But I see that girl," Madame Liu said. "Tonight."

Aimée froze.

"Man follow her on street."

"One of Tso's men?"

Madame Liu shook her head. "Maybe Frenchman. I don't know."

"What did he look like?"

"Coat, hat, I don't see face. Bag of crumbs, like he feed the pigeons."

Few people fed pigeons this late at night in the winter. The RG or the *flics*? Or . . .

"Which way did she go, Madame?"

"Toward Métro."

AIMÉE RAN, CELL PHONE to her ear. "René, please tell me Meizi's with you."

"With me? I'm meeting her near Square du Temple." René's voice mounted in worry. "Meizi told me everything. The diagram . . ."

This felt wrong. "You mean Meizi told you over the phone, on the street?"

"*Bien sûr*. It's safer for her to come to the tower, that's why . . ."

Bread crumbs to feed the swans in the square's pond. Of course. And it was coming together. Samour's killer's next victim.

"A man's following her, René," Aimée said. "Hurry, I'll meet you there."

She clicked off. Saved her breath, wishing with every step she hadn't smoked that cigarette.

At rue du Temple she met a locked gate; the Square du Temple closed early in winter. She looked both ways, then hoisted herself over the side fence. Through the spindle of bare tree branches she saw the glass-roofed, green-metal band shell, home to classical music in summer, now forlorn in the mist.

The frost-tipped grass, the playground, and the statue of Béranger obscured by the low-lying fog.

The waterfall gurgled, slipping over stones and feeding into the pond, whose surface was a dull, opaque shimmer of broken ice. A lone swan glided and disappeared. Somewhere a bird trilled. The park, deserted in the dark, cold evening, held night sounds: splashing water, framed by distant traffic.

Aimée shivered, stamped her feet. Nervous, she continued around the pond's mud-rimmed edge. Saw floating bread crumbs.

"Meizi?" she called, alarmed.

No answer.

Aimée exhaled a plume of frost.

A dark figure moved in the shadows. She heard footsteps, snapping branches. Coming closer.

An attacker?

Then splashing farther away. A scream.

Aimée broke into a run, her heart racing.

"Meizi?"

Furious splashing. A figure ran from the bushes, but she could only make out a dim outline in the darkness.

Meizi yelled, thrashing in the water.

Aimée reached down and grabbed Meizi's arm. Pulled her up on the mud bank from the pond. Frightened, Meizi backed up, catching her foot on a root.

"Aimée? Someone tried to at—attack me," said a shaking Meizi.

Tso, or someone else? "Hurry, someone's watching you."

Her teeth were clicking in the cold, her jeans dripping at the pond's edge. "I twisted my ankle, I can't make it."

"You need to try." Aimée nodded toward the low fence. The glow of a cigarette tip by the bare branches. "I've worked out a deal with the *flics* to protect you, Meizi. But we have to hurry. You're being followed."

Meizi's eyes glittered in fear. Aimée pulled her back into the bushes, put her arm around her shaking shoulders, and guided her through the damp foliage.

Trying not to make a sound, Aimée propelled her to the mound by the grilled fence.

"Climb over."

Meizi winced. "You're kidding, right?"

Instead of arguing with her, Aimée gripped Meizi's shoulder tighter, pointed to the foothold in the low grillwork. "Put your good foot here, see? Then swing your other leg up."

Before Meizi could protest, Aimée boosted Meizi up, then climbed over, herself. "Give me your hand . . . *et voilà.*"

Down on the pavement, every step Meizi took squelched water from her dripping shoes. Aimée gripped Meizi's shoulder tighter. The frigid air made breathing hard. She struggled not to slip on the ice and to keep Meizi, shivering and soaked, moving forward. "We're almost there."

So dark, and the street blanketed in fog.

"Where's the diagram, Meizi?"

"I threw it away," she said, her voice trembling. "Don't you see, it's all trouble since . . ." She stumbled, leaned hard into Aimée.

Something glinted ahead. "René's up there," Aimée said. "Just to the corner, you can make it."

Then the start of an engine. A car's headlights blinded her. The wheels crunched ice. *Merde.* They'd been seen.

With a burst of energy, she ran, pulling Meizi along with her.

"My ankle!" Meizi cried.

"Half a block, not far."

Meizi let go.

"The car!" René shouted. "Watch out."

Aimée heard an *ouff* as Meizi stumbled on the street, shoving Aimée forward. Aimée's heel caught in the cobble cracks, and then she was flying through cold air. A thump as her head hit the lamppost. Lights spinning. And she crumpled, dazed, on the wet pavement.

The car's engine whined.

Aimée heard Meizi's scream. A sickening thud. Shots.

René was firing and running.

The car pulled away. Red brake lights evaporated in the fog.

"*Non . . . non*," she heard René's voice break. Saw the gun in his hand.

THE REST PASSED in a blur. Vaguely, she was aware of the surveillance van, the flashing blue lights from the *flics'* cars, her examination in the emergency room of Hôtel-Dieu, the public hospital. Sometime later, the waiting room, Meizi in the operating room, René's pacing, and Prévost's long face.

"But I wrote down the license plate number," René was saying in the waiting room.

"We found the car," Prévost said. "Stolen and abandoned at Place de la République."

"But Tso's men followed her," René said, insistent. His fingers drumming the blue plastic chair.

"We apprehended them approximately fifteen minutes prior to the incident."

"Incident?" René shouted. "Attempted homicide!"

Prévost cast a look at the *flics* by the reception desk. "We took them into custody at Théâtre Dejazet's back entrance. But I think Mademoiselle Leduc knows more about that."

Thanks to Madame Liu.

Aimée nodded. Pain shot through her temple. She shouldn't have done that. The doctor had diagnosed a raging headache, not even a mild concussion, and had counseled against foot races or long division.

"Did you get anything from dumping Samour's phone?"

She hadn't heard back from Saj on the microcassette yet.

"Different SIM card," Prévost said. "Replaced."

Useless now.

She wished her head didn't ache. Wished the nurse would update them on Meizi's surgery. "But the killer's still out there," she said.

"Tso's under interrogation, Mademoiselle," Prévost said. "He'll talk."

Enjoying his cake and claiming the credit too. But she didn't care. "Don't you understand? A Frenchman followed Meizi. Ask Madame Liu. Aren't you investigating—?"

"Monsieur Friant, I'm sorry." The surgeon in green scrubs appeared, taking off his surgical mask. "We did everything we could to save her. But she suffered massive internal bleeding."

René blanched. Staggered. Aimée caught his arm.

She stared at Prévost. "It's homicide now." Prévost turned, strode past the white curtains to the *flics* down the green-tiled hall.

IN THE OPERATING room, René took a stool and climbed on it. He pulled back the sheet, revealing Meizi's ashen pallor, the bruises, the blue tinge already formed around her lifeless mouth. Aimée trembled. So senseless.

She reached for his hand but he shook her off.

"I meant for her to have this." He pulled the red velvet box from his pocket. Took out the ring. The pearl glinted under the harsh operating table lights. Aimée forced herself to watch René as he slipped it on Meizi's stiff, dirt-covered finger.

Aimée's gut wrenched. "I'm sorry, René. I should have . . ." Her voice cracked. All the things she could have done flashed in her mind: bolted Meizi to the bed, given her the damn phone, gained her trust.

René reached on his toes and kissed Meizi's forehead.

"It's not your fault, Aimée," he said, his eyes wide and dry.

Aimée looked down. Meizi's spattered blood on the green

tile, the oxygen machine tubes trailing on the floor. She made a sign of the cross.

"I'll take you home, René."

"Meizi made me feel things. Things I didn't know I'd feel again for anyone. Almost as much as . . ." He paused. "And I thought . . ."

What was that look on his face? "What, René?"

His voice had changed when he spoke again. "I want to say good-bye. To be alone with her."

"But René . . ."

He raised his hand. "Do one thing for me, Aimée."

"Anything, partner," she said.

"Get the bastard."

She blinked at the hardness in his voice.

"That's a given, René."

ARMED WITH EXTRA-STRENGTH Doliprane, she left Hôtel-Dieu and stood across from floodlit Notre Dame. No tourists, just bare-branched trees and the speckles of light from the Gothic window. Opposite lay the prefecture.

Her headache had subsided to a dull throb. She could walk for hours and still not erase the ache, the pointlessness of Meizi's death. Or the hardness in René's voice.

She needed to talk to someone. And she bet that someone sat in his office on the quai behind the prefecture.

She pulled out her cell phone.

"Morbier, turns out I'm free for dinner."

A clearing of his throat. "Ever hear of advance notice, Leduc?"

"Knowing you, you're at your desk with a cigarette burning and a half-drunk cup of espresso."

She heard what sounded like the closing of a door.

A pause. "Something wrong, Leduc?"

"Why don't I stop at Le Soleil, bring up a *casse-croûte?*" she said. "You're paying, right? I'll put it on your tab."

Pause. "Forget it."

"Didn't *you* want to talk to me, Morbier?" she said, kicking a cobblestone. "No matter if you don't have Clodo's file. He didn't make it."

"I meant forget Le Soleil." Voices, a loudspeaker in the

background. Sounded like a train station. "L'Astier. Give me twenty minutes."

He hung up.

SHE WALKED BACK to her Île Saint-Louis apartment knowing this only postponed the sleepless night ahead of her. Reliving the sickening thud, Meizi's ashen face, her spattered blood on the green hospital tiles. The fact she hadn't found Samour's murderer and he'd struck again.

In the bathroom she applied arnica to her bruises and anti-biotic cream to the still-stinging cuts on her face, then a heavy dose of concealer to the bump on her forehead. In her armoire she found the little black vintage Chanel, still in its plastic dry-cleaning bag. On her way out she grabbed her long copper coat and hailed a taxi down on Pont Neuf. She touched up her mascara on the short ride.

The driver let her off at Place des Vosges. Her red-soled Louboutin heels echoed under the dark, vaulted arcade. Several black limos double-parked, as unobtrusively as possible, waiting for the dining ministers inside.

She'd discovered part of Samour's project. Too bad she hadn't found all the DST wanted. But tomorrow she'd make a deal with them. Ignore the hollowness inside. Right now she needed Morbier's help to fine-tune her dealings with them. To find the killer.

The tuxedoed maître d' glided her past late-night diners to a secluded corner table. Morbier was sitting there, drinking something red. His basset-hound eyes were ringed with deeper circles than usual. His jowls sagged. The corduroy jacket with elbow patches and the crumpled tie looked even shabbier than usual. Xavierre's death had hit him harder than she'd thought.

"A three-star Michelin *resto* without reservations? You've come up in the world, Morbier. Or you've got something on the maître d'." She summoned a smile. At least the Doliprane was working.

"A little of both."

A waiter appeared with a deep bow.

"Mademoiselle, *un aperitif* before ordering?"

She glanced at the bottle of Burgundy on the table. Wine and Doliprane? "That looks fine."

"She'll have what I'm having, Paul," Morbier said, reaching over to pour her a glass from the half-full bottle. "I'll do the honors. We'd like a little quiet, if you don't mind."

"*Oui, Monsieur le Commissaire.*" He bowed again, more discreetly this time, and vanished.

Aimée clinked her glass to Morbier's. "Call me impressed. His first bow almost scraped the floor." She hesitated. Didn't know how else to say it. "Grieving takes time, Morbier."

"So the world tells me, Leduc." He waved his hand, then stared at her. "What happened to you?"

So her makeup hadn't done its job? Her hand paused at her temple. "Stupid. I ran into a lamppost."

"Anything to do with the roundup near Arts et Métiers?"

He'd heard.

She nodded. "It got messy," she said, fingering the white linen napkin on her lap. "A major casualty."

"Not what I heard," he said. "They're calling it a success. Weren't you involved?"

"René's girlfriend didn't make it," she said. Bit her lip. "But that's part of why I'm here."

Again he waved his liver-spotted hand. "We're here to eat. For once. This place costs the earth."

"You've called in a favor, more like it," she said, "or the maître d's your informer." She noticed the burgundy spots on the lapel of his jacket. "Killed half a bottle already, I see."

"I'd like to enjoy it, Leduc. Looks like you could do with some food in your stomach."

But she told him anyway. And about Pascal Samour.

Morbier pulled out an unfiltered Gauloises. Cast a warning glance at a waiter, who had promptly appeared with a lighter, then lit it with a matchbox from his pocket.

Aimée stared. Why hadn't she seen it? Stupid again.

"All these years you've worked with the DST and never told me?" she said, controlling her voice with effort. "Shame on you, Morbier."

Shock painted his lined brow. "Where does that come from?"

"A little under-the-sheets time with the DGSE too? Too bad the DGSE agent success rate is only twenty-eight percent."

He blinked. She'd surprised him for once.

"I thought their rate was thirty-two percent."

Her turn for surprise. And then it faded.

"Your leaked report's more current than mine," she said. "Don't play dumb. You're my contact instead of Sacault tonight."

"The lamppost knocked you harder than you thought," Morbier said. "Not my people at all. The opposite." Shrugged. "There are things I need to tell you."

Something in his voice made her sit up.

Two plates of white asparagus dotted with caviar appeared. He paused until the waiter backed away.

Morbier pushed his cell phone toward the wineglass, tucked his linen napkin in his collar. A member of the proletariat like him would enjoy a three-star *resto* in his own way. He speared an asparagus tip with his salad fork.

"Eat while it's hot, Leduc," he said, glancing at the other diners.

"Asparagus is served cold, Morbier. So you wanted to have dinner, eh? Talk?"

He nodded. Always a good liar.

"Then convince me."

"You're more than unusually feisty tonight." He glanced at her untouched plate.

"Murder does that to me."

"Homicide's not my turf. Not anymore, you know that."

She stared at the white asparagus. Couldn't eat. Her stomach churned. She heard a choking, looked up.

Morbier paled. Swallowed several times.

What was wrong with him?

She saw an uneasy flicker in his basset-hound eyes.

"Got a stalk stuck in your throat?"

He shook his head.

"Lift your hands up in the air," she said.

"Leduc, keep my eye contact. In a minute or so, drop your napkin. Glance at the fourth table, the couple sitting over a bottle of Vouvray."

She dropped her linen napkin, turned as she reached down for it.

"Him or her?"

"Operatives of this caliber work in couples. Better cover."

Now she had a lump in her throat.

"This vintage comes from a northern vineyard," he said, all of a sudden. "You can taste the *terroir*, the rich soil."

Morbier knew as much about vintage as a street cleaner.

"The *terroir*? We're not describing vine-growing conditions in sandy or acidic soil here, but people."

"Lower your voice, Leduc." He leaned closer. "Certain branches have expressed great interest in you. I don't know what pot you've stirred up . . ."

"It's what I'm doing at the Musée des Arts et Métiers," she said. "Or not doing, as I told you. But they don't know that. I've got a theory."

"Theory?" Surprise painted Morbier's face. "Connected to Samour?"

"Good, you've been listening," she said. "You're not usually so informative. Funny, since you haven't answered your phone. Or returned my messages in weeks."

"Paranoid, Leduc?"

"You're the one seeing operatives at the fourth table." She sat back. Noticed a high-end satellite phone poking out from the napkin on the woman's lap.

All the signs were there: Morbier's evasiveness, a hurried meeting. The DST had kicked this into high gear.

She felt him grab her hand under the table and place a piece of paper in it.

"Read it later. Trust me."

Since when had she trusted him? Any favor he'd done her demanded payment. She turned her back, blocking anyone's view, and slit open the sealed envelope. Found a small pale-blue notecard with cramped writing.

Amy, believe no one. They're using you to find me. I've done things I'm not proud of. But I've watched you from afar, tried to shield you. Thanks to your father, I found a new life. Now for once, I'm doing something right. It means I can't protect you. Not anymore. You're the only person who can take care of you. Remember that. I told you this when you were little and in my letters for years. Know that I care for you.

—Mommy (DESTROY THIS)

"My mother?" Her insides wrenched. "When did you get this?"

"You know how your father felt."

Papa pretended Sydney had never existed.

"She's my mother." Aimée bit her lip. "What does she mean, protect me?"

"It's complicated." Morbier looked as comfortable as a hen held under a knife.

"That's all you can say? Diagram it for me, Morbier." She seethed inside. "Better yet, give me her letters."

"I destroyed them."

She swallowed. Her mother's letters and he destroyed them. "Because Papa . . ."

"You're naive."

"Call me what you want. I don't hate my mother. How could I? How can you? I want to see her." Her eyes teared. "Just once."

"A woman hunted, persona non grata, on the World Security watch list?"

In the end, what did it matter? All she remembered were those warm arms that held her when she'd had a fever, the drawings scribbled on old envelopes to make her laugh. That smile, those carmine-red lips.

"Quit putting me off, like always. You've never told me the truth, Morbier. When I was little I knew when you lied."

Morbier hadn't answered her calls. What had changed?

"You've got a red face," she said. "The tops of your big ears are pink."

"But I'm not lying, Leduc. Not this time."

"You think I believe you?" Aimee clutched at a hope, as always. "If Maman's life is in danger, she needs me. Now."

"She abandoned you."

That hole opened up. Wide and empty. The years of not knowing.

"Maybe she had to." The lie she told herself. "Not all women can handle raising a child," she said. "I just want to see her, talk with her. Once. Then if she doesn't want to know me—"

"She knows you, Leduc," he said, his voice low. "What you do, how you live."

Pain lanced her heart. She thought of the times she'd sensed a presence, a shadow on the quai. That hurt even more. "Why not contact me, Morbier?"

"Try to understand." His shoulders sagged. "They'd implicate you in aiding and abetting terrorism. Arrest you." Morbier expelled a sigh. "Children. Always so selfish."

Part of her always felt eight years old, that little girl waiting for her mother in the empty apartment after school.

"So you appointed yourself judge and jury, eh, Morbier? Decided long ago." A terrible thought hit her. "Or you're hiding the truth because the truth's too ugly. And your part in the reason she left? And Papa . . . you lied to him?"

"But you know what happened. The facts."

"I had to find them out years later. Myself. You could have told me."

"That your mother's a convicted terrorist, served time in prison until your father worked a deal?" he said. "Deported. Banned from France. The rest she did herself. She picked the wrong horse. Had to ride it."

Little details, pieces fit together. "What if she's playing both sides?"

Morbier averted his eyes.

"Maybe she had to. And won't anymore."

"If I tell you, will you leave it alone?"

He expected a promise? But she nodded.

"She's gone rogue."

Aimée had expected anything but that. "Rogue?" Was he lying? "That's what she meant in the letter?"

"She doesn't want you in danger. Or under pressure to reveal—"

"You think I'd turn in my own mother?"

"Politicos, drug lords, arms dealers, old terrorists. Her speciality. Let's call it her area of expertise, Aimée."

"Why can't she tell me in person?"

He glanced at his cell phone.

"She's going to call?"

"*Alors*, Leduc, you wouldn't believe it, like another letter from your brother. Typical Company tactic."

"My brother . . . the Company, the CIA? That's all made up?"

Morbier checked his phone again. Took her hand. "Listen,

it's important. She wants you free, not making the mistake she did. A mistake she's had to live with. The only other choice was to compromise you. And she cared too much to do that."

Aimée's hand trembled on the wineglass. Was that the real reason? "But you're using the past tense, Morbier. You're talking like she's dead."

He glanced at his watch. "She was supposed to call ten minutes ago. Confirm. Speak with you."

"You mean . . . ?"

He shrugged. Looked away. Then leaned forward, intent.

"Don't believe the DST, DGSE, or Interpol," he said, his voice urgent. "Just asses with tails between their legs. When you go rogue, no one's in your corner."

The chandelier's crystals reflected the candlelight, the hushed service. The hypocrisy of the three-star clientele. "Doesn't the smell of what human beings do to each other get in your nostrils, Morbier? Doesn't it bother you?"

His shoulders sagged. For a moment he looked like the old man he was. "In my business, I never get rid of it."

He took her hand. Held it tight. "You have to watch your back. She disowned you so they couldn't use you to get to her."

A tidal wave hit her, all the old hurt surfaced. She didn't know which way was up.

A patsy. Desperate, she'd fallen for it.

"But they did, Morbier," she said. "I took their bait."

"Spit it out, Leduc." Morbier shook his head. "Or do you want to be under surveillance all your life?"

No way in hell that would happen.

She grabbed Morbier's phone. Scrolled down the last calls received. A UK country code. "She called you, didn't she?"

The couple at the next table stared.

She punched the call return. And waited the longest minute of her life: the ringing, the slow motion of Morbier's pained expression, the clink of cutlery, more ringing, the long-ago image of her mother's face floating in front of her.

Ringing, ringing. A click. Her heart leapt.

"*Maman?*" she breathed.

"The number you've reached is no longer in directory service," a clipped British accent informed her. "Please check the—"

She put the phone down.

"They got her, Leduc," he said. "I'm sorry."

"Who's they?" She stifled a sob.

He turned away. "Does it matter?"

She flung her plate at him. Stood. At the couple's table, she emptied the bottle of Vouvray over their laps, drenching their high-end satellite phones. Out of commission. For a little while.

She ran past waiters with plates of food who scattered in her path, meeting the maître d', who blocked her exit at the door. "Mademoiselle, please sit down, *restez tranquille* . . ."

A hard kick to the shin sent him reeling into an arrangement of white roses. She was out the door, running under the vaulted arcade. Her heels clicking, tears streaming down her face, freezing on her cheeks.

It all reeled in front of her. Her mother, the DST, Samour's murder, Meizi, the attack that almost killed her last night, the alchemical formula, the secret to the fiber optics. She grabbed the freezing stone arcade, racked by sobs. Shaking, trying to draw strength from the ancient stone. She forced herself to take deep breaths of slicing cold. Again and again, until determination surfaced. Her mind cleared in the freezing cold night. Now, she knew what she had to do.

"STORM PREDICTED, *ma chère*," the homeless man said. Thunder shook the sky. Straining, the weather channel came from the vent under his m

Her shoulders shook. "Too bad I don't have my raincoat," she said, scanning the area around the Carreau du Temple.

"Have a dinner date?" His gaze ran over her outfit.

"Past tense. I didn't care for the company." She pushed down her emotions. An entwined couple stood in front of Café Rouge by the rue de Picardie door to the courtyard of the tower.

"Fifty francs for you if you keep an eye on them," she said. "Another fifty if you go along with me when I get back."

"But *ma chère*, I have a new radio," he said.

"Then something for your daughter, eh?"

He grinned.

She pulled her copper-colored coat tighter, kept to the shadows. Within five minutes she had entered the courtyard and unlocked the door of Samour's tower room.

Saj sat on the floor surrounded by burning candles and several laptop screens.

"Meizi's dead, Saj," she said, her voice cracking. If only she'd protected Meizi. Hadn't failed René.

"*Mon Dieu*. That's terrible." He shook his head. "How's René?"

"He won't leave the hospital."

Another shake of his head. "We have to let him grieve in his own way, Aimée," Saj said. "You know we're missing a piece, don't you?" Saj hadn't looked up from the screens, his eyes darted from one to another. "That's what I've been trying to find."

"Whatever Meizi had, it's gone."

He nodded. Took a deep breath. "Samour left a trail of crumbs."

"You think

Saj sat up. "[Wa]sn't a brilliant mind with his skill set back up the steps of [the fiber]-optic process? His notes, his formulas? He'd store it awa[y like a] squirrel."

Made sense. "But on Friday he was desperate, he tried to contact Coulade—"

"Coulade's hard drive's a wash," Saj interrupted. "Nothing."

Her mind went back to Coulade's words in his office. "Samour left his last message for Coulade at five P.M.," she said. "At seven P.M. Samour passed Chez Chun on his way to meet his killer."

"*Et alors?*"

"What did he do in those two hours?"

Saj hit a few keys on Samour's keyboard. "His laptop shows no activity," he said, "so he didn't come here."

"Pull up the diagram copy René made."

Saj stared, his eyes widening. "That's it." More key clicks and it popped up on the screen. "See? We need to think in two directions, not just the one.

"What?" Aimée said, frustrated. "I still don't get it."

"This tower, his flat, and extend the line."

She took a deep breath so she wouldn't shout. "What do you mean?"

"Pascal followed the diagram—that's his message. Followed it to the other end of this line. That's where the rest of the manuscript lies. And it looks to me like . . ." Saj superimposed a clear street map over the diagram and traced his finger. "Here."

The Musée. Aimée nodded. "He followed the diagram. will I." She stuck her laptop in her bag. Noticed his br wool Tibetan cap with earflaps. "Mind if I borrow this?"

"As long as both of you come back in one piece."

OUT IN THE courtyard, she pulled the cap's e low, turned her metallic coat inside out to show the bl ing, lit up a cigarette from the pack of filtered Gaul hat the blonde had given her. Felt the jolt of nicotine

Now or never.

Head down, she stepped out of the doorway and kept to the right. A church bell chimed in the distance. A moment later she'd joined the homeless man under the sleeping bag, trying to ignore his pungent aroma. Impossible. She'd make this quick.

"Any action?"

"Only they used their cell phones after you went inside."

Just as she'd thought. Watchers.

But chances were they hadn't keyed in on her location. Otherwise they'd have a crew waiting.

"What's your name, Monsieur?"

"Hippolyte," he said. "Would you be interested in exchanging coats, *ma chère?*"

"You read my mind, Hippolyte. But only if you take this too," she said, handing him the last of Tso's francs.

SHE LEFT THE warm vent, confident no one would follow her.

She kept to the narrow side streets below Place de la République. She felt invisible. No one looked twice at a clochard shuffling along in a Tibetan hat and moth-eaten raccoon coat—more fragrant now after a spritz of Chanel No. 5.

She hit Martine's number on her cell phone. Martine answered on the first ring.

"About time, Aimée," she said. "When can I meet Meizi?"

"Bad news, I'm afraid," she said, her chest tightening. That aw taste of guilt clutched the back of her throat.

"at now, Aimée?"

Sh k a breath and filled Martine in as she walked.

"De Meizi's dead? Poor René." Martine exhaled. A cough.

"Not to l mercenary, but it shoots down my exposé," she said. "Lib interested in a three-part series documenting conditions r. But for that I need a connection in the sweatshops. who will talk to me. Open doors. Proof."

Aimée's he

Martine couldn't pull out now.

"She's not the only one, Martine."

"Get real, Aimée. It's a closed world. They live in fear, held hostage by their families in China. Who'd talk to me?"

Aimée had to make her understand. And she didn't have time. "I found Meizi chained, Martine," she said. "Treated worse than a dog. The *flics* snared a few snakeheads to ante up on their taxes."

Pause.

"No one cares about the women or the men living ten to a room, sleeping under the machines," Aimée said. "Who's fighting for them? Or for the unnamed dead in paupers' graves at Ivry. I sent Prévost proof, he just doesn't know it yet."

Another pause.

"But Prévost has connections at *Libération*," Aimée continued.

Martine let out a *phfft*. "Proving what?"

She had no idea. "I met him there on the roof, stunning view," she said. "You figure it out."

A longer pause.

"I doubt he was renewing his subscription, Martine," she said.

"So you'd like me to take on the Ministry of Labor with a possible ally at the newspaper—some *flic* you met on a rooftop?"

Aimée gripped the phone in her gloved hand. "Prizes for investigative journalism don't come from fluff pieces," she said. "Got a pencil?"

Pause. "Why do I feel I'll regret this?"

"You won't." She gave Martine the addresses, the refuge at the Chinese evangelical church, Nina's name. "Now anything stopping you, Martine?"

A longer pause. "Just my car. I totalled it yesterday. Gilles threw a fit."

Aimeé sucked in her breath. "You okay?"

"Shaken up." Aimée heard the jingle of keys. "But I'll take Gilles's Range Rover. Safer."

Aimée used her security access to gain entry to the Musée des Arts et Métiers. Vardet, the security guard, nodded from his guardroom.

"Ah, Mademoiselle, *un express?* Fresh, too. Join me before I do rounds."

Just what she needed. "You're a lifesaver, Monsieur."

He poured her a steaming demitasse. Added a trickle of *eau-de-vie*. "Let me add *un fortifiant*, as we say in Lyon."

A Lyonnais, of course.

"Gorgeous country." Vardet's eyes misted. "I miss it. The Rhône gurgling past."

Perhaps he'd had a little too much *eau-de-vie* already.

She popped another Doliprane and sipped the espresso laced with pear liquor. Heaven. Vardet pointed out his grandchildren in photos. His old-fashioned alarm clock rang. "Time for my rounds."

Under the Gothic nave, Aimée connected her laptop to the museum's desktop and logged on. Thank God for the space heater. She scrolled the museum's archaic database. It was hidden here somewhere.

Impatient, she raced over the keys, scrolling through the documents she'd digitized. Nothing. She, René, and Saj had gone over all of these.

the floor. She narrowly avoided the old, dusty glass display cases, empty and forlorn, in the long corridor.

But it wasn't the wind; chanting came from somewhere ahead in the dark. The hair rose on the back of her neck. The ghosts of old monks?

"*Allo?* Someone there?" Her voice echoed.

She turned left and continued in the direction of the chanting. Wouldn't the students studying late be in the same predicament as she was? The chanting sounds grew. Choral practice? But this late at night?

She found herself in a humid vaulted corridor, and almost walked into an ancient wooden door with rusted hinges and grimy metal studs. She lifted the hinge handle and parted the velvet drapery. Candles flickered in holders on the bookcases, on the reading tables. Her eyes adjusted from the darkness to see seven or so figures in hooded black robes gathered around a table, chanting in what sounded like Latin. Metallic odors wafted from a glass globe in front of them.

Good God, had she walked into a ritualistic cabal, some ancient occult rite? Or stepped into a Knights Templar ritual like those depicted in the medieval paintings she'd cataloged? Her nose itched from the candle smoke and she sneezed.

The chanting stopped, the last low echo rising in the vaulted Gothic refectory.

"Who's there?"

She swallowed hard and almost dropped her laptop bag. "*Excusez-moi*, the power's out in the museum . . . and I thought the door here would . . ."

"Open from here?" said a brown-haired man. He smiled, his face illuminated by a candle, and approached her. "*Alors*, if the electricity's out, we're all stuck. Might need to spend the night here."

Not in her lifetime. Not with him and these robed figures. They looked like grim reapers to her. All they needed were scythes.

"Time enough for us to get to know you," he said, with a wink.

Fat chance. "Look, I work here," she said.

"You don't look like a construction worker," he said, sniffing. "Interesting coat. You sure the raccoon's dead?"

"Digital inventory archive," she said, impatient. "But who are you?"

By now the robes had come off, and surrounding her were young men in pinstripe suits. The candlelight flickered over their faces. "Gadz'Arts," one of them said as if assuming she'd understand.

Like Pascal Samour, Jean-Luc, and de Voule, but a few years younger. "What's going on?"

"One of our traditions," the brown-haired one said, as if chanting in robes were commonplace. "We're recent Conservatoire graduates, but part of a long history. One of our customs. Many think them arcane and silly, but we've been here since 1789, so to speak."

With their robes off in the flickering candlelight, they looked like any three-piece suits in the nearby Bourse bars.

He grinned. "We're trained technical engineers, I'm afraid. This meeting, well, it's what we Gadz'Arts have done for centuries, nothing so exotic as the Freemasons." He turned to one of the others, now on his cell phone. "Or so I've heard."

"If you're engineers, you can figure a way out, *non*?"

The one with the phone nodded. "Bad news. The hail's knocked out the grid for several streets."

Great. "But with your technical savvy, I'd imagine you know how to jimmy the electrical door lock."

"Why?" the brown-haired one said.

She had no intention of spending the night here with these . . . whatever they were.

"I'm late," she said, wishing she'd come up with something more original. Part of her hesitated, held back from mentioning Jean-Luc.

The men exchanged glances.

"Or do I need to learn the secret handshake?"

"Follow us."

"To where?"

"The tunnel to the street exit." Two of them moved carved chairs aside, revealing a coved door that clicked open on a spring latch. Beyond it, narrow steps wound down to a subterranean tunnel. Vaulted and dry.

"But how do you know about this?" She didn't like this plan. On the other hand, she wanted to get out of here.

"Part of our initiation rites," the smiling brown-haired man said. "After you."

The tunnel followed the refectory layout above. The men carried candles, illuminating the dirt ground, the blackened stone archways.

"We're concluding our ritual," one of them said.

Filing through one cavern, each of the men deposited something from their pockets in a human skull. She backed up against the wall.

"Your turn."

"I don't think so." But before she could turn, he'd pushed her and slammed an old oak door she hadn't noticed in the shadows. She heard clinking metal as the door locked.

Stupid again! "What the hell! Let me out!"

Laughter. "Part of our rites, Mademoiselle."

"Rites? Some prank? You're sick."

"*Non*, we expected you."

Expected her? In rising panic, she pounded on the door.

Then stopped and listened. Nothing. She turned her penlight to the human skull. She shuddered. Inside were wooden matchsticks, written all over with miniscule black script.

Mademoiselle Samoukashian's words came back to her: the cruel medieval rites of hazing. An overcoat hung dripping on the dirt. A camel-hair coat. Like the one worn by the man darting in the street, the man who'd attacked her.

Her head ached. She had to get out of here. Her penlight battery would last only so long. She inserted her double-sided lock pick and jiggled. The door opened. Thank God centuries-old locks had simple mechanisms.

Meizi had been run down before her eyes, both of them targets. She'd discovered Morbier to be a *traître*, her mother likely dead. The clueless DST was on her tail for a lead to her mother, or maybe for Samour's formula. But they weren't the only ones.

Footsteps pounded behind her in the dirt.

She ran through the tunnel's forks and twists, trying to visualize what lay above.

She came to a bricked-up wall. Nowhere to go.

Her fingers scrabbled inside her bag for a tool, a weapon. Only the lock pick.

"Are you lost?"

She knew that voice. And in that moment, all the puzzle pieces fit. Her lip trembled. She should have put it together before. But after the attack . . . Revulsion took over. Now she was trapped. But let him win? No way. She fought the shaking in her legs, her hands. She had to talk her way out of here. "Thank God, Jean-Luc. The power's out, the Gadz'Arts said—"

"And they were right," Jean-Luc said. A strong flashlight beam blinded her. Her blood ran cold. Cornered like a rat, no way out and the killer in front of her.

"You expected me, Jean-Luc?" Her hand gripped the lock pick in her bag. She slid it up her sleeve. "So you know I just found the document Samour stole from you."

"*Bien sûr*," he said, his voice soaked up by the densely

packed earth. She couldn't see him behind the flashlight beam. "We can't have you interrupting our ritual, you know. That's not allowed."

"My mistake. I need to show you this, upstairs." She tried to sound more confident than she felt with her back to the wall. "There's more light, still some power in my laptop," she said, trying to buy time.

"I told them I'd deal with you," he said.

Like he dealt with Pascal? Her heels hit the wall, nowhere to go, no way to see him. Did he have a gun?

Her breath came in short spurts.

Jean-Luc had wanted to steal the formula from Pascal Samour, not the other way around. He was desperate to jump ahead in fiber optics. Why hadn't she put it together? How could she have ignored the obvious signs? She was furious with herself.

"You don't understand," Jean-Luc said. "Pascal didn't follow rules. Never had. He wouldn't listen. I caged him up, like we'd always done. But he'd changed."

Caged him? So for once Pascal stood up to him, refused to act the doormat. And paid.

"As his Mentu, his mentor, you tried, didn't you?" she said.

"You found the backup he promised me, like I knew you would," he said, his tone matter-of-fact.

"Promised you?" She had to keep talking. "But you told me he stole this."

How much longer until he attacked her? Here, vulnerable, with the light blinding her as the car's headlights had blinded Meizi.

"*C'est vrai*, but I'm the only one who ever listened to Pascal."

"Becquerel believed in him." Then it hit her. "But you took care of Becquerel," Aimée said, taking a guess. "Smothered him with a pillow in the nursing home, didn't you?"

"That shouldn't have happened." His bittersweet tone surprised her. "We're trained engineers, not killers."

"But Pascal was brilliant," she said. "He discovered the ancient stained-glass formula and applied the concept to the principles of fiber optics." She was perspiring in the coat.

"So simple, when you think about it. The greatest discoveries are. The rest, so unnecessary." Jean-Luc's voice dropped, almost sad now. "I listened to Pascal, I was the only one."

"Wrong again. The DST listened," she said. "He worked for them."

"The DST? Too late to the party." His voice hardened. "The Chinese military offered me a contract. It's the Year of the Tiger, auspicious."

"Chinese? Was Meizi involved?"

He snorted. "A sweatshop girl? But convenient for me. Who'd care about an illegal immigrant like her but Pascal? The bleeding-heart Communist."

Anger filled her. The pompous ass. Meizi had been an unknowing pawn in his game. It made her sick. He'd planned it to the last detail.

"With your technical know-how, you worked the plastic wrap machine like a snap," she said, her high heel working the dirt. "Yet you made a mistake. You were surprised when Clodo appeared. You dropped your cell phone."

"Who?"

"Don't tell me you forgot the homeless man you pushed onto the Métro tracks?"

"Vermin," Jean-Luc spat. "He stank."

"But Clodo sold your phone. Now the *flics* have it."

He didn't have to know Clodo replaced the SIM card.

Close humid air mixed with the wet fur smells from Hippolyte's coat. She heard the patter of crumbling dirt.

"Now you'll put down the laptop," he said.

She crouched with the laptop bag. One hand behind it,

fingers scrabbling for clumps of dirt. The dense air in this narrow tunnel and the ragged, stinking fur nauseated her.

"Closer," he said.

Still blinded by the beam, she pushed the laptop bag forward.

"Unzip the case."

Shaking, she took the laptop out. Prayed Saj had received the file she sent.

The flashlight beam focused on the laptop, revealing Jean-Luc's leaning silhouette. She flung the handful of dirt in his face. Catching him off guard, she lunged and shoved him against the wall.

"Bitch!" His arm lashed out, whacking her ribs and throwing her off balance. Struggling, she shook him off, stumbled and ran, pushing herself off the wall. Her adrenalin kicking in.

Darkness except for her thin penlight beam. Perspiration, the hot fur coat, the thick air. She saw the ramp. Ran up it, pushed the door open. Back in the refectory, a few candles sputtering, the odor of melted wax.

She slipped behind the first thing she saw, a bookcase, eyed the stone steps leading to the pulpit. Her adrenalin ebbing, she grabbed her side. This pain.

"We're playing *cache-cache* now? Hide-and-seek?"

She couldn't see him in the shadows. Her mouth felt like cotton, bile rose in her stomach. Her legs wobbled.

"Don't you understand?" Jean-Luc said. "Pascal lied. That's how he repaid me. No gratitude after I helped him learn to weld, mold, machine-design, to calculate, to construct machines."

Keep focused. Keep him talking. Find his inner geek. "You mean like the guilds?"

"Our heritage comes from the guilds," he said, his voice impassioned. "Even the classic freshman problem of how to drill a hole at a ninety-degree angle in a piece of metal. An old guild secret." A short bark of laughter echoed. "But I tried to guide him, be a *parrain*, a godfather to him at school."

"So you caged him?"

Weakness sapped her. Pain knifed through her side.

"Pascal wanted to give this formula away free!" Jean-Luc shouted. "To the world! Can you imagine?"

The glass globe and a leather scientific tome the size of Miles Davis lay within reach on the table. Either one could . . .

Jean-Luc shoved the bookcase back and smiled. He wore glasses now. Thick lenses. For the first time, she saw his face up close, saw the violent anger contorting his eyes. His dilated pupils. Why had she ever considered him handsome, vulnerable? She'd even felt sorry for him.

"Scream as loud as you like," he said. "No power. We shorted the power grid."

Smart ass. She maneuvered the lock pick from her sleeve. "You brainwashed your disciples. Pitiful. You attacked me."

His knife blade glinted in the candlelight. "Too bad things didn't work out more smoothly. I wish I had taken care of you then."

Pascal, Meizi, now her. She felt blood rush to her face. She tried again to stall him. "You ran over Meizi . . ."

He snorted. "Like she matters. Or you, for that matter. All you did was complicate the means to the end. But nothing I can't handle."

He rushed at her with his knife. She threw up her arms to ward off the blow. His glasses went flying.

But his knife blade pinned Hippolyte's ragged coat sleeve to the bookcase. An odd look spread on his shadowed face. His mouth twitched, contorted. "What did . . . you do?" he gasped.

She twisted and turned, but she couldn't move. Stuck.

And she realized the lock pick in her other hand had gone into his eye. All fifteen centimeters of it, up to the handle. His eye was a mashed purple globe.

"Call it luck," she said. "Auspicious."

Horror sticken, she shoved his body away. Jean-Luc sagged

in a little pirouette, then crumpled against the bookcase, life-less. A thin line of vitreous and blood trailed onto the stone.

The red light shone on her laptop's reserve battery, one bar of power remaining. She grabbed her cell phone. Shook it, and lifted it as high as she could for reception. Pecked Saj's number. Fuzz. Her vision fading, she hit René's speed dial. It rang and rang. Finally, she heard a buzzing. "Refectory," was all she could manage.

Light-headedness filled her, the bookcases spun. Her fingers came back sticky, and she saw the keyboard was smeared red with blood. Her blood. Jean-Luc had sliced his knife through the coat into her side. And her dress. Her vintage Chanel.

How would she get the blood out? Her thoughts drifted, swirled with bits of code, Latin, the picture of the woman on the Pont Marie. Then the rushing cold, such bone-chilling cold in her legs, her arms. The howling wind in the nave filled her ears until blackness took over.

"YOU LIKE US, do you? Second time tonight," the white-uniformed nurse consulted her chart. "As if we needed another emergency intake, with the ward this full."

The gold glow of dawn crept in from under the hospital window shade. "Technically, it's morning, nurse." Aimée groaned at the smarting stitches. "But you should have seen the other *mec*."

"I'd call you trouble, Mademoiselle." The nurse gave her a little smile. "And that's the morphine talking."

"That's what I like to hear," said Saj, "after all our medita-tion work. Drugs."

"Mademoiselle, you're lucky no vital organs were punctured."

Aimée felt like she'd been run over by a truck.

"The X-rays indicate the knife hit your vertebra," the nurse continued, reading her chart. "Bone and muscle tissue protected your spinal column. A nice *umph* but no lasting damage."

She became aware of Sacault, all in brown, standing next to Saj. "As long as you're talking, let's continue the conversation. We're ambulancing you to Val de Grâce."

"The military hospital?" she said, wincing in pain. "No way."

René was holding her hand, his green eyes wide. "You called me?"

"Sorry for the bad reception, René," she said. "But I took care of him. Sorry it was too late."

René looked down. "Morbier's out in the waiting room."

Hurt pinched her heart. She couldn't deal with Morbier now. If ever.

"Mademoiselle Leduc, you'll debrief with our team," Sacault said. "Go over the files recovered from Jean-Luc Narzac's office at Bouygues. Furnish us with Samour's work."

She shook her head, and everything swam.

"Tell him, René," she said. "Fill it in for the DST. Then consider me done. All done."

Saj nodded, pulled his madras scarf around his shoulders. "First I suggest we center . . ."

Sacault blinked.

"Pascal Samour applied lost medieval stained-glassmaking principles to fiber optics," René said. "But you know that." René handed Sacault a disc. "It's all here. But he wanted to give the fiber-optic formula away free. A gift from the fourteenth century. And we have." René smiled. "However, since only seventy-eight scientific engineers in the world will understand it, no great alarm." He smiled again. "Saj designed an obscure website. Not even the Chinese will find it for six months, Monsieur."

Three Days Later

RENÉ TRIED AIMÉE'S number again. Busy. No doubt conferring with Melac on their Martinique trip. Dejected, he buttoned his Burberry raincoat in the dusk outside the shuttered luggage shop on rue au Maire. Next door, red banners proclaiming the Year of the Tiger ruffled in the wind outside the tofu shop. He remembered Meizi speaking of the festivities and how they would—

A loud pop startled him, made him jump and duck for cover by the bin of husked lychees. Sharp pain shot up his hip.

A shot? But he smelled the acrid smoke, heard a continuous pop and crackle, then laughing children. Fireworks.

The thumping of a drum. *Dum . . . da da dum . . . dum . . . da da dum.* Crashing cymbals, growing louder and echoing in the narrow street. Then the bright head of the lion, his twisting silk body supported by a trail of people. The New Year parade.

René straightened up, feeling foolish and more alone than ever. He limped over the glistening cobbles, inhaling the cooking smells from Chez Chun. Past excited children running toward the parade to catch the candy thrown from the lion's mouth, the red lanterns shaking in the wind. At the corner, the stained-glass windows glinted from the walls of the museum.

He turned left on rue Beaubourg toward his Citroën. Crowds, shadows, charcoal clouds promising more rain. Where had he parked his car?

His eye caught on the travel agency window: a poster with

a blazing sun, palm trees, and a white beach advertising specials to California. He stood for a long time in the cold February evening, staring at the poster. He recalled the latest e-mail from the start-up in Silicon Valley offering him a job. And then he opened the travel agency door.

THE LAST RAYS of winter light shone on rue du Louvre as Aimée left the office. She passed the arcaded rue de Rivoli, took her time over the Pont Marie, thinking. Along the Quai d'Anjou, she felt that familiar frisson. As if someone were watching her. She turned around. Only a hovering mist.

Miles Davis scampered out of Madame Cachou's loge in the courtyard and barked a greeting. She walked upstairs and, after turning her key, paused in the doorway. Her heart hesitated, wondering if Melac would understand.

She couldn't leave René like this. Martine would call her crazy, giving up Martinique, the sun and Melac. She unsnapped Miles Davis's tartan sweater, wiped his paws clean, and took courage from his wagging tail. "You and me, furball, no matter what."

Miles Davis licked her face.

She took off her wet heels, pulled on wool socks, and set her shoulders. Time to return Melac's message and cancel Martinique. And if this meant he'd end up finding someone else . . . maybe that was the way it was meant to be.

But first she needed a drink.

Something sweet drifted from the salon. Frangipani?

She parted the half-open door. A large tropical beach umbrella opened over the Aubusson carpet, which sat on a straw beach mat, surrounded by mini potted palm trees. Beside it sat a wine decanter filled with something pink and floating lemon rounds, along with two tall glasses and paper drink umbrellas. Sounds of breaking waves and surf came from the CD player.

"This is what you meant by Martinique, Melac?"

Melac shrugged, gave a little grin. "No boarding pass needed." He lifted up her YSL beaded turquoise bikini from the sales. "Why don't you put this on?"

"Matches my socks, eh?"

"Island rum, hibiscus, our own umbrella, even tropical fish." He gestured to a fish tank, beside which she noticed Miles Davis's bowl appeared to be filled with filet mignon strips. He'd gone all out.

"So you're on a case." She shook her head, hands on her hips.

He ducked his head. "It's not always going to be like this. *Desolé*, I had to cancel the tickets." When he looked up, there was sadness in his gray eyes. "Can you understand?"

She wanted to tell him. Maybe she would. Someday.

Instead she unbuttoned her black cashmere sweater, unzipped her pencil skirt, and stepped out of it. "I knew I needed that bikini."

Melac stared at her. Blinked. "Are those stitches?"

"Two rules *en vacances*. I don't talk about work," she said. "And I get a pink umbrella in my drink." She grinned. "Later you can rub oil on my back."

"First things first," Melac said.

SHADOWS LENGTHENED OUTSIDE the window. Yellow light from the quai glowed in the mist. The empty decanter sat between them on the beach mat under the umbrella.

She ran her fingers through Melac's hair and stuck an orange umbrella behind his ear.

"There are things I can't tell you, too, Melac."

He propped himself up on his elbows. "You mean *you* joined MI6 or Israeli intelligence? I'd have to arrest an enemy agent?"

She averted her eyes. "Someday I'll need to make a choice."

Worry creased Melac's brow. "About us? So you're really married? Or have a lover in Rouen?"

Startled, she laughed. "Not that simple." Shook her head, stood and looked out into the dusk. "Choosing sides, that's all. We could end up on opposite ones."

A long silence broken only by the rain drizzling on the wrought-iron balcony outside, the toot of a barge on the Seine. And she found herself in Melac's arms. Understanding shone in his gray-blue eyes. "Blood ties?"

"Life's not black and white." Her gaze went beyond his shoulder, past the bare plane-tree branches, to the rain-swollen Seine.

"Don't borrow trouble, we Bretons say. It finds you soon enough."

She nodded. From the window she caught a glimpse of a figure shrouded in mist on the Pont Marie.

ACKNOWLEDGMENTS

My huge gratitude goes to the many brilliant and patient
people who helped with this story: Dot; Barbara; Jan; Max;
Susanna; John; Mary; Libby Hellmann; Jassy Mackenzie;
Steven Bunting; Isabelle and Andi; forensic pathologist Terri
Haddix, M.D.; the amazing Jean Satzer; and generous inspiration of Remy Sanouillet, graduate of *Ecole Nationale Supérieure
d'Arts et Métiers*.

Mercis in Paris to Carla Bach; Sauveur Chemouni; the
Archives National; Monsieur X in the RG who told me "no
one dies in Chinatown"; Adrian Leeds; Benoît, Nathalie and
Gavroche Pastisson; Naftali Skrobek, a true *Rèsistant*; Andre
Rakoto, *Chef de cabinet, service historique de la Défense*; Kati, Jo
and Elise for *les Bains*; the real Chez Chen; Gilles Thomas;
Julian Pepinster, Metro master; the gardeners at Square du
Temple; Bijoux Fantasie on rue du Temple; Gilles Fouque for
les crevettes raviolis; Donna Evleth; Sarah Tarille; and toujours
Anne-Françoise Delbegue.

And always to the treasures in my corner: Linda Allen;
James N. Frey, without whom; Ailen Lujo; Michelle Rafferty;
my publisher, Bronwen Hruska and editor, Juliet Grames; Jun
and my son, Tate.

Turn the page for a sneak preview from the next
Aimée Leduc investigation

MURDER BELOW
MONTPARNASSE

Monday, Late February 1998, Paris, 5:58 P.M.

AIMÉE LEDUC BIT her lip as she scanned the indigo dusk, the shoppers teeming along rain-slicked Boulevard du Montparnasse. the scent of daffodils drifted from the corner flower shop. Her kohl-rimmed eyes zeroed in on the man hunched at the window table in the café. Definitely the one.

Gathering her courage, she entered the smoke-filled café and sat down across from him. She crossed her legs, noting the stubble on his chin and the half-filled glass of *limonade*.

He sized up her mini and three-inch leopard-print heels. "Going to make me happy?" he asked. "They said you're good."

"No one's complained." She unclipped the thumb drive from her hoop earring and slid it across the table to him. "Insert this into your USB port to download the file," she said, combing her red wig forward with her fingers. *"Et voilà."*

"You copied the entire court file to that?" The thick eyebrows rose above his sallow face.

"Cutting-edge technology not even patented yet," she said with more confidence than she felt. She wished her knees would stop shaking under the table.

"How do you do it?"

"Computer security's my business," she said, glancing at her Tintin watch. This was taking too long.

"We'll just see to make sure, *non?*" He pulled a laptop from his bag under the table and inserted the thumb drive. More tech savvy than he'd let on. Thank God she'd prepared for that.

"Satisfied?" She fluffed her red wig.

A grin erupted on his face. "The Cour d'Assize witness list with backgrounds, addresses, and schedule. Nice work." He'd lowered his voice. "Perfect to *nique les flics*." Screw the cops.

She grinned. Glanced at the time. "Don't you have something for me?"

Under the table he slipped an envelope, sticky with lemonade residue, into her hands. In her lap she counted the crisp, fresh bills.

"Where's the rest?" Perspiration dampened the small of her back. "You trying to cheat me?"

"That's what we agreed to," he said, slipping another envelope under the table. Winked.

Thought he was a player.

"Count again," he said.

She did. "No tip? *Service compris?*"

"Let's do business again, Mademoiselle. You live up to your reputation. Glad I outsourced this." He smiled again. "I couldn't be more pleased."

She smiled back. "Neither could Commissaire Morbier."

His shoulders stiffened. "Wait a minute. What. . . ?"

"Would you like to meet my godfather?" She gestured to the older man sitting at the next table. Salt-and-pepper hair, basset-hound eyes, corduroy jacket with elbow patches.

"Godfather?" he said, puzzled.

"Did you get that on tape, Morbier?"

"On camera, too. Oh, we got it all," Morbier said.

Two undercover *flics* at the zinc counter approached with handcuffs. Another turned from a table with a laptop, took the thumb drive and inserted it.

The man gave a short laugh and pulled a cell phone from his pocket. "*Zut*, that's entrapment plain and simple. Never fly in court, fools. My lawyer will confirm. . . ."

"Entrapment's illegal, but a sting's right up our alley,

according to the Ministry's legal advisor." Morbier jerked his thumb toward a middle-aged man at a neighboring table, who raised his glass of grenadine at them. "Don't worry, I had the boys at the Ministry of the Interior clear the operation technicalities, just to err on the safe side. Makes your illegal soliciting and paying for and reading confidential judicial documents airtight in court."

"Lying slut," the man said, glaring at Aimée. "But you're not a *flic*."

She nodded. "Just another pretty face."

"To think I trusted you."

"Never trust a redhead," she said, watching him be led away. Aimée removed the red wig, scratched her head, and slipped off her heels.

"Not bad, Leduc." Morbier struck a match and lit a cigarette. The tang of his non-filtered Gauloise tickled her nose.

"That entrapment business, you're sure?" She leaned forward to whisper. "I won't get nailed somehow? *Alors*, Morbier, with such short notice. . . ."

"Quick and dirty, Leduc. Your specialty, *non*? I needed an outsider."

"Why?" What hadn't he told her in his last-minute plea for help?

"But I told you." A shrug. "He broke my last officer's knees."

She controlled a shudder. "You forgot to tell me that part."

He shrugged. Not even a thank-you. And still no apology for what had happened last month, the lies he'd told about the past, her parents. A hen would grow teeth before he apologized. But she'd realized it was time to accept that he'd protected her in his own clumsy way. And made up for her outburst—she'd thrown caviar in his face at the four-star *resto*.

"So we're good, Leduc?" The lines crinkled at the edge of his eyes, the bags under them more pronounced. His jowls sagged.

She blinked. Coming from Morbier, that rated as an apology.

She pulled on her red high-tops, laced them up. Scratched her head again.

"*Au contraire.*" She stood, slipped the wig and heels in her bag, buttoned the jean jacket over her vintage black Chanel. "Now you owe me, Morbier."

Monday, 7:30 P.M.

IN THE QUARTIER below Montparnasse, the Serb shivered in his denim jacket, huddled in the damp doorway, watching Yuri Volodya close and lock his atelier door. Why do they lock the doors and leave the windows open? Just foolish.

Yuri Volodya walked across the wet cobbles and disappeared up the dark lane. The old man kept right on schedule—he'd be out for the evening. Now for this simple snatch-and-grab job. The Serb noted a few passersby taking the narrow thread of a street—the shortcut to the boulevard—the general quiet and the cars parked for the night. Perfect.

He peered over the cracked stone wall of the back of the old man's place—part atelier, part living space. A small garden wreathed in shadows, the windows dark. He heaved himself up and over.

The garden was redolent with rosemary. The Serb waited a few seconds, moved without making a sound on his padded soles to the side window. He slid it fully open and slipped in. He reached into his pocket and checked the syringe filled with the tranquilizer, just in case the old man came back. All capped tight.

"Don't kill him," they had said. Would have been easier.

A couple of lamps were lit, so the Serb didn't need his flashlight. The atelier was small enough to search quickly. He looked behind the worktable and under it, too—but *nyet*—no one would store a painting flat.

He had to think. . . . What was wrong here? His eyes scanned the room, and he noticed some fresh scuffing in front of the armoire, as if it had been moved back and forth—more than once, too.

He moved the armoire aside to find a locked door. He searched the armoire drawers for a key, and when he found it, he put it into the lock.

Then he heard a switch click, and the room plunged into darkness. The Serb sensed someone behind him. He flung out an arm, hoping to strike before being struck, but he tripped instead. Someone kicked him in the stomach. He felt gut-wrenching pain and the hypodermic needle rolled in his pocket.

His attacker went down on his knees and roped him around his neck, but the Serb fought him off. That's when he felt the jab in his rear. The liquid ran cold into his muscle, and he felt the freeze go up his body. He went limp.

His attacker let him go, thinking his job was done. A small penlight went on and the key turned in the lock. The wall cabinet opened to reveal . . . nothing. The painting was gone.

The Serb's attacker turned on his heel and walked out. The Serb, disturbed by the strange buzzing in his ears, knew he had to leave, too. The simple snatch-and-grab complicated by a rival intruder, and then no painting. He stood, unsteady, and realized it was much harder to breathe. He needed to go outside into the fresh air. . . .

He managed to unlock the door and stumble onto the side-walk before he realized he couldn't catch his breath at all. A rock-like weight pressed into his chest. Gasping, he reached out between the parked cars. His sleeve caught on something and the world went black.

Monday, 8 P.M.

IN THE OVERHEATED *commissariat*, Aimée signed her police statement. She took the last sip of Morbier's burgundy, then dabbed Chanel No. 5 on her pulse points and slipped the flacon into her bag.

"You'll need to testify against him, Leduc," said Morbier from behind his desk. "So the rat won't get up the drainpipe again."

"Not part of our deal, Morbier." She shook her head.

He waved his age-spotted hand. "Legally you're covered. Sanctioned from the top. It's all in my report."

"Against the Corsican mafia?" She snapped her bag shut. "My identity becomes public knowledge and then a thug appears on my doorway. I disappear. Didn't you tell me his history of intimidating witnesses?"

"Your testimony takes place in closed judges' chambers. No leaks. No media." Morbier stabbed out a Gauloise in the overflowing ashtray. "For three years the rat's boss has evaded every conviction. Now the Corsican's going down and I need you as a witness."

She figured it linked to the corruption investigation that had almost cost him his career.

"More like someone you can trust," she said. And someone he could dupe into assisting him. It always went like this with Morbier. As if she didn't have enough on her plate right now after losing her business partner, René, to Silicon Valley.

The light of the desk lamp on Morbier's sagging jowls illuminated how he'd aged. Despite her annoyance with him, her heart wrenched a little.

"Then you double owe me, Morbier." She kissed him on both cheeks, then grabbed her jean jacket from the rack. She nodded to an officer she recognized from his undercover unit before she noticed Saj de Rosnay, the cash-poor aristocrat and Leduc Detective's part-time hacker, standing at reception.

"You need bail, Aimée?" Saj worried the sandalwood beads around his neck.

"*Non*, just a ride, Saj. And I borrowed your thumb drive—owe you a new one. We've got work to do tonight. Feel like takeout?"

"But I thought you'd been arrested." He sniffed. "Drinking?" His jaw dropped. "What the hell have you been doing?"

"Morbier and I made up, but I had to play his game."

"Didn't look like poker to me." His eyebrow rose.

"He needed last-minute help with a sting. Long story."

Outside on the dark, narrow street, the locked exit of the Catacombs glowed under a street lamp. The car was parked in front of an old forge, horseshoes visible high on the façade. Saj unlocked the door for her. He took the wheel of René's beloved vintage Citroën DS, a classic entrusted to Saj temporarily until René had a chance to settle in San Francisco. Saj readjusted the custom seat controls, which were usually fitted for René's short legs. A pang went through her.

"You know, that could have gone very badly," Saj told her. "You took my technology without asking—what if I had had important client files on that drive? Warn me next time, Aimée, when you're putting the business at risk."

Her cheeks reddened as the Citroën's heated leather seat began to warm her derrière. "*Desolée*, Saj, I didn't think—"

"*Comme toujours*," Saj interrupted, exasperation in his tone. "Isn't it time you started thinking of the consequences before you jump into these dangerous schemes?"

Guilt assailed her. This was worse than her usual tactlessness—she'd been plain stupid. She needed Saj more than ever right now; she couldn't afford to lose him. Or stress him out. "Saj, I only had two hours to put this together. But you're right," she said, trying to sound contrite.

"What about my thumb drive prototypes? I'm supposed to test them."

"I only borrowed one." She unclipped her hoop earrings, wondering how to make it up to him. "*La police* kept it in evidence. You'll get it back with the court files erased and good as new."

A crow cawed from outside the car window. There it was, overlooking the church, perched on the charcuterie's façade.

She caught its beady black-eyed stare. Bad luck, her *grand-mère* would say.

"I won't hold my breath," Saj said, shifting into first.

"Consider the thumb drive a rental. Morbier needs me to testify." She cringed at the thought. She hated the cold marble-floored tribunal, the smell of fear and authority.

Saj didn't reply, just nudged the Citroën out into the street. Aimée ran her fingers through her blonde-streaked shag cut hair, wishing she hadn't run out of mousse. An evening of reports stretched ahead. They were barely coping with René's workload.

"It's a good time for you to start being honest with me about your other side jobs." A thick envelope landed in her lap. The second tonight.

"What's this?" she asked, surprised.

"You tell me," Saj said.

Inside the envelope she found a bundle of worn franc notes and a card embossed with YURI VOLODYA, 14 VILLA D'ALÉSIA and a phone number. On the back: *Accept this retainer. Contact me. Urgent.*

She had no idea who this Yuri Volodya was. "Out of the blue, this man gives you . . . when?"

"This afternoon."

"*Une petite seconde,* did you speak with him?"

Saj said, "I told him to call you."

She'd turned her cell phone ringer off. Now she checked for messages. The same number had called twice but left no message.

"Some scam?" Another five thousand francs tonight. "We're busy. How could you accept this without an explanation?"

"I didn't—he mentioned being a family friend. Protecting his painting. Said you'd understand."

"Understand?" She shook her head. "What did he mean, family friend? You think an old colleague of my father's?"

"Your mother, he said."

For a moment everything shifted; she felt the oxygen being sucked from the car. Her pulse thudded. Her American mother, who was on the world security watch list? "How did he know my mother?"

Saj downshifted. "So he's trouble, *non?*"

She hit the number. No answer. "What else did he say?"

"That's all." Saj shrugged. "Even if his money's good, this smells bad. *Alors*, Aimée, we need to stay on track. We need to spend our time figuring out how to juggle all René's projects and keep our existing clients happy. We don't have time for whatever this is."

Anxious, she tried the man's number again. She needed to know more. A friend of her mother's? But no answer.

"We will sort it all out, Saj. But turn around. Let's meet this Monsieur Volodya."

"Didn't you say takeout?" Saj said.

The last thing Aimée was in the mood for was food. But she needed to do something for Saj. She also needed to talk to this man Yuri, and return his money. Her nerves jangled.

"Yes, takeout," she said. "My treat."

Saj downshifted off the boulevard into the honeycomb of tiny lanes of small houses, ateliers, and old warehouses. A long-time resident, he knew the best routes to take at this time of night. The quartier was a less well-heeled bourgeois-bohemian version of adjoining Montparnasse, complete with mounting rents. Saj complained that the former ateliers of famous Surrealists like Picasso now belonged to bohemian-chic residents whose trust funds couldn't quite afford the 6th arrondissement.

Twenty minutes later the couscous *végétarien* takeout sat on the backseat, the turmeric and mint smells reminding Aimée she'd forgotten dinner. But she had no appetite. Yuri Volodya still didn't answer his phone. Was it worth going to the address on the card? Part of her wanted Saj to drop her off at the Métro so she could head home and collapse in her bed. The other part knew she wouldn't be able to rest until she discovered why he'd sent this, and what his connection was to her mother.

The Citroën bumped over the cobbles. She wished Saj would slow down. He unclipped his seat belt, reached in the backseat for his madras cloth bag. Popped some pills from a pill case.

"What's wrong? Your chakra's misaligned again?"

"Try some." He dropped a fistful of brown pellets into her hand. "Herbal stress busters. Works every time, remember?"

"*Bien sûr,*" she said, chewing her lip. His fungus-scented pellets reminded her of rabbit droppings. "We'll make it work without René," she added. "We should think of his amazing job offer. This opportunity for him."

Inside she thought only of the hole he'd leave. Selfish, Aimée, as usual.

"René didn't trust me, or the business, Saj. *Avec raison,*" she said, hating to admit it. She couldn't compete with René's job offer—six figures, stock options, and the title of CTO, chief technology officer.

"Maybe René doesn't trust himself right now," Saj said, pensive. Apart from the purring motor, quiet filled the car. He was right; René had moped around, couldn't concentrate after his broken heart.

"We should do some more asana breathing sessions," Saj went on. "It will exand your awareness and you'll feel less stressed."

Not this again. She almost threw the pellets at him.

"Make a right here, Saj." She hoped they hadn't made a wasted trip.

He turned into Villa d'Alésia, a tree-lined lane lit by old-fashioned lampposts. Suddenly, a white van lurched in front of them. Saj honked the horn and downshifted. The van shot ahead, its hanging muffler scraping the cobbles, and turned out of sight.

Aimée scanned the house numbers for number fourteen.

From the corner of her eye she caught a figure in front of the Citroën's grill. A man's blue jean jacket shone in the head-lights' yellow beam.

"Look out, Saj!" she shouted.

Horrified, her right arm shot out against the dashboard, while out of instinct, she threw her other arm protectively across Saj's chest.

Saj punched the brakes. Squeals and then a horrible thump as the man hit the windshield. For a second, the man's pale face pressed against the glass, his half-lidded eyes vacant, his palms splayed.

The man crumpled off the side of the car as Saj veered left. Too late. The Citroën jolted, hitting an old parked Mercedes. The metal screeched as it accordioned; the car shuddered. Cold air tinged by the smell of burning rubber poured over her face.

The impact set off the alarms of parked cars, a shrill honking cacophony. A hiss of steam escaped the Citroën's crushed radiator.

Her bag had fallen from the dashboard—mascara, keys, and encryption manuals spilling onto the floor. Saj's body hung over the steering wheel. Good God, he'd taken off his seat belt.

"Saj, can you hear me?"

He stirred, rubbed his head.

"The *mec* came out of nowhere," he said. And before she could struggle out of her seat belt, Saj pushed open the dented door. He staggered in shock, his pale dreadlocks hanging in the yellow slants of the headlights. "*Mon Dieu,* I killed him."

Aimée's door jammed against the Mercedes. She climbed out of the driver's seat, then realized her phone was somewhere on the car floor. Stunned, she tried to take in the dark, wet lane, the body lying beside the car. Saj limping and clutching his neck.

A woman down the street gripping a gym bag, ran toward them. Green surgical scrubs showed under her short brown jacket.

"Call for help," Aimée shouted. "Ambulance!"

"*Quelle catastrophe*," said the woman. She pulled out her cell phone. "And I just finished my shift at the hospital."

The nurse knelt down beside the steaming car, the hem of her green scrubs trailing on the oil-slicked cobbles. With the nurse attending to the victim, Aimée hurried toward Saj. "What hurts? Can you move your neck?"

"Where did he come from? I didn't see him until he. . . ."

Dazed, Saj touched his temple and grimaced in pain. She realized he was in shock and guided him to a low stone wall.

"Stay here, Saj," she said.

"Help's coming," the nurse was saying to the motionless man. Apart from the cuts on his face, the man appeared to be asleep. "The hospital's two blocks away. Can you hear me?"

Not even a groan.

It had happened so fast, one minute she and Saj were talking and then. . . . Aimée realized she might be in shock herself. She struggled to focus, became aware of the nurse's thrusts to the man's chest. The whining echo of a siren. Approaching red flashes splashed the walls. Lights went on in the windows of the adjoining alley.

Suppressing a shudder, Aimée watched the nurse put her index and middle finger on the man's carotid artery.

"No pulse," she said.

Aimée gasped. She looked closer at the man's pallor, his fresh facial cuts and scratches. "But he's not bleeding anywhere."

The shifting of the fire truck's gears swallowed the nurse's reply. The red lights reflected on the water pooled between the cracks in the road and on the roof tiles of the two-story ateliers.

Saj shivered in his thin muslin shirt, his sandalwood prayer beads tangled with his dreads. He had a glassy look as he spoke to the first response team. As if in a nightmare Aimée watched the helmeted *sapeurs-pompiers* confer with the nurse beside René's Citroën. The arriving medic tried for vitals and shook his head.

They lifted the body onto the stretcher. The man's torn jeans were oil-spattered; his lifeless, pale arm fell limp, exposing the blue tattoos peeking from beneath the rolled-up sleeve of his Levi's jacket. Cyrillic letters intertwined in an elaborate figure of a wolf.

Нада и вера

"He's Russian?" she said to the medic who was putting a blood pressure cuff on Saj's arm.

"Worse," said the medic, a thin mustached twenty-something. "A Serb."

Shivering, Aimée stared closer at the tattoo. "How can you tell?"

"Believe me, as the son of a Ukrainian dissident, I'm supposed to hate both Russians and Serbs." He pointed to the script. "See there? Serbian uses Cyrillic and Latin script. The Serb mafia tattoo themselves in prison like that."

Her blood ran cold. Serb mafia?

The medic clipped a Styrofoam brace around Saj's neck, then draped a blanket across his shivering shoulders. Then he took her aside. "You look pale. We'll bring you in for observation."

"I'm fine." Aimée was loath to share how shaken she felt. How her stomach churned at the image of the man's white face, his half-lidded eyes reminding her of the fish on ice in the market. His palms splayed on the windshield. His tattoo.

"If we hadn't driven up this street to find. . . ." Her words left her. It spun in her mind that a man she didn't know who knew her mother had sent her an envelope of cash.

"Fate. Accidents happen, terrible," the medic said. He took her vitals. "Your blood pressure's a bit high." He put a stethoscope to her chest.

"But we ran him over," she said, hesitating. "There's something wrong—"

"You feel guilty, that's natural," he interrupted. "But if it happened as you say, it's not your fault."

Her shoulders shook. She couldn't get the words out, but any medic should be able to see the Serb didn't look like a man who'd been hit by a car.

"*Alors.*" The medic leaned forward. "We've treated Serbs who were injured after bar brawls and knife fights here in the quartier."

"How's that supposed to make me feel better?"

He scanned the street, nodded to a colleague who assisted Saj toward the ambulance. "Between us," he said, lowering his voice, "I'd say watch your back."

But who was this Serb? Why hadn't anyone come out to identify him after the sirens, the commotion?

Her jacket whipped in the rising wind. She turned to see the van waiting for the corpse, engine running, as the *flics* arrived. Before she could get past the crowd, the medic bundled Saj into a waiting blue-and-white SAMU van. The engine rumbled, backing out down the lane.

Too late.

A *flic* escorted the nurse to a police van that had been set up for questioning. Aimée followed. "Wait your turn, Mademoiselle."

"But my friend's hurt." Shaken up, tired, and cold, she wanted to get this over with. "I need to get to the hospital."

"Where he's going you can't visit him."

The hair stood up on her neck. "You've taken him in *garde à vue?*"

"*C'est de rigueur*, questioning and treatment, Mademoiselle."

She knew the criminal ward at Hôtel-Dieu, the public hospital.

"But it was an accident, this man came out of nowhere and landed on our windshield."

"That's up to our investigation," he said, checking for messages on his cell phone. "Right now we're calling it a *homicide involontaire.*"

Her heart dropped. Saj could face a charge of manslaughter. Saj? A gentle soul who meditated and spent months in ashrams in India. A hacker genius who could paralyze the French bourse, bring a Ministry database to its knees, but wouldn't hurt a fly. It made her sick to think they suspected him.

"*Zut alors*, Saj swerved trying to avoid this man."

"So he'd had a few drinks, eh?"

Again, the *flic* was off base. "Saj drinks green tea."

"Immediate blood tests and alcohol level analysis will confirm that." He nodded to the crime scene unit to tape off the area. "What's your worry?"

"The victim's injuries." She pointed to the dry cobbles. "Do you see any blood here?"

But he'd already gone to join several officers near the ambulance.

She hated waiting. Hated thinking of Saj being questioned in the criminal ward. The Mercedes' smashed grill leaked water; escaping radiator steam hovered cloud-like over the hood. At least the car alarms had subsided.

A stocky man of medium height, bundled into a black lamb fur coat—the kind she hadn't seen since the seventies—and a Russian fur hat ran toward them. His gaze took in the ambulance. Short of breath, he paused and shook his head. "*Mon Dieu.* Someone hurt?" There was shock and concern in his voice.

"Dead," muttered someone in the crowd. A finger pointed at her. The Mercedes.

"My car? Think you can get away with smashing my car, too?"

Aimée flinched.

Just what she needed. René's insurance would go sky-high. Another layer of guilt descended on her. René hadn't been gone twenty-four hours and they'd run over a Serb and totaled his prized car.

"An angry little Cossack," said one of the firemen under his breath. "The only thing missing are his boots."

"*Restez tranquil*, Monsieur," Aimée said. "I'll take care of the damages."

Aimée noted a long-haired young man, a cell phone to his ear, rushing up behind the older man. An armband encircled his khaki jacket sleeve. "What's happened to your car?"

The old man waved him away. "I'll handle this, Damien."

His brows knit in worry. "But you need my help."

"Go back to the hospital," the old man said. "Your aunt's more important."

"You're sure?" said Damien, his tone conflicted.

The old man nodded. Aimée heard the slap of Damien's footsteps as he disappeared in the shadows.

"So you don't have insurance, Mademoiselle?" The man's face flushed. "I know your type, you want to rip me off. Offer to fix my car but sell the parts. You some gypsy?"

"Do I look like a gypsy?" He grated on Aimée's nerves. Saj injured, a man dead, and now this callous car owner. "I'll have your car repaired."

"Think I'll fall for that old trick?" Suspicion showed in his watery blue eyes. He gave a quick shake of his head. "Don't think you're leaving, Mademoiselle."

She had no intention of leaving—not until she did everything she could to save René's insurance. But before she could respond, a *flic*, notepad out, asked for the car registration. She opened the intact door on the driver's side and reached into the glove compartment. Felt René's kid leather driving gloves. Size *petit*. A pang went through her.

After handing the *flic* René's car registration and scooping up the contents of her bag from the floor, she shifted on her high-tops, awaiting questioning. The crime scene unit photographer's flash emitted bursts of light. She caught sight of the old man a few meters away—he was opening the door to number

14. He had to be the man she'd come to see, Yuri Volodya! She hurried after the old man just as he disappeared behind the gate.

"Monsieur . . . Monsieur Volodya?" she called out.

No answer. As she reached the darkened front door of the atelier, Aimée heard the tinkle of broken glass. A cry. She reached out but felt only cold air.

"Monsieur?" Her eyes tried to adjust to the dank vacuum in front of her. "What happened?"

"My door was open, the lights don't work," he said, his voice quavering. "I've been robbed."

Aimée's spine tingled. Smart thieves short-circuited electricity these days. With a tickle of intuition, she wondered if this was connected to the Serb they'd run over outside his door.

She rooted in her secondhand Vuitton bag until she found her penlight. Shined it on the man's face. Confusion filled his watering blue eyes. A trickle of blood trailed on his cheek. He'd cut himself on broken glass.

"Where's your fuse box, Monsieur?"

"What good will that do?"

Did he want to argue now? "I'll try to switch the power back on."

She followed the old man across the creaking floorboards, glass crackling underfoot. A musty scent of paper emanated from the shadows. In the thin yellow beam she saw the problem right away. She pulled on her leather gloves and with a quick flick switched the fuse box levers upright.

Light flooded the sparsely furnished turn-of-the-century atelier. A worn velvet armchair had been overturned. A vase lay on its side, orange marigold petals scattered and water pooled on a long worktable.

Horrible. She pitied the old codger. His car, now his house.

"Monsieur Volodya? That's you, *non*? I'm Aimée Luduc, you sent for me. I'm so sorry about your car, but I hope—"

"Forget about the car." He grabbed at a dark wood beam in the wall, his bony white wrists shaking. Reminding her of her grandfather. She righted the chair, took his elbow to help him sit down. Dazed, he resisted, refusing to sit. With his thick fingers, he smeared the blood on his cheek. Shock painted his face.

"I think you should see a doctor."

"Wait. . . ."

With surprising agility he hurried to the armoire, which had been shoved aside. She followed, noticing the small door behind it. Like a broom closet. A dark red stain smeared the wood door.

Blood.

He pulled the creaking door open. Empty. Anguish painted his face. "You're too late. My painting's stolen."

"You kept a painting in a broom closet? A valuable painting?"

"But I locked it. It was only until the formal appraisal tomorrow." His lip quivered. "My legs feel not so steady."

His face had gone white. This time, he let her help him to the chair. "Let me get you water."

He shook his head. "Vodka." He pointed to the galley kitchen. A show of bravado, or to calm his nerves? But he looked like he needed it. She'd humor him until he explained. Then alert the *flics*.

The dark wood-walled atelier held an open loft mezzanine above, a cramped kitchen off to the side, an alcove with faded flowered wallpaper, and a bed covered by a rumpled duvet.

At the empty sink she wetted an embroidered towel, noticed the dish rack with a single plate, cup, and fork. The old man lived alone. Tidy. In the one cupboard she found a bottle of Stolichnaya, two glasses.

Could the Serb have been the one who robbed the old man? Caught in the act, she figured. But he hadn't been carrying anything. Definitely not a painting.

"Now how do you feel?" She uncapped and poured the vodka. Handed him the towel.

"A scratch," he said, clinked her shot glass. "I'm Yuri Volodya."

"I know. You sent me five thousand francs." She set down her card on the side table.

"So of course you came," he said. "But too late. Hand me my glasses."

Stubborn old Cossack, all right.

"There's a pair hanging from your neck," she said. "What's this all about?"

He put on his glasses, and his voice changed. "You look just like her."

Hope fluttered in her heart. "*Maman?* She's alive?"

He shook his head. Winced in pain. "Forgive me. I thought you could help. You see, I owe your mother."

"I don't understand. Help how? And owe my mother what? When did you last see her?"

He averted his eyes and swigged the vodka. "I'm a book-binder, I craft special editions. A commission takes a year." He rubbed his thumb and fingertips together.

Why had he changed the subject? Nerves? He seemed anxious now, worried. Like he was saying one thing but meaning another.

"*Alors*, Monsieur Volodya, if we could talk about my mother, this painting. . . ."

"My craft's for *les connaisseurs, vous savez*," he said, as if she hadn't spoken. "A certain clientele who appreciate the feel of a hand-bound book, the presentation of prints inside. Salvador Dalí commissioned my work, *des gens comme ça*." Apart from his odd sentence structure—as if he translated from Russian construction—he spoke with a pure Parisian pronunciation.

Under her boot she felt something hard and round. A brass button embossed with LEVI'S on it. Like the brass buttons on the Serb's jean jacket. Her heart skipped. "What if this fell off the Serb's jacket?"

"That man you ran over?" Yuri's eyes widened. "Blame it on the Serb curse."

"Meaning?"

"We have a saying about Serbs: An unfortunate man would be drowned in a teacup. But of that man I know nothing. Nothing."

She doubted that. "I think this button came from his jean jacket. Maybe he trashed this place and came up empty."

Yuri's shoulders sagged, the lines framing his mouth more pronounced. A quick scan told her the intruder knew exactly what to look for and where. The leather-bound books lining the shelves were untouched, as was an antique iron book press on the worktable. An open calendar and notepad lay undisturbed on the desk.

"Life kicks one in the gut and we're surprised?" he said. "As if one is the exception, not the rule?"

Since when did people refer to themselves in the third person, she wondered. An old-world thing?

"Monsieur Volodya, I'm here to return your money."

"Keep it. Find my painting."

"Art recovery's not my line of work," she said, suspecting he'd mentioned her mother as a ruse. This smelled off.

"I'll make up a list, tell you everything."

Everything? "Tell me how you know my mother."

His left hand trembled slightly. "Please, in my own way. Give me a moment."

It was foolish to rush him. Of course he was still in shock. He'd seen a man die, his car damaged, and his home burglarized all within a short time.

"Damien, my neighbor, the political boy, just brought me back from dinner at Oleg's place. Oleg's my stepson, as he calls himself. My wife's child. Not mine." Yuri's voice rose, petulant. "Oleg's wife served burnt blinis, like cement—can you imagine?"

Aimée contained her impatience with effort. "Why contact me to protect your painting?"

"Pour me another."

Frustrated, she reached for the bottle. His liver-spotted hand clamped on her gloved one with surprising strength. His eyes narrowed. His confusion was gone.

"If the Serb left empty-handed," he said, "someone else didn't."

He knew something. She saw it in his eyes. Suspicion filled her.

"So you claim a painting is missing, but the man who appears to have broken into your house didn't have it. Strange, Monsieur. And I still don't understand what any of this has to do with my mother." She sipped the vodka. "Why do I feel like all this is some ruse?"

There was fear in his eyes. He downed the vodka. His hand clenched in a fist, his knuckles white. "I've been rude to you, I'm sorry."

He was wasting time she should have been using to help Saj. "*S'il vous plaît*, Monsieur Volodya, quit the guessing games." She was angry with herself for getting caught up in this, for buying into his fishy story just because he'd mentioned her mother.

"So help me. I know you're a detective. I wanted to hire you to protect the painting, but now it's too late for that. I'm hiring you instead to get it back for me."

Like she needed to add to Leduc Detective's workload. They were already drowning. "Like I said, Monsieur, we don't do art recovery." She couldn't resist adding, "You didn't really know my mother, did you?"

"Of course I knew your mother. The American."

Aimée gripped his hand. "How?"

"It's complicated." He stiffened. "I didn't know her well."

Aimée didn't know her well, either. Sydney Leduc had abandoned them when Aimée was eight years old. "But you knew her. When?" Hope fluttered despite his vagueness.

"Of course, she was much younger then. Changed a little, but . . . it's been years."

Years? Her heart sank. "Where. . . . how?"

"Now I wanted to make good on my debt."

"Debt?" Why wouldn't he give her a straight answer? "Is this about the painting?"

Footsteps crackled over the glass, and a draft of cold air rushed through the atelier. "Monsieur?" It was the *flic* with the clipboard.

"Please, Monsieur, where do you know my mother from?"

"Not now." Yuri put his finger to her lips. Dry, rough skin.

She'd had enough. She reached in her bag for the francs, about to tell him to forget involving her, when he whispered, "I'm being watched." He held her hand. "Tomorrow. Wait for my call. I'll tell you about her."

"But I can't take your money—"

"Recover my painting."

"Monsieur, I need your car registration," said the *flic*. He glanced around, noticing the scattered objects. "Your house was broken into as well? Is anything missing?"

"My wife. She died last year."

"Desolé," he said. "But I'll need to take down the accident details before I make a robbery report."

"No report," Yuri said, shaking his head. His defiance belied the fear in his eyes. "I'm remodeling."

She wondered why the old man was lying.

The *flic*'s eyes narrowed. Maybe he wondered the same thing. Yuri pulled open a drawer in the art nouveau chest, the most expensive-looking piece in the room. took out a folder and handed it over.

As the officer noted the vehicle info, Aimée watched Yuri sit hunched in his chair, his mouth set, the blood clotting on his cheek. She wasn't sure she believed him about her mother, or trusted him about his missing painting, but she felt pity for him.

"Let me ask a medic to look at your cut, Monsieur."

He waved his wrinkled hand in dismissal. "Now both of you get out."

About the Author

Cara Black lives with her husband and their son in San Francisco. Her novels in the Aimée Leduc Investigations have been nominated for several Anthony and Macavity mystery awards and the Northern California Book Award. She's a member of the Marais Historical Society and Histoires de Vie of the 10th arrondissement and the recipient of the Medaille de la Ville de Paris. She visits often for research, cat-sitting, and couch surfing, to follow the cobbled streets, talking to *flics*, detectives and café owners, and exploring the darker side of the City of Light. Her website is www.carablack.com.

OTHER TITLES IN THE SOHO CRIME SERIES